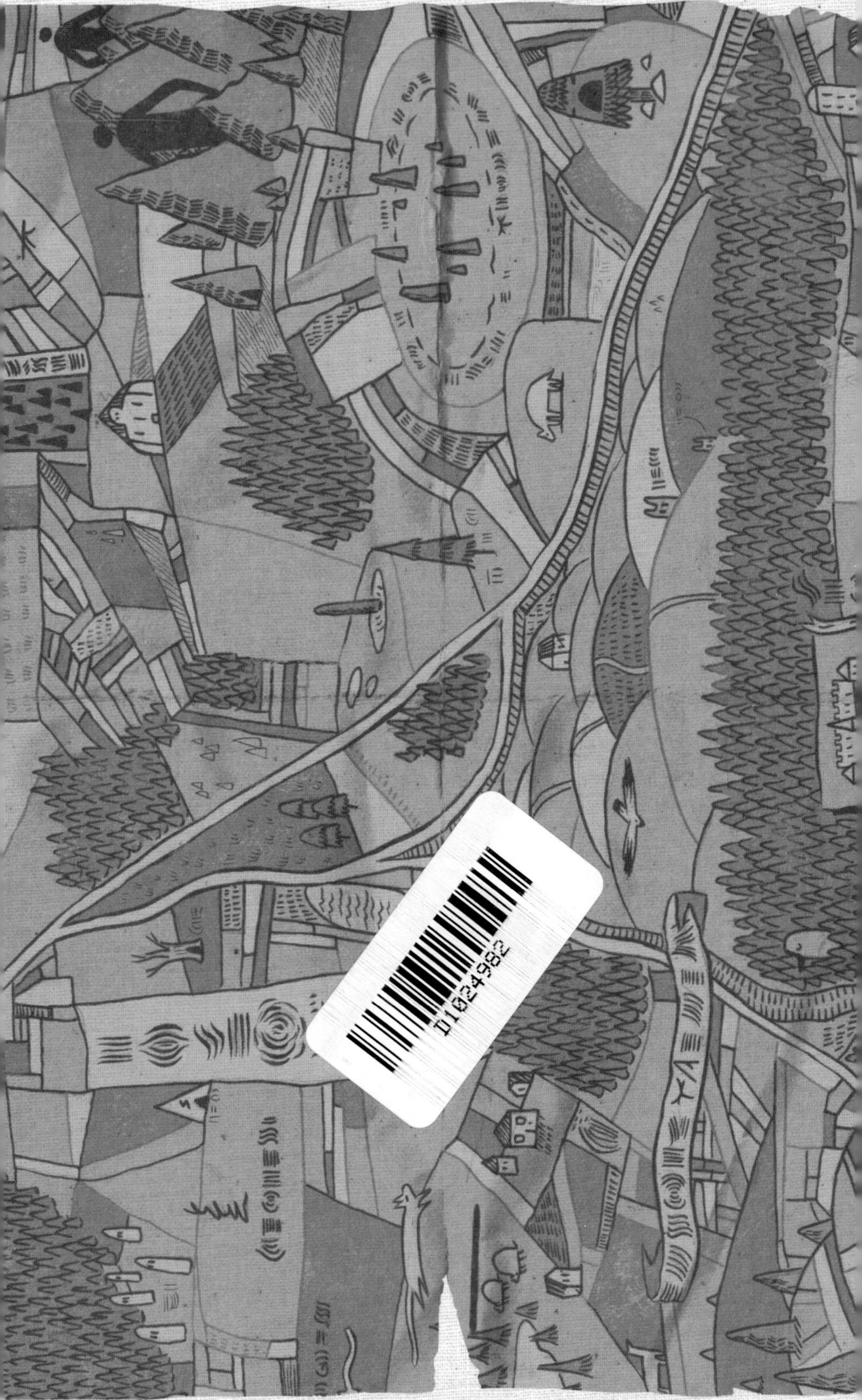

THIS BOOK

and the spirited adventures contained within

BELONGS TO:

....

Spera ™

JOSH TIERNEY

VANDERKLUGT • HWEI • CARROLL • PICHARD • CHAN

ARCHAIA ENTERTAINMENT LLC
WWW.ARCHAIA.COM

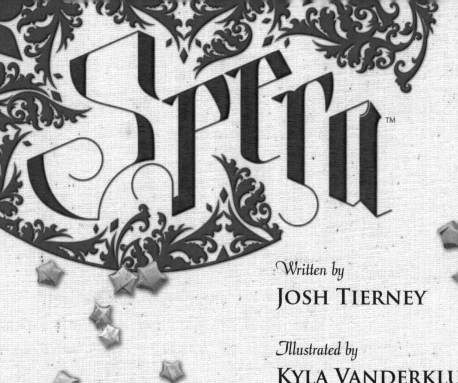

SPERA™

Written by
JOSH TIERNEY

Illustrated by
KYLA VANDERKLUGT
HWEI
EMILY CARROLL
OLIVIER PICHARD

Character Designs and Cover Art by
AFU CHAN

Rebecca Taylor, *Editor*
Scott Newman, *Production Manager*

Archaia Entertainment LLC

PJ Bickett, *CEO*
Mark Smylie, *CCO*
Mike Kennedy, *Publisher*
Stephen Christy, *Editor-in-Chief*

Published by **Archaia**

Archaia Entertainment LLC
1680 Vine Street, Suite 1010
Los Angeles, California, 90028, USA
www.archaia.com

ARCHAIA™
NEW STORIES. NEW WORLDS.

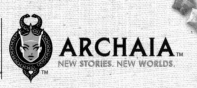

SPERA Volume One. Original Graphic Novel Hardcover. December 2011. FIRST PRINTING

10 9 8 7 6 5 4 3 2 1

ISBN: 1-936393-30-1
ISBN 13: 978-1-936393-30-5

Printed in China.

TABLE OF CONTENTS

CHAPTER ONE
Under the Stars

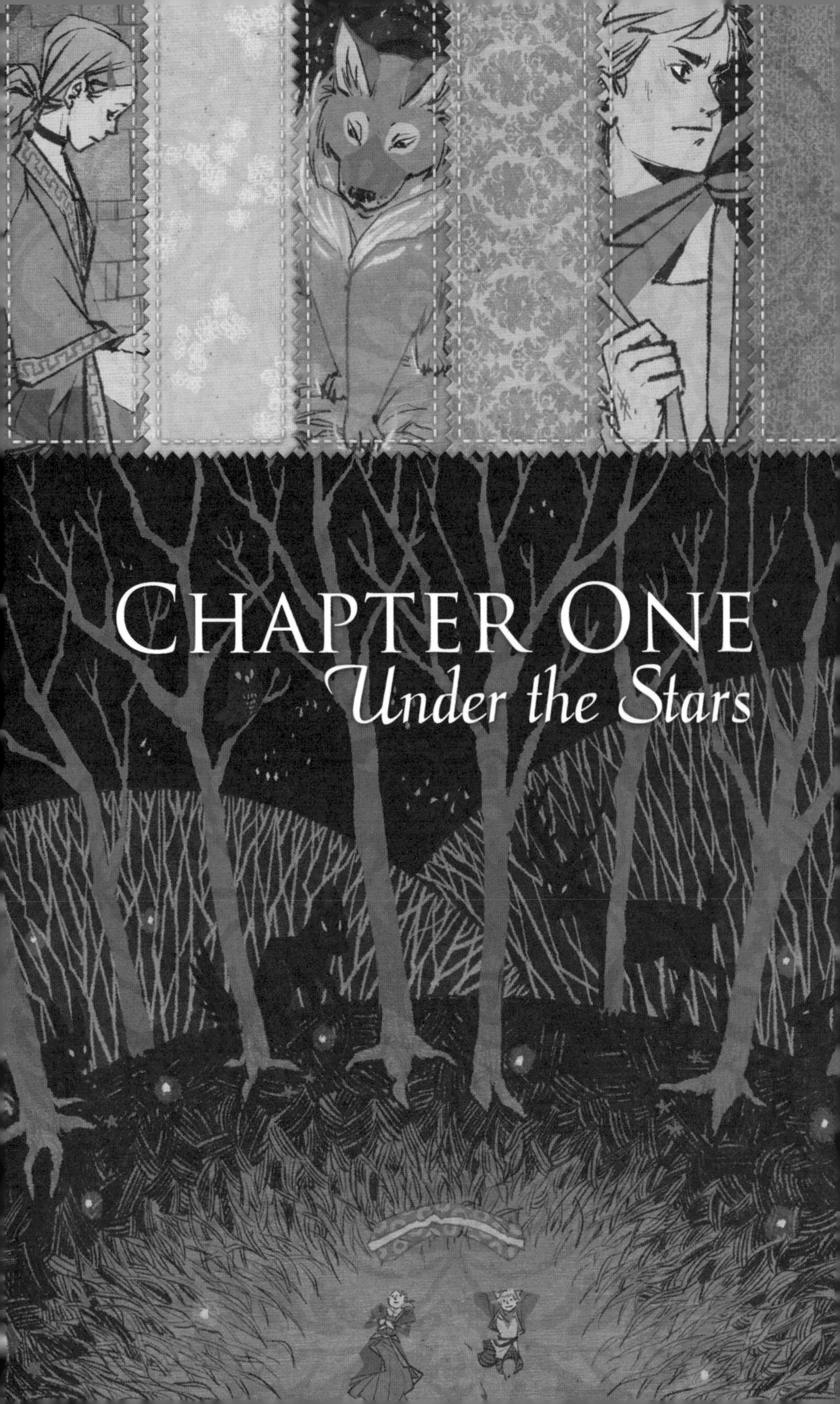

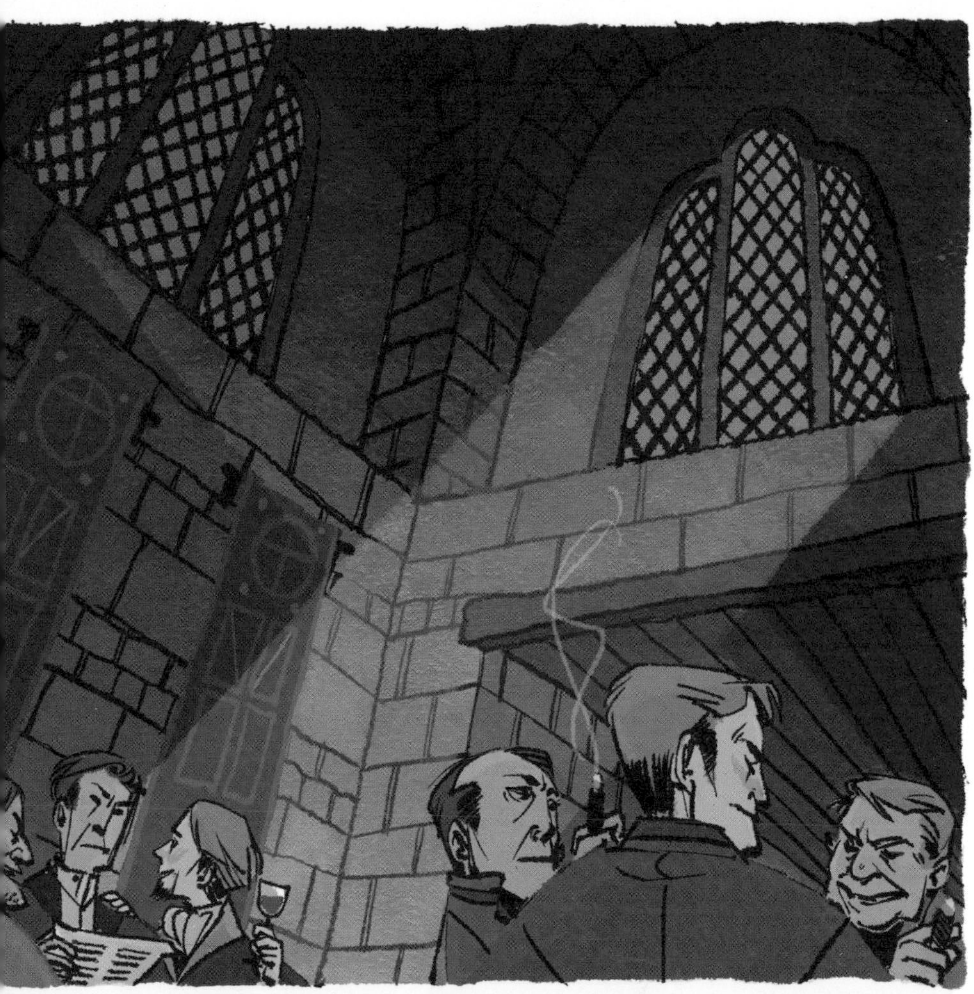

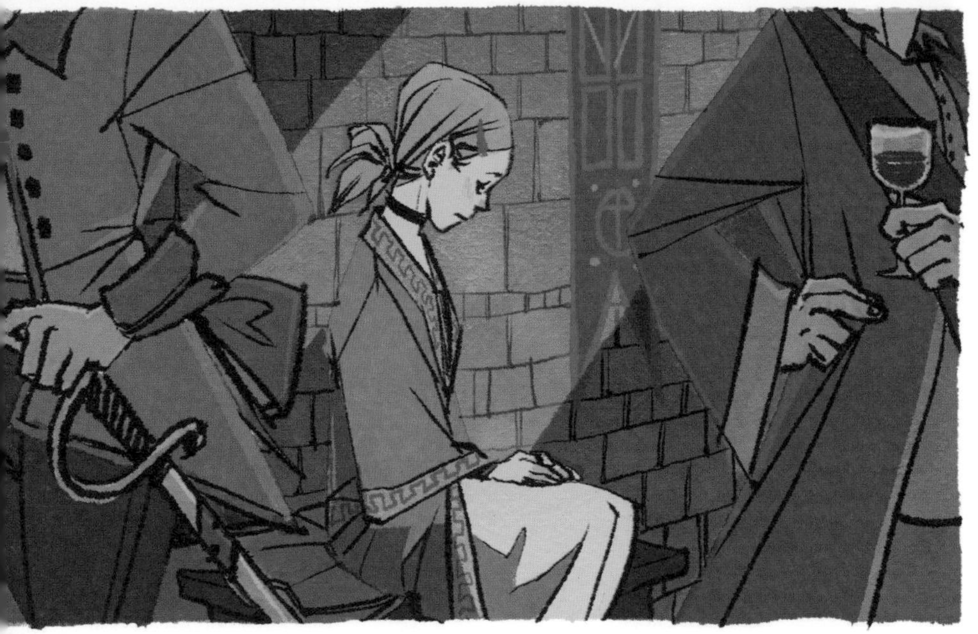

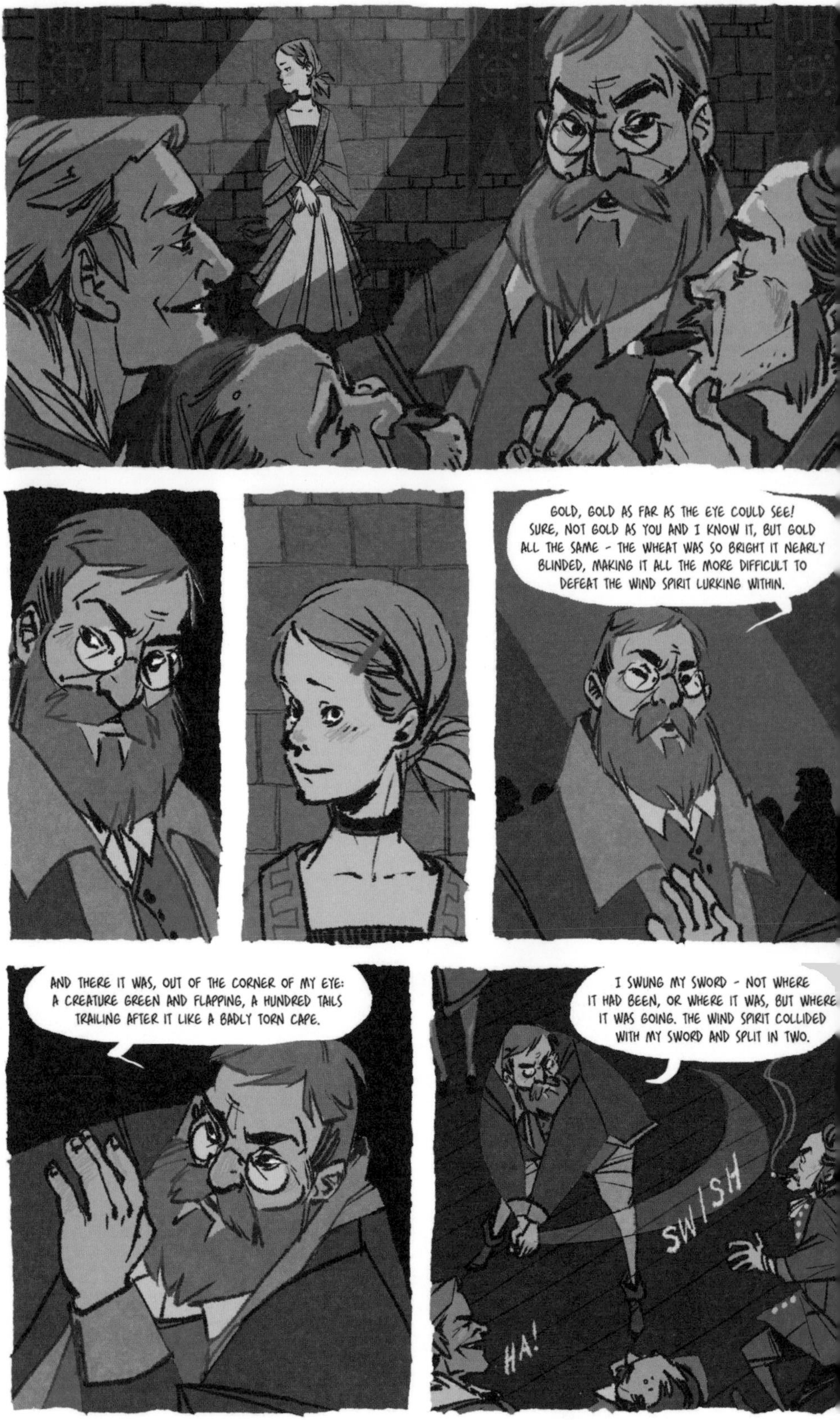
GOLD, GOLD AS FAR AS THE EYE COULD SEE! SURE, NOT GOLD AS YOU AND I KNOW IT, BUT GOLD ALL THE SAME - THE WHEAT WAS SO BRIGHT IT NEARLY BLINDED, MAKING IT ALL THE MORE DIFFICULT TO DEFEAT THE WIND SPIRIT LURKING WITHIN.
AND THERE IT WAS, OUT OF THE CORNER OF MY EYE: A CREATURE GREEN AND FLAPPING, A HUNDRED TAILS TRAILING AFTER IT LIKE A BADLY TORN CAPE.
I SWUNG MY SWORD - NOT WHERE IT HAD BEEN, OR WHERE IT WAS, BUT WHERE IT WAS GOING. THE WIND SPIRIT COLLIDED WITH MY SWORD AND SPLIT IN TWO.
SWISH
HA!

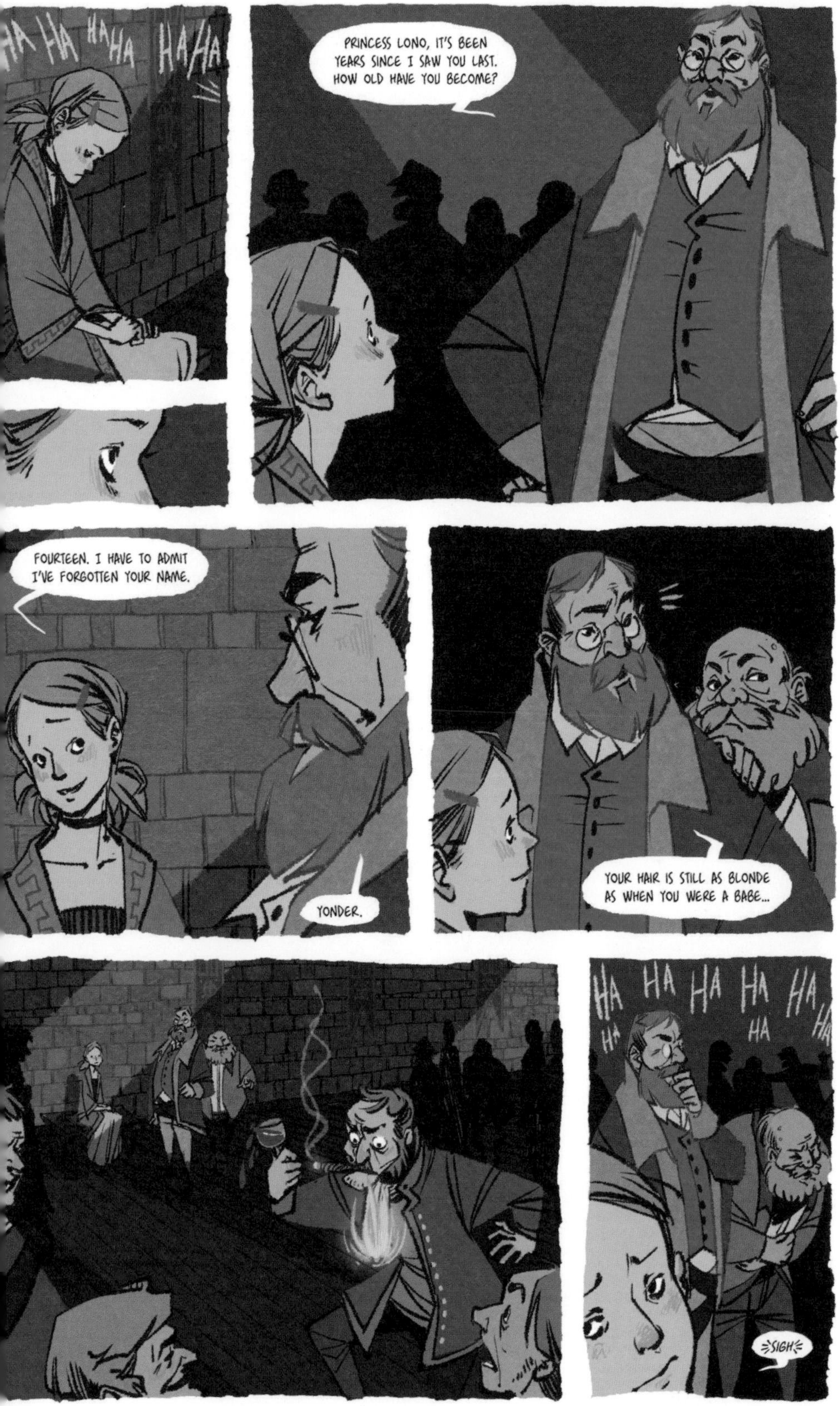
HA HA HAHA HAHA
PRINCESS LONO, IT'S BEEN YEARS SINCE I SAW YOU LAST. HOW OLD HAVE YOU BECOME?
FOURTEEN. I HAVE TO ADMIT I'VE FORGOTTEN YOUR NAME.
YONDER.
YOUR HAIR IS STILL AS BLONDE AS WHEN YOU WERE A BABE...
HA HA HA HA HA HA HA HA HA
SIGH

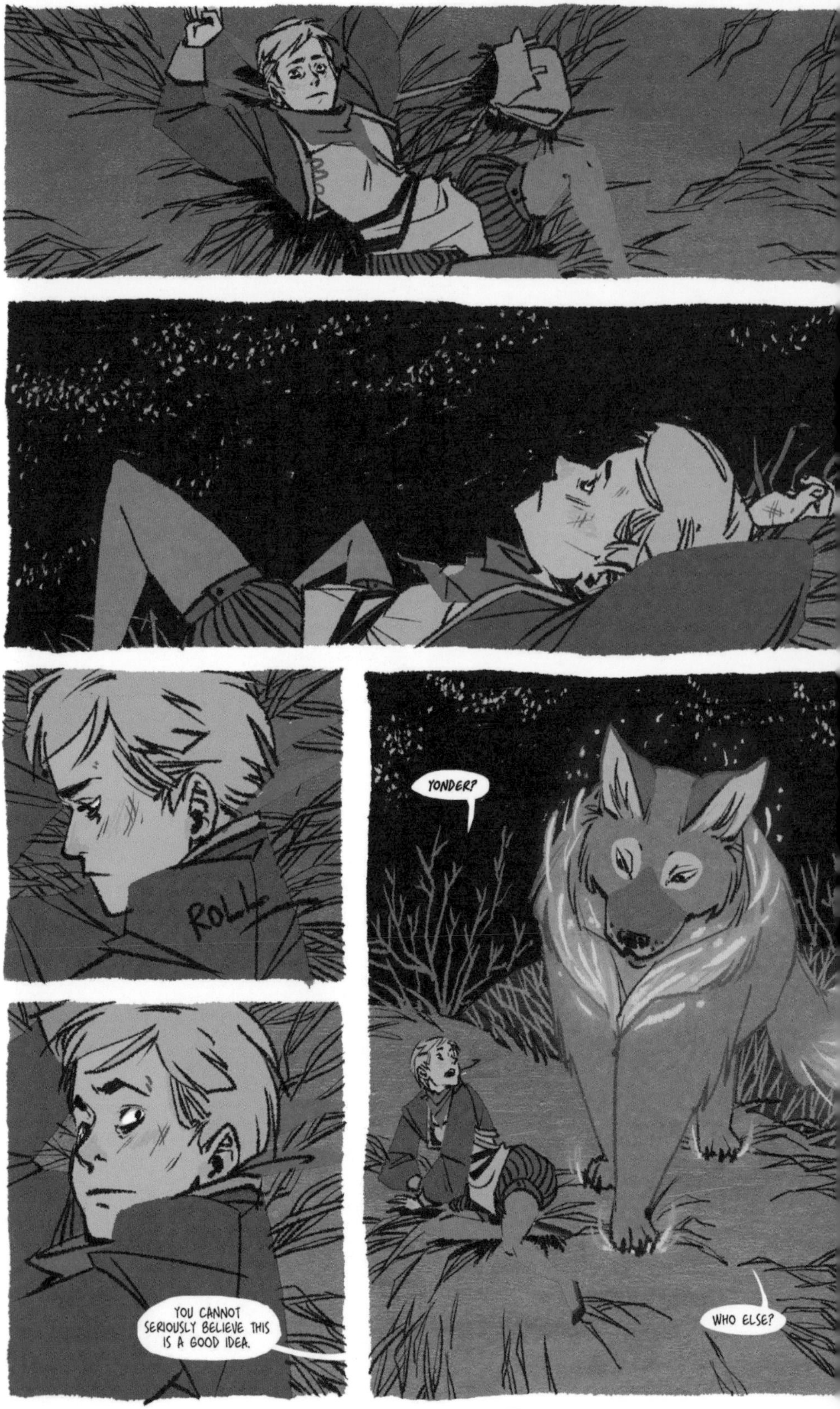
YOU CANNOT SERIOUSLY BELIEVE THIS IS A GOOD IDEA.
YONDER?
WHO ELSE?

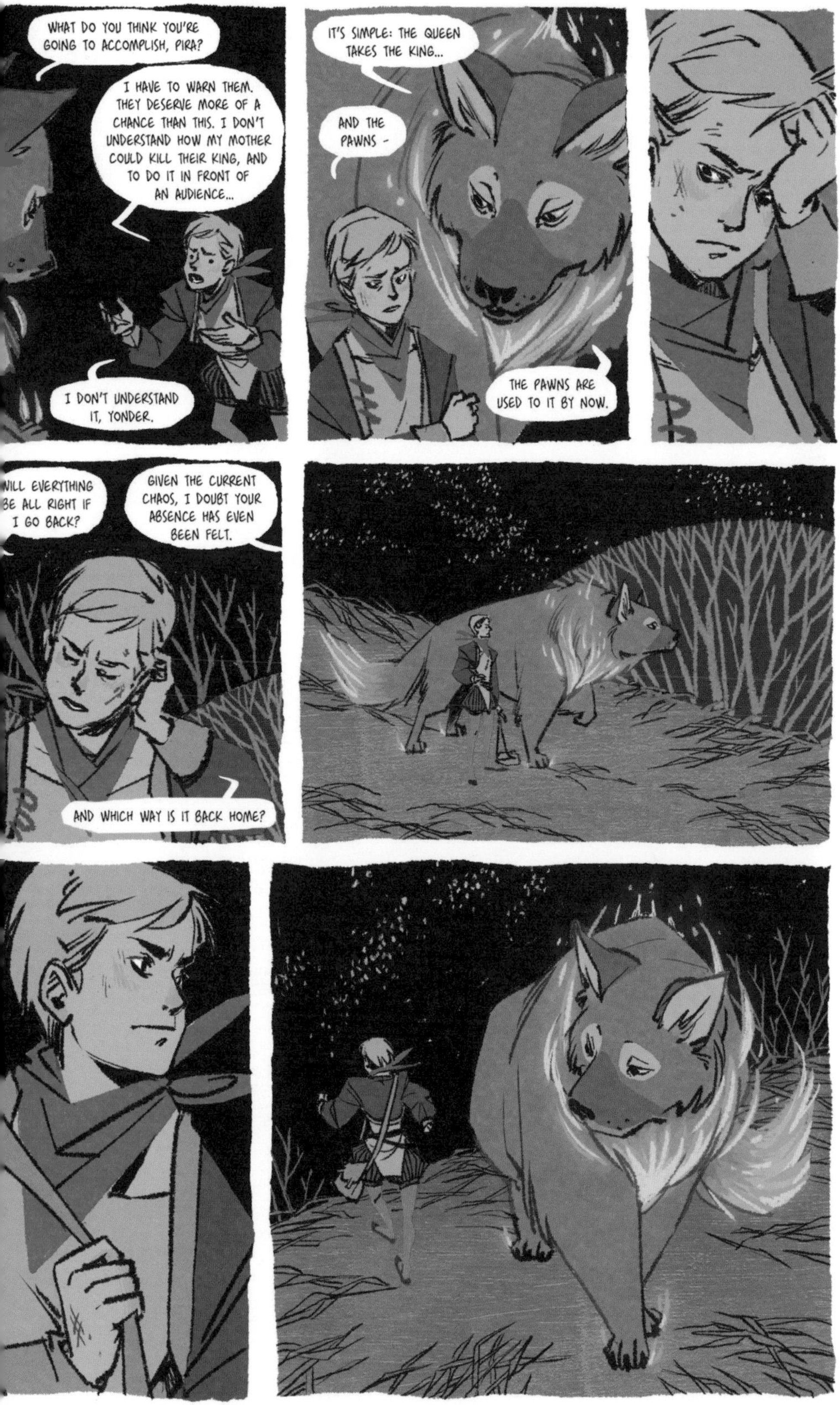
WHAT DO YOU THINK YOU'RE GOING TO ACCOMPLISH, PIRA?
I HAVE TO WARN THEM. THEY DESERVE MORE OF A CHANCE THAN THIS. I DON'T UNDERSTAND HOW MY MOTHER COULD KILL THEIR KING, AND TO DO IT IN FRONT OF AN AUDIENCE...
I DON'T UNDERSTAND IT, YONDER.
IT'S SIMPLE: THE QUEEN TAKES THE KING...
AND THE PAWNS -
THE PAWNS ARE USED TO IT BY NOW.
WILL EVERYTHING BE ALL RIGHT IF I GO BACK?
GIVEN THE CURRENT CHAOS, I DOUBT YOUR ABSENCE HAS EVEN BEEN FELT.
AND WHICH WAY IS IT BACK HOME?

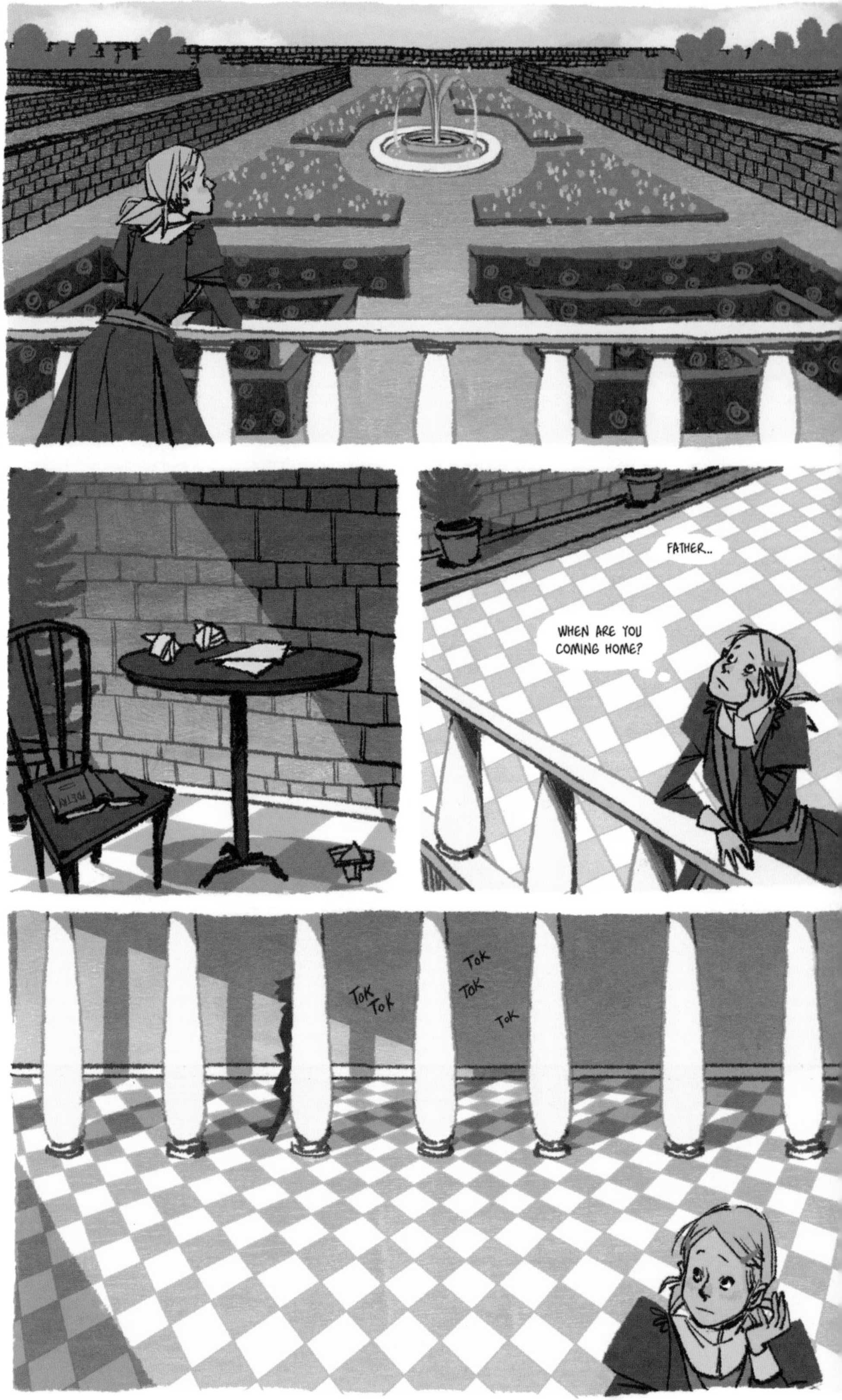
POETRY
FATHER..
WHEN ARE YOU COMING HOME?
TOK TOK
TOK
TOK
TOK

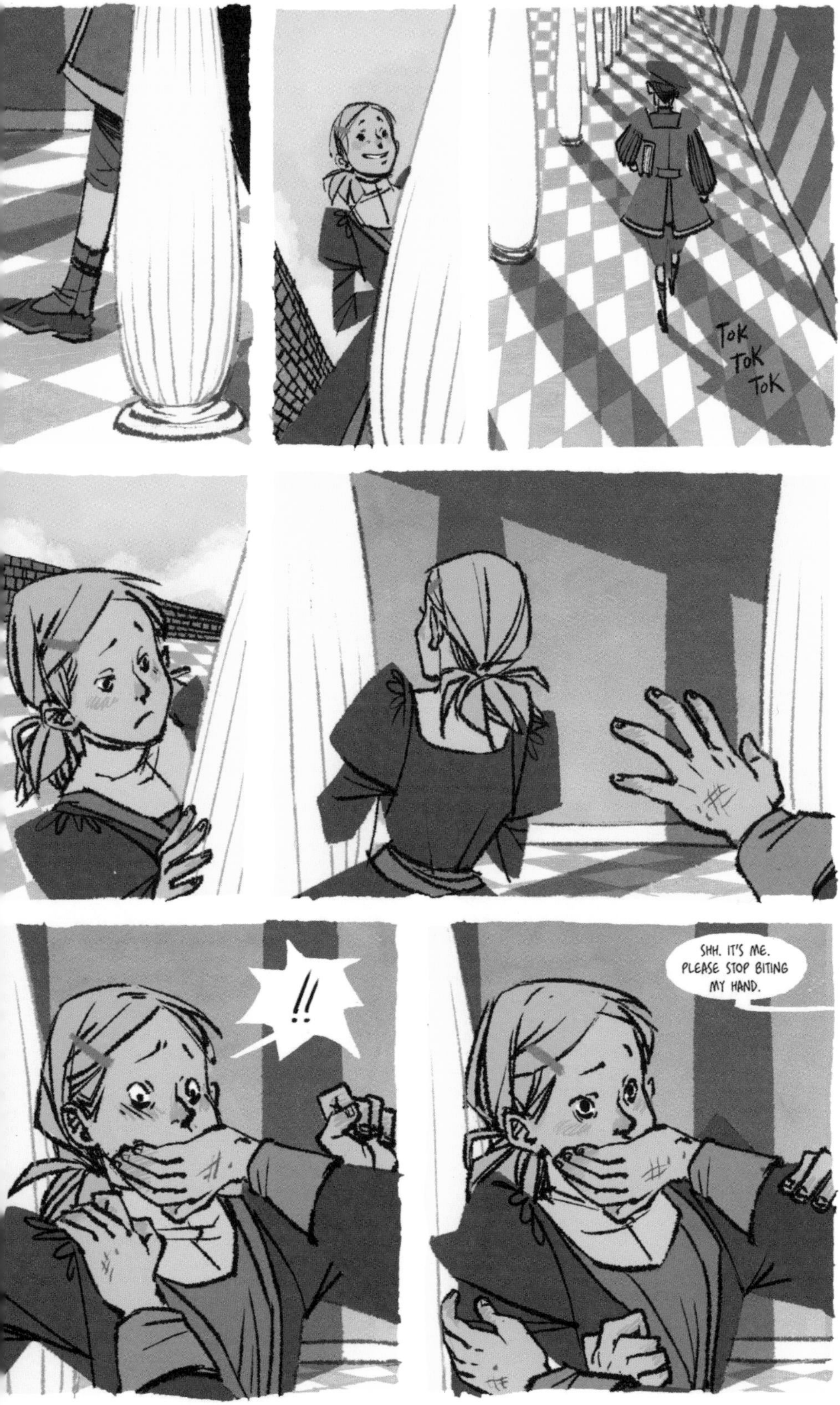
TOK
TOK
TOK
!!
SHH. IT'S ME. PLEASE STOP BITING MY HAND.

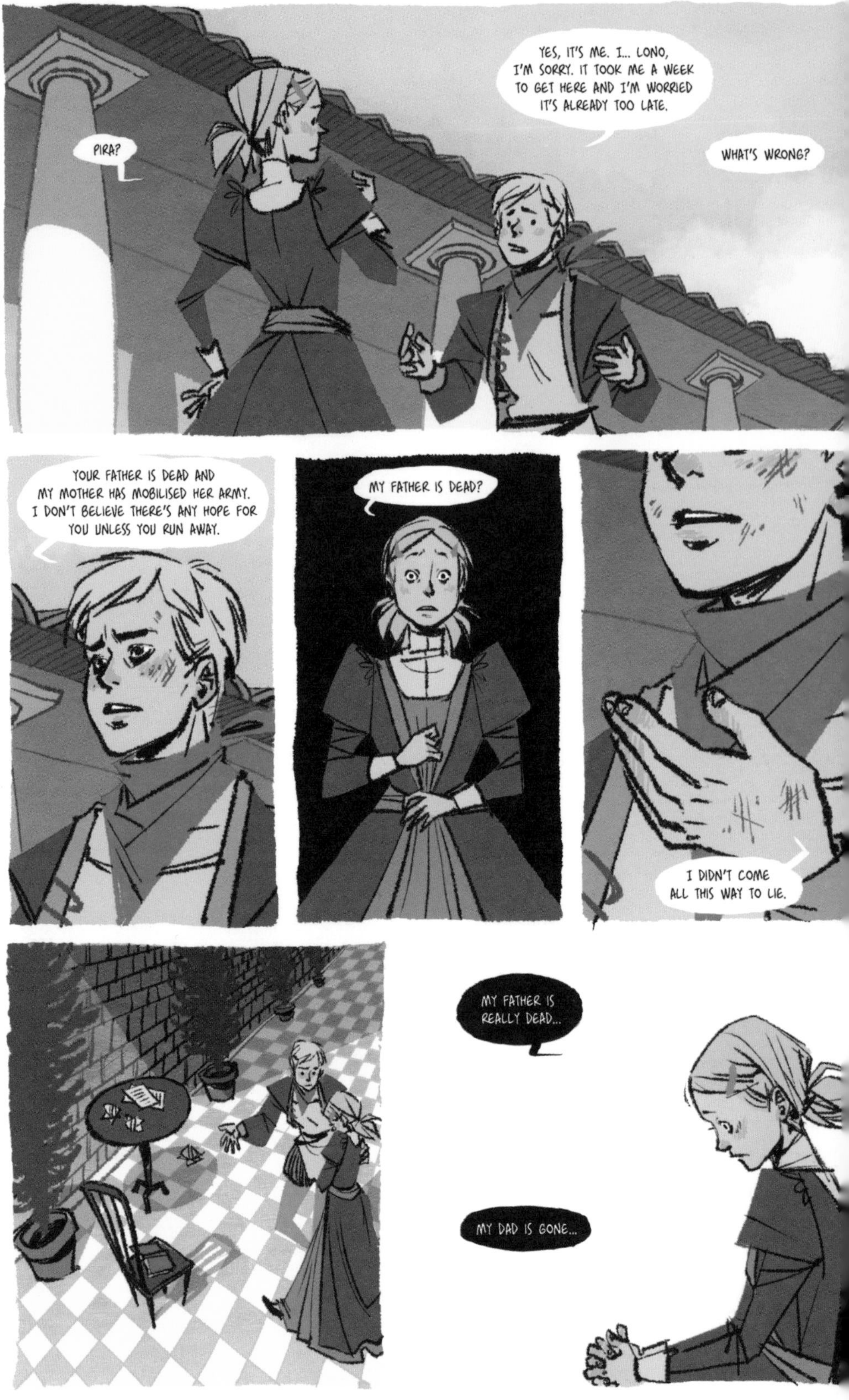
PIRA?
YES, IT'S ME. I... LONO, I'M SORRY. IT TOOK ME A WEEK TO GET HERE AND I'M WORRIED IT'S ALREADY TOO LATE.
WHAT'S WRONG?
YOUR FATHER IS DEAD AND MY MOTHER HAS MOBILISED HER ARMY. I DON'T BELIEVE THERE'S ANY HOPE FOR YOU UNLESS YOU RUN AWAY.
MY FATHER IS DEAD?
I DIDN'T COME ALL THIS WAY TO LIE.
MY FATHER IS REALLY DEAD...
MY DAD IS GONE...

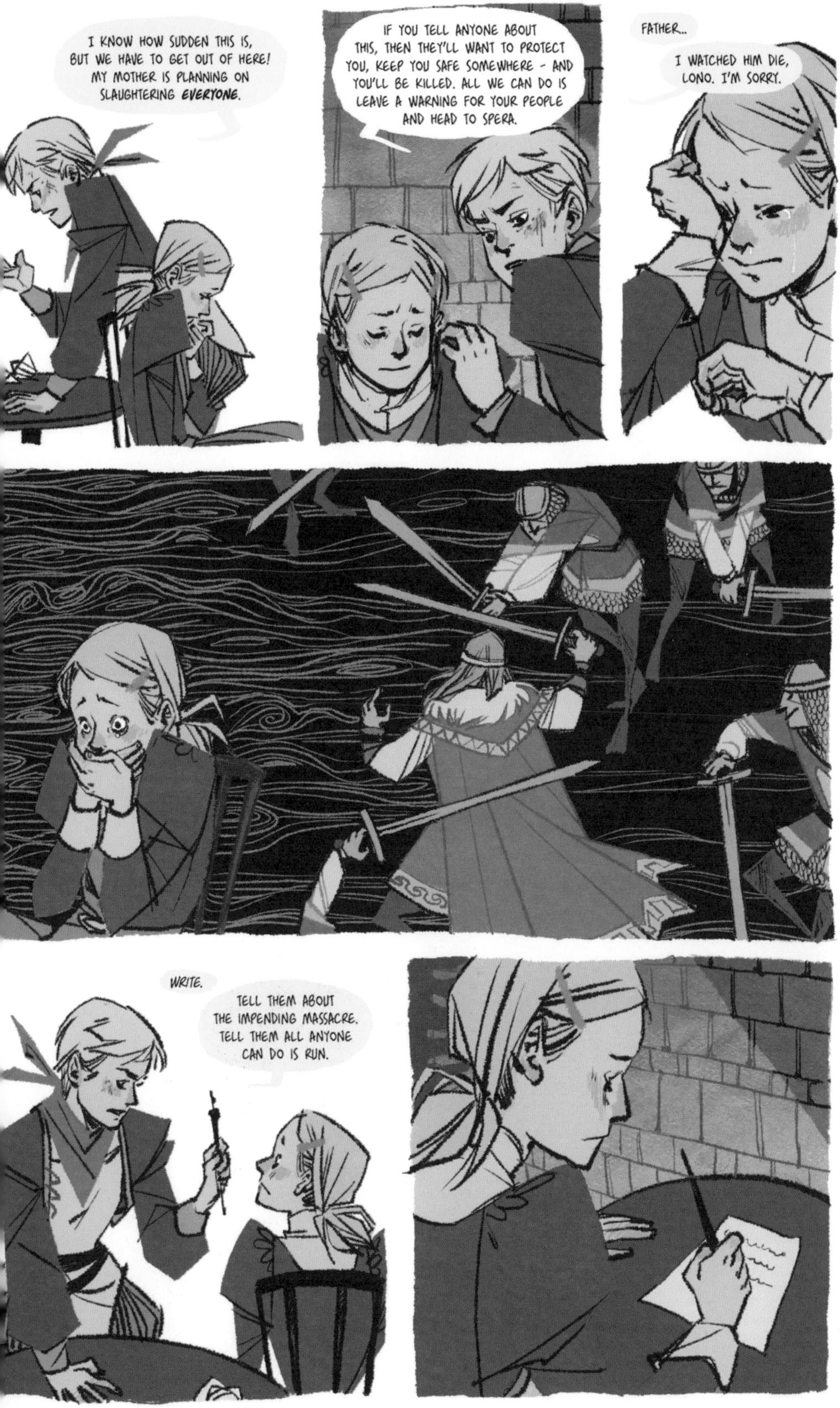
I KNOW HOW SUDDEN THIS IS, BUT WE HAVE TO GET OUT OF HERE! MY MOTHER IS PLANNING ON SLAUGHTERING *EVERYONE*.
IF YOU TELL ANYONE ABOUT THIS, THEN THEY'LL WANT TO PROTECT YOU, KEEP YOU SAFE SOMEWHERE - AND YOU'LL BE KILLED. ALL WE CAN DO IS LEAVE A WARNING FOR YOUR PEOPLE AND HEAD TO SPERA.
FATHER..
I WATCHED HIM DIE, LONO. I'M SORRY.
WRITE.
TELL THEM ABOUT THE IMPENDING MASSACRE. TELL THEM ALL ANYONE CAN DO IS RUN.

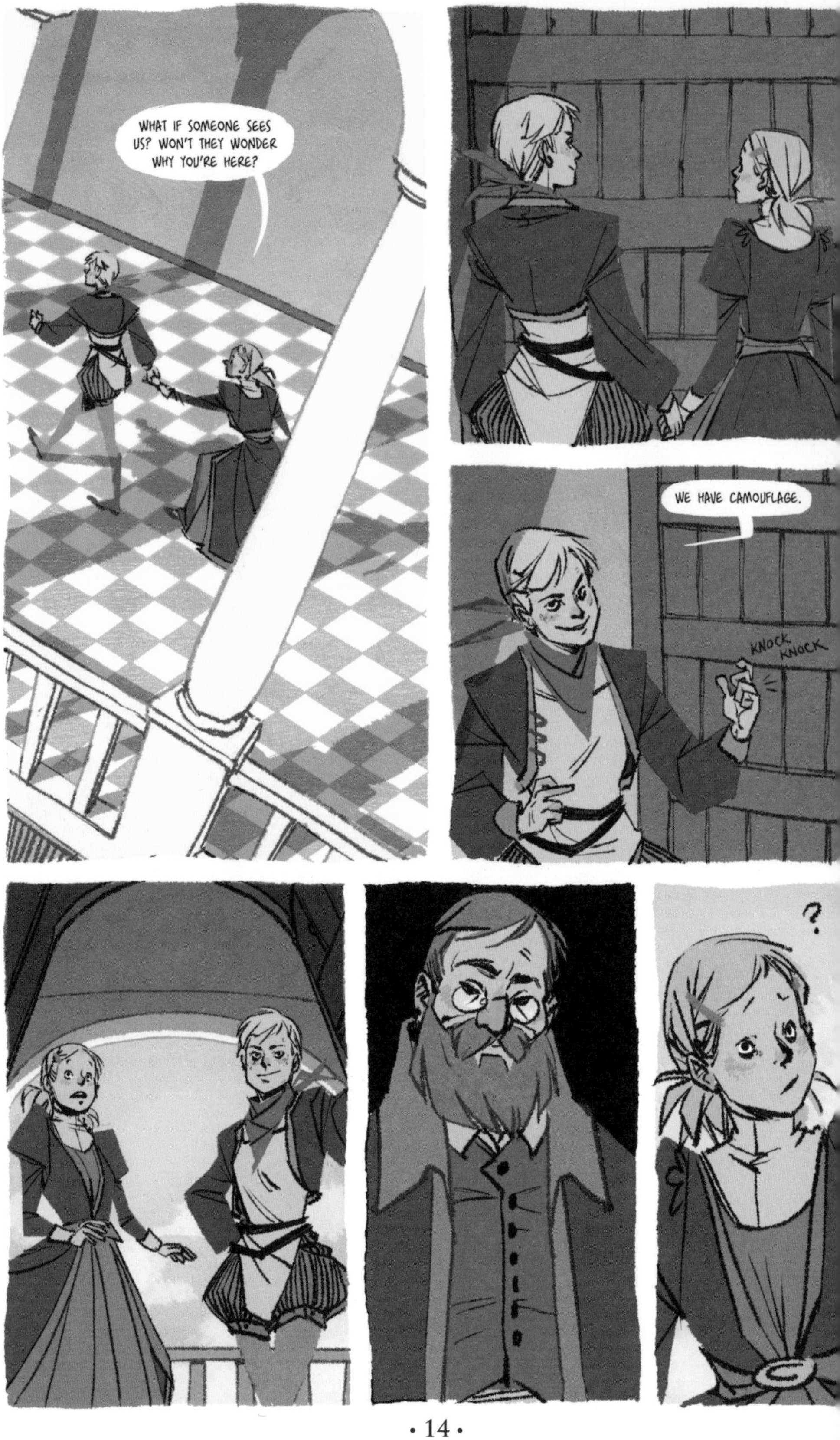
WHAT IF SOMEONE SEES US? WON'T THEY WONDER WHY YOU'RE HERE?
WE HAVE CAMOUFLAGE.
KNOCK KNOCK
?

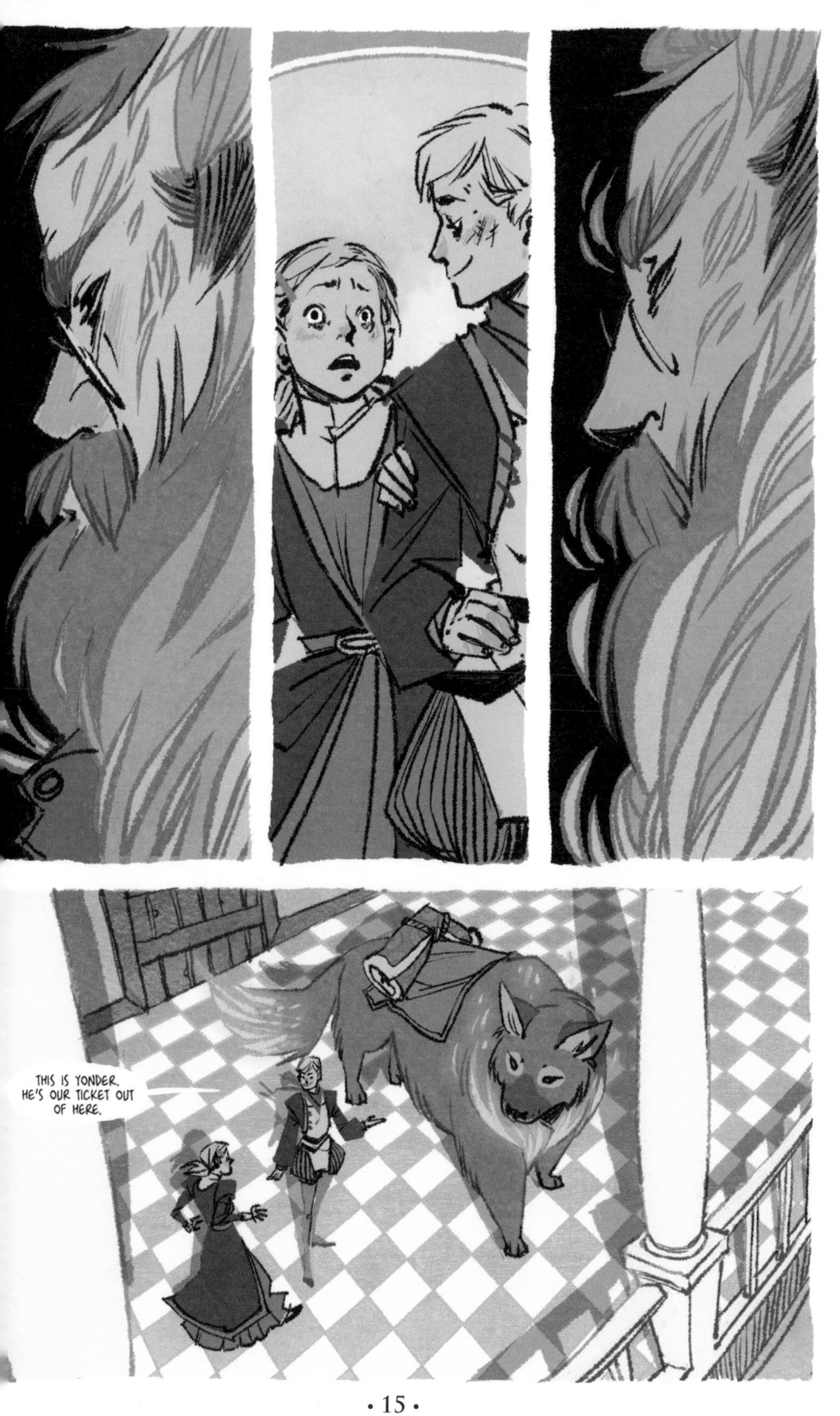
THIS IS YONDER.
HE'S OUR TICKET OUT
OF HERE.

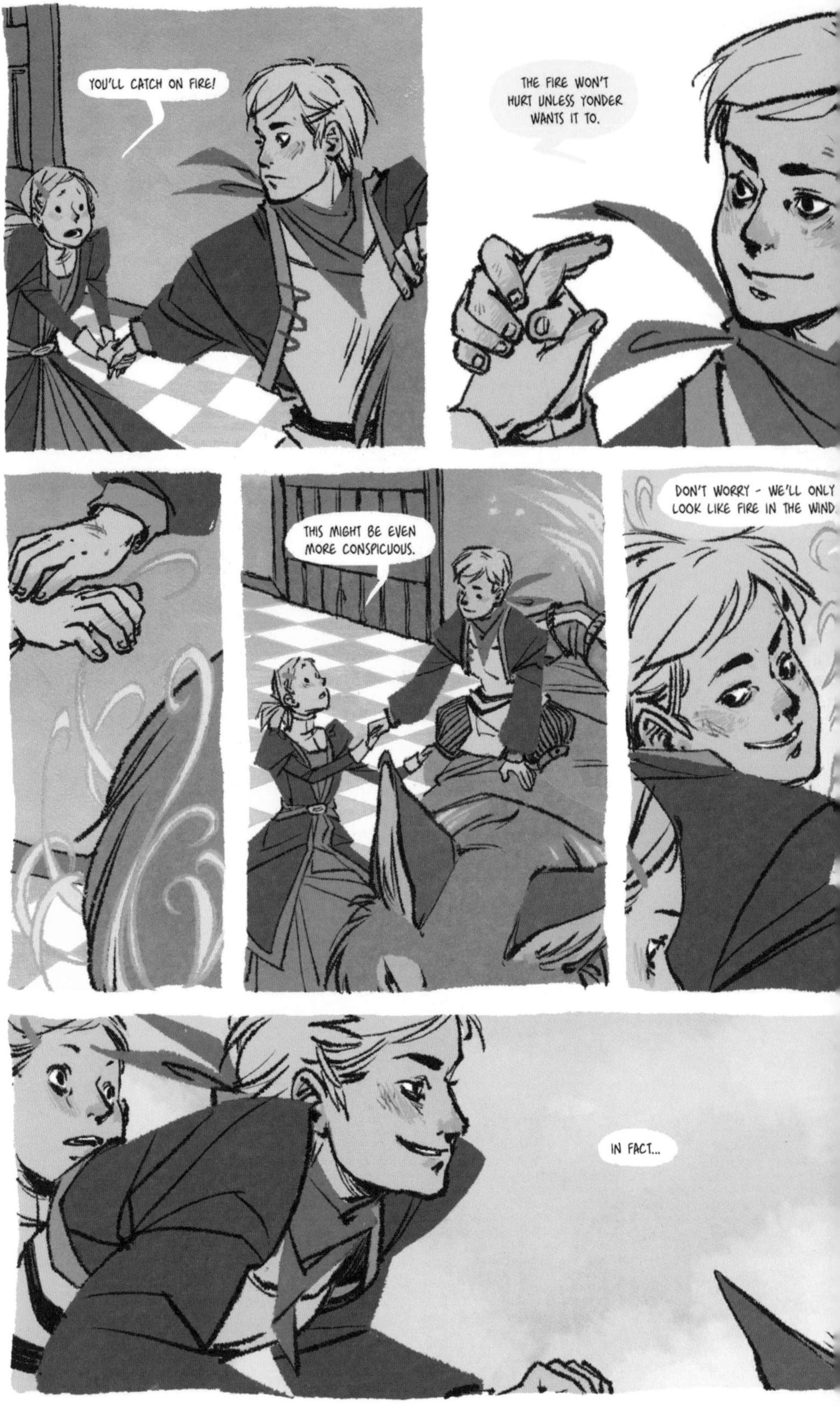
YOU'LL CATCH ON FIRE!
THE FIRE WON'T HURT UNLESS YONDER WANTS IT TO.
THIS MIGHT BE EVEN MORE CONSPICUOUS.
DON'T WORRY - WE'LL ONLY LOOK LIKE FIRE IN THE WIND.
IN FACT...

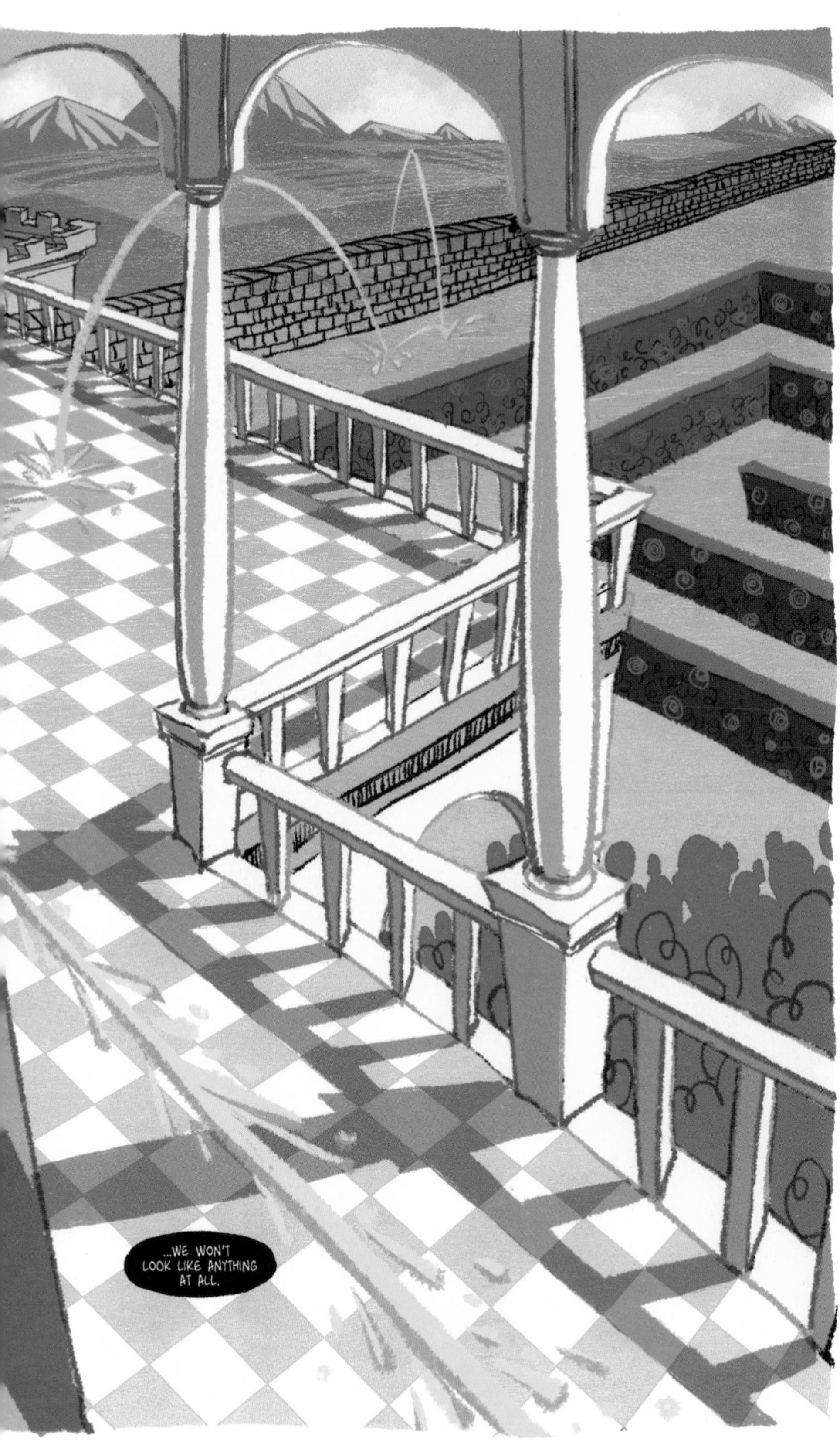
...WE WON'T LOOK LIKE ANYTHING AT ALL.

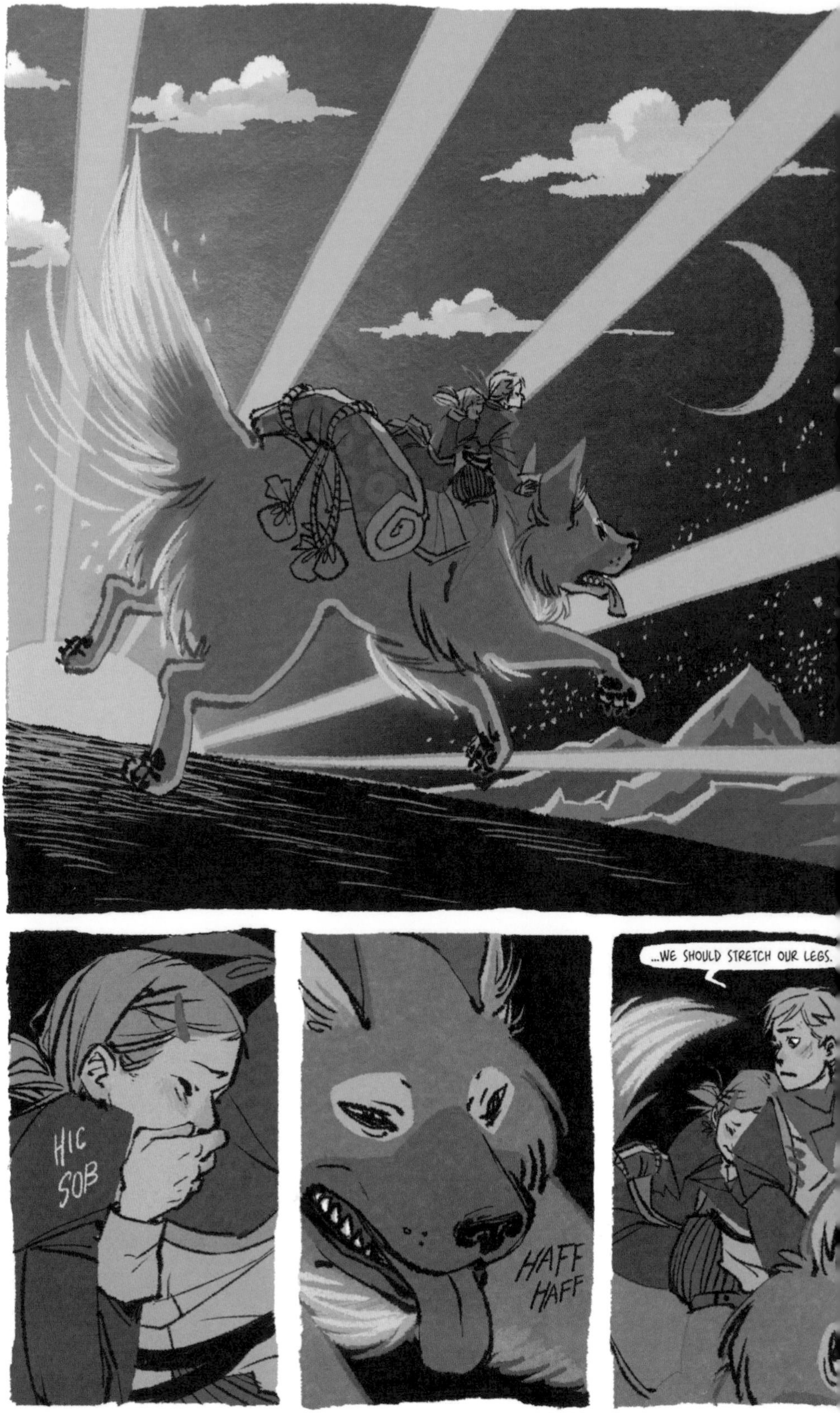
HIC
SOB
HAFF
HAFF
...WE SHOULD STRETCH OUR LEGS.

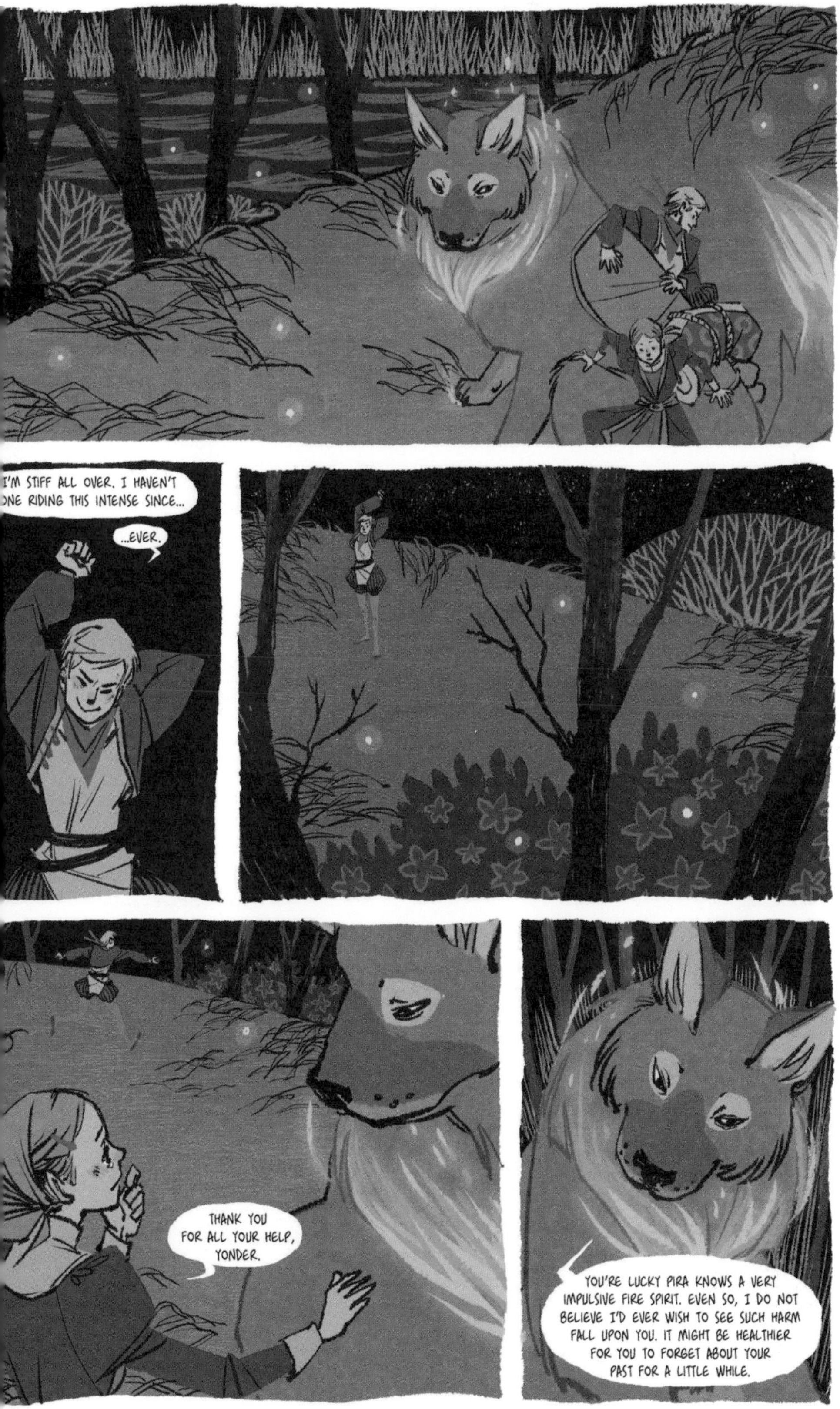
I'M STIFF ALL OVER. I HAVEN'T
ONE RIDING THIS INTENSE SINCE...
...EVER.
THANK YOU FOR ALL YOUR HELP, YONDER.
YOU'RE LUCKY PIRA KNOWS A VERY IMPULSIVE FIRE SPIRIT. EVEN SO, I DO NOT BELIEVE I'D EVER WISH TO SEE SUCH HARM FALL UPON YOU. IT MIGHT BE HEALTHIER FOR YOU TO FORGET ABOUT YOUR PAST FOR A LITTLE WHILE.

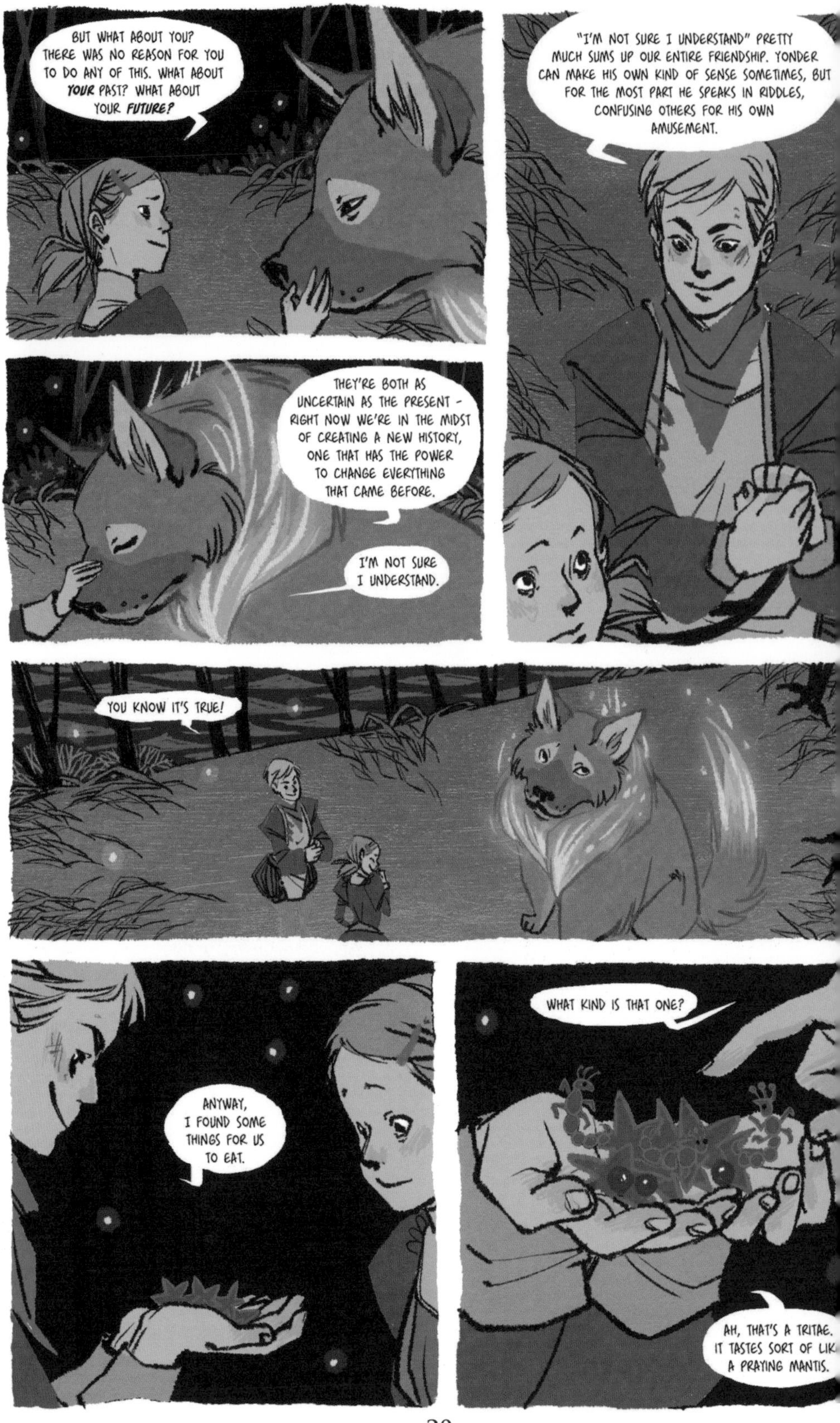
BUT WHAT ABOUT YOU? THERE WAS NO REASON FOR YOU TO DO ANY OF THIS. WHAT ABOUT YOUR PAST? WHAT ABOUT YOUR FUTURE?
THEY'RE BOTH AS UNCERTAIN AS THE PRESENT - RIGHT NOW WE'RE IN THE MIDST OF CREATING A NEW HISTORY, ONE THAT HAS THE POWER TO CHANGE EVERYTHING THAT CAME BEFORE.
I'M NOT SURE I UNDERSTAND.
"I'M NOT SURE I UNDERSTAND" PRETTY MUCH SUMS UP OUR ENTIRE FRIENDSHIP. YONDER CAN MAKE HIS OWN KIND OF SENSE SOMETIMES, BUT FOR THE MOST PART HE SPEAKS IN RIDDLES, CONFUSING OTHERS FOR HIS OWN AMUSEMENT.
YOU KNOW IT'S TRUE!
ANYWAY, I FOUND SOME THINGS FOR US TO EAT.
WHAT KIND IS THAT ONE?
AH, THAT'S A TRITAE. IT TASTES SORT OF LIK A PRAYING MANTIS.

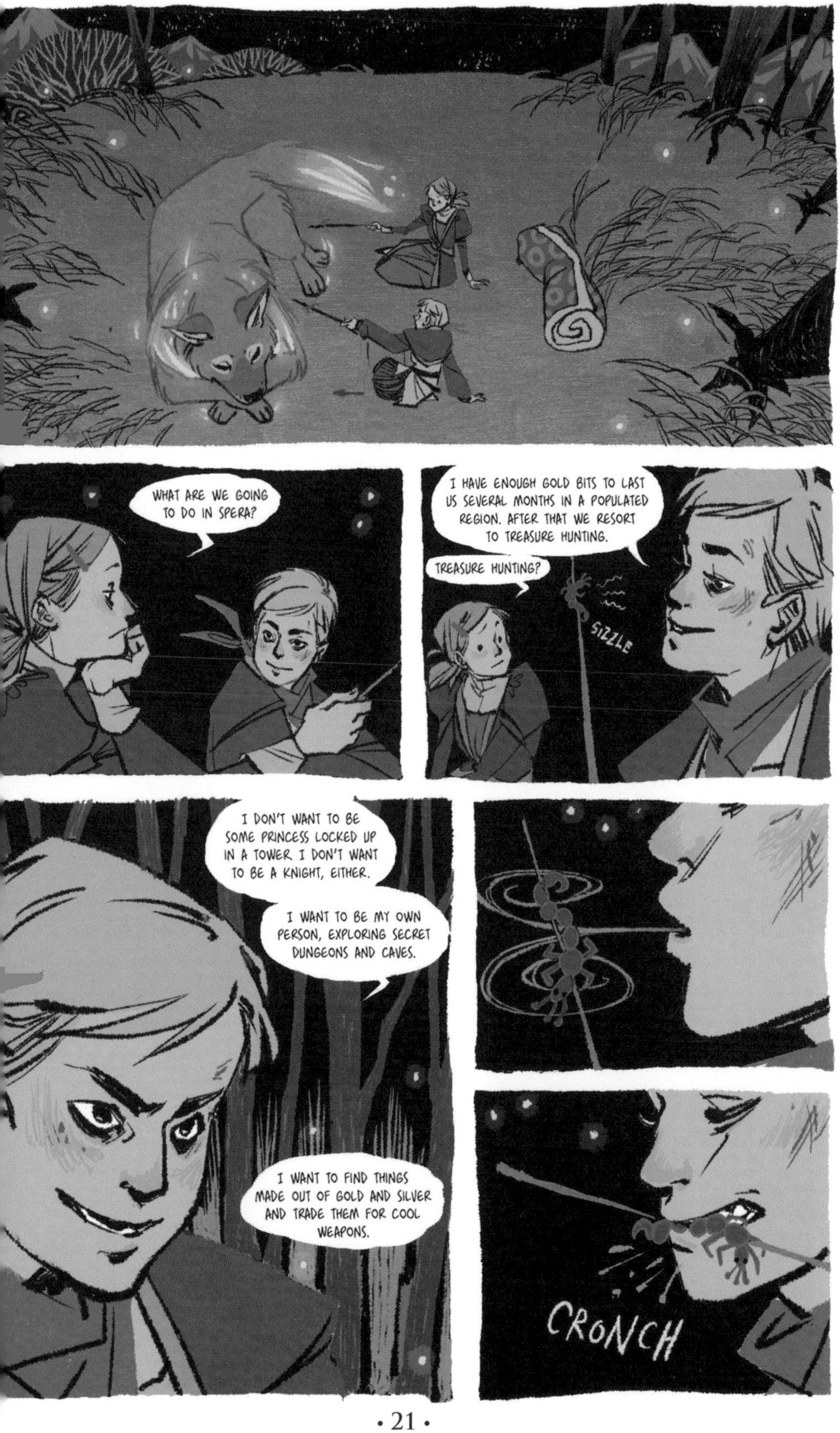
WHAT ARE WE GOING TO DO IN SPERA?
I HAVE ENOUGH GOLD BITS TO LAST US SEVERAL MONTHS IN A POPULATED REGION. AFTER THAT WE RESORT TO TREASURE HUNTING.
TREASURE HUNTING?
SIZZLE
I DON'T WANT TO BE SOME PRINCESS LOCKED UP IN A TOWER. I DON'T WANT TO BE A KNIGHT, EITHER.
I WANT TO BE MY OWN PERSON, EXPLORING SECRET DUNGEONS AND CAVES.
I WANT TO FIND THINGS MADE OUT OF GOLD AND SILVER AND TRADE THEM FOR COOL WEAPONS.
CRONCH

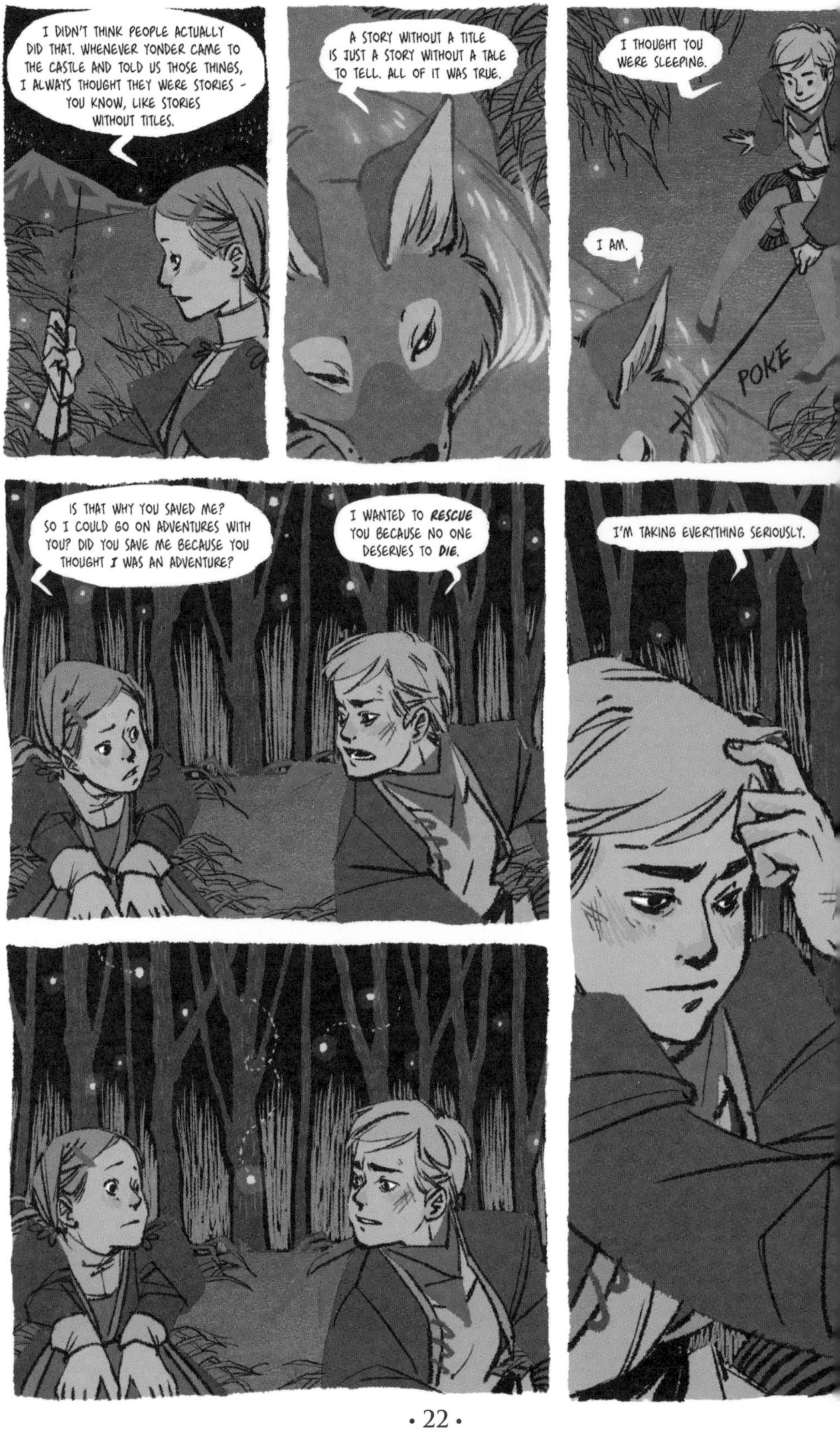
I DIDN'T THINK PEOPLE ACTUALLY DID THAT. WHENEVER YONDER CAME TO THE CASTLE AND TOLD US THOSE THINGS, I ALWAYS THOUGHT THEY WERE STORIES - YOU KNOW, LIKE STORIES WITHOUT TITLES.
A STORY WITHOUT A TITLE IS JUST A STORY WITHOUT A TALE TO TELL. ALL OF IT WAS TRUE.
I THOUGHT YOU WERE SLEEPING.
I AM.
POKE
IS THAT WHY YOU SAVED ME? SO I COULD GO ON ADVENTURES WITH YOU? DID YOU SAVE ME BECAUSE YOU THOUGHT *I* WAS AN ADVENTURE?
I WANTED TO ***RESCUE*** YOU BECAUSE NO ONE DESERVES TO ***DIE***.
I'M TAKING EVERYTHING SERIOUSLY.

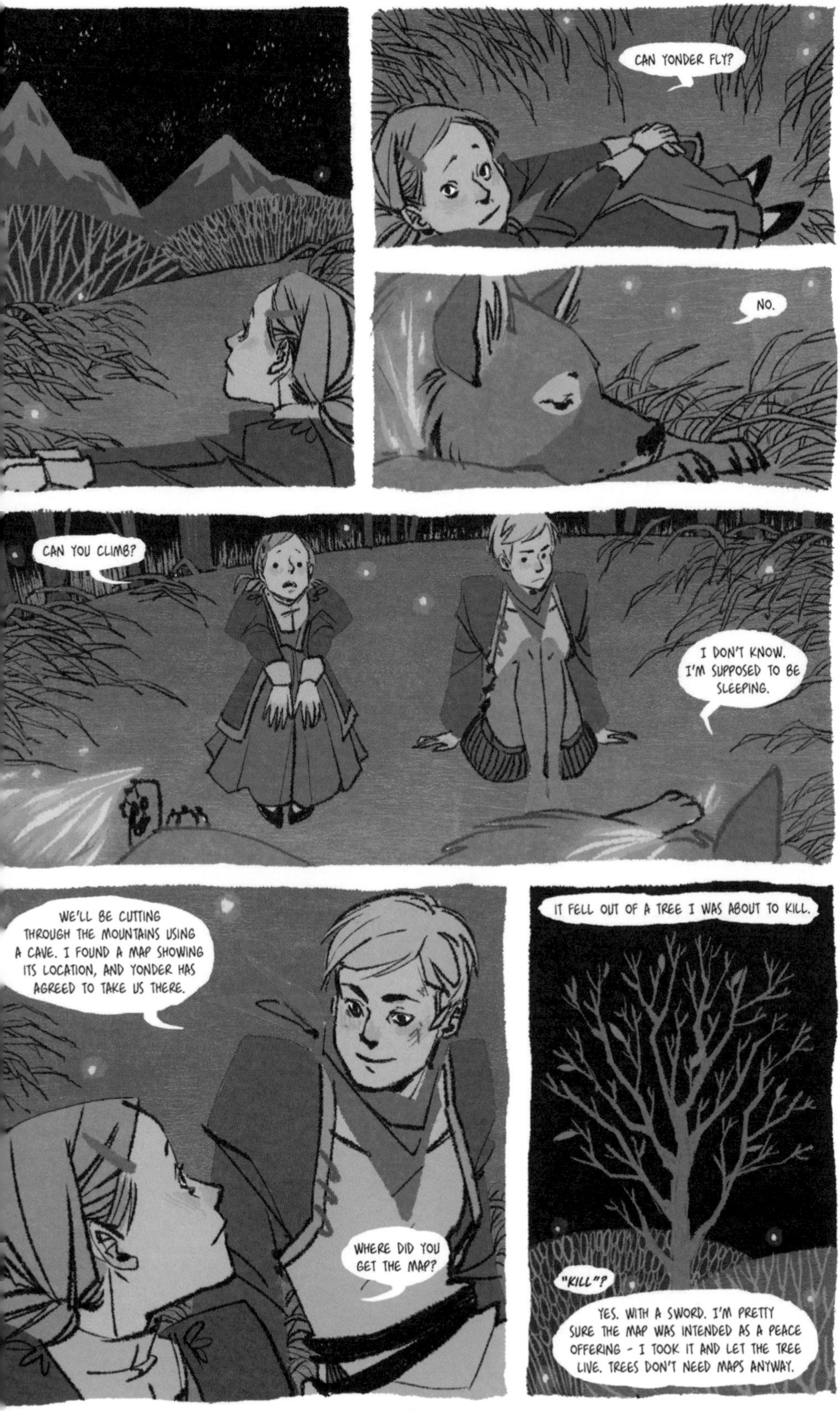
CAN YONDER FLY?
NO.
CAN YOU CLIMB?
I DON'T KNOW. I'M SUPPOSED TO BE SLEEPING.
WE'LL BE CUTTING THROUGH THE MOUNTAINS USING A CAVE. I FOUND A MAP SHOWING ITS LOCATION, AND YONDER HAS AGREED TO TAKE US THERE.
WHERE DID YOU GET THE MAP?
IT FELL OUT OF A TREE I WAS ABOUT TO KILL.
"KILL"?
YES. WITH A SWORD. I'M PRETTY SURE THE MAP WAS INTENDED AS A PEACE OFFERING - I TOOK IT AND LET THE TREE LIVE. TREES DON'T NEED MAPS ANYWAY.

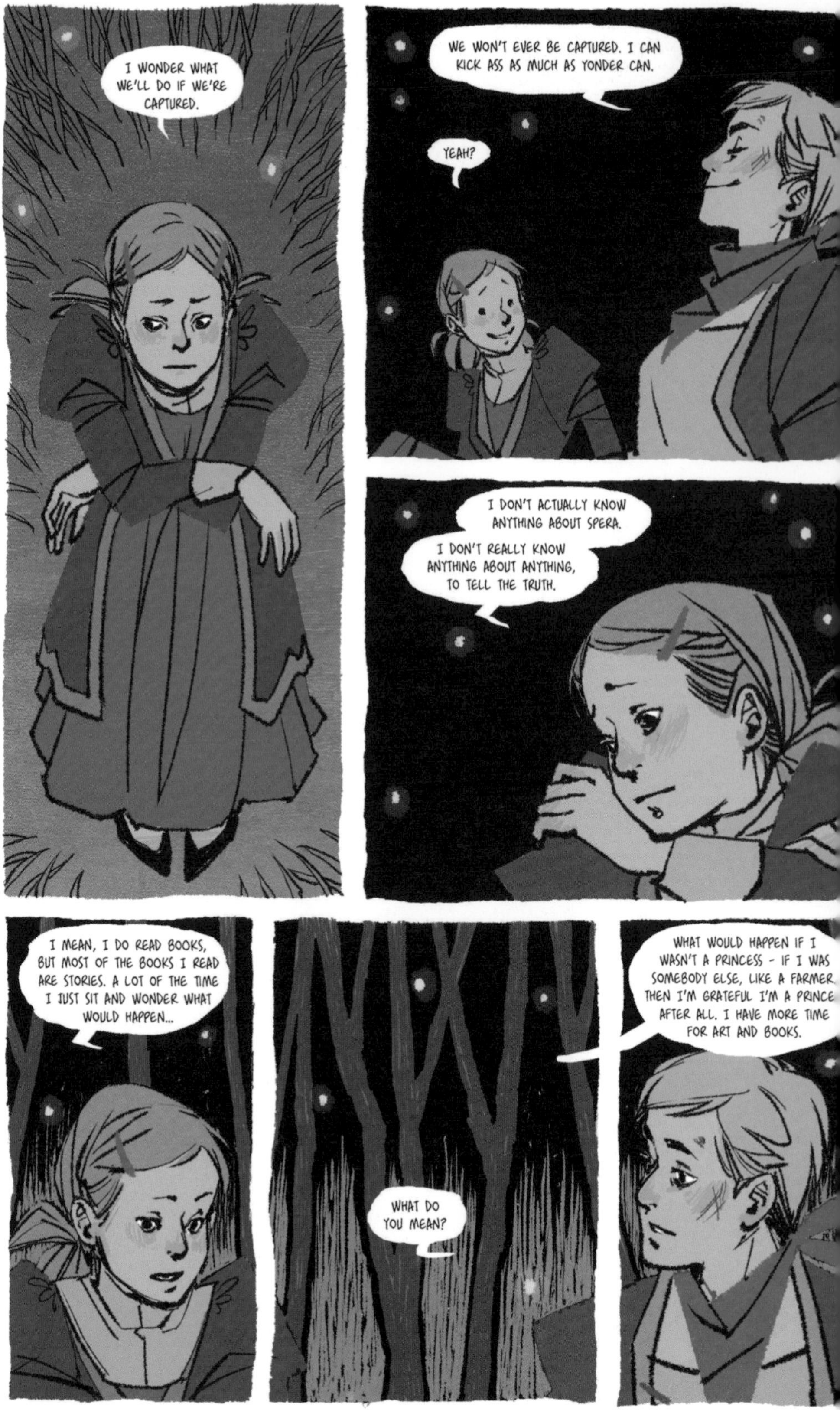
I WONDER WHAT WE'LL DO IF WE'RE CAPTURED.
WE WON'T EVER BE CAPTURED. I CAN KICK ASS AS MUCH AS YONDER CAN.
YEAH?
I DON'T ACTUALLY KNOW ANYTHING ABOUT SPERA.
I DON'T REALLY KNOW ANYTHING ABOUT ANYTHING, TO TELL THE TRUTH.
I MEAN, I DO READ BOOKS, BUT MOST OF THE BOOKS I READ ARE STORIES. A LOT OF THE TIME I JUST SIT AND WONDER WHAT WOULD HAPPEN...
WHAT DO YOU MEAN?
WHAT WOULD HAPPEN IF I WASN'T A PRINCESS - IF I WAS SOMEBODY ELSE, LIKE A FARMER THEN I'M GRATEFUL I'M A PRINCE AFTER ALL. I HAVE MORE TIME FOR ART AND BOOKS.

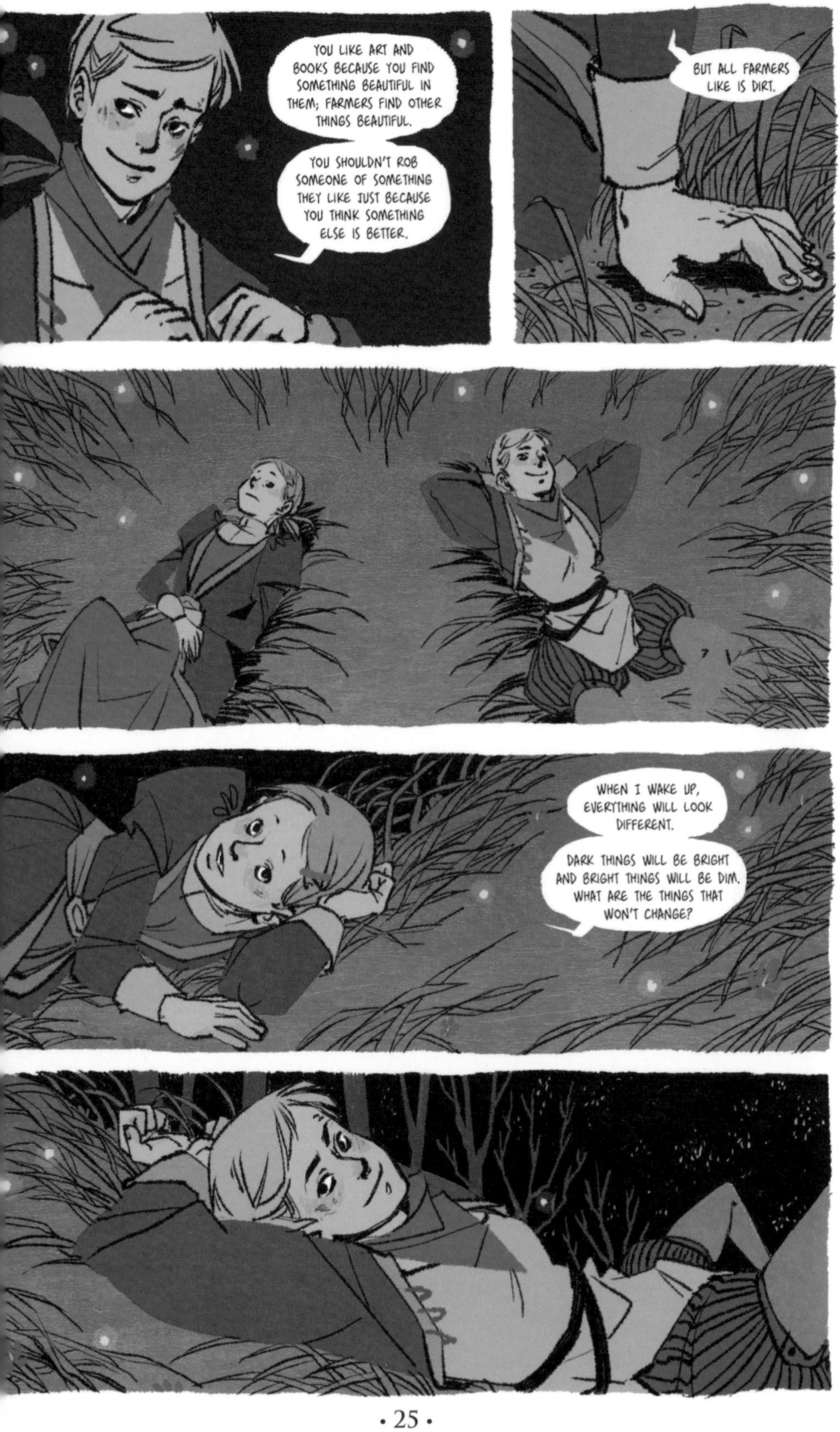
YOU LIKE ART AND BOOKS BECAUSE YOU FIND SOMETHING BEAUTIFUL IN THEM; FARMERS FIND OTHER THINGS BEAUTIFUL.
YOU SHOULDN'T ROB SOMEONE OF SOMETHING THEY LIKE JUST BECAUSE YOU THINK SOMETHING ELSE IS BETTER.
BUT ALL FARMERS LIKE IS DIRT.
WHEN I WAKE UP, EVERYTHING WILL LOOK DIFFERENT.
DARK THINGS WILL BE BRIGHT AND BRIGHT THINGS WILL BE DIM. WHAT ARE THE THINGS THAT WON'T CHANGE?

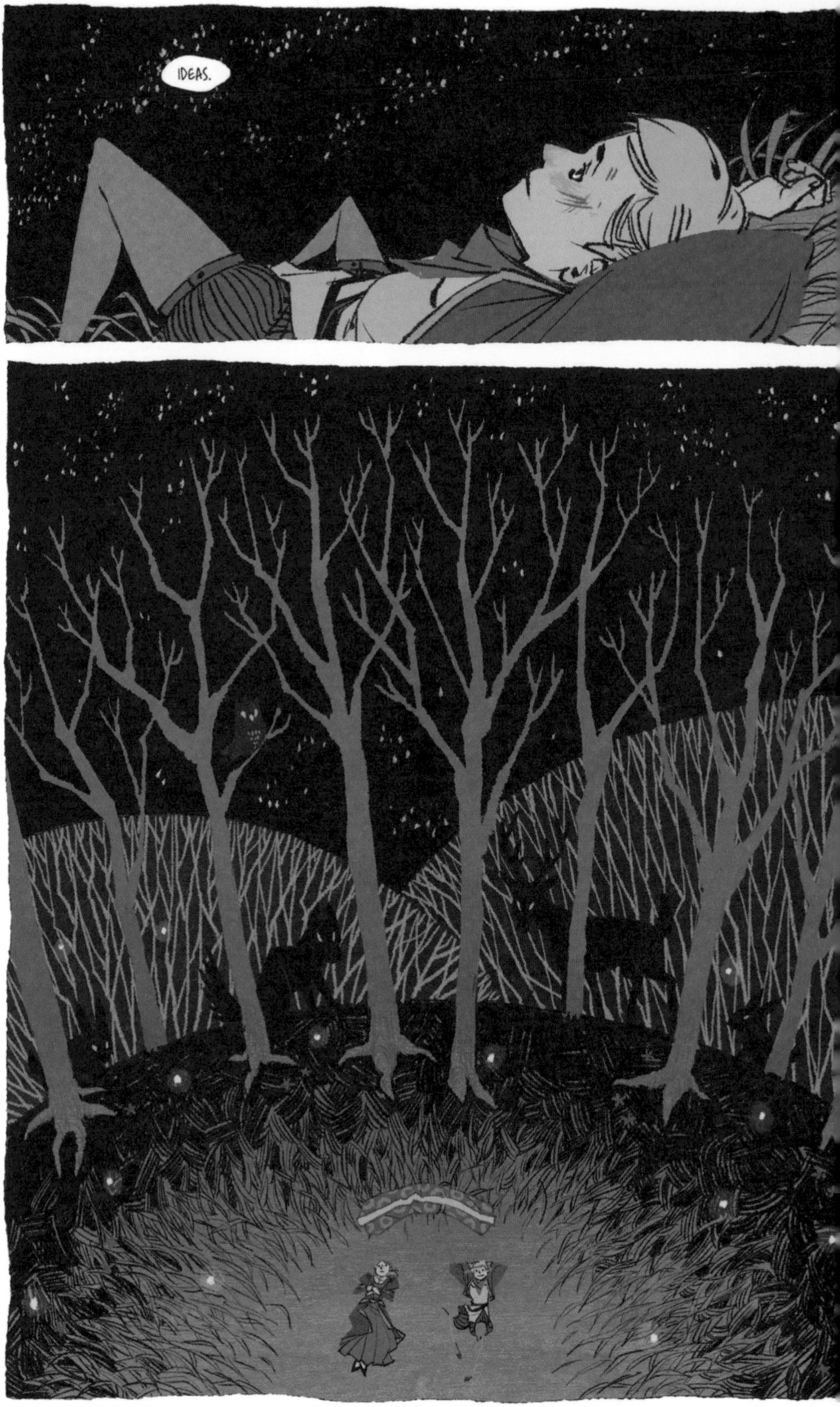
IDEAS.

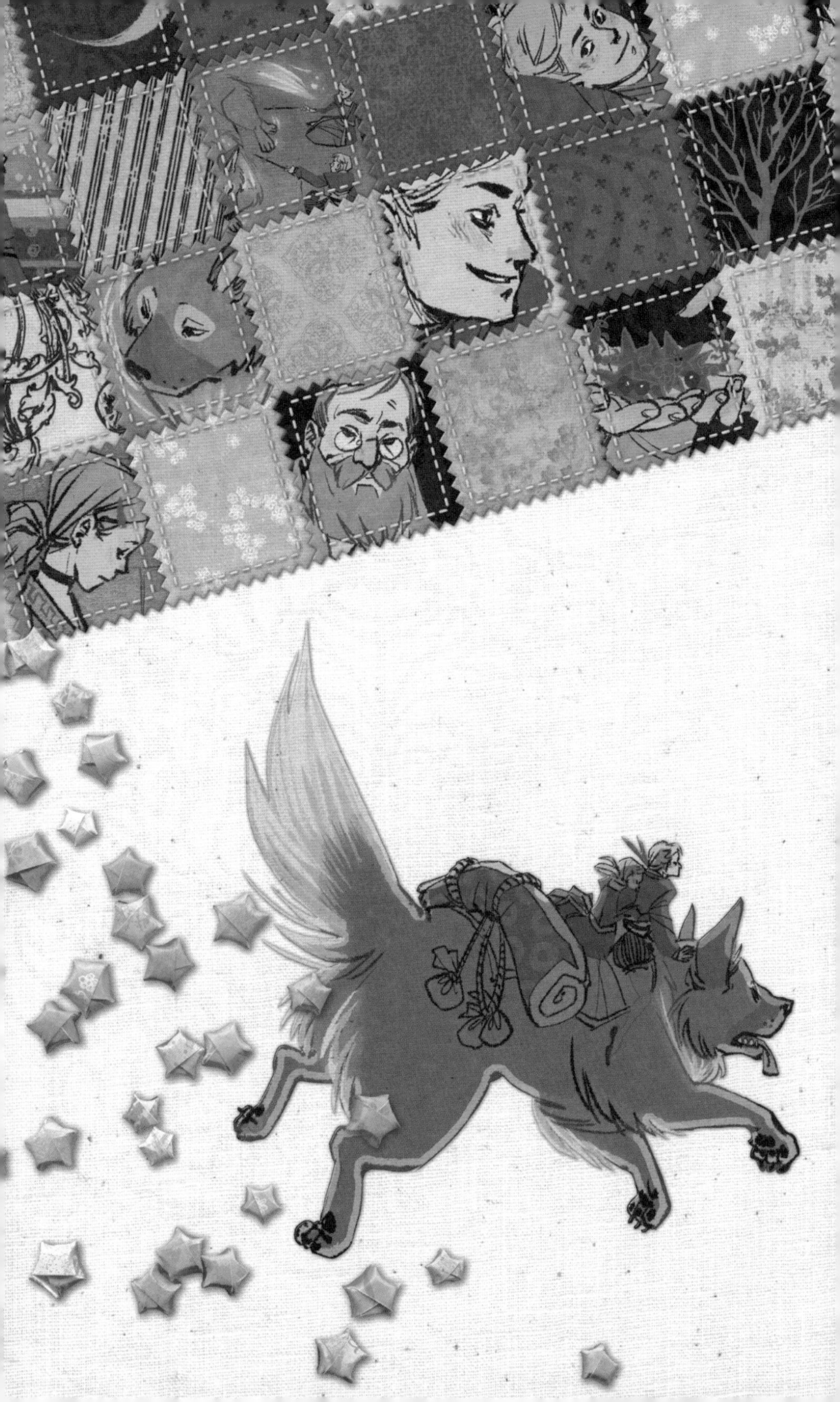

CHAPTER TWO
Spirits of the Mountain

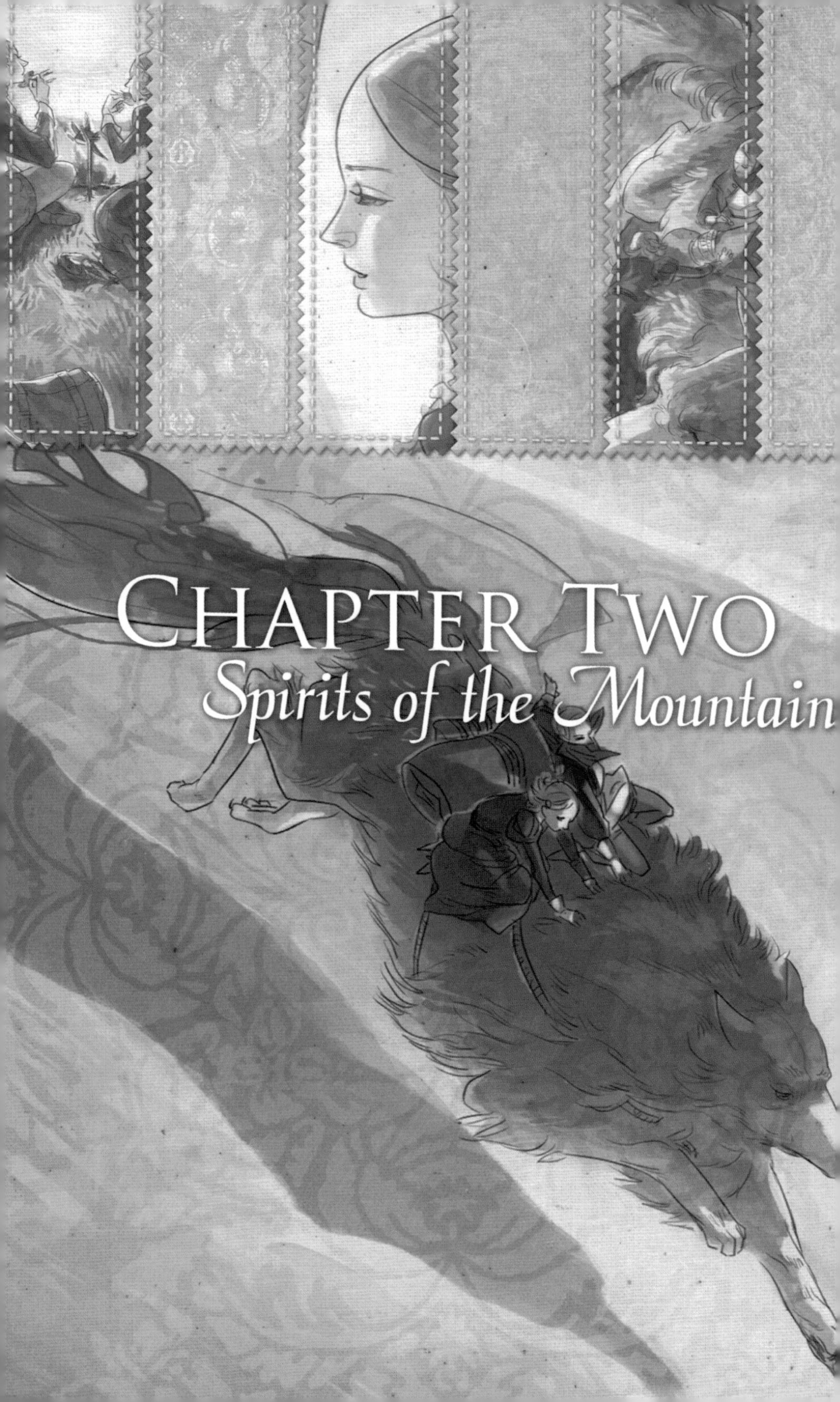

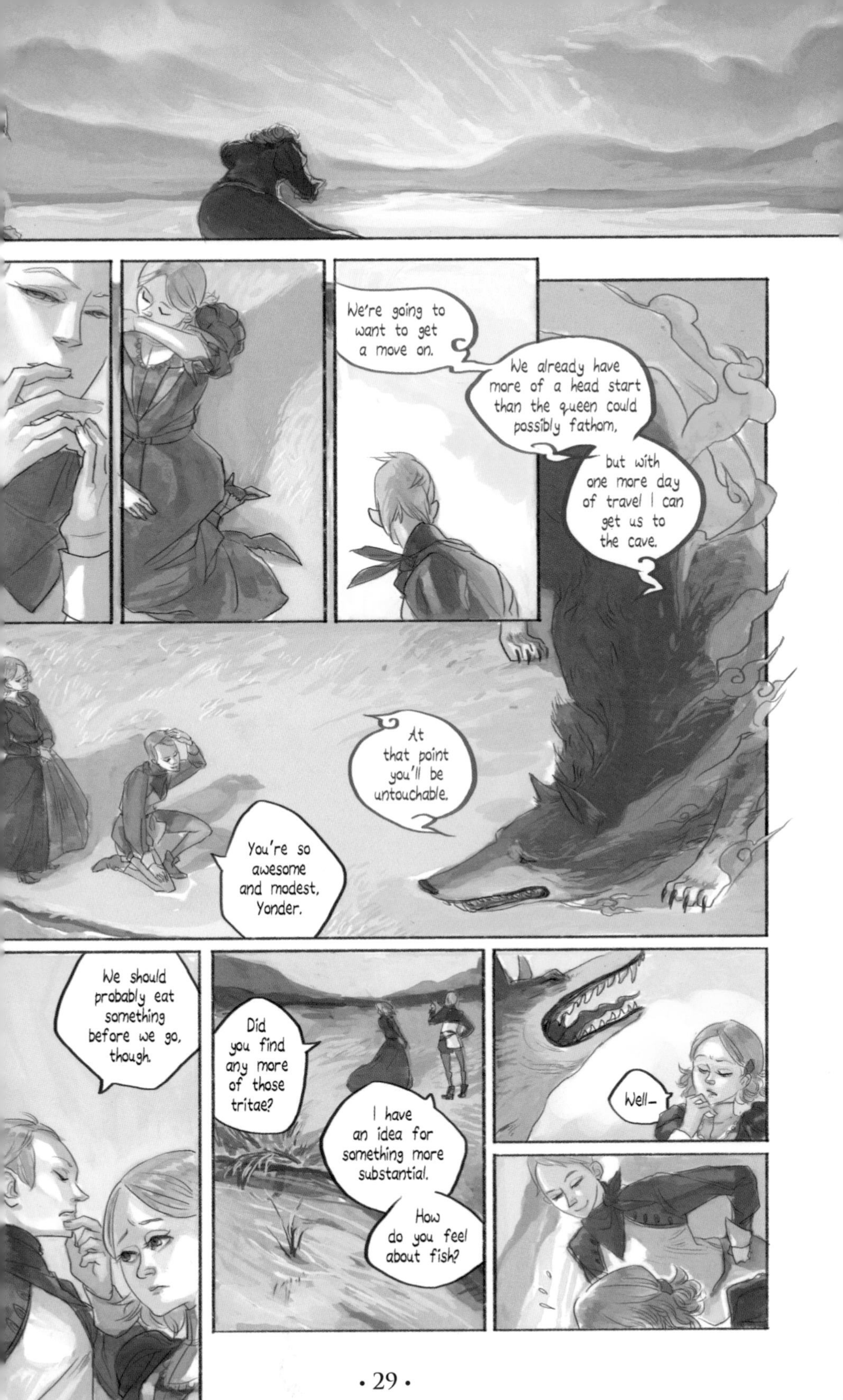
We're going to want to get a move on.
We already have more of a head start than the queen could possibly fathom,
but with one more day of travel I can get us to the cave.
At that point you'll be untouchable.
You're so awesome and modest, Yonder.
We should probably eat something before we go, though.
Did you find any more of those tritae?
I have an idea for something more substantial.
How do you feel about fish?
Well–

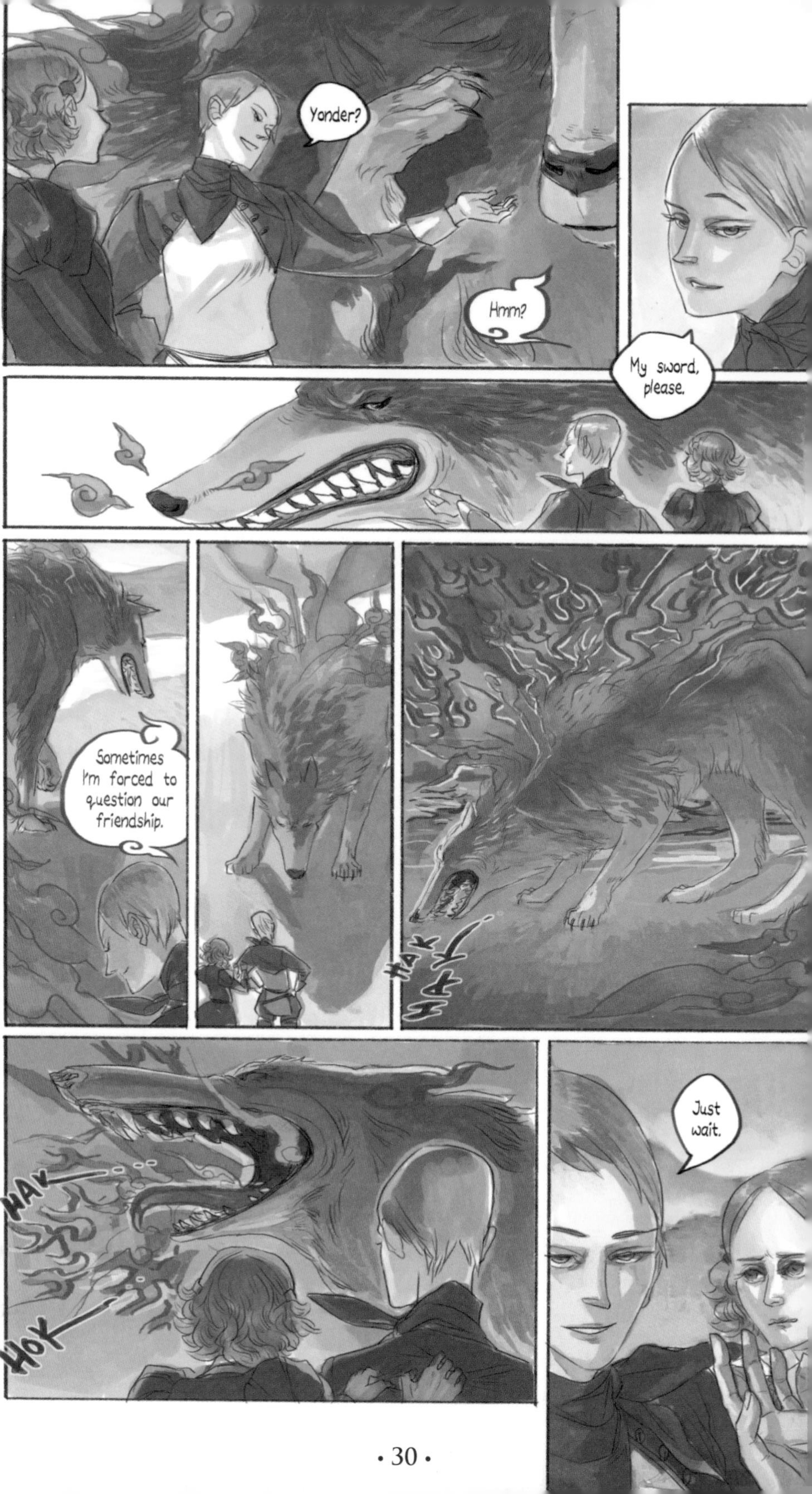
Yonder?
Hmm?
My sword, please.
Sometimes I'm forced to question our friendship.
HAK HAK
HAK
HOK
Just wait.

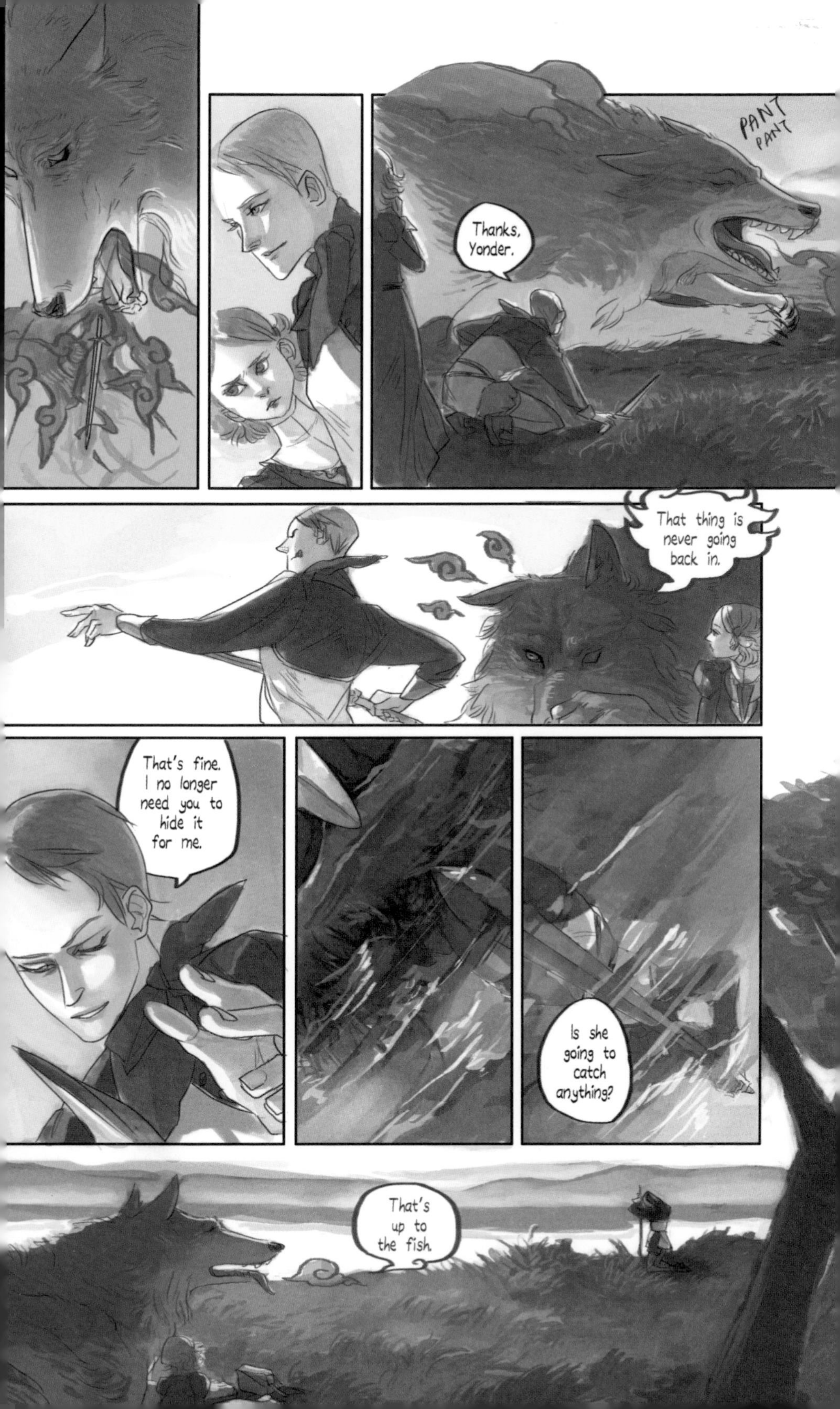
PANT
PANT
Thanks, Yonder.
That thing is never going back in.
That's fine. I no longer need you to hide it for me.
Is she going to catch anything?
That's up to the fish.

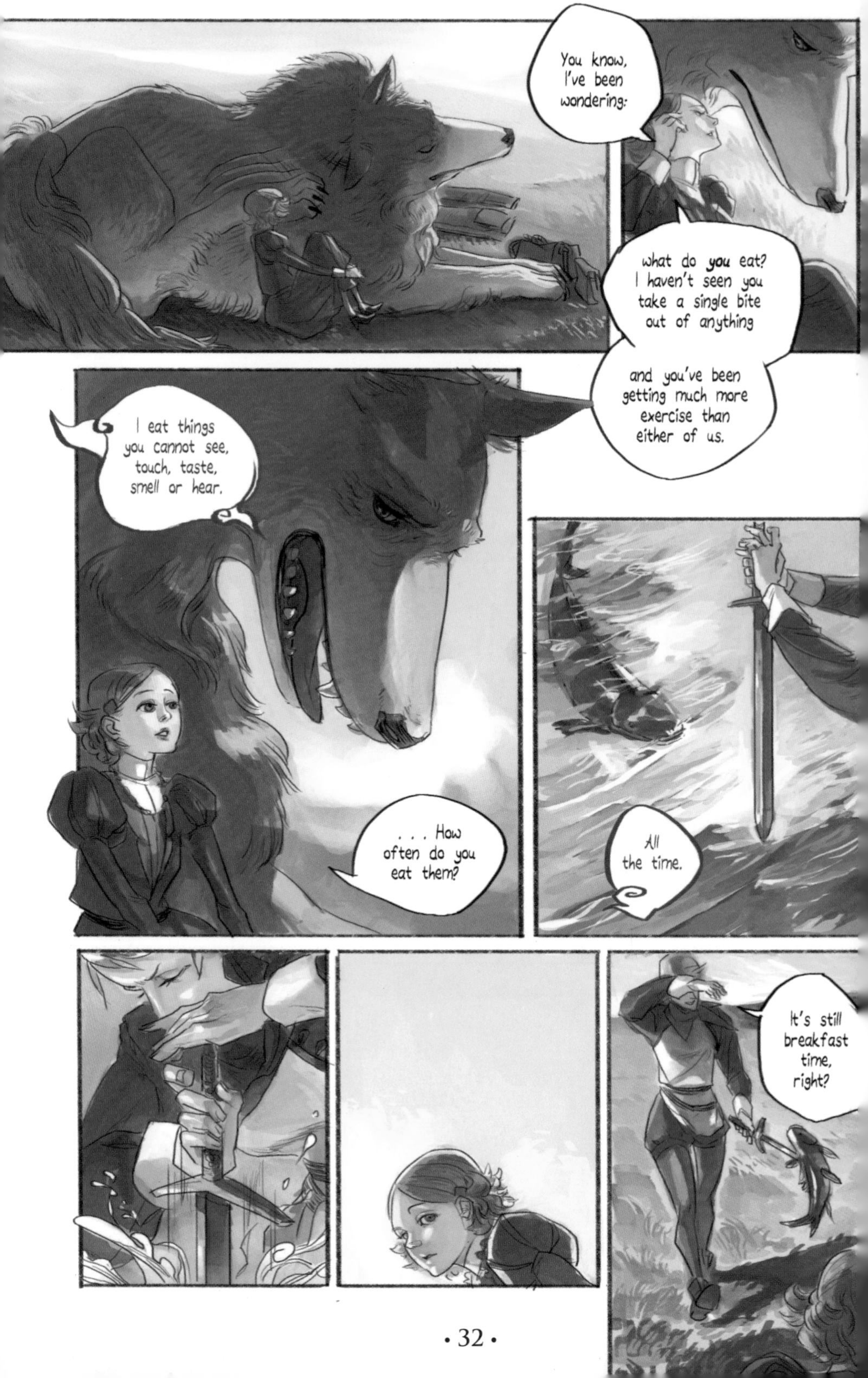
You know, I've been wondering:
what do **you** eat? I haven't seen you take a single bite out of anything
and you've been getting much more exercise than either of us.
I eat things you cannot see, touch, taste, smell or hear.
. . . How often do you eat them?
All the time.
It's still breakfast time, right?

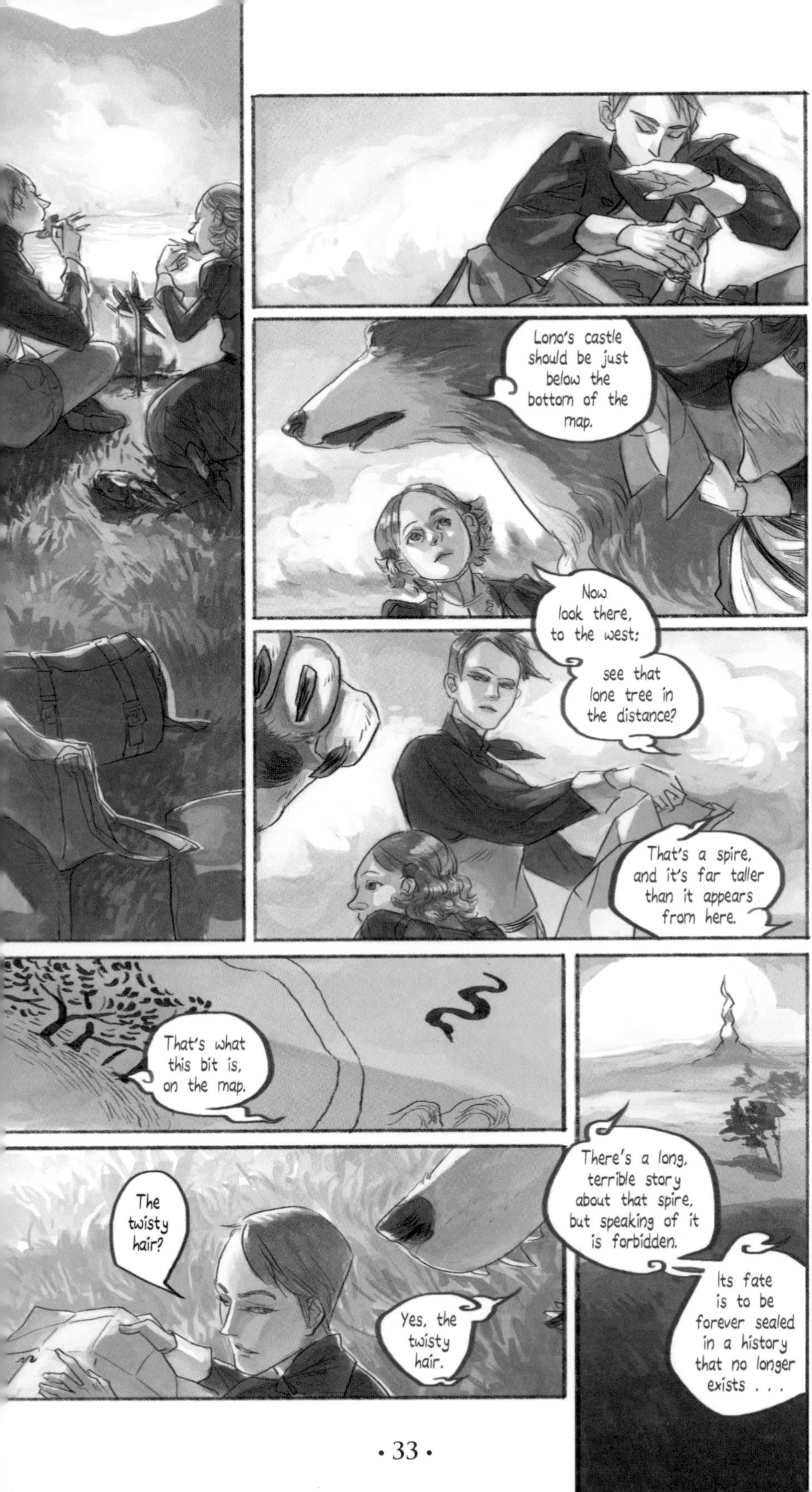
Lono's castle should be just below the bottom of the map.
Now look there, to the west;
see that lone tree in the distance?
That's a spire, and it's far taller than it appears from here.
That's what this bit is, on the map.
There's a long, terrible story about that spire, but speaking of it is forbidden.
Its fate is to be forever sealed in a history that no longer exists . . .
The twisty hair?
Yes, the twisty hair.

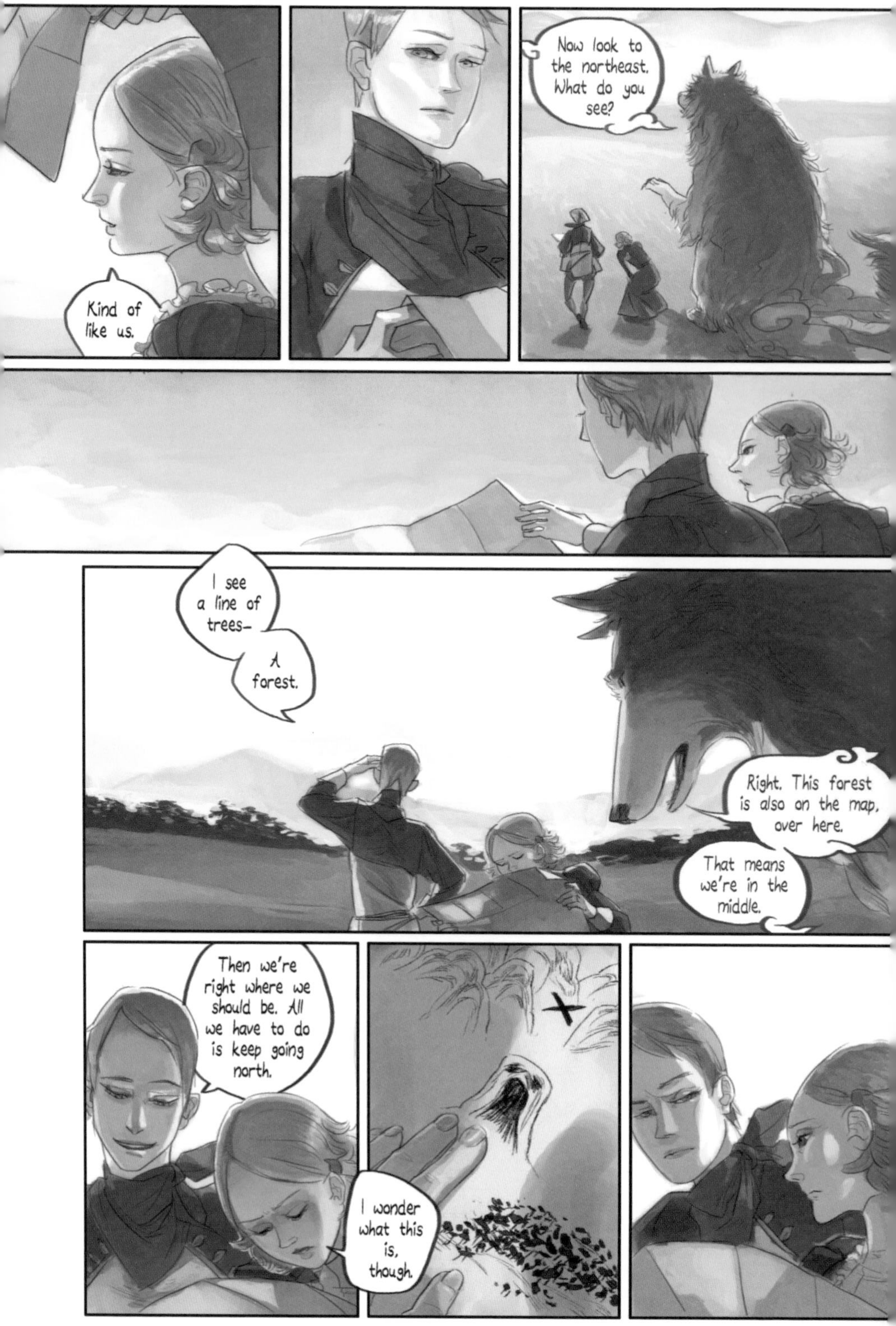
Kind of like us.
Now look to the northeast. What do you see?
I see a line of trees—
A forest.
Right. This forest is also on the map, over here.
That means we're in the middle.
Then we're right where we should be. All we have to do is keep going north.
I wonder what this is, though.

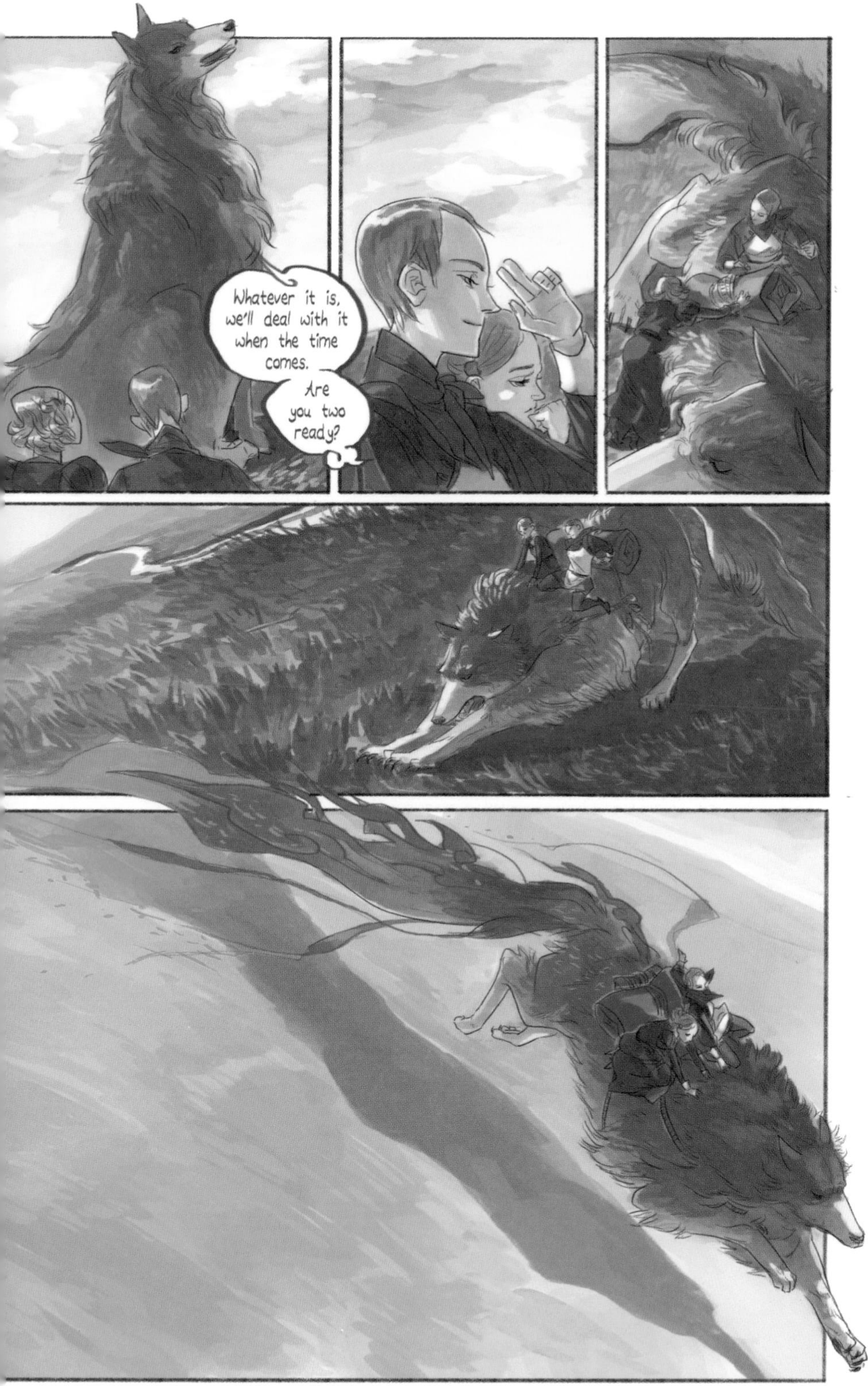
Whatever it is, we'll deal with it when the time comes.
Are you two ready?

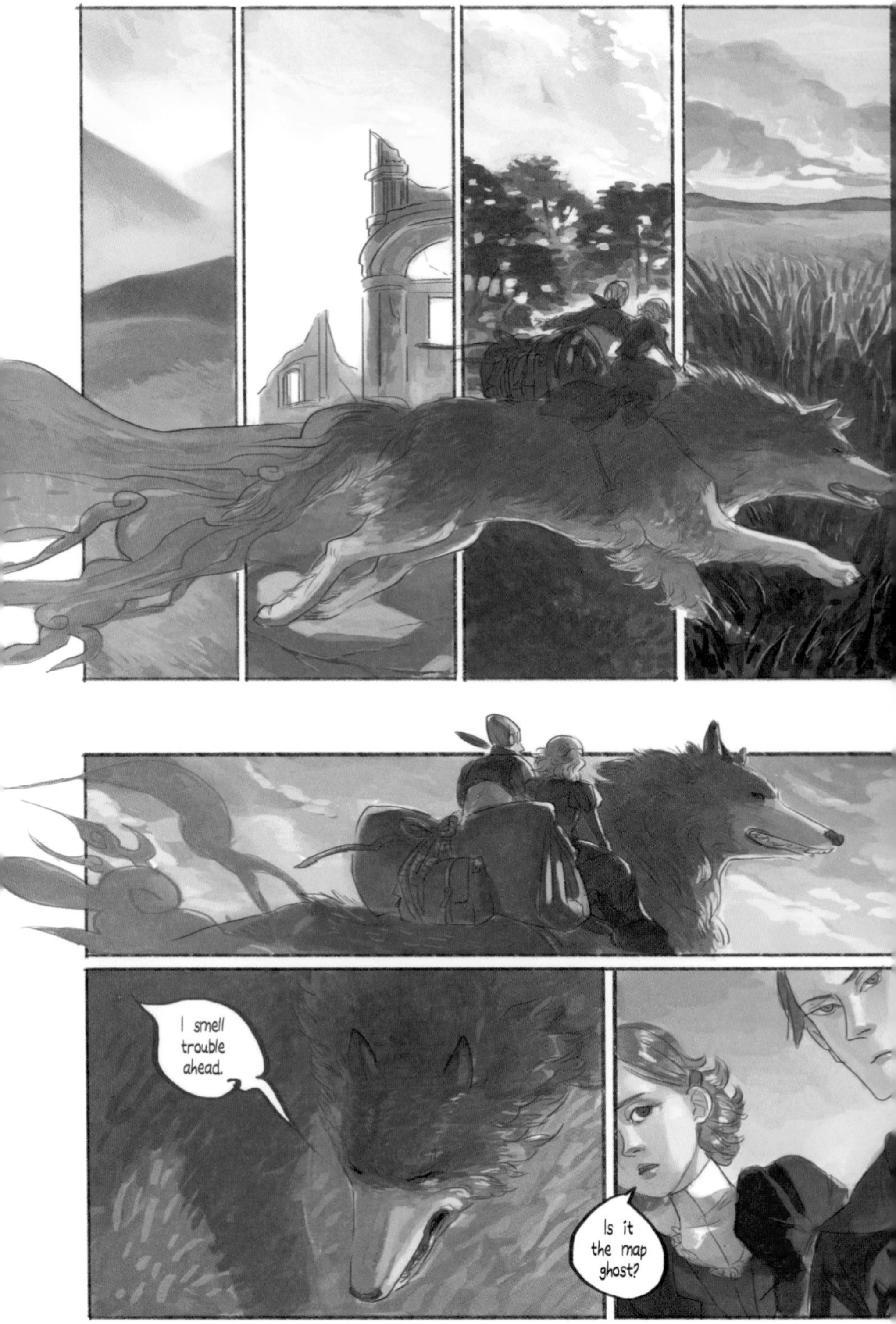
I smell trouble ahead.
Is it the map ghost?

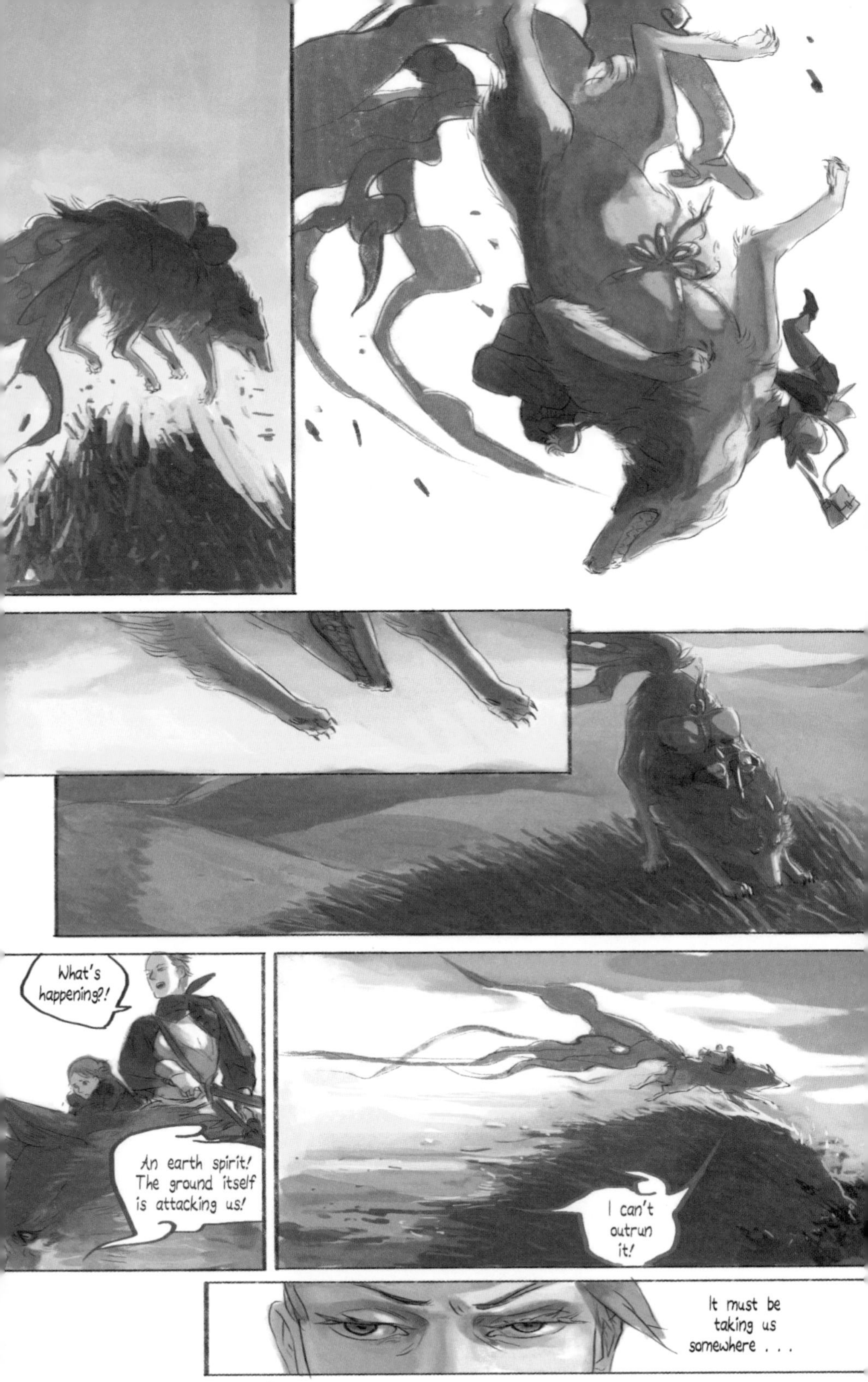
What's happening?!
An earth spirit! The ground itself is attacking us!
I can't outrun it!
It must be taking us somewhere . . .

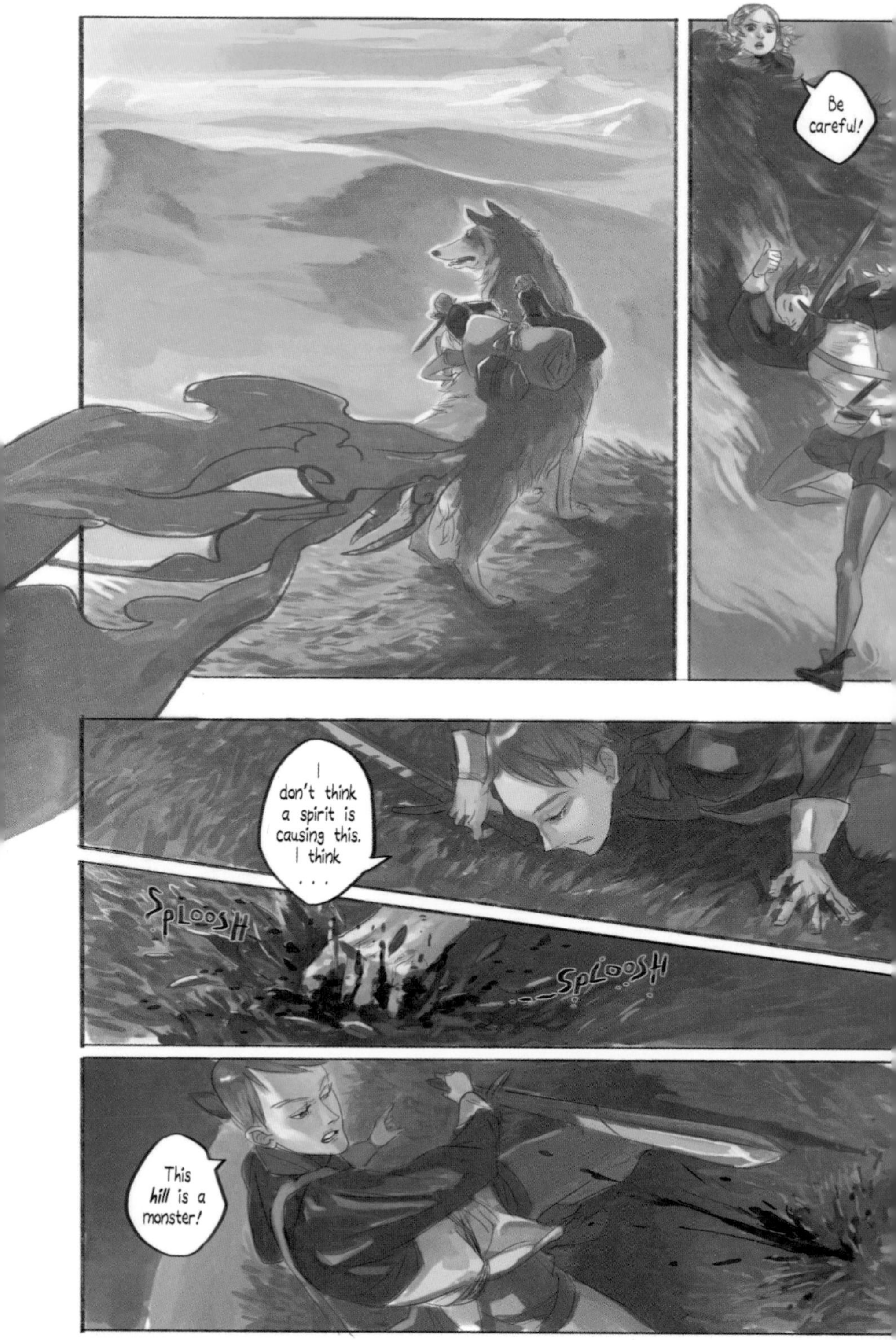
Be careful!
I don't think a spirit is causing this. I think . . .
SPLOOSH
SPLOOSH
This hill is a monster!

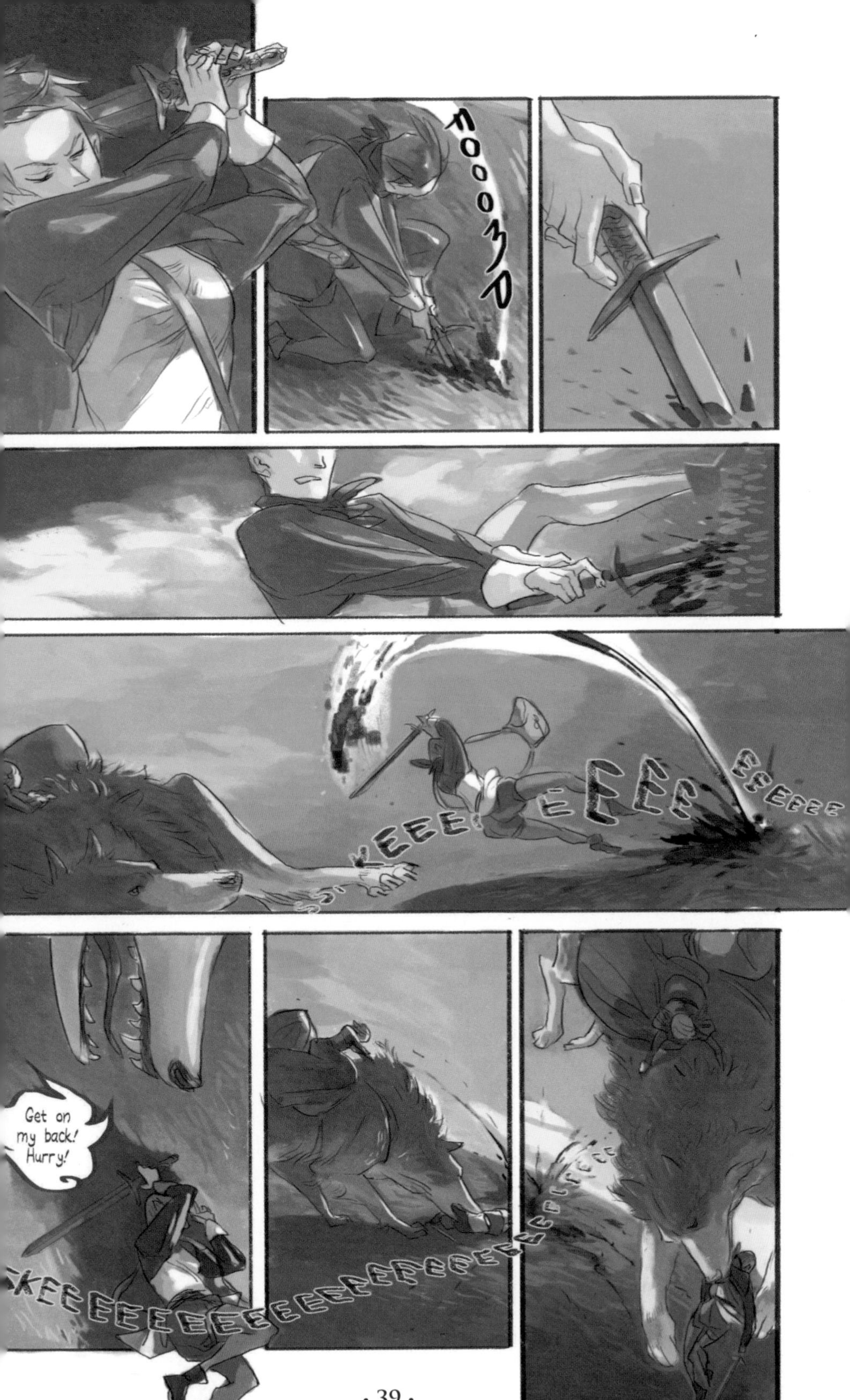

FOOOMP
KEEEEEEEEEEEEEEE
Get on my back! Hurry!
KEEEEEEEEEEEEEEEEEEEEEEEEEE

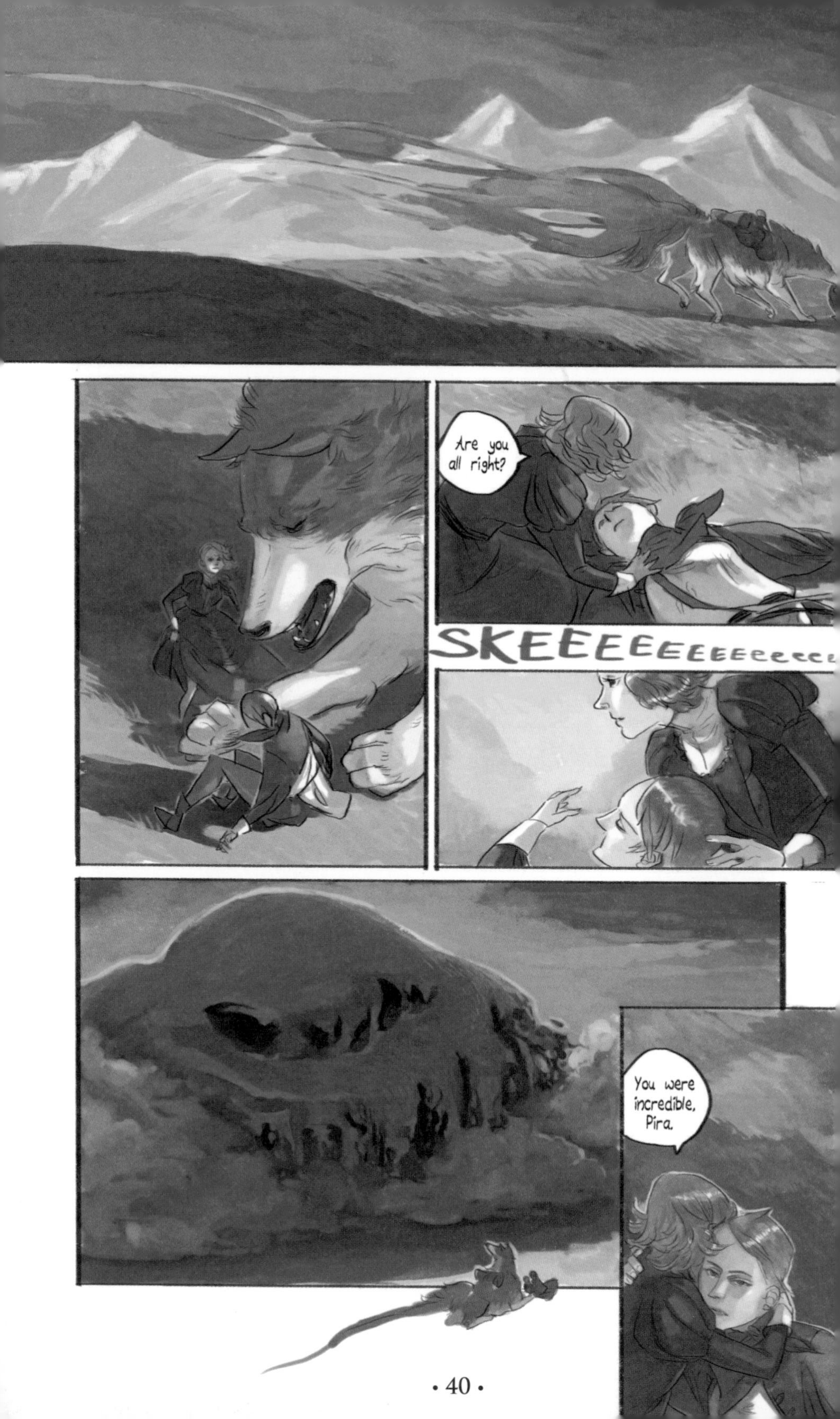
Are you all right?
SKEEEEEEEEEeeee
You were incredible, Pira.

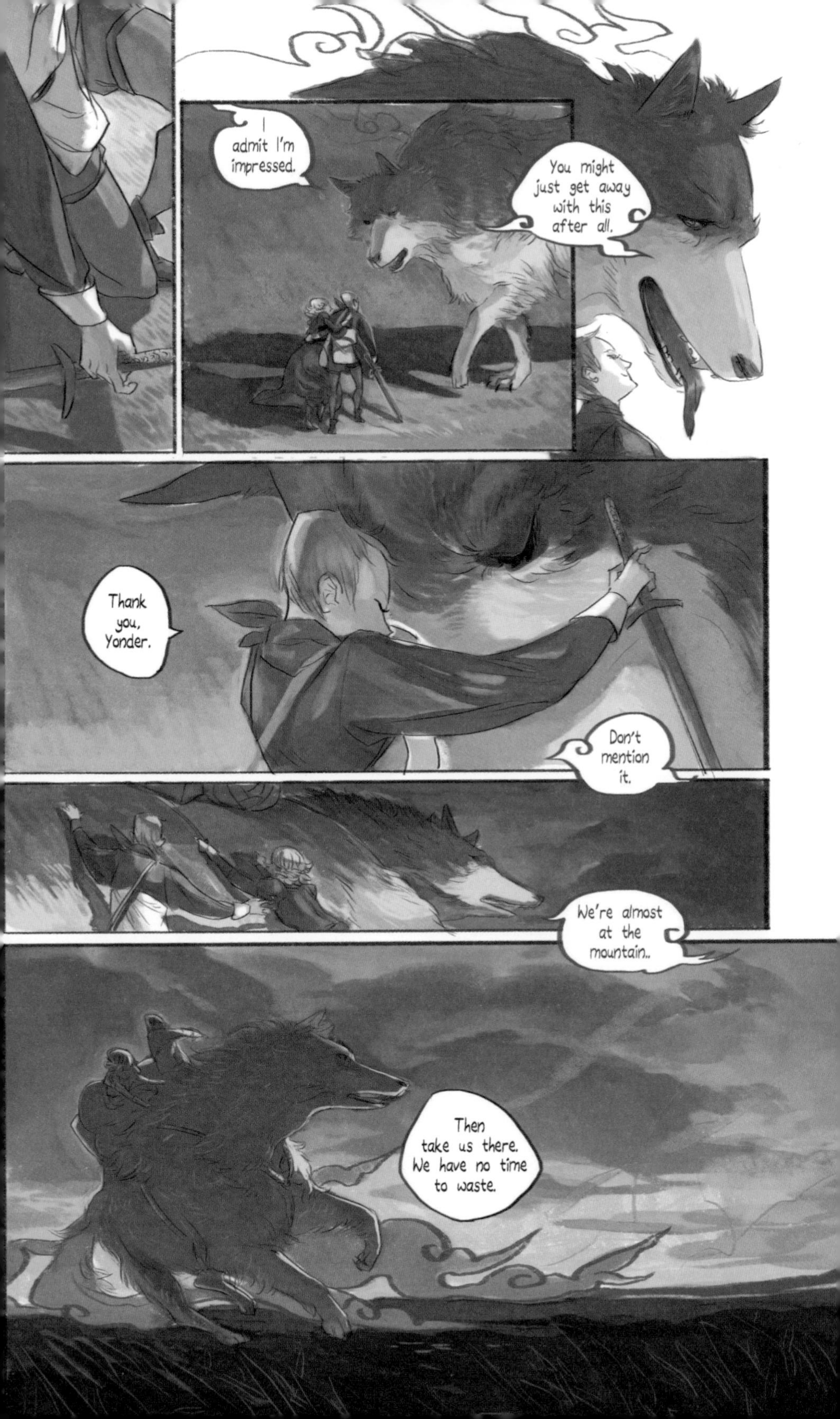
I admit I'm impressed.
You might just get away with this after all.
Thank you, Yonder.
Don't mention it.
We're almost at the mountain..
Then take us there. We have no time to waste.

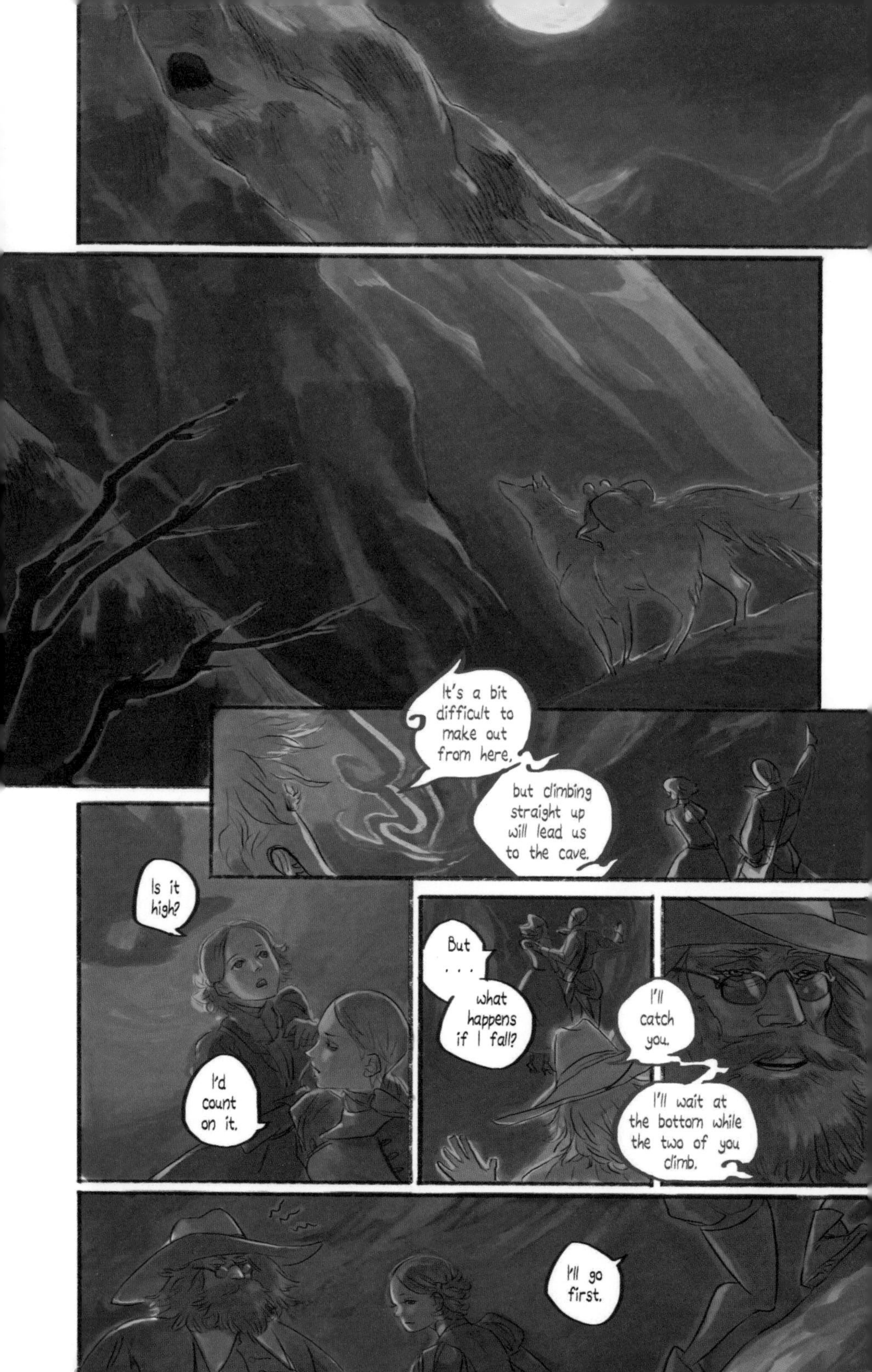
It's a bit difficult to make out from here,
but climbing straight up will lead us to the cave.
Is it high?
I'd count on it.
But . . .
what happens if I fall?
I'll catch you.
I'll wait at the bottom while the two of you climb.
I'll go first.

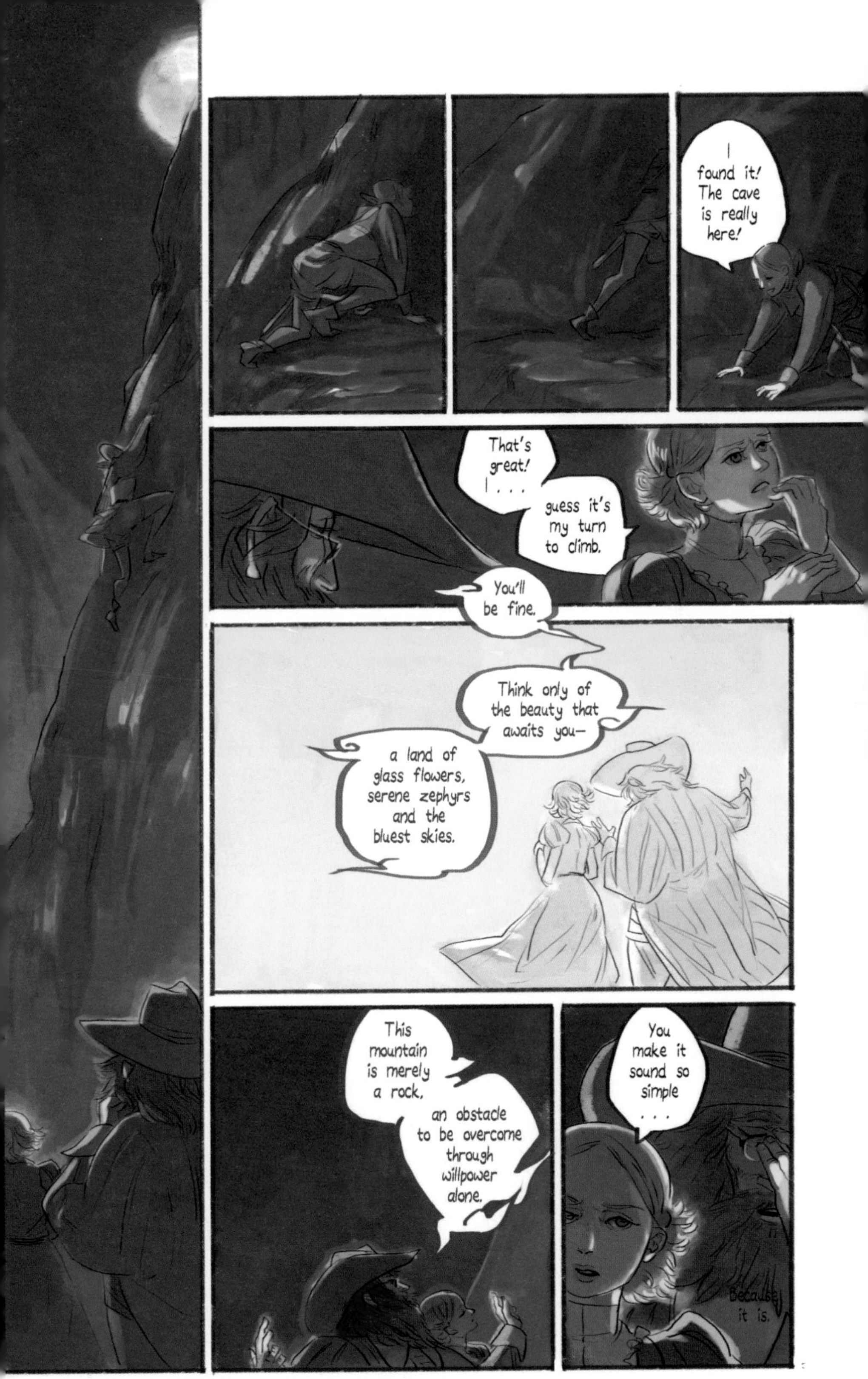
I found it! The cave is really here!
That's great! I . . .
guess it's my turn to climb.
You'll be fine.
Think only of the beauty that awaits you—
a land of glass flowers, serene zephyrs and the bluest skies.
This mountain is merely a rock,
an obstacle to be overcome through willpower alone.
You make it sound so simple . . .
Because it is.

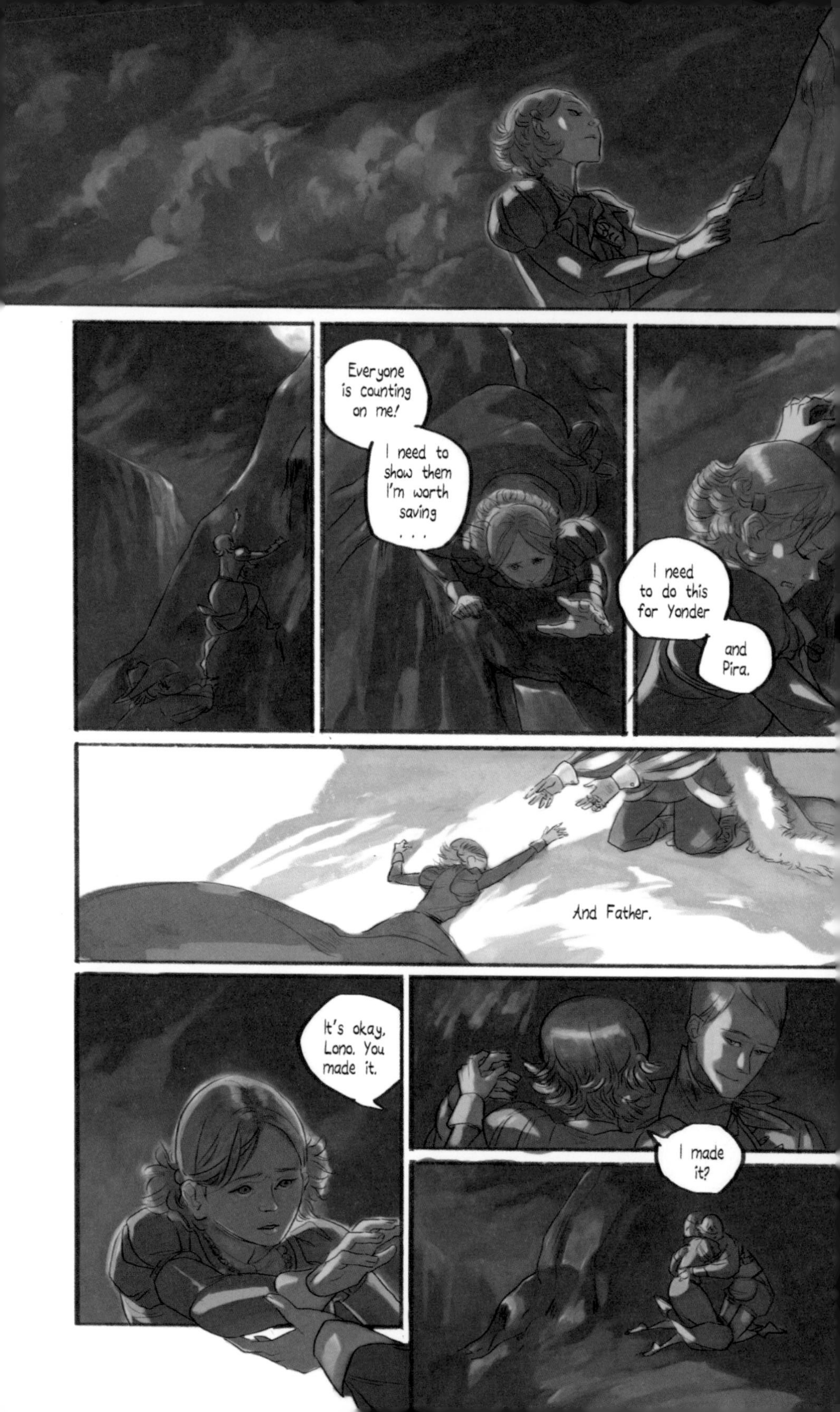
Everyone is counting on me!
I need to show them I'm worth saving . . .
I need to do this for Yonder
and Pira.
And Father.
It's okay, Lono. You made it.
I made it?

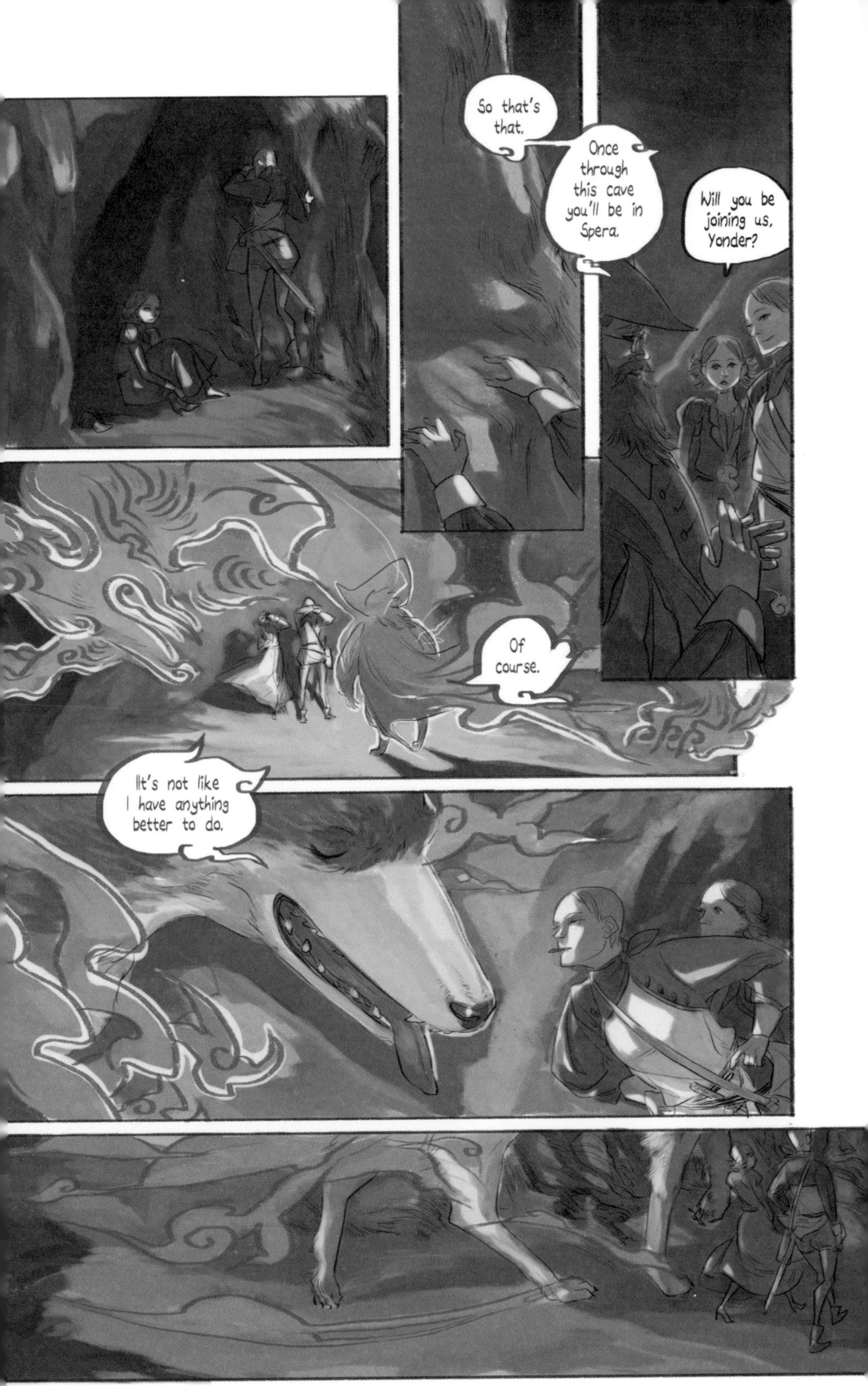
So that's that.
Once through this cave you'll be in Spera.
Will you be joining us, Yonder?
Of course.
It's not like I have anything better to do.

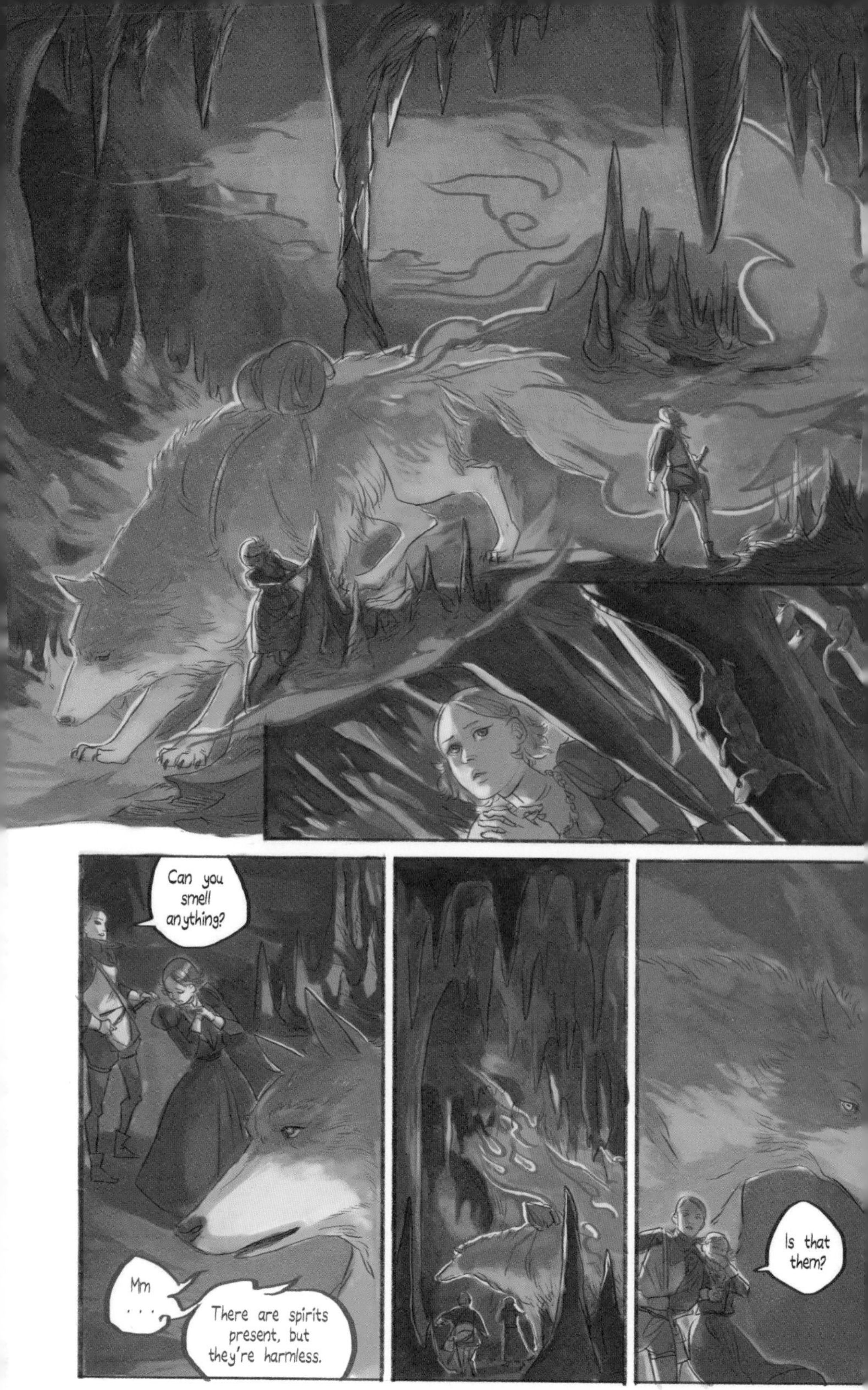

Can you smell anything?
Mm . . .
There are spirits present, but they're harmless.
Is that them?

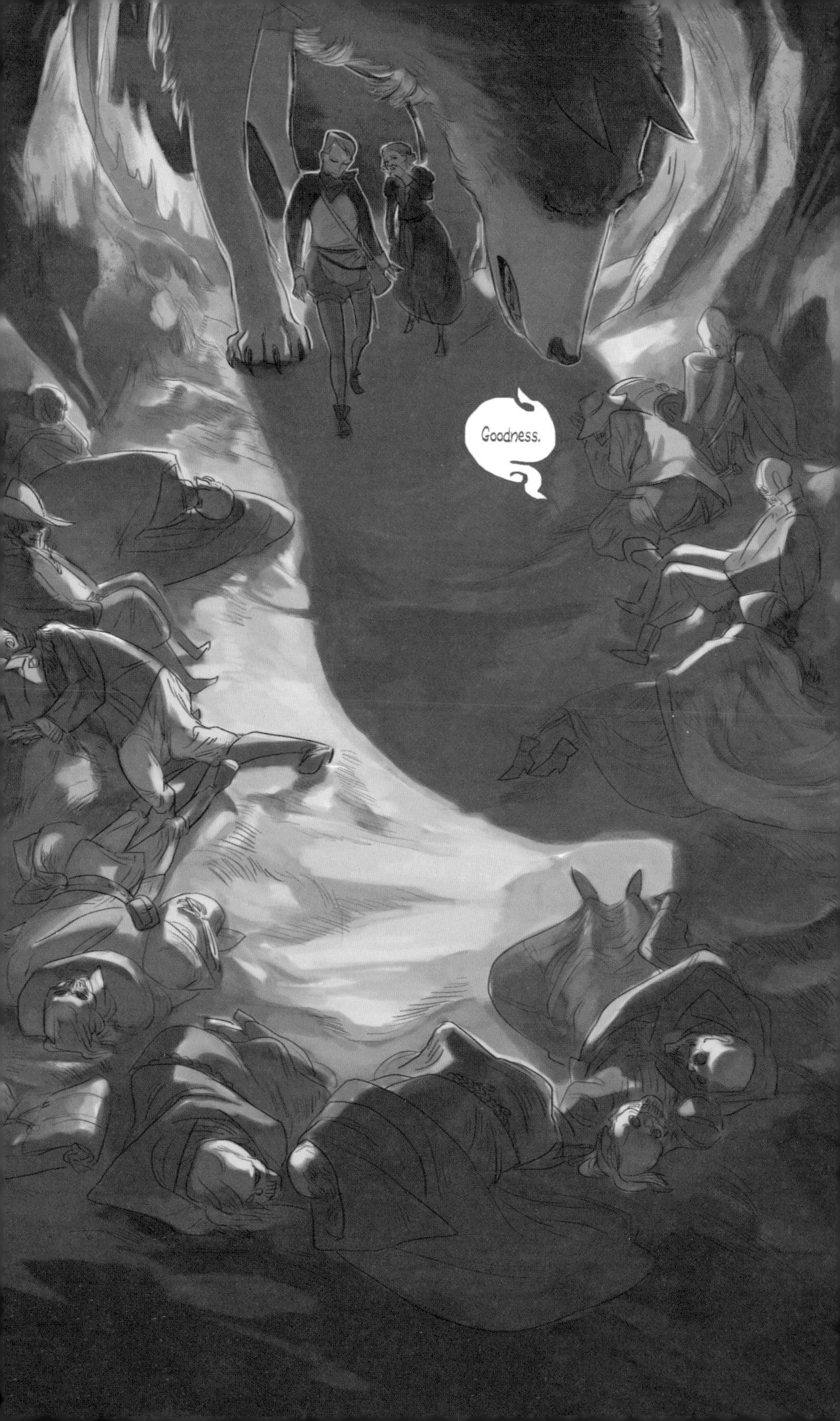
Goodness.

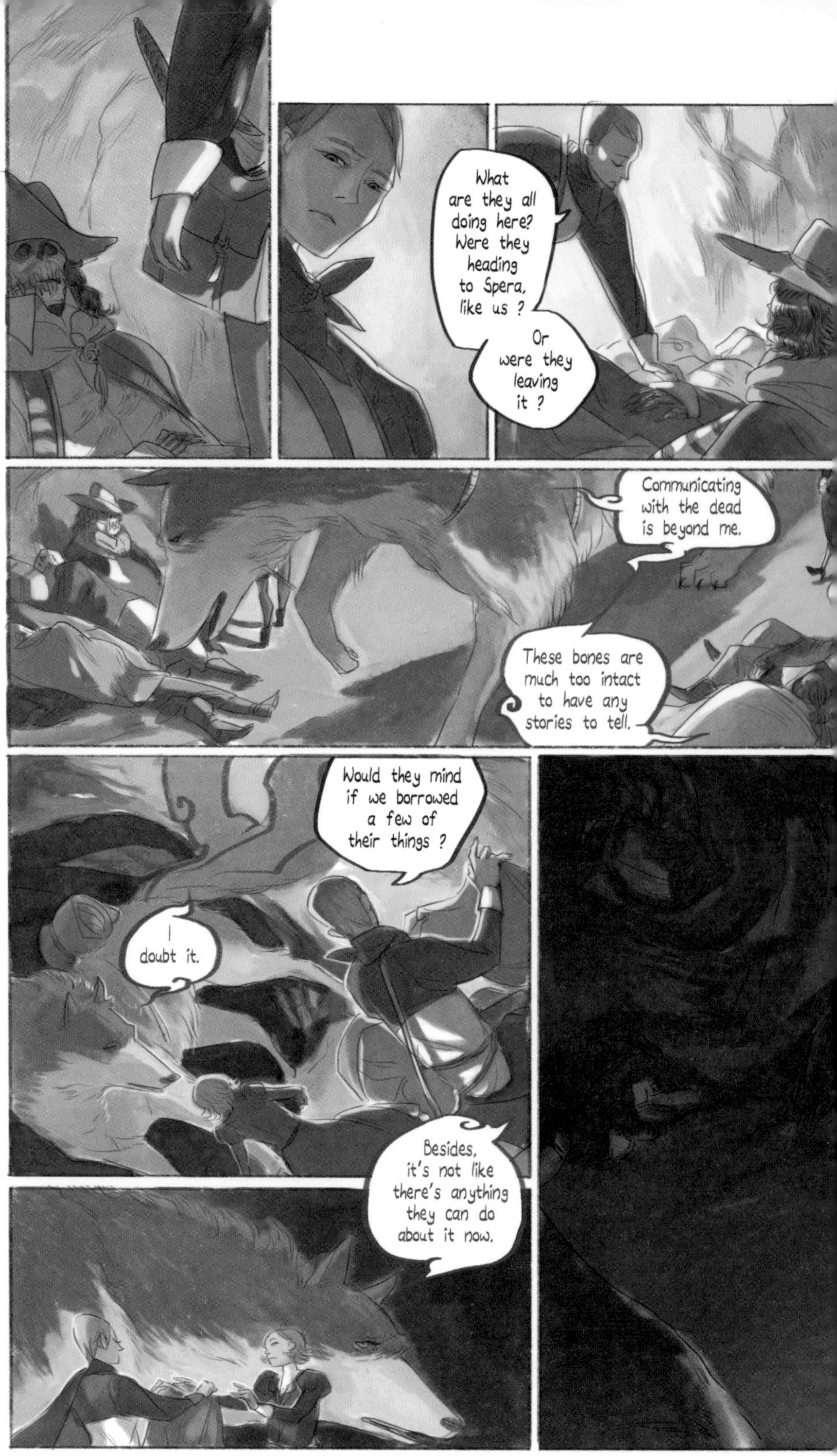
What are they all doing here? Were they heading to Spera, like us ?
Or were they leaving it ?
Communicating with the dead is beyond me.
These bones are much too intact to have any stories to tell.
Would they mind if we borrowed a few of their things ?
I doubt it.
Besides, it's not like there's anything they can do about it now.

CHAPTER THREE
A Warm Hearth

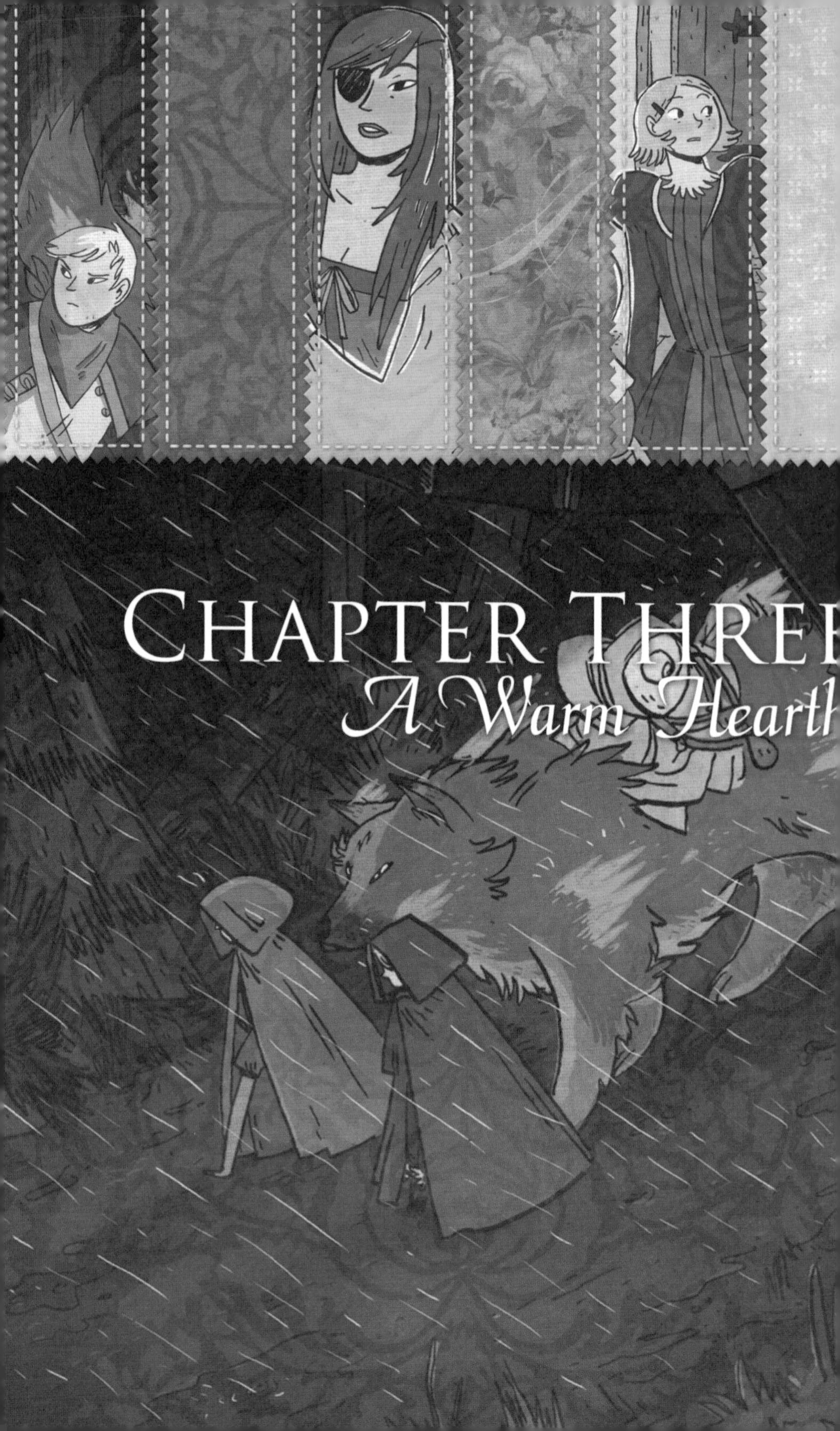

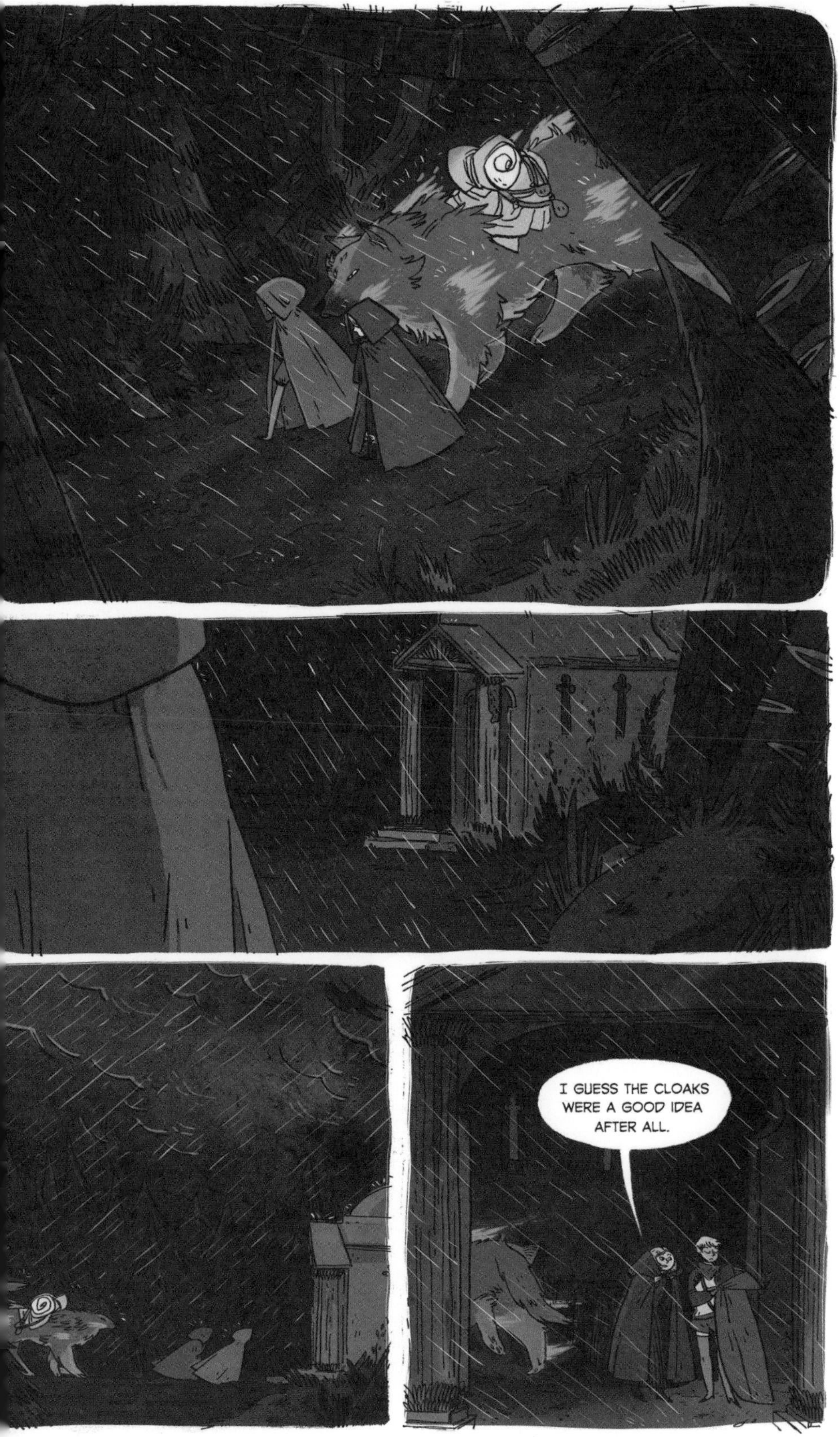
I GUESS THE CLOAKS WERE A GOOD IDEA AFTER ALL.

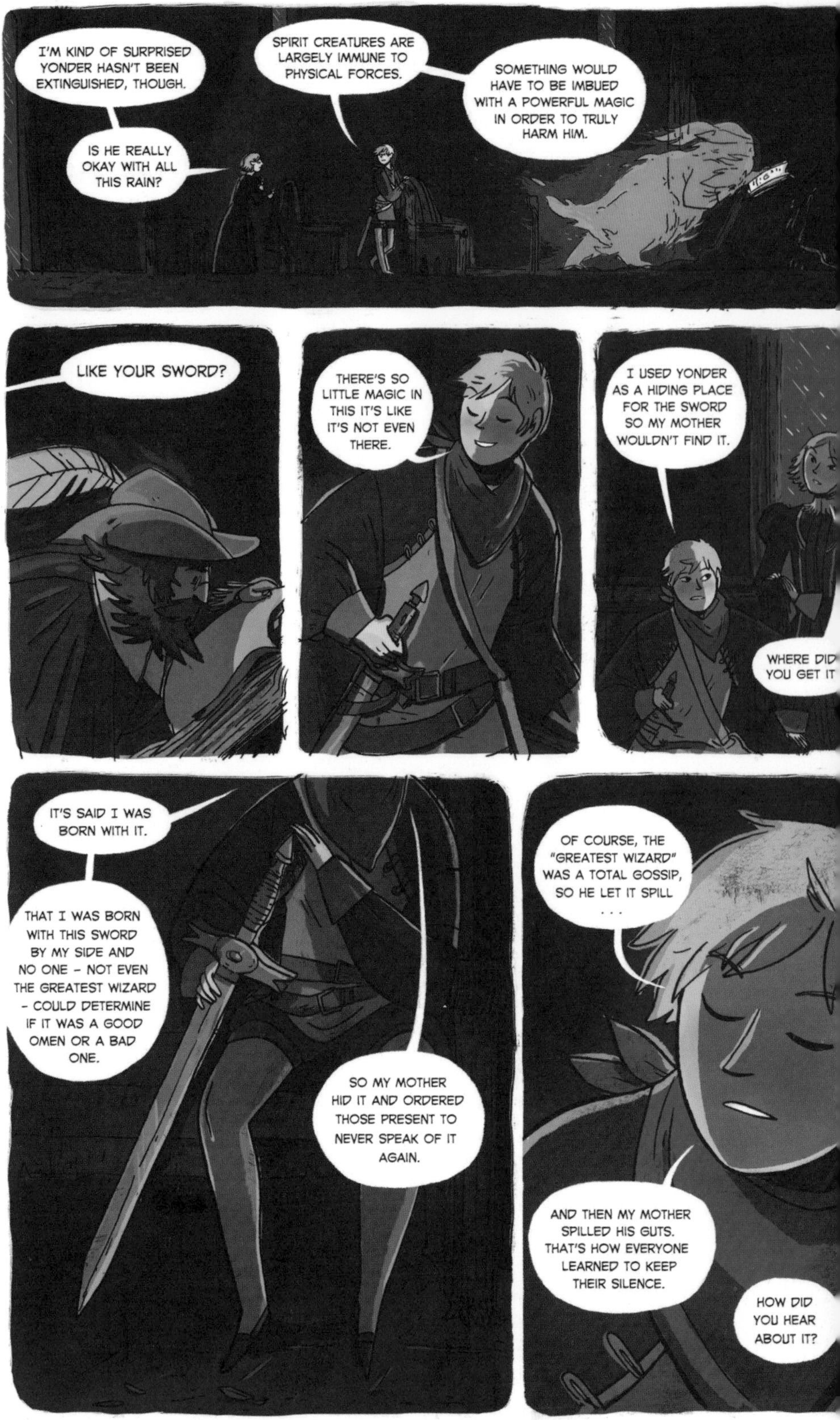
I'M KIND OF SURPRISED YONDER HASN'T BEEN EXTINGUISHED, THOUGH.
IS HE REALLY OKAY WITH ALL THIS RAIN?
SPIRIT CREATURES ARE LARGELY IMMUNE TO PHYSICAL FORCES.
SOMETHING WOULD HAVE TO BE IMBUED WITH A POWERFUL MAGIC IN ORDER TO TRULY HARM HIM.
LIKE YOUR SWORD?
THERE'S SO LITTLE MAGIC IN THIS IT'S LIKE IT'S NOT EVEN THERE.
I USED YONDER AS A HIDING PLACE FOR THE SWORD SO MY MOTHER WOULDN'T FIND IT.
WHERE DID YOU GET IT
IT'S SAID I WAS BORN WITH IT.
THAT I WAS BORN WITH THIS SWORD BY MY SIDE AND NO ONE - NOT EVEN THE GREATEST WIZARD - COULD DETERMINE IF IT WAS A GOOD OMEN OR A BAD ONE.
SO MY MOTHER HID IT AND ORDERED THOSE PRESENT TO NEVER SPEAK OF IT AGAIN.
OF COURSE, THE "GREATEST WIZARD" WAS A TOTAL GOSSIP, SO HE LET IT SPILL . . .
AND THEN MY MOTHER SPILLED HIS GUTS. THAT'S HOW EVERYONE LEARNED TO KEEP THEIR SILENCE.
HOW DID YOU HEAR ABOUT IT?

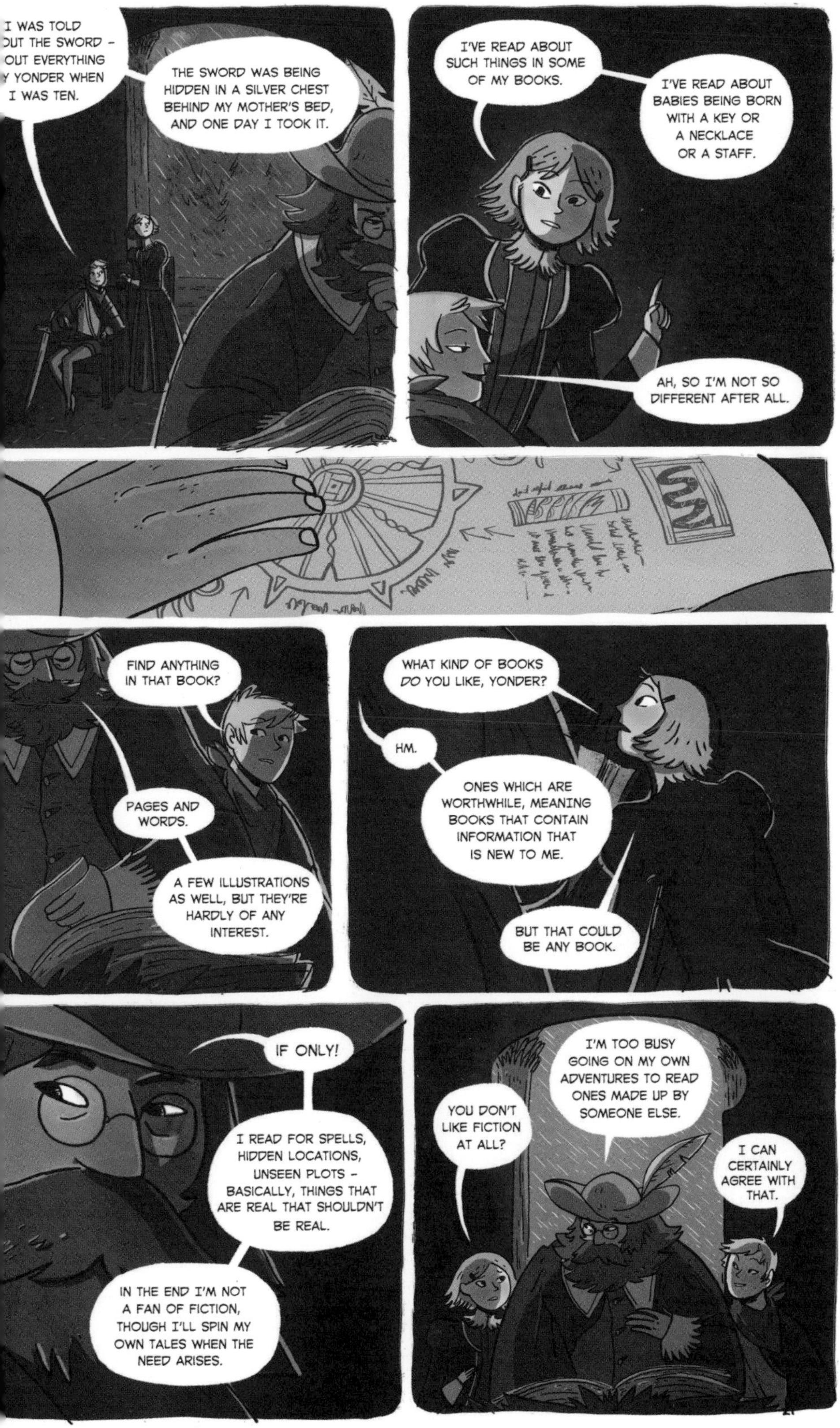
I WAS TOLD
OUT THE SWORD -
OUT EVERYTHING
Y YONDER WHEN
I WAS TEN.
THE SWORD WAS BEING HIDDEN IN A SILVER CHEST BEHIND MY MOTHER'S BED, AND ONE DAY I TOOK IT.
I'VE READ ABOUT SUCH THINGS IN SOME OF MY BOOKS.
I'VE READ ABOUT BABIES BEING BORN WITH A KEY OR A NECKLACE OR A STAFF.
AH, SO I'M NOT SO DIFFERENT AFTER ALL.
FIND ANYTHING IN THAT BOOK?
PAGES AND WORDS.
A FEW ILLUSTRATIONS AS WELL, BUT THEY'RE HARDLY OF ANY INTEREST.
WHAT KIND OF BOOKS *DO* YOU LIKE, YONDER?
HM.
ONES WHICH ARE WORTHWHILE, MEANING BOOKS THAT CONTAIN INFORMATION THAT IS NEW TO ME.
BUT THAT COULD BE ANY BOOK.
IF ONLY!
I READ FOR SPELLS, HIDDEN LOCATIONS, UNSEEN PLOTS - BASICALLY, THINGS THAT ARE REAL THAT SHOULDN'T BE REAL.
IN THE END I'M NOT A FAN OF FICTION, THOUGH I'LL SPIN MY OWN TALES WHEN THE NEED ARISES.
YOU DON'T LIKE FICTION AT ALL?
I'M TOO BUSY GOING ON MY OWN ADVENTURES TO READ ONES MADE UP BY SOMEONE ELSE.
I CAN CERTAINLY AGREE WITH THAT.

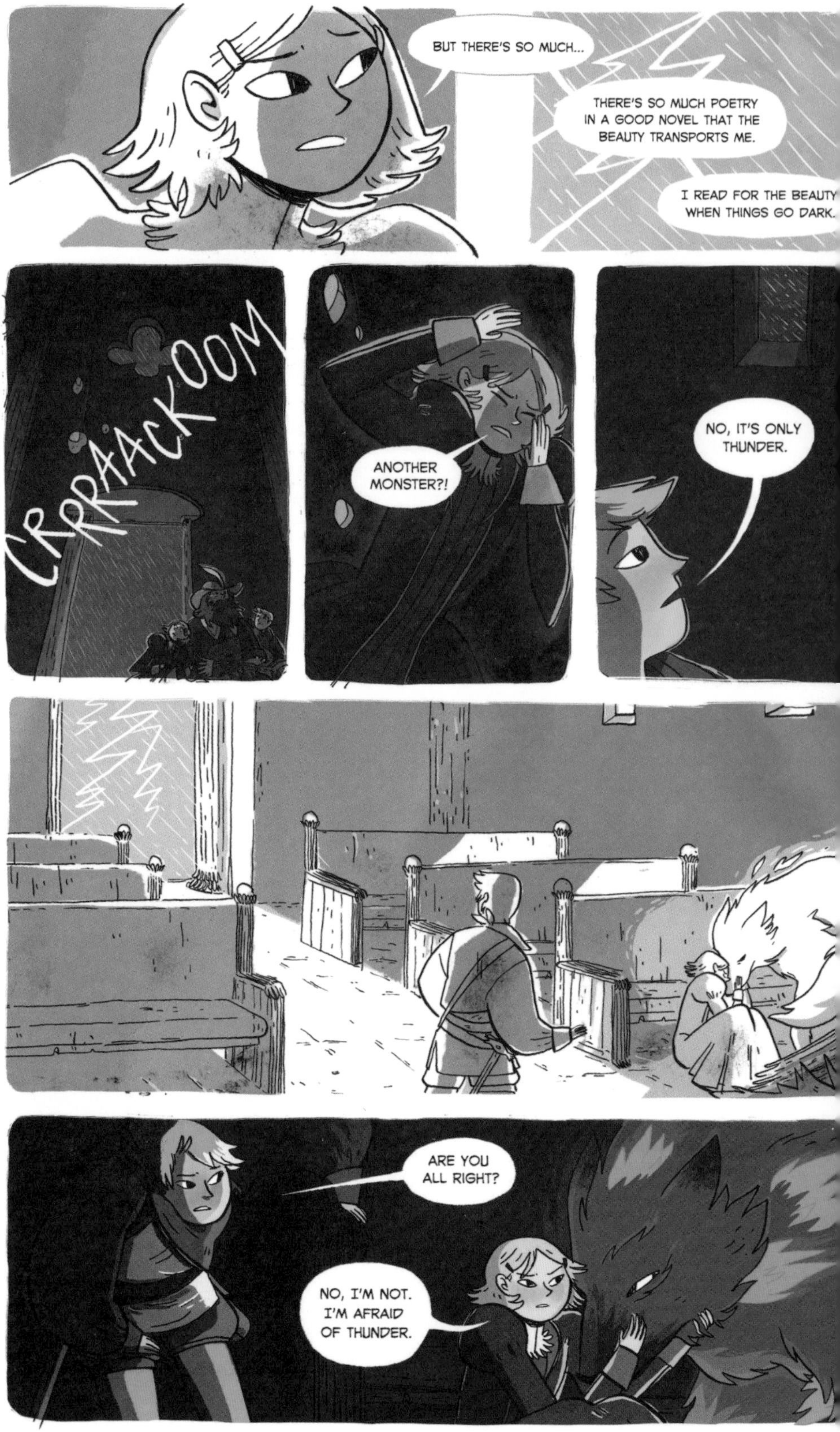
BUT THERE'S SO MUCH...
THERE'S SO MUCH POETRY IN A GOOD NOVEL THAT THE BEAUTY TRANSPORTS ME.
I READ FOR THE BEAUTY WHEN THINGS GO DARK.
CRRAACKOOM
ANOTHER MONSTER?!
NO, IT'S ONLY THUNDER.
ARE YOU ALL RIGHT?
NO, I'M NOT. I'M AFRAID OF THUNDER.

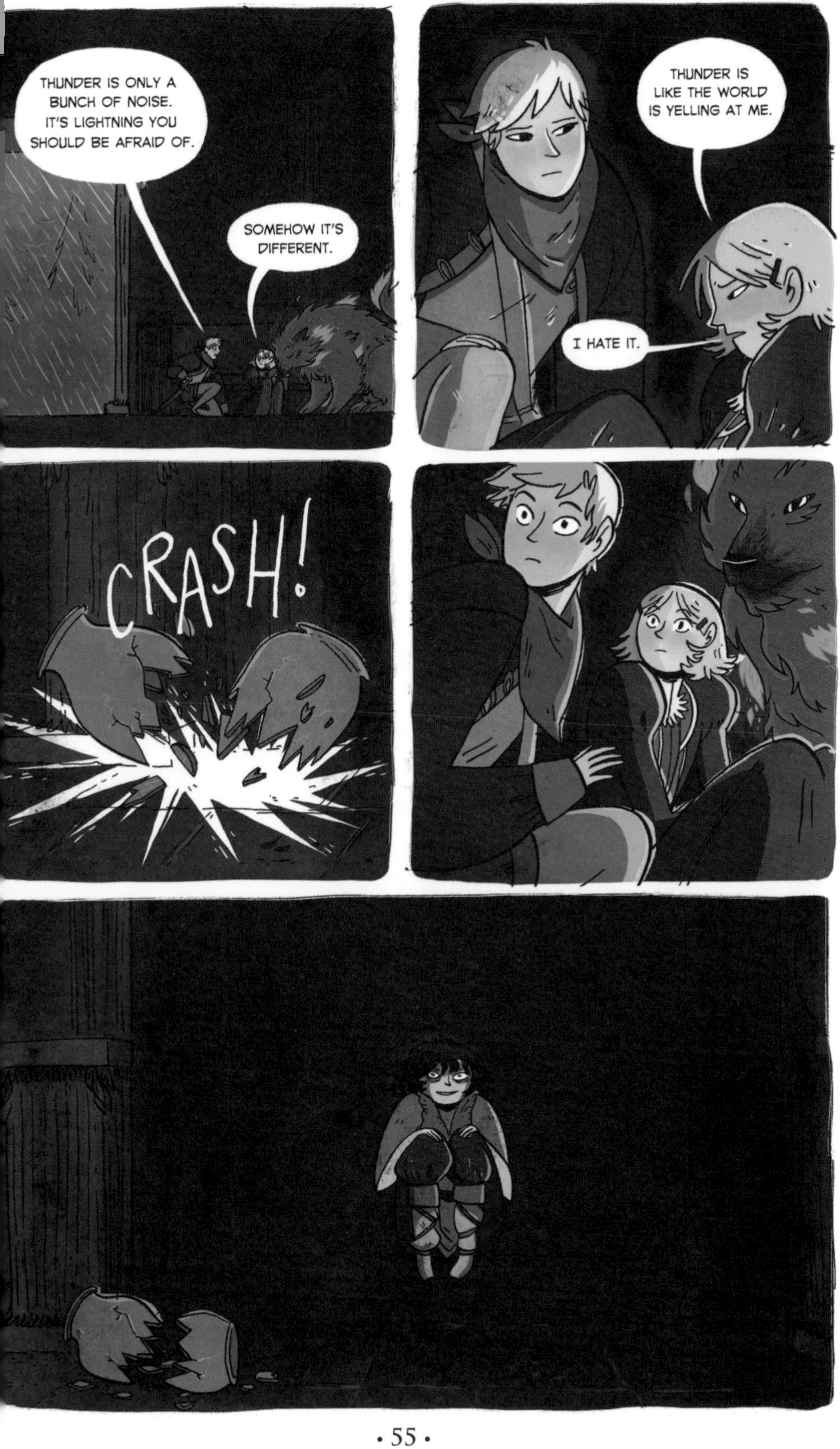
THUNDER IS ONLY A BUNCH OF NOISE. IT'S LIGHTNING YOU SHOULD BE AFRAID OF.
SOMEHOW IT'S DIFFERENT.
THUNDER IS LIKE THE WORLD IS YELLING AT ME.
I HATE IT.
CRASH!

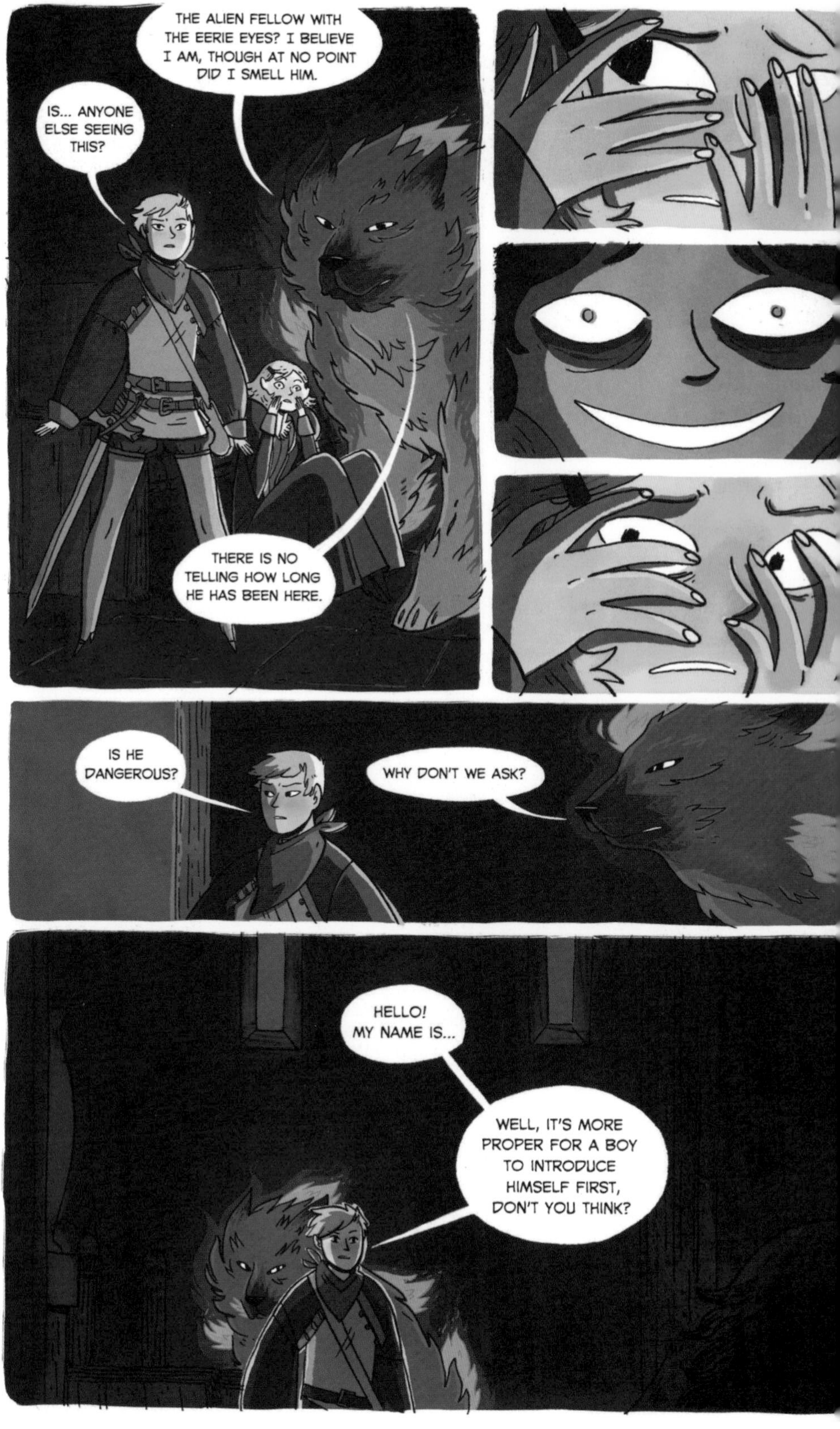
IS... ANYONE ELSE SEEING THIS?
THE ALIEN FELLOW WITH THE EERIE EYES? I BELIEVE I AM, THOUGH AT NO POINT DID I SMELL HIM.
THERE IS NO TELLING HOW LONG HE HAS BEEN HERE.
IS HE DANGEROUS?
WHY DON'T WE ASK?
HELLO! MY NAME IS...
WELL, IT'S MORE PROPER FOR A BOY TO INTRODUCE HIMSELF FIRST, DON'T YOU THINK?

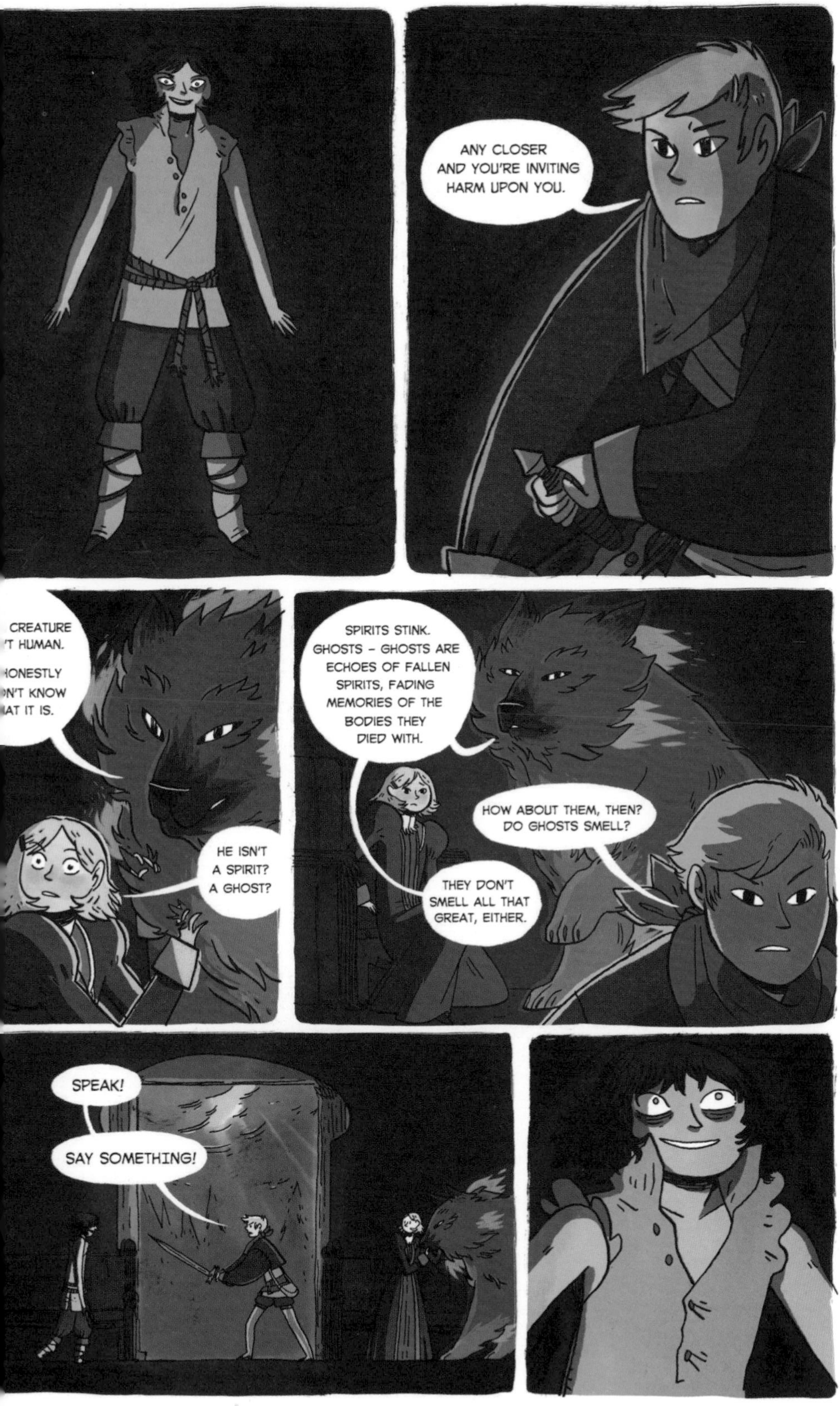
ANY CLOSER AND YOU'RE INVITING HARM UPON YOU.
CREATURE 'T HUMAN. HONESTLY N'T KNOW AT IT IS.
HE ISN'T A SPIRIT? A GHOST?
SPIRITS STINK. GHOSTS - GHOSTS ARE ECHOES OF FALLEN SPIRITS, FADING MEMORIES OF THE BODIES THEY DIED WITH.
HOW ABOUT THEM, THEN? DO GHOSTS SMELL?
THEY DON'T SMELL ALL THAT GREAT, EITHER.
SPEAK!
SAY SOMETHING!

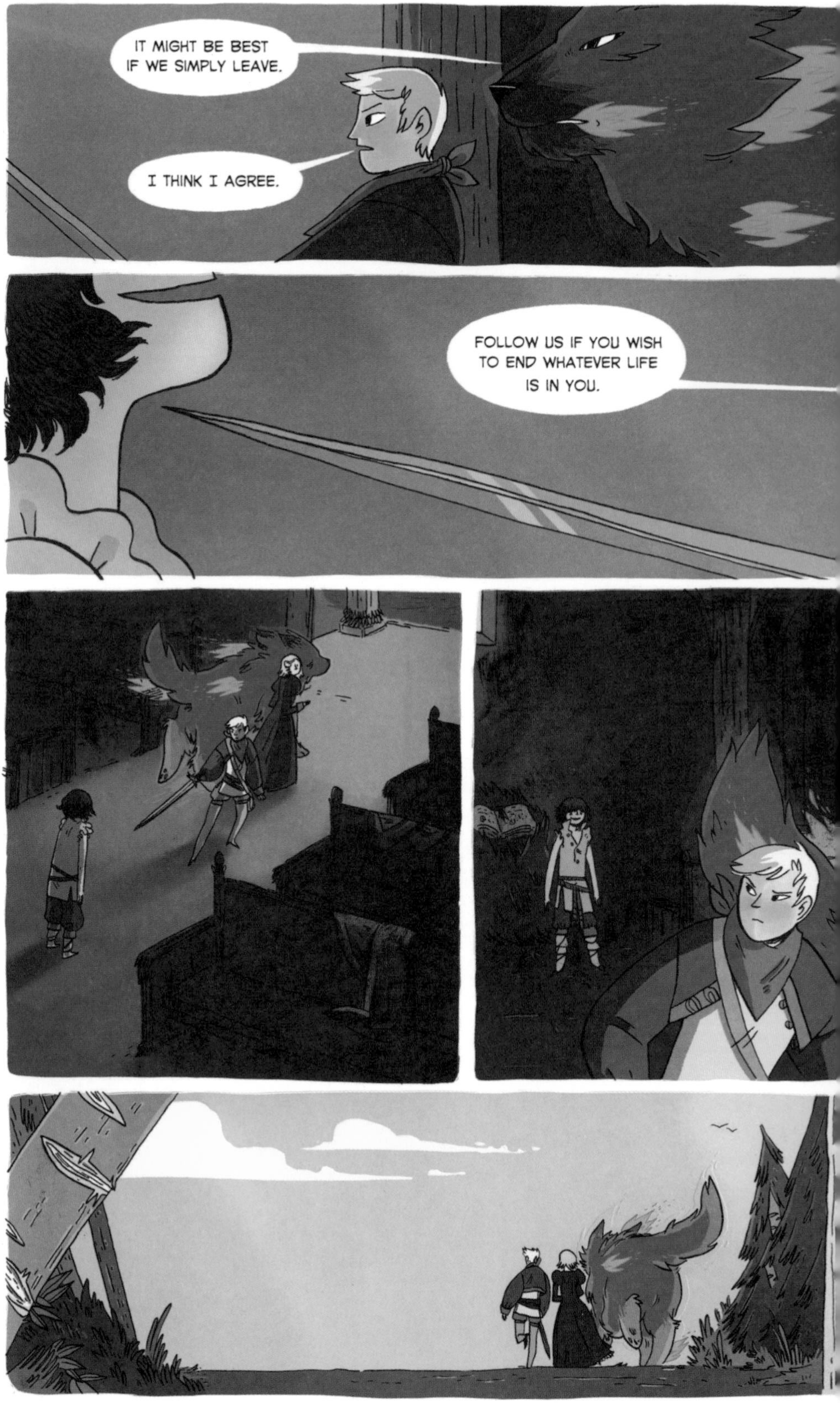
IT MIGHT BE BEST IF WE SIMPLY LEAVE.
I THINK I AGREE.
FOLLOW US IF YOU WISH TO END WHATEVER LIFE IS IN YOU.

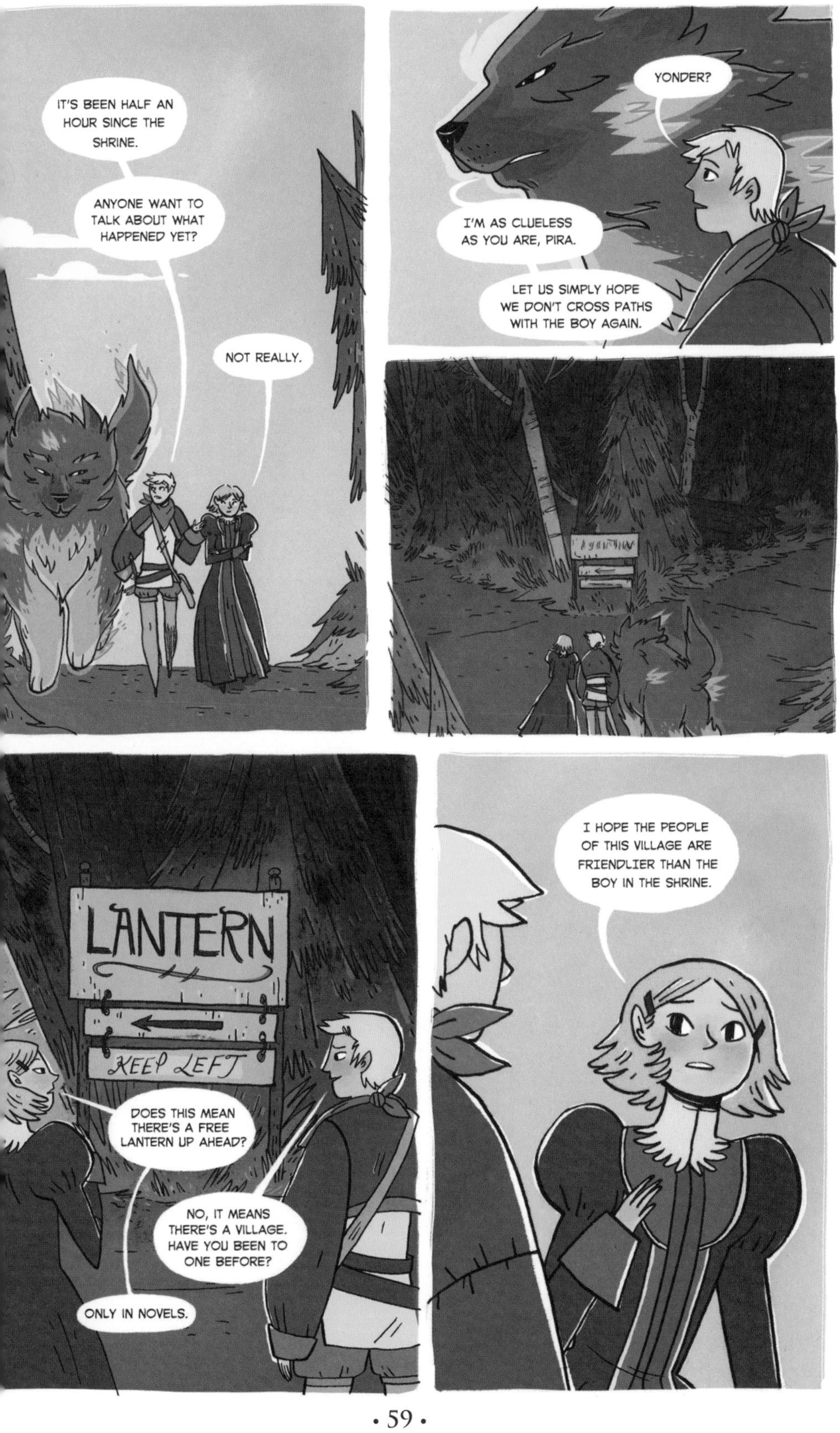
IT'S BEEN HALF AN HOUR SINCE THE SHRINE.
ANYONE WANT TO TALK ABOUT WHAT HAPPENED YET?
NOT REALLY.
YONDER?
I'M AS CLUELESS AS YOU ARE, PIRA.
LET US SIMPLY HOPE WE DON'T CROSS PATHS WITH THE BOY AGAIN.
LANTERN
KEEP LEFT
DOES THIS MEAN THERE'S A FREE LANTERN UP AHEAD?
NO, IT MEANS THERE'S A VILLAGE. HAVE YOU BEEN TO ONE BEFORE?
ONLY IN NOVELS.
I HOPE THE PEOPLE OF THIS VILLAGE ARE FRIENDLIER THAN THE BOY IN THE SHRINE.

NOW REMEMBER: YOU'RE PRINCESSES NO LONGER, SO PLEASE REFRAIN FROM ACTING LIKE ONES.

GREETINGS!

LOOKS TO ME YOU HAVE A MOST IMPORTANT ROLE FOR TODAY.

I AM YONDER, WHILE THE TWO WITH ME ARE LONO AND PIRA.

WE ARE MOST INTERE IN EXPERIENCING DELICACIES AND LODG OF LANTERN, IF YOU W BE SO KIND AS T DIRECT US TOWARDS

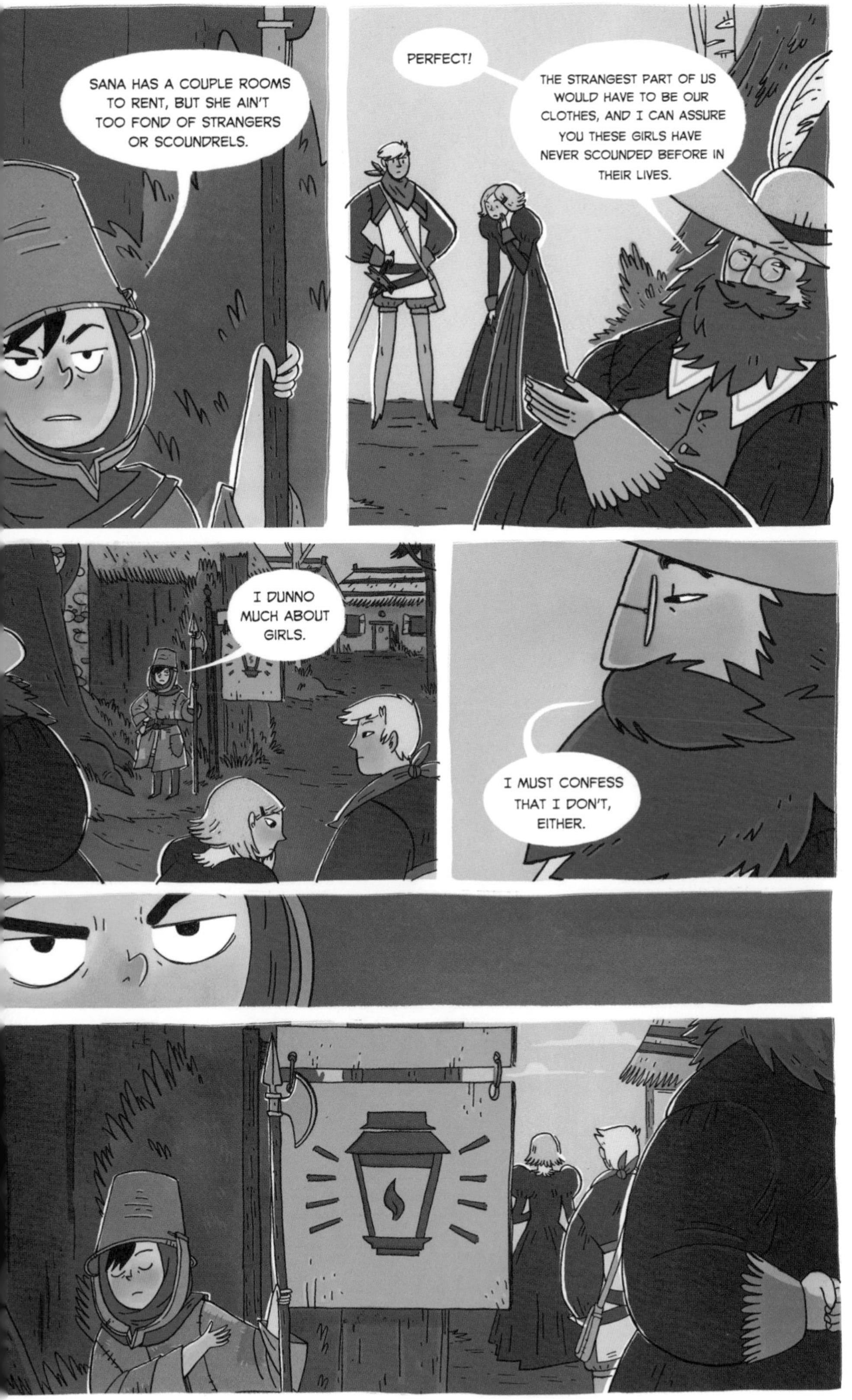
SANA HAS A COUPLE ROOMS TO RENT, BUT SHE AIN'T TOO FOND OF STRANGERS OR SCOUNDRELS.
PERFECT!
THE STRANGEST PART OF US WOULD HAVE TO BE OUR CLOTHES, AND I CAN ASSURE YOU THESE GIRLS HAVE NEVER SCOUNDED BEFORE IN THEIR LIVES.
I DUNNO MUCH ABOUT GIRLS.
I MUST CONFESS THAT I DON'T, EITHER.

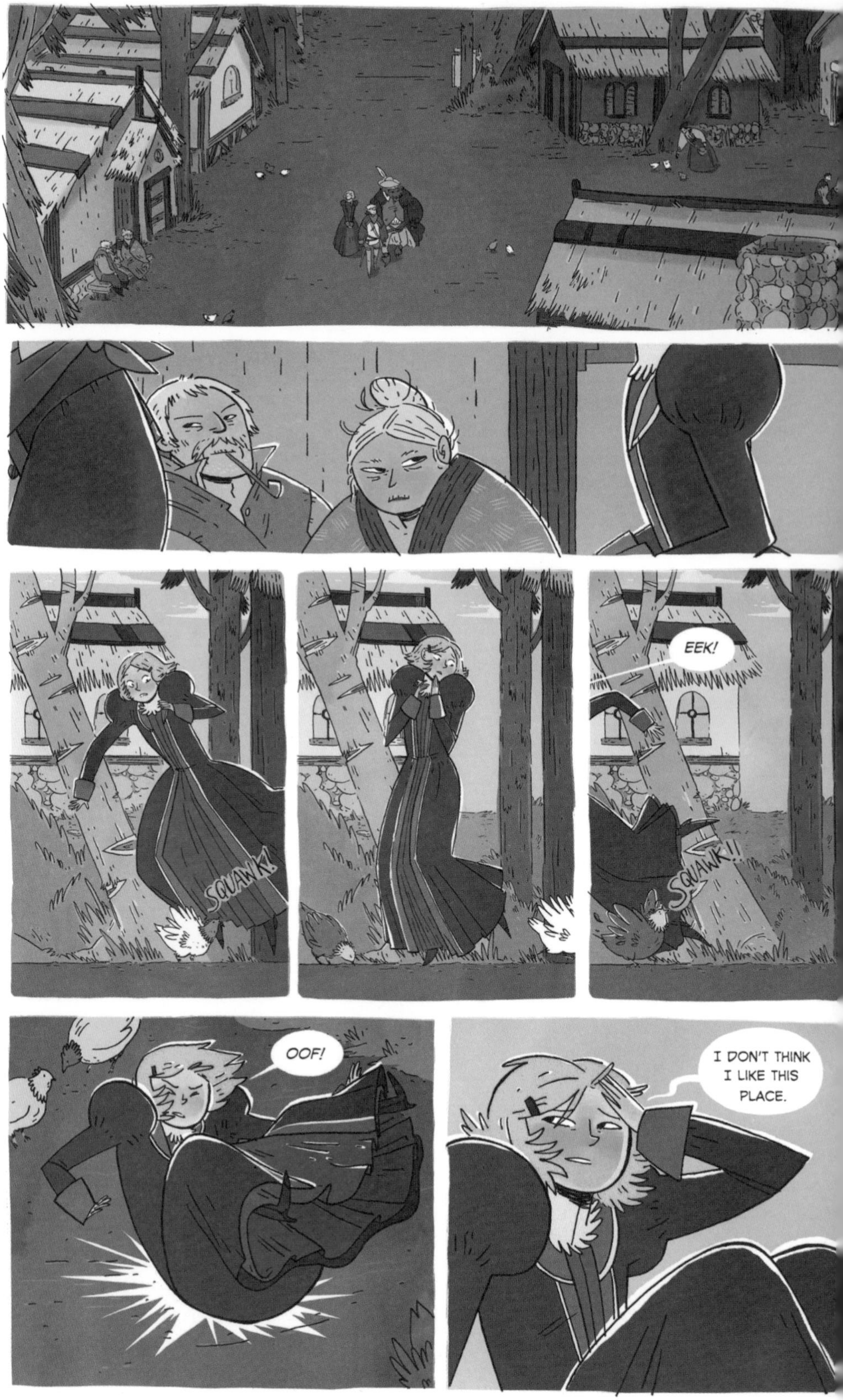
SQUAWK!
EEK!
SQUAWK!!
OOF!
I DON'T THINK I LIKE THIS PLACE.

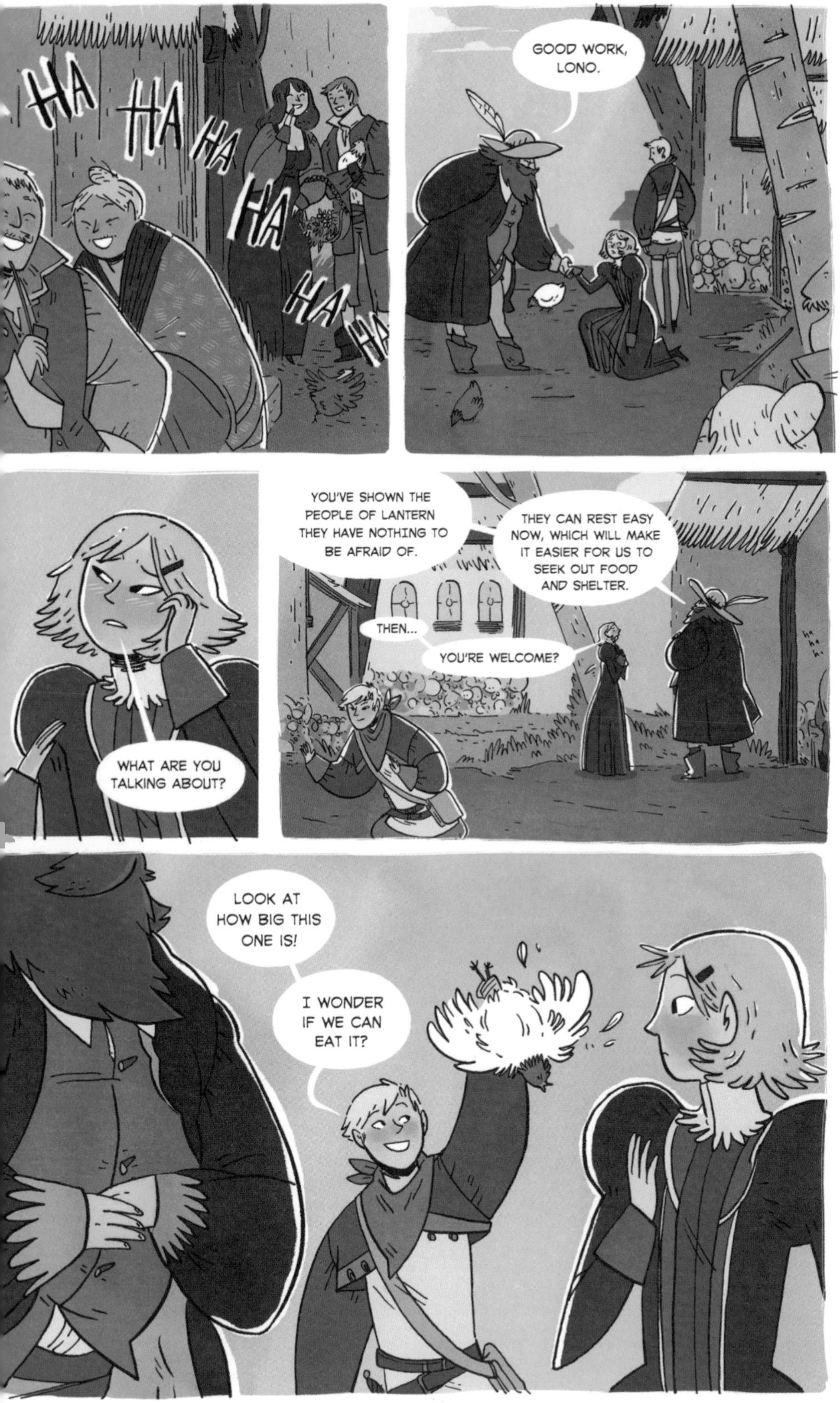
HA HA HA HA HA HA
GOOD WORK, LONO.
WHAT ARE YOU TALKING ABOUT?
YOU'VE SHOWN THE PEOPLE OF LANTERN THEY HAVE NOTHING TO BE AFRAID OF.
THEY CAN REST EASY NOW, WHICH WILL MAKE IT EASIER FOR US TO SEEK OUT FOOD AND SHELTER.
THEN...
YOU'RE WELCOME?
LOOK AT HOW BIG THIS ONE IS!
I WONDER IF WE CAN EAT IT?

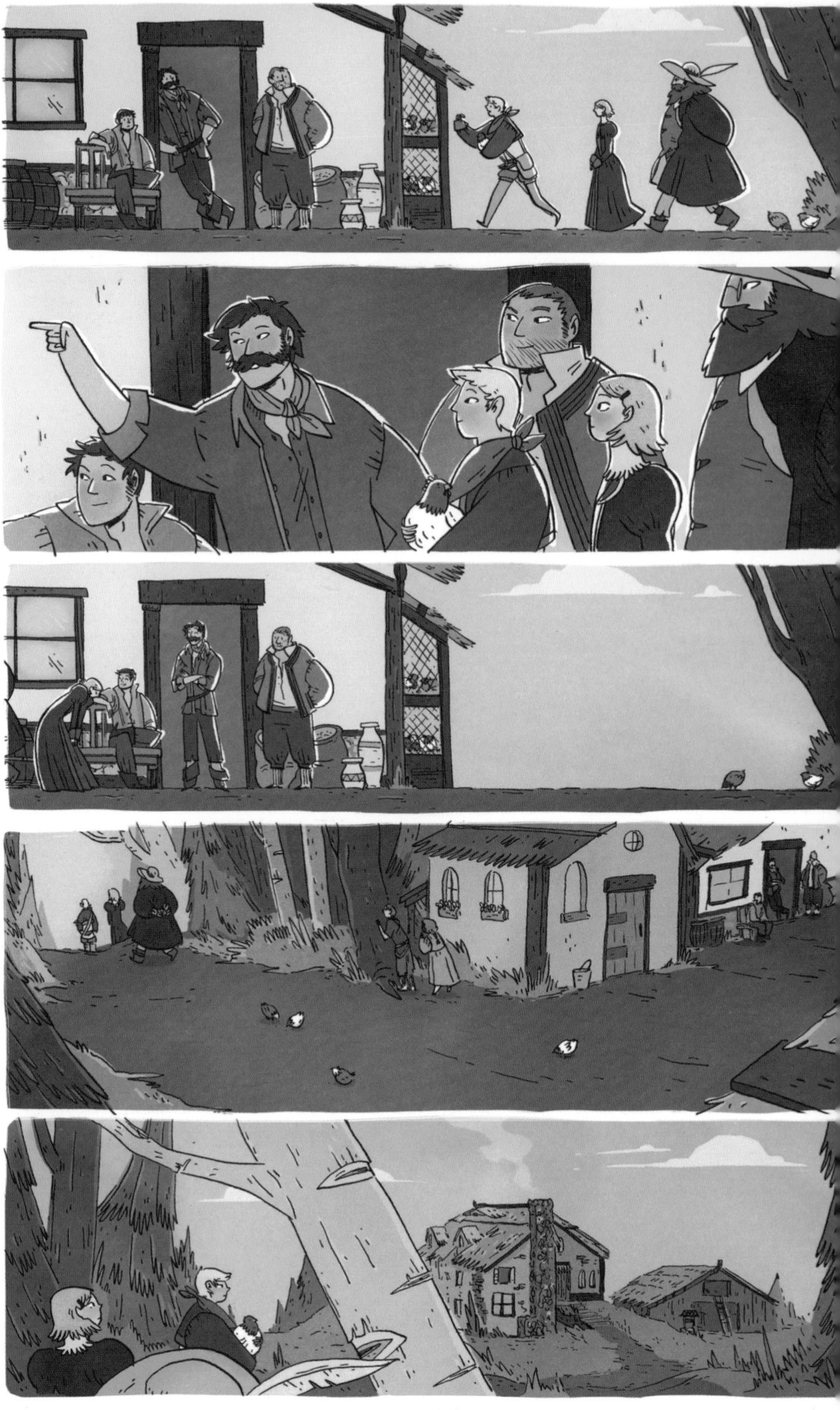

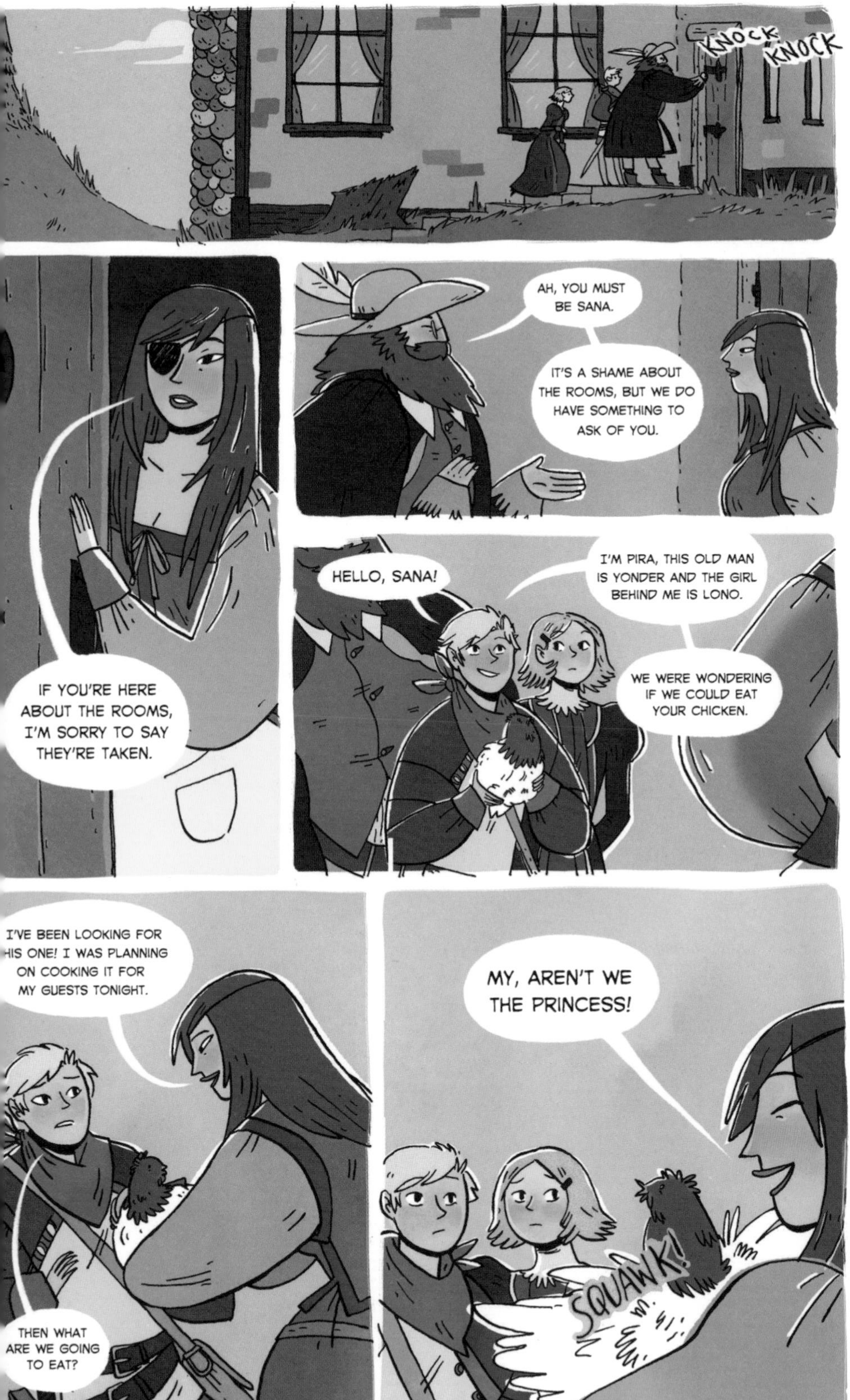
KNOCK KNOCK
IF YOU'RE HERE ABOUT THE ROOMS, I'M SORRY TO SAY THEY'RE TAKEN.
AH, YOU MUST BE SANA.
IT'S A SHAME ABOUT THE ROOMS, BUT WE DO HAVE SOMETHING TO ASK OF YOU.
HELLO, SANA!
I'M PIRA, THIS OLD MAN IS YONDER AND THE GIRL BEHIND ME IS LONO.
WE WERE WONDERING IF WE COULD EAT YOUR CHICKEN.
I'VE BEEN LOOKING FOR HIS ONE! I WAS PLANNING ON COOKING IT FOR MY GUESTS TONIGHT.
THEN WHAT ARE WE GOING TO EAT?
MY, AREN'T WE THE PRINCESS!
SQUAWK!

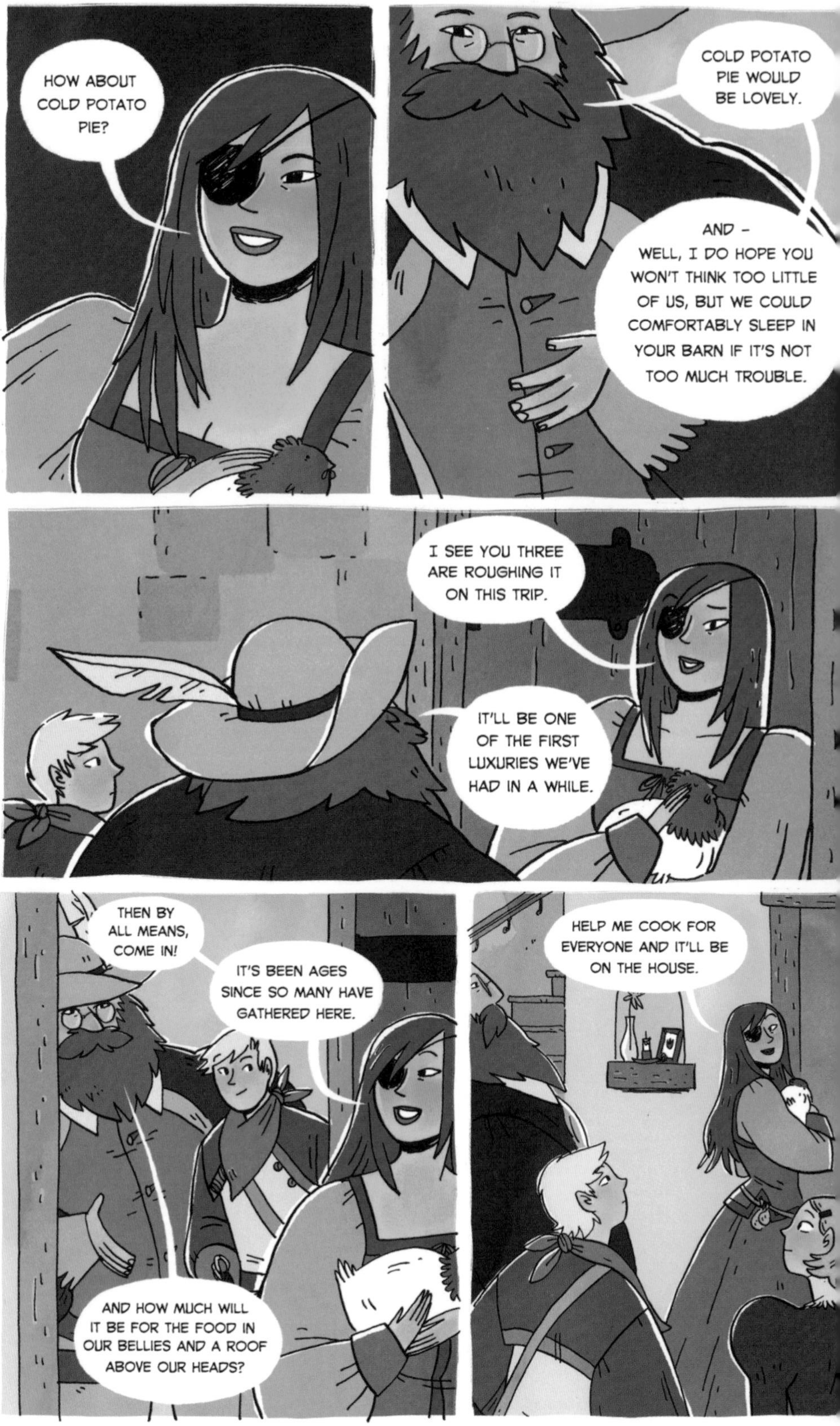
HOW ABOUT COLD POTATO PIE?
COLD POTATO PIE WOULD BE LOVELY.
AND - WELL, I DO HOPE YOU WON'T THINK TOO LITTLE OF US, BUT WE COULD COMFORTABLY SLEEP IN YOUR BARN IF IT'S NOT TOO MUCH TROUBLE.
I SEE YOU THREE ARE ROUGHING IT ON THIS TRIP.
IT'LL BE ONE OF THE FIRST LUXURIES WE'VE HAD IN A WHILE.
THEN BY ALL MEANS, COME IN!
IT'S BEEN AGES SINCE SO MANY HAVE GATHERED HERE.
AND HOW MUCH WILL IT BE FOR THE FOOD IN OUR BELLIES AND A ROOF ABOVE OUR HEADS?
HELP ME COOK FOR EVERYONE AND IT'LL BE ON THE HOUSE.

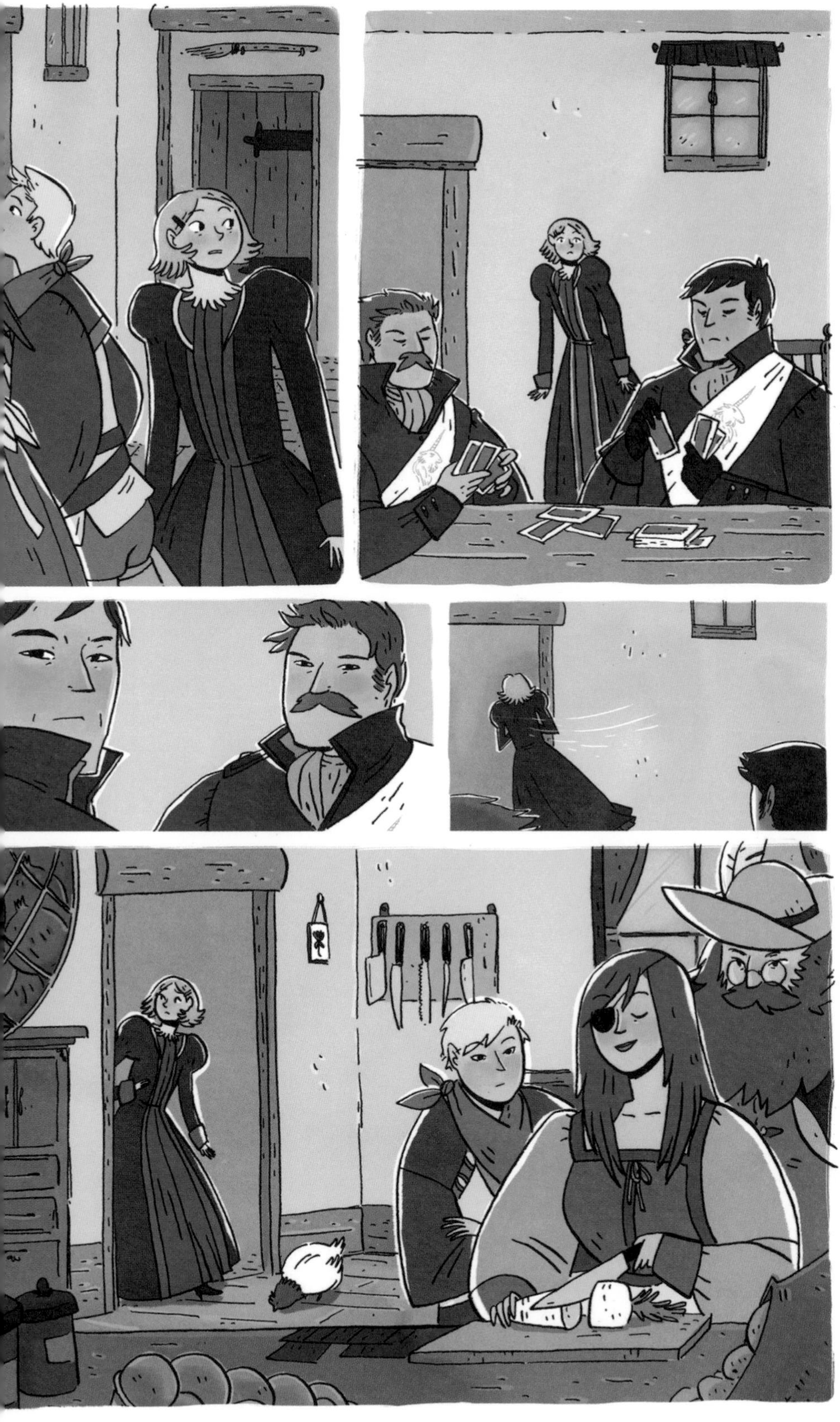

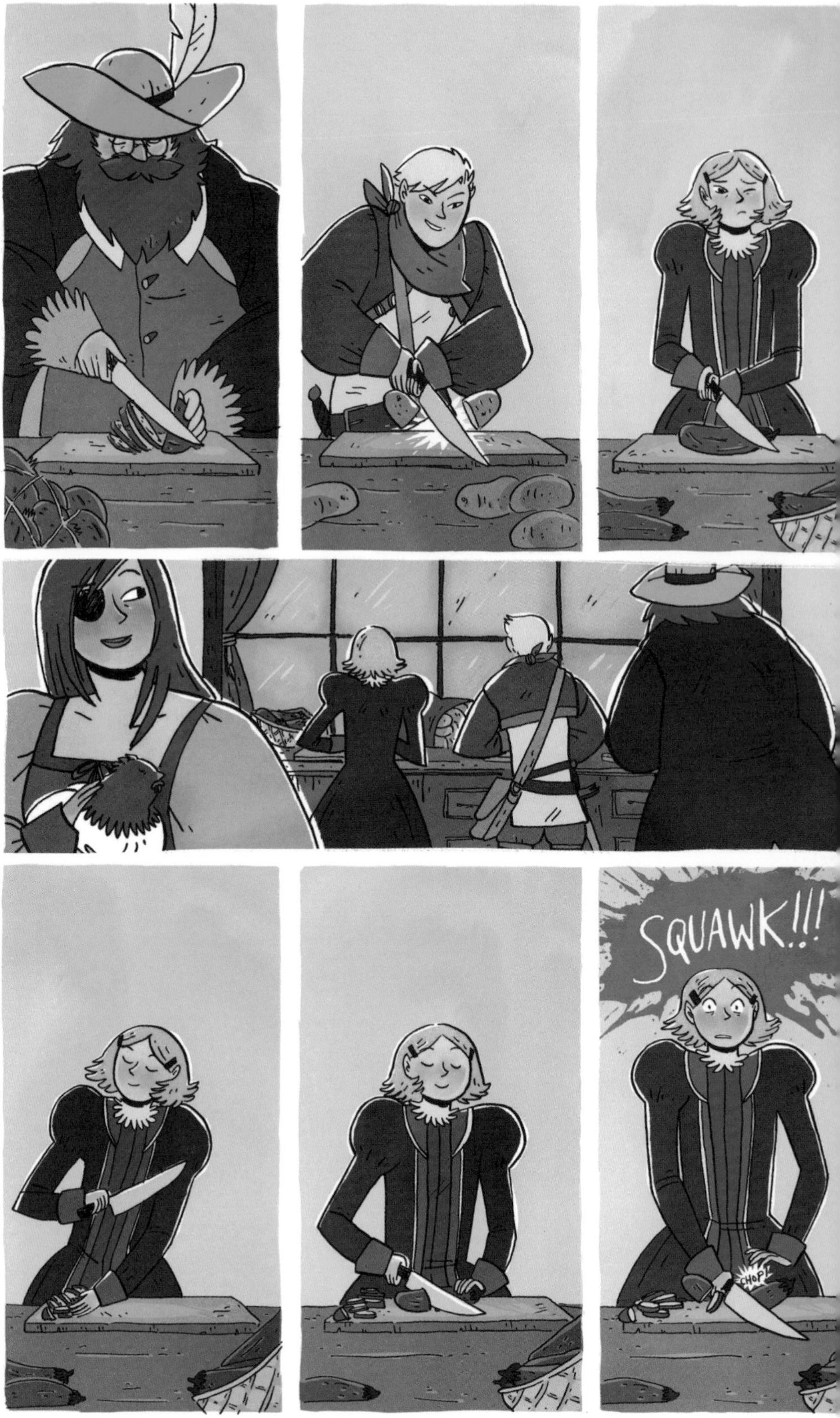
SQUAWK!!!
CHOP!

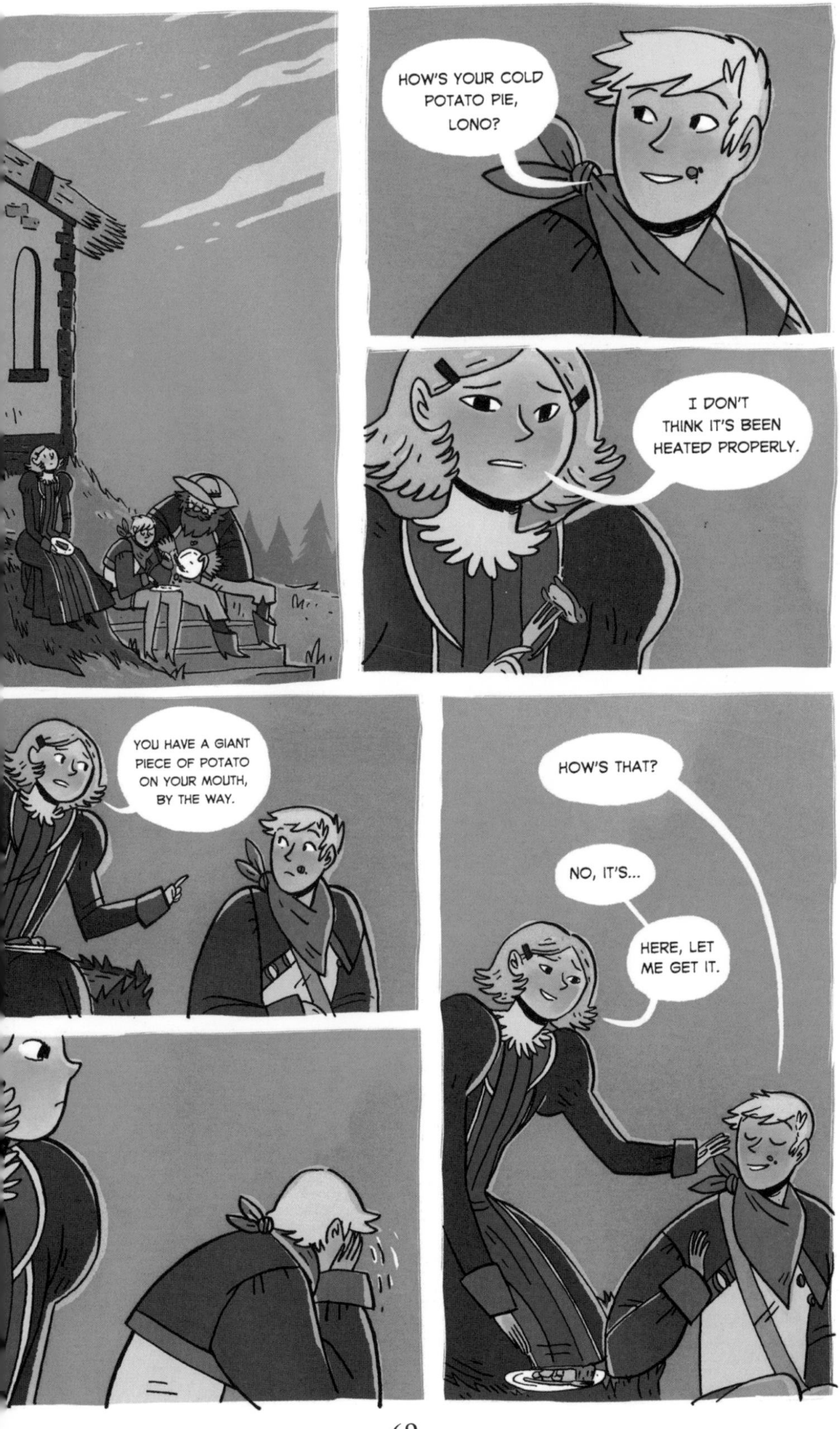
HOW'S YOUR COLD POTATO PIE, LONO?
I DON'T THINK IT'S BEEN HEATED PROPERLY.
YOU HAVE A GIANT PIECE OF POTATO ON YOUR MOUTH, BY THE WAY.
HOW'S THAT?
NO, IT'S...
HERE, LET ME GET IT.

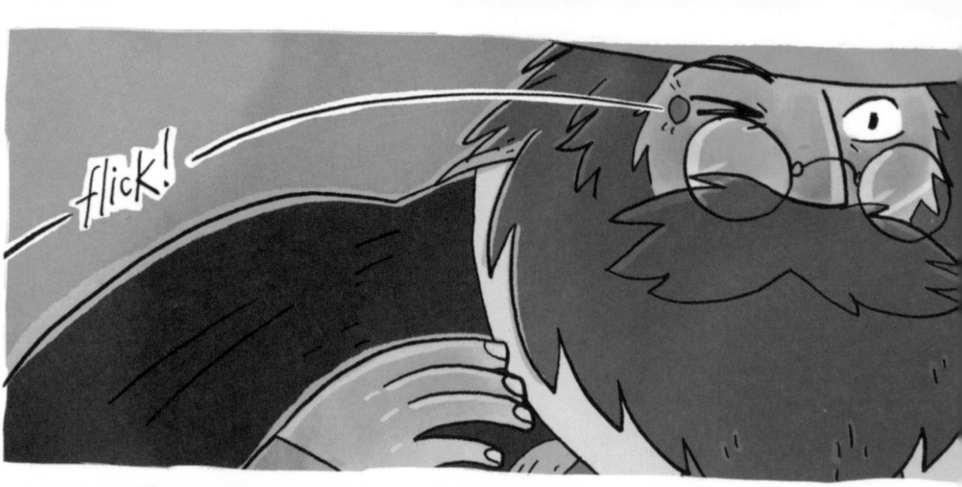
flick!

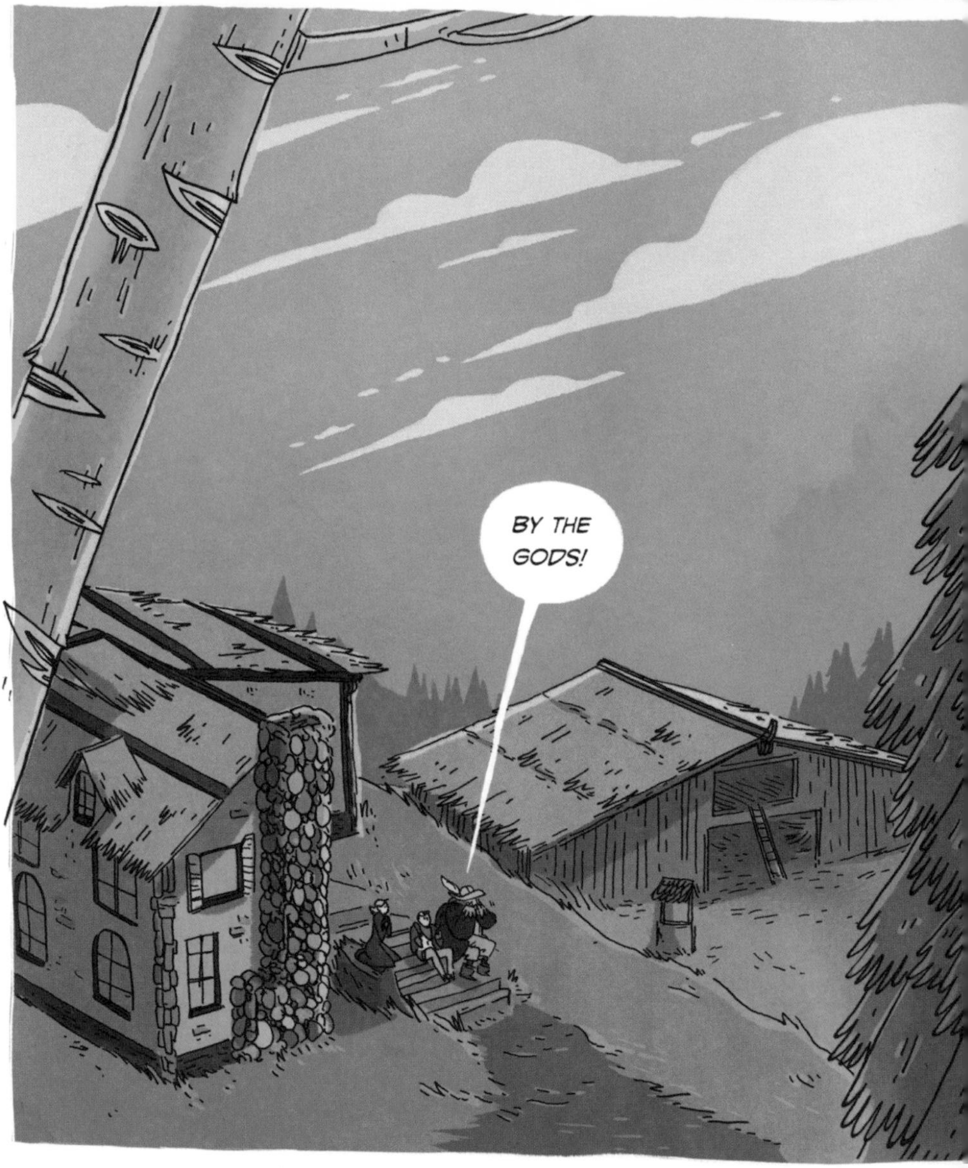
BY THE GODS!

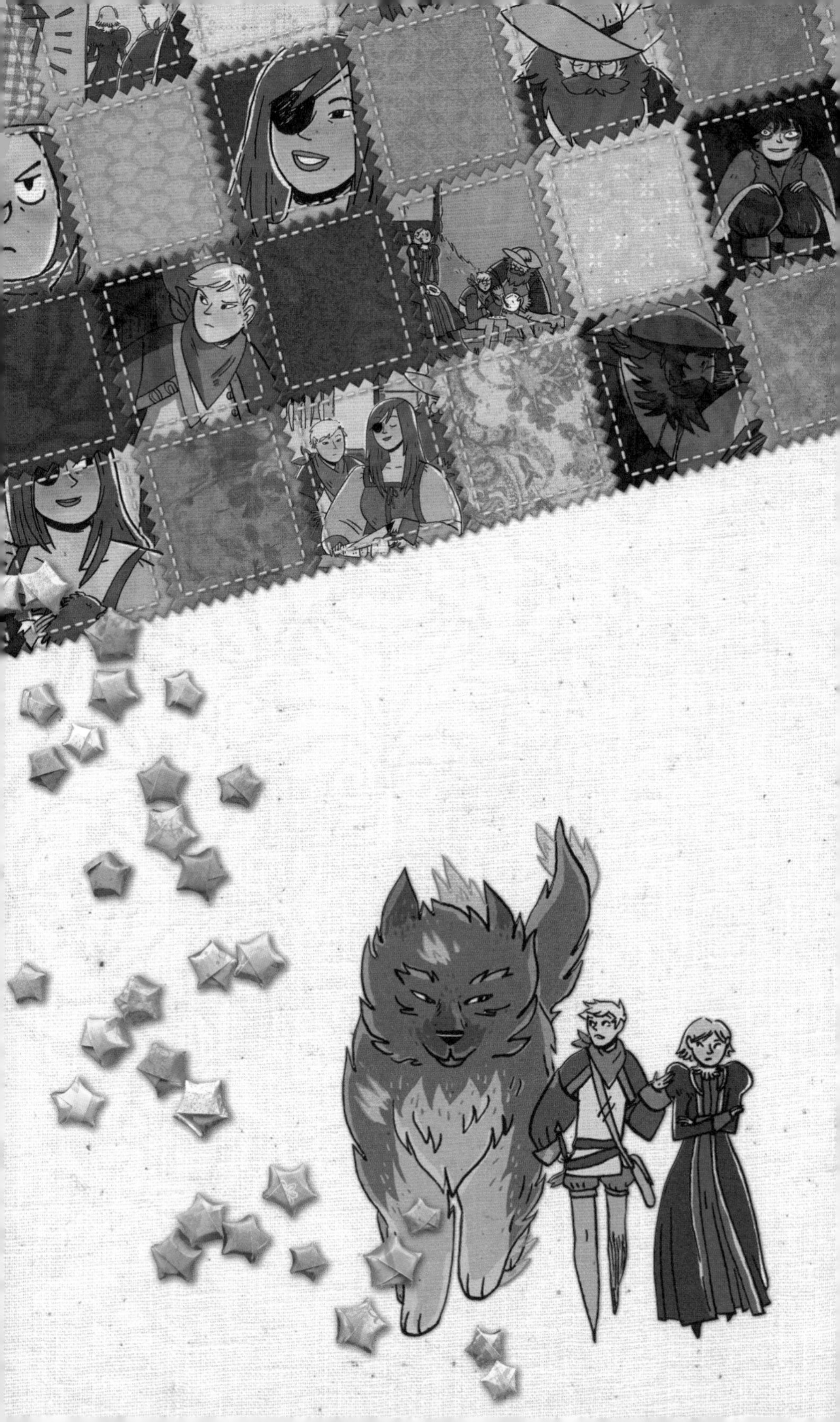

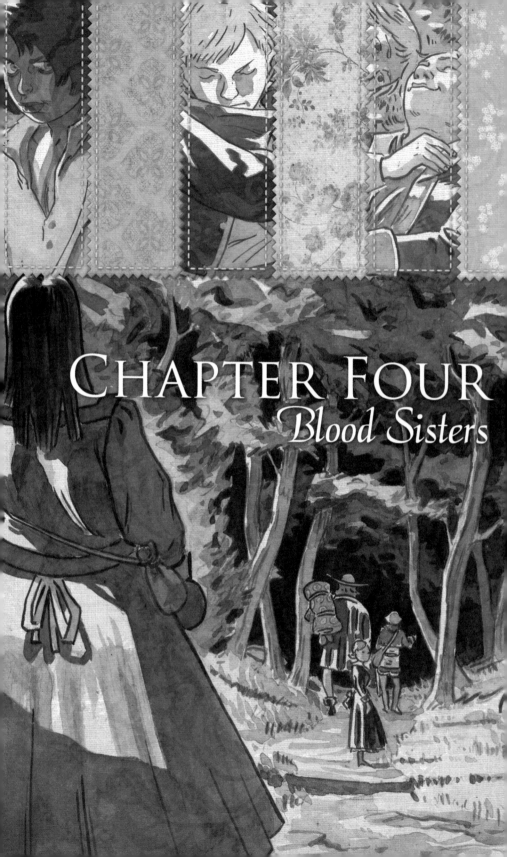

CHAPTER FOUR
Blood Sisters

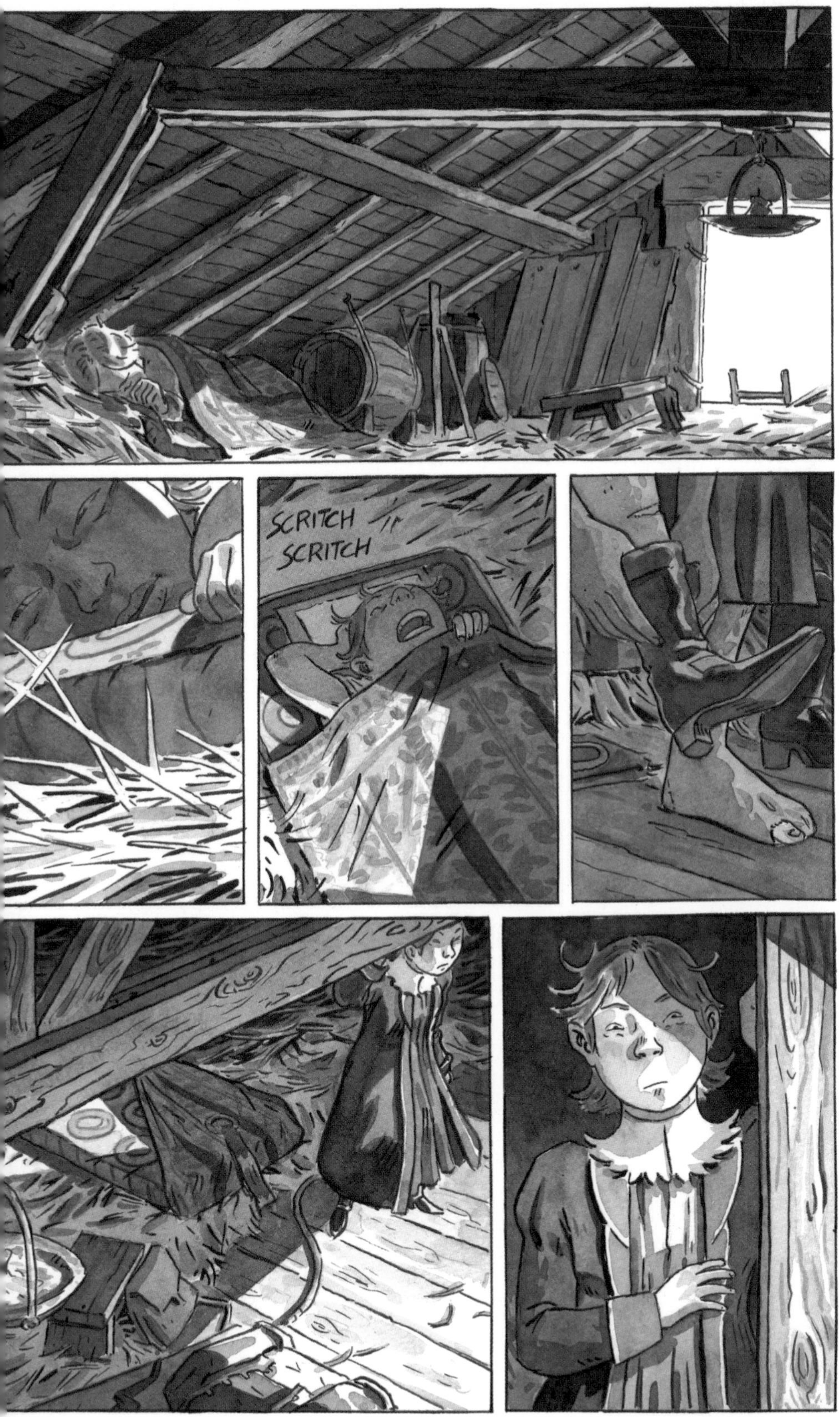
SCRITCH
SCRITCH

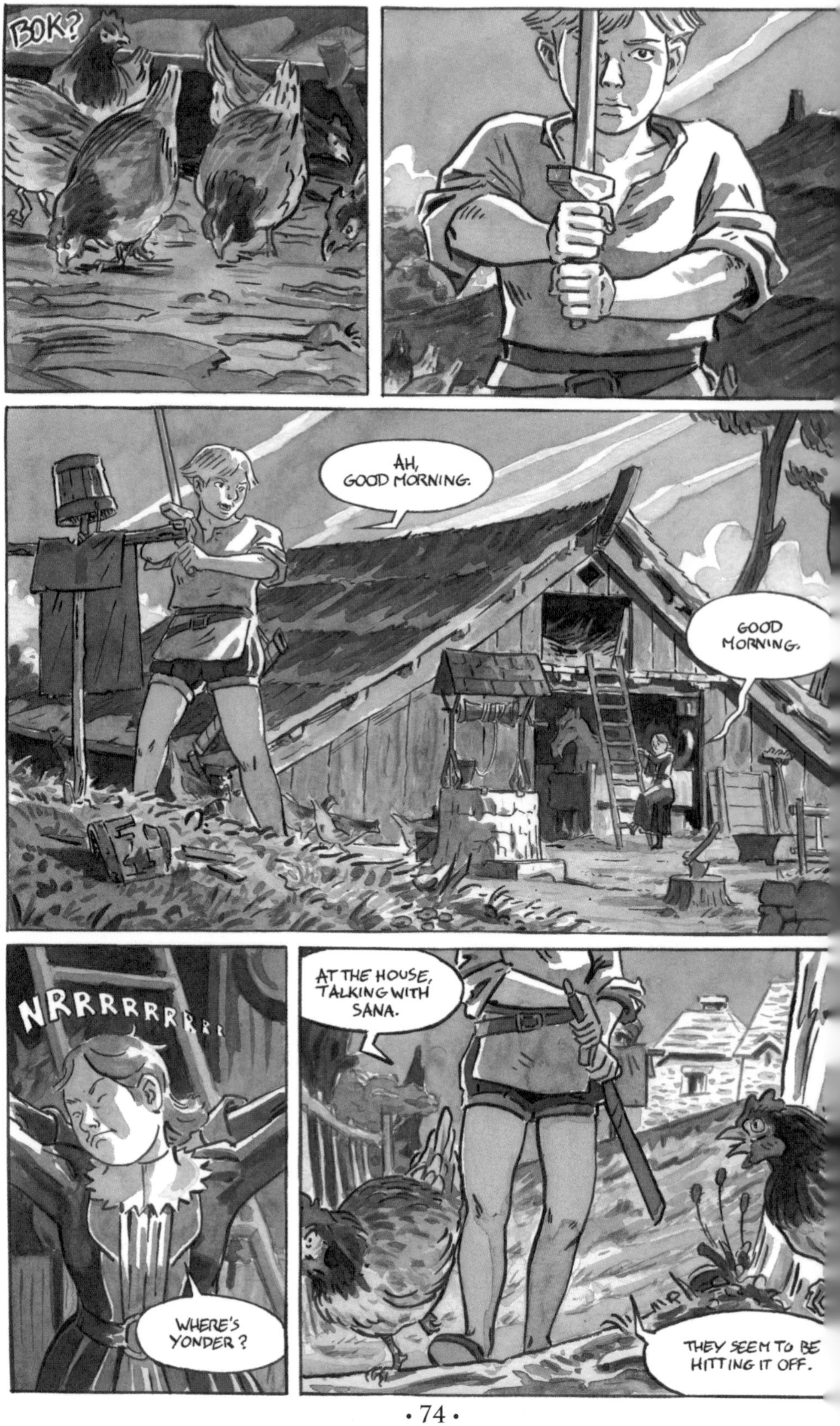
BOK?
AH, GOOD MORNING.
GOOD MORNING.
NRRRRRRRRR
WHERE'S YONDER?
AT THE HOUSE, TALKING WITH SANA.
THEY SEEM TO BE HITTING IT OFF.

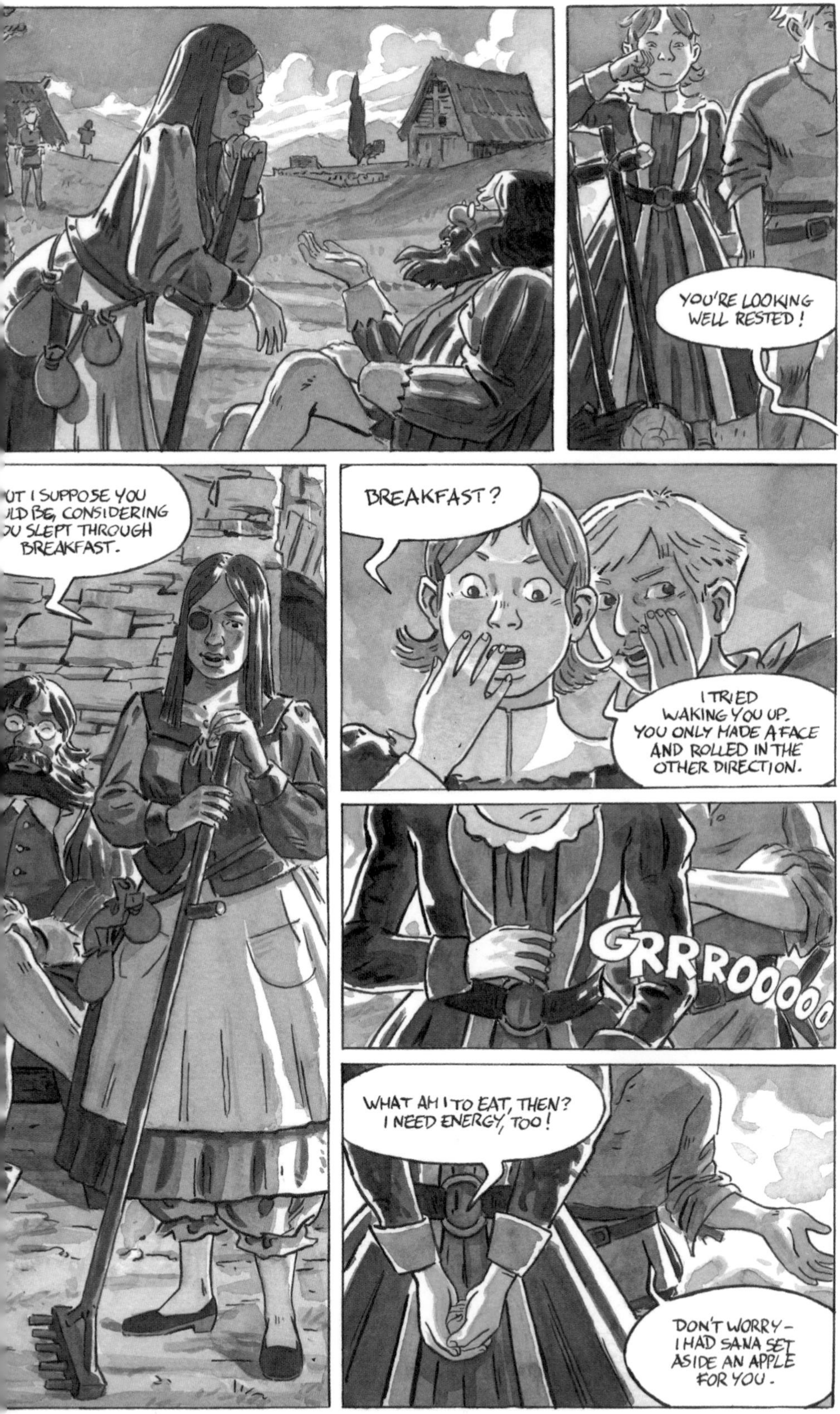
YOU'RE LOOKING WELL RESTED!
...UT I SUPPOSE YOU ...ULD BE, CONSIDERING ...OU SLEPT THROUGH BREAKFAST.
BREAKFAST?
I TRIED WAKING YOU UP. YOU ONLY MADE A FACE AND ROLLED IN THE OTHER DIRECTION.
GRRROOOOOO
WHAT AM I TO EAT, THEN? I NEED ENERGY, TOO!
DON'T WORRY - I HAD SANA SET ASIDE AN APPLE FOR YOU.

YOU CAN HAVE IT BEFORE TAKING A BATH. I'LL MEND YOUR CLOTHES AS YOU'RE WASHING AWAY ALL THE BUGS THAT HAVE PROBABLY LATCHED ONTO YOU.

THAT'S VERY KIND OF YOU, SANA.

MY DRESS WILL SURELY APPRECIATE IT.

IT'S THE LEAST I CAN DO - PIRA HAS GIVEN ME AN ENTIRE GOLD BIT, AND FOR THAT I'LL ENSURE YOU GIRLS ...

... GET THE ROYAL TREATMENT.

IS SOMETHING WRONG?

OH NO - I WAS JUST WONDERING ABOUT YOUR OTHER GUESTS.

THEM ? THEY LEFT EARLY THIS MORNING.

IT SEEMS THEY GOT LOST ON THEIR WAY TO A SKIRMISH.

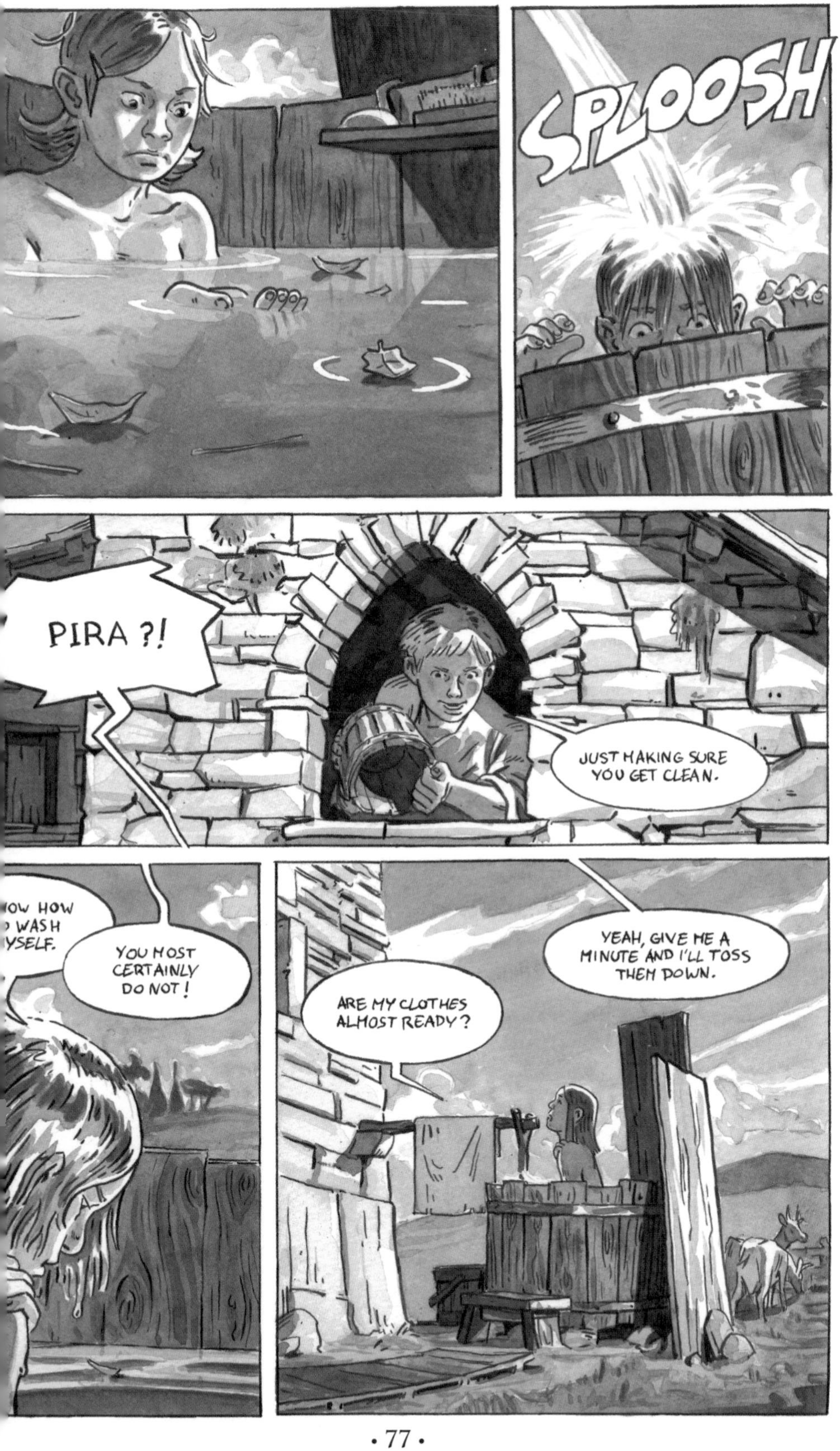
SPLOOSH
PIRA ?!
JUST MAKING SURE YOU GET CLEAN.
YOU MOST CERTAINLY DO NOT!
ARE MY CLOTHES ALMOST READY?
YEAH, GIVE ME A MINUTE AND I'LL TOSS THEM DOWN.

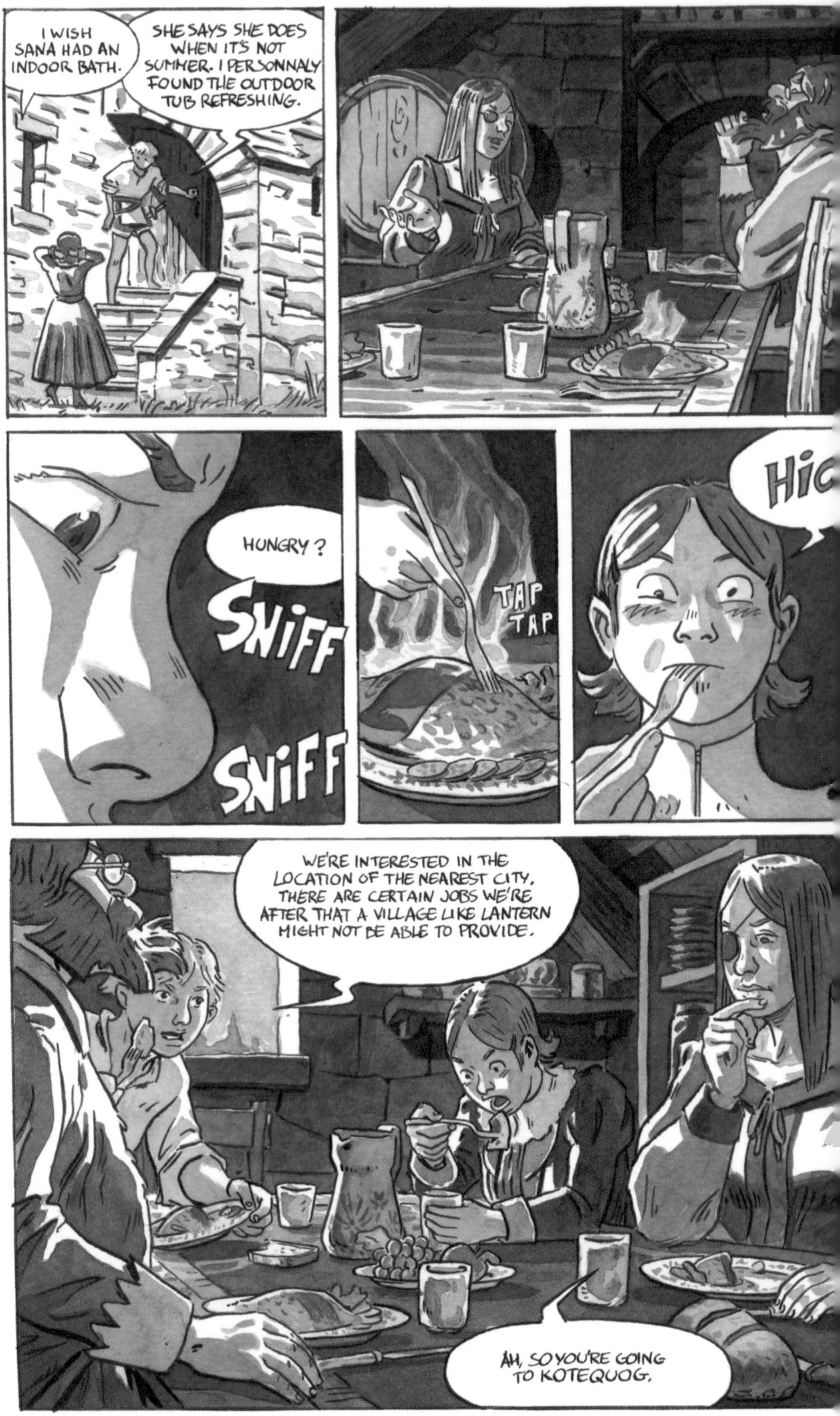
I WISH SANA HAD AN INDOOR BATH.
SHE SAYS SHE DOES WHEN IT'S NOT SUMMER. I PERSONNALY FOUND THE OUTDOOR TUB REFRESHING.
HUNGRY?
SNIFF
SNIFF
TAP TAP
Hic
WE'RE INTERESTED IN THE LOCATION OF THE NEAREST CITY. THERE ARE CERTAIN JOBS WE'RE AFTER THAT A VILLAGE LIKE LANTERN MIGHT NOT BE ABLE TO PROVIDE.
AH, SO YOU'RE GOING TO KOTEQUOG.

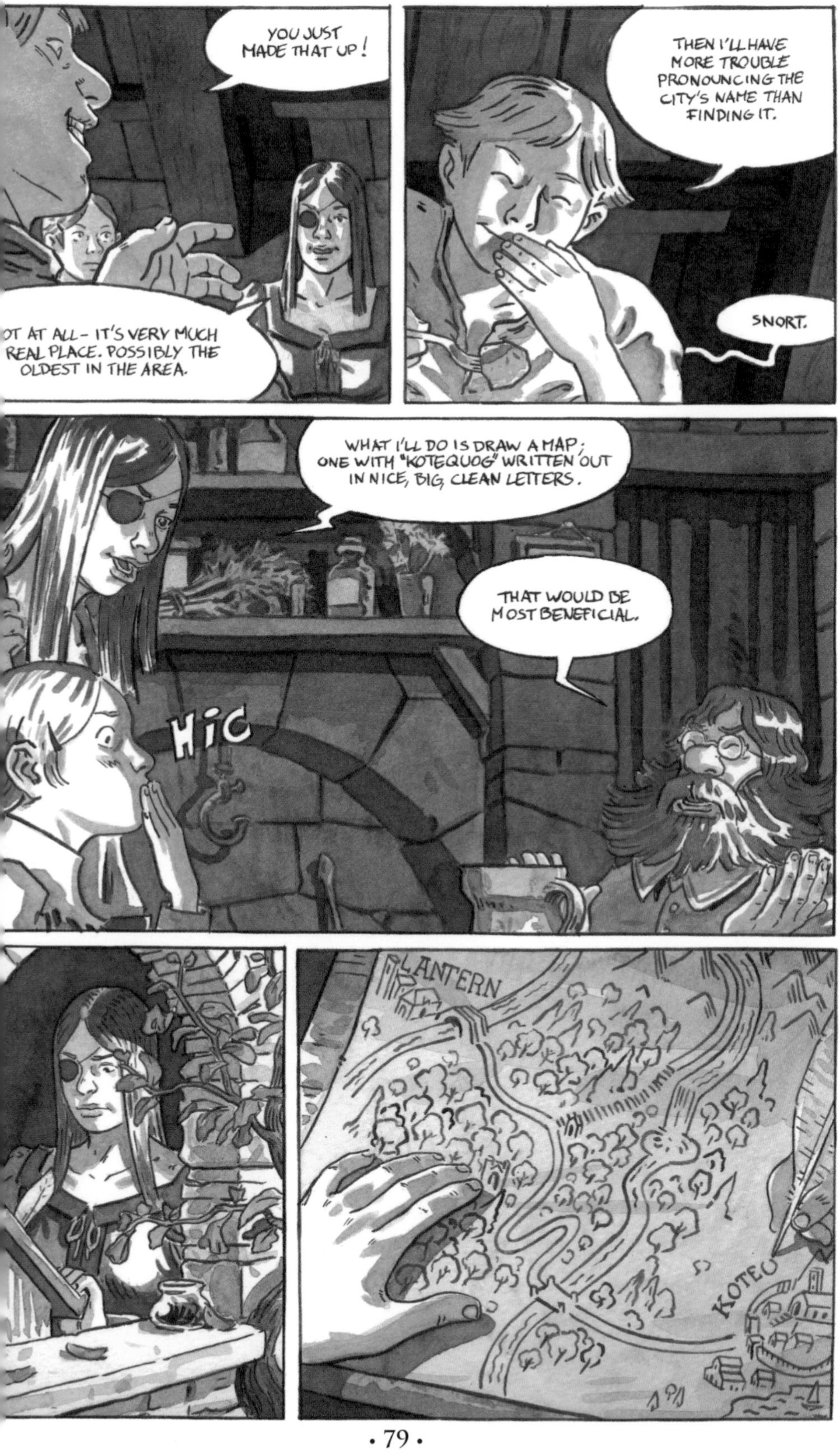
YOU JUST MADE THAT UP!
OT AT ALL- IT'S VERY MUCH REAL PLACE. POSSIBLY THE OLDEST IN THE AREA.
THEN I'LL HAVE MORE TROUBLE PRONOUNCING THE CITY'S NAME THAN FINDING IT.
SNORT.
WHAT I'LL DO IS DRAW A MAP; ONE WITH "KOTEQUOG" WRITTEN OUT IN NICE, BIG, CLEAN LETTERS.
THAT WOULD BE MOST BENEFICIAL.
HIC
LANTERN
KOTEQ

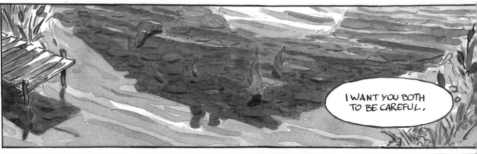

I WANT YOU BOTH
TO BE CAREFUL.

YOU MIGHT HAVE YONDER
TO PROTECT YOU FOR NOW
BUT HE'S NOT GOING TO
BE AROUND FOREVER.

YOU'RE NOT AWARE
OF JUST HOW STUBBORN
HE CAN BE.

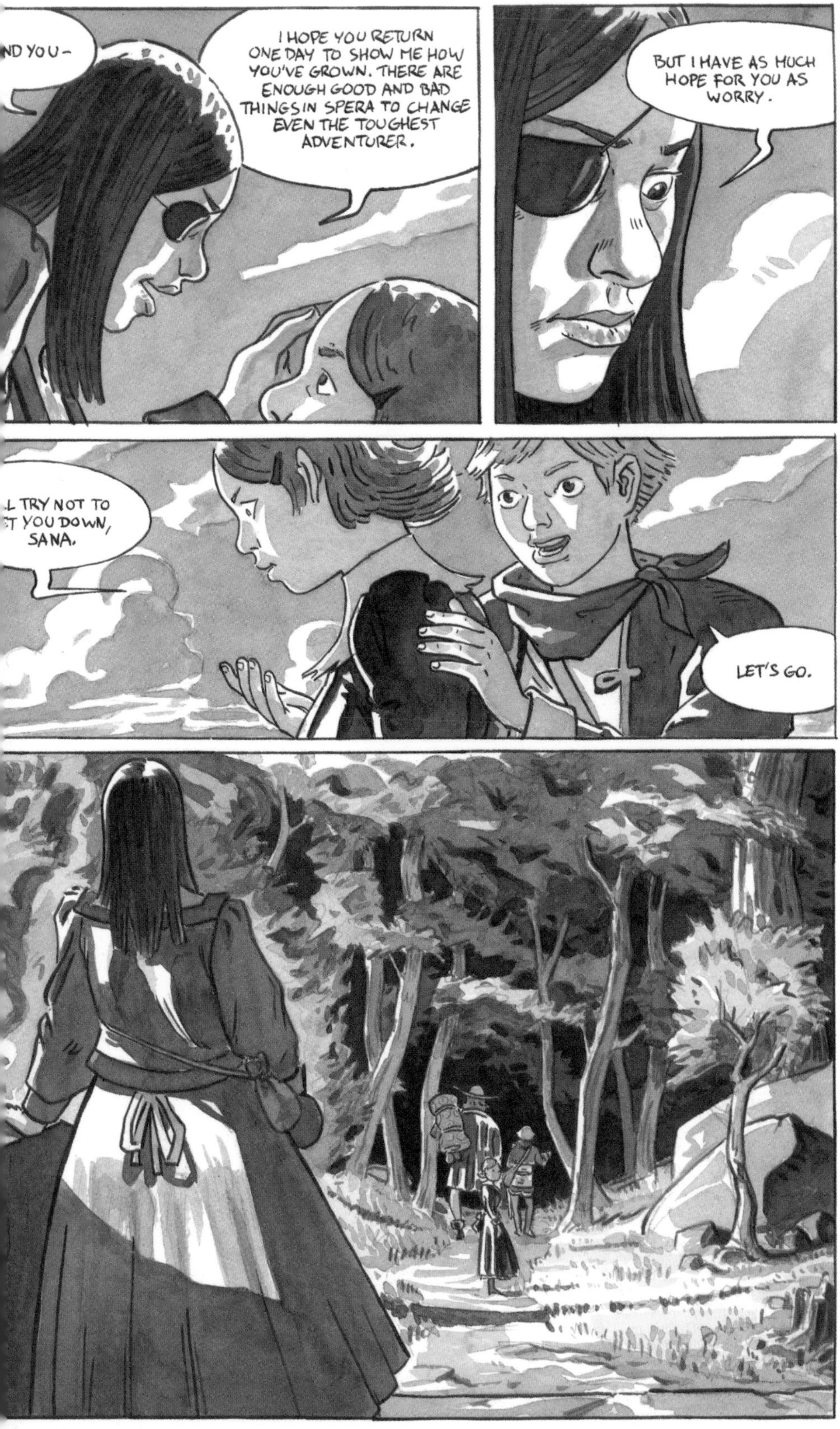
ND YOU-
I HOPE YOU RETURN ONE DAY TO SHOW ME HOW YOU'VE GROWN. THERE ARE ENOUGH GOOD AND BAD THINGS IN SPERA TO CHANGE EVEN THE TOUGHEST ADVENTURER.
BUT I HAVE AS MUCH HOPE FOR YOU AS WORRY.
L TRY NOT TO
T YOU DOWN,
SANA.
LET'S GO.

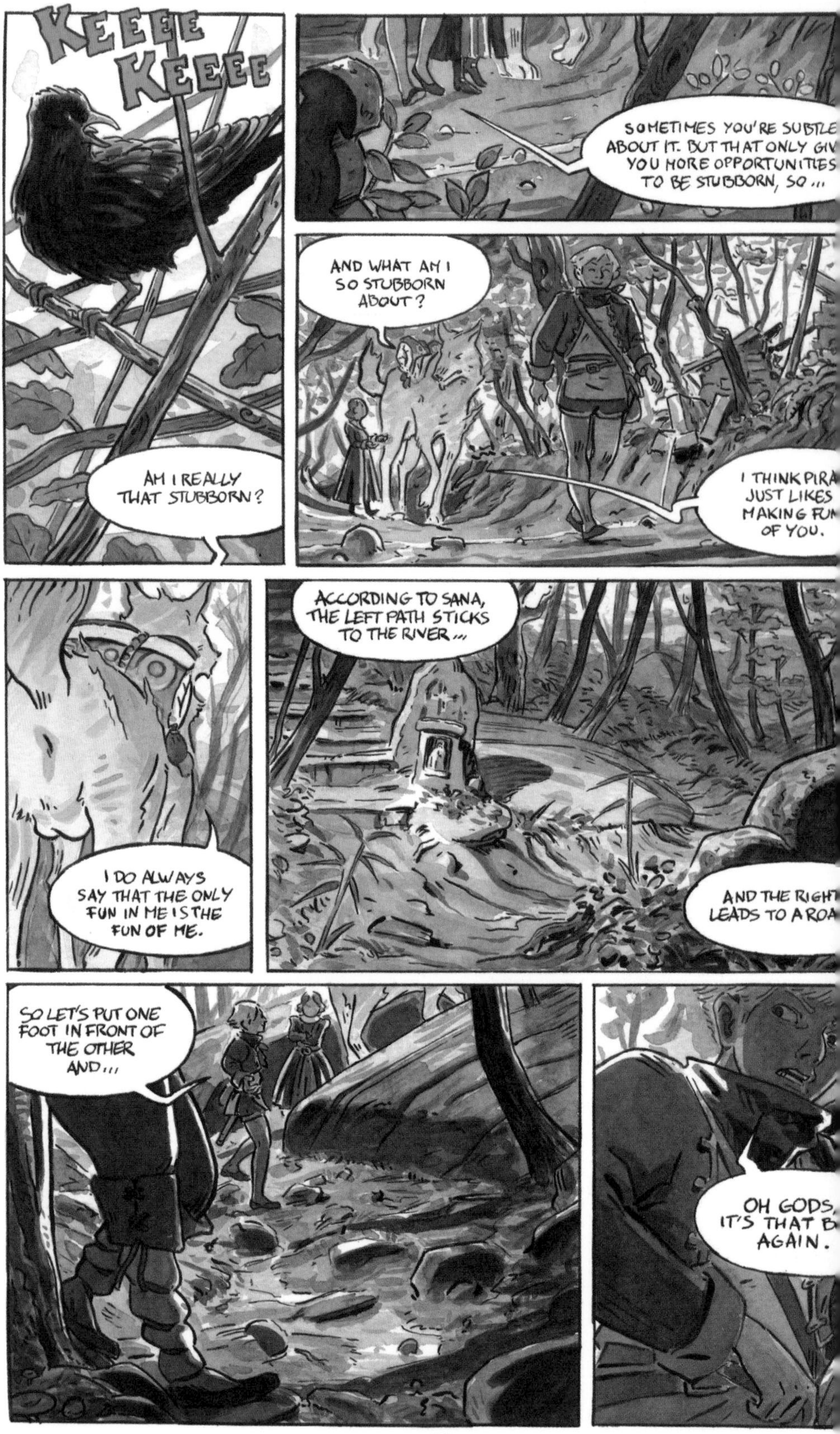
KEEEE KEEEE
AM I REALLY THAT STUBBORN?
SOMETIMES YOU'RE SUBTLE ABOUT IT. BUT THAT ONLY GIV YOU MORE OPPORTUNITIES TO BE STUBBORN, SO...
AND WHAT AM I SO STUBBORN ABOUT?
I THINK PIRA JUST LIKES MAKING FU OF YOU.
I DO ALWAYS SAY THAT THE ONLY FUN IN ME IS THE FUN OF ME.
ACCORDING TO SANA, THE LEFT PATH STICKS TO THE RIVER...
AND THE RIGH LEADS TO A ROA
SO LET'S PUT ONE FOOT IN FRONT OF THE OTHER AND...
OH GODS. IT'S THAT B AGAIN.

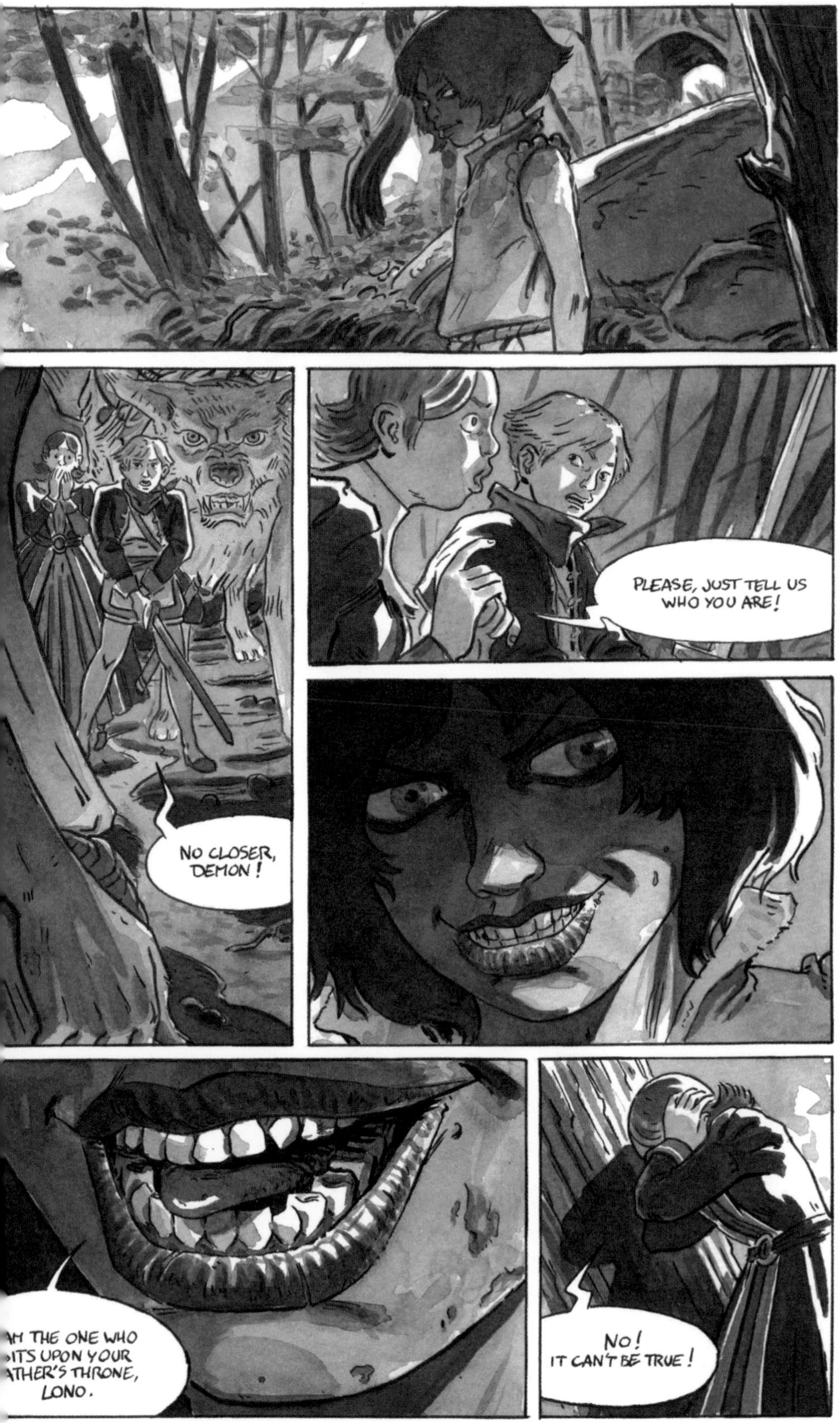

NO CLOSER, DEMON!
PLEASE, JUST TELL US WHO YOU ARE!
AM THE ONE WHO ITS UPON YOUR ATHER'S THRONE, LONO.
NO! IT CAN'T BE TRUE!

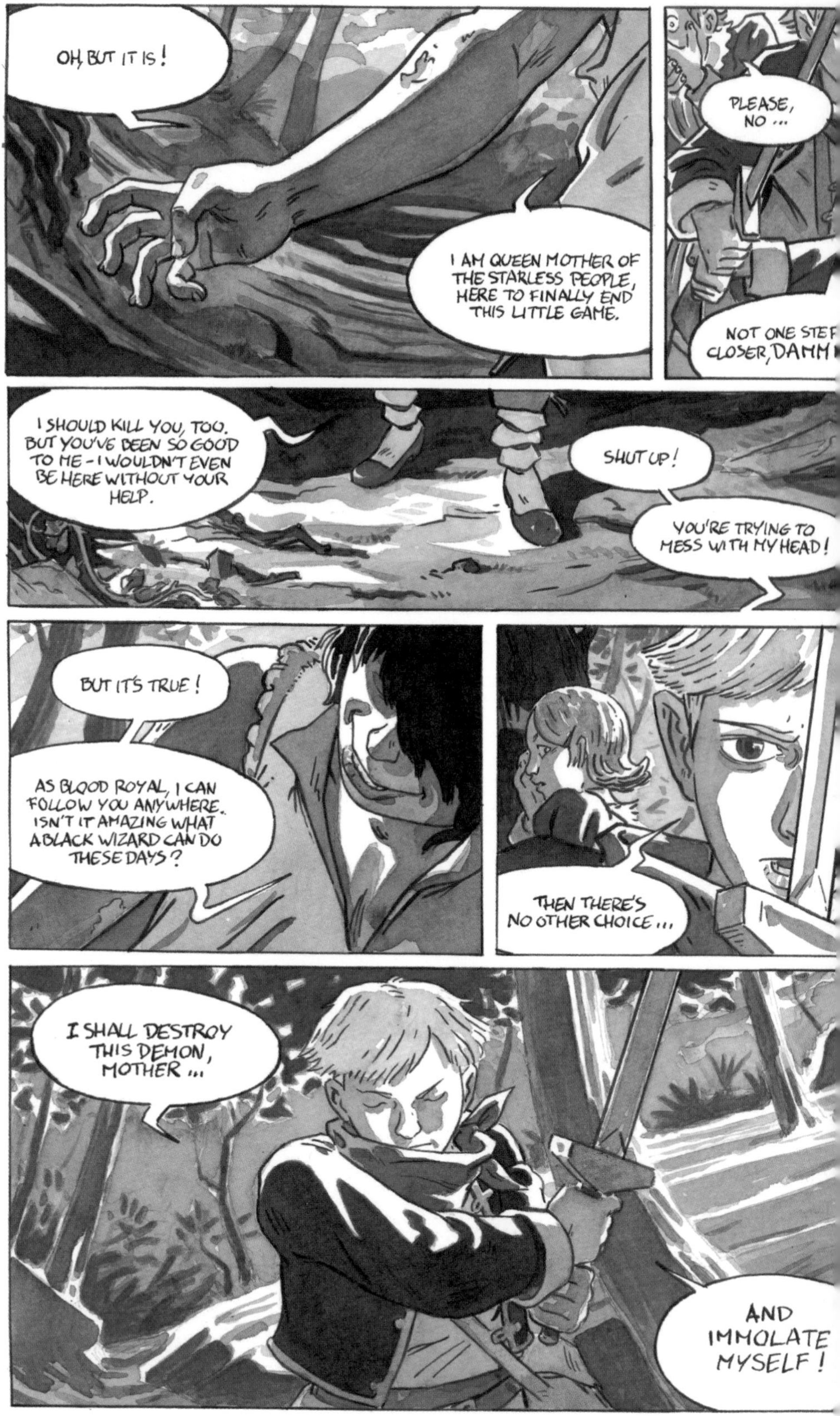
OH, BUT IT IS!
I AM QUEEN MOTHER OF THE STARLESS PEOPLE, HERE TO FINALLY END THIS LITTLE GAME.
PLEASE, NO ...
NOT ONE STEP CLOSER, DAMM
I SHOULD KILL YOU, TOO. BUT YOU'VE BEEN SO GOOD TO ME - I WOULDN'T EVEN BE HERE WITHOUT YOUR HELP.
SHUT UP!
YOU'RE TRYING TO MESS WITH MY HEAD!
BUT IT'S TRUE!
AS BLOOD ROYAL, I CAN FOLLOW YOU ANYWHERE. ISN'T IT AMAZING WHAT A BLACK WIZARD CAN DO THESE DAYS?
THEN THERE'S NO OTHER CHOICE ...
I SHALL DESTROY THIS DEMON, MOTHER ...
AND IMMOLATE MYSELF!

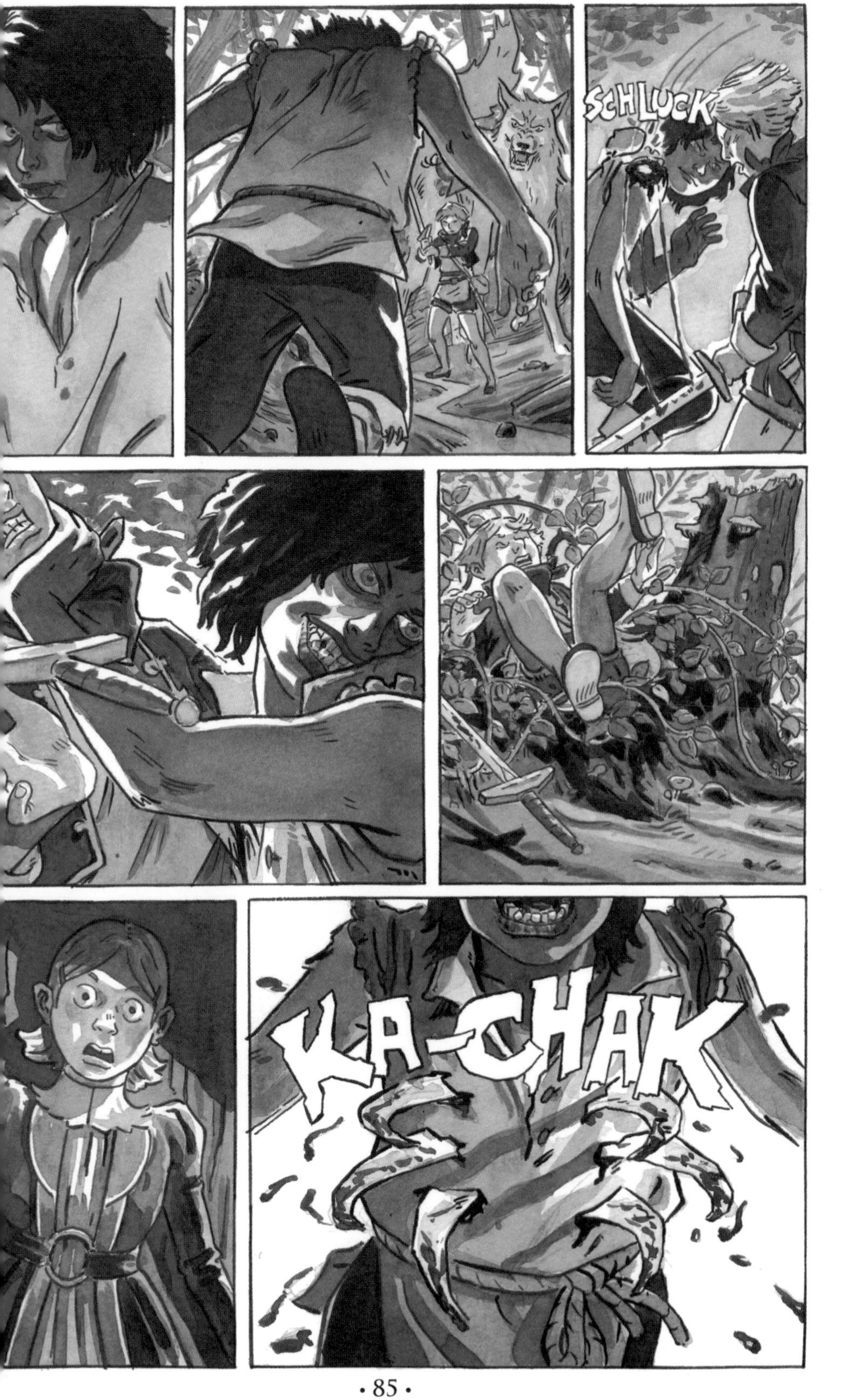
SCHLUCK
KA-CHAK

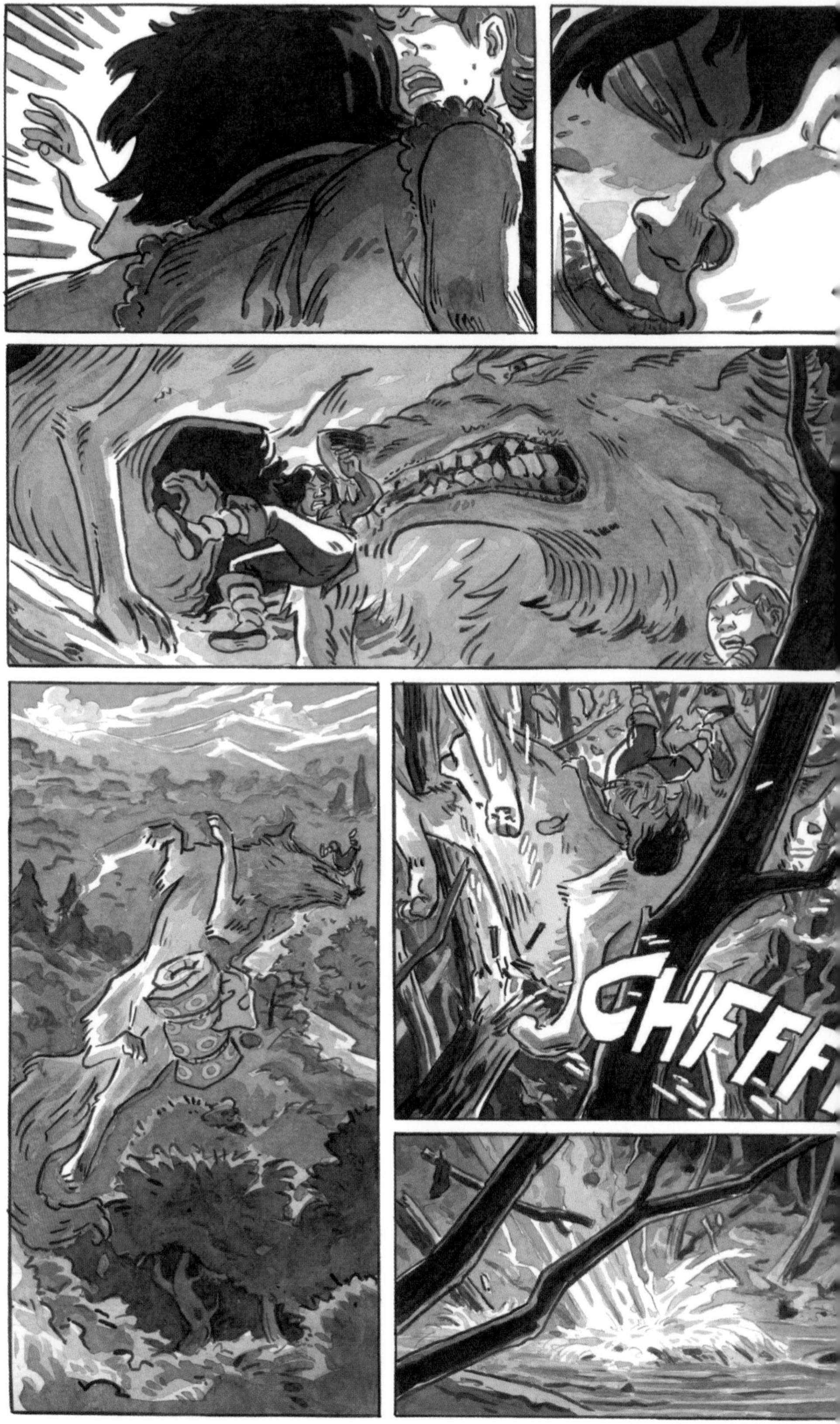
CHFFF

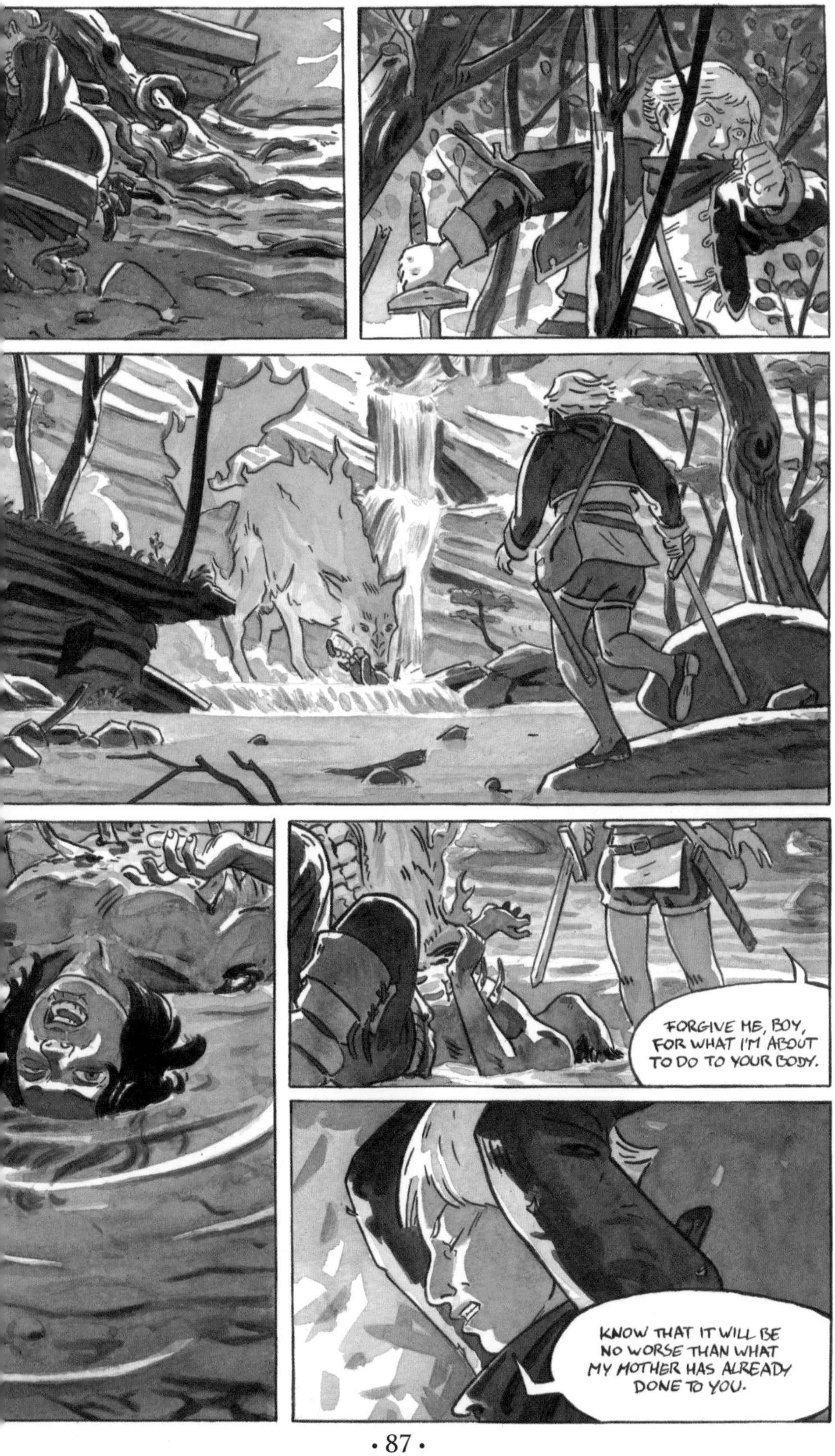
FORGIVE ME, BOY, FOR WHAT I'M ABOUT TO DO TO YOUR BODY.
KNOW THAT IT WILL BE NO WORSE THAN WHAT MY MOTHER HAS ALREADY DONE TO YOU.

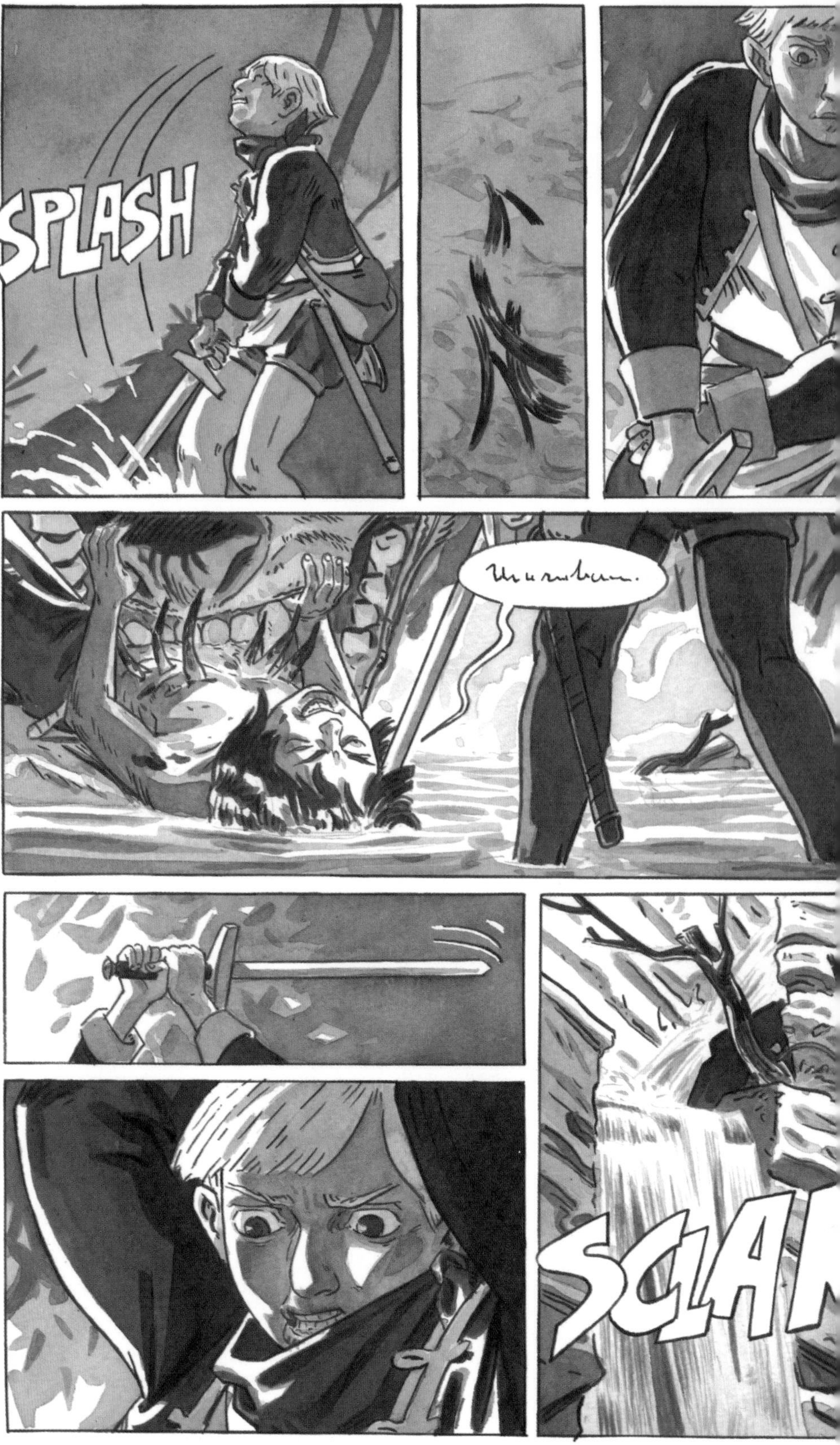
SPLASH
SCLA

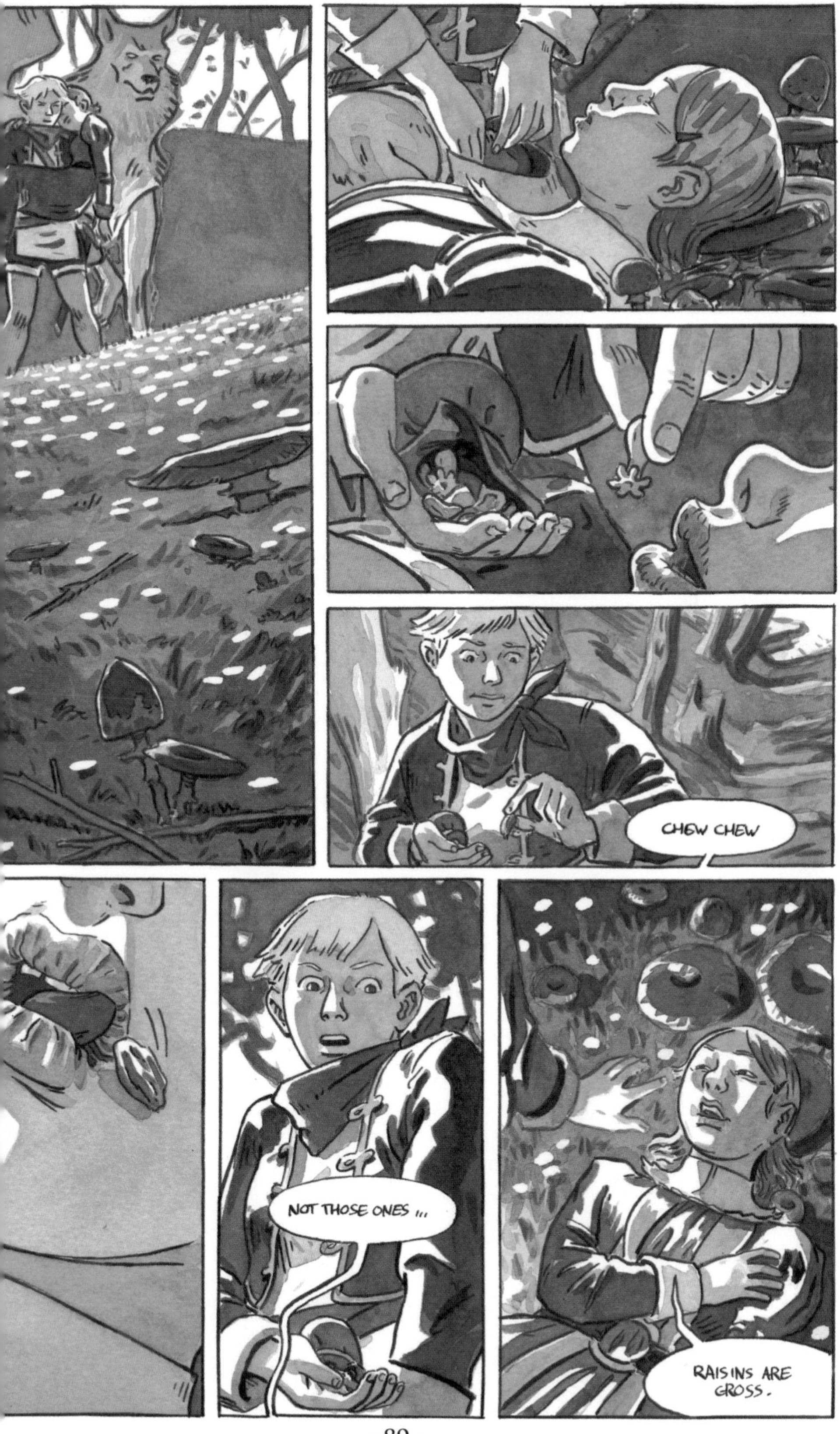
CHEW CHEW
NOT THOSE ONES ...
RAISINS ARE GROSS.

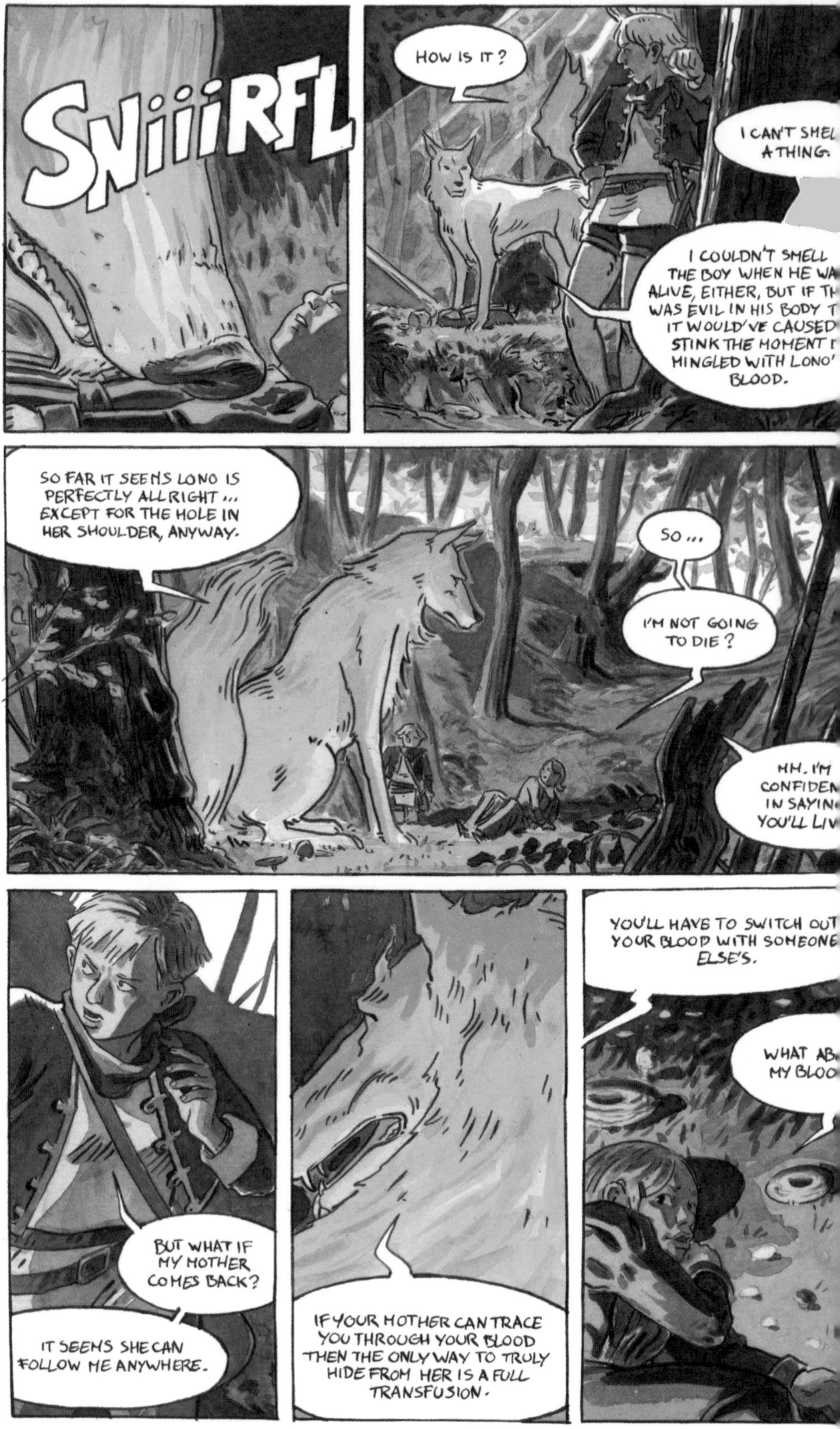
SNIIIRFL
HOW IS IT?
I CAN'T SHEL A THING.
I COULDN'T SMELL THE BOY WHEN HE WA ALIVE, EITHER, BUT IF TH WAS EVIL IN HIS BODY T IT WOULD'VE CAUSED STINK THE MOMENT I MINGLED WITH LONO' BLOOD.
SO FAR IT SEEMS LONO IS PERFECTLY ALLRIGHT... EXCEPT FOR THE HOLE IN HER SHOULDER, ANYWAY.
SO...
I'M NOT GOING TO DIE?
MH. I'M CONFIDEN IN SAYIN YOU'LL LIV
BUT WHAT IF MY MOTHER COMES BACK?
IT SEEMS SHE CAN FOLLOW ME ANYWHERE.
IF YOUR MOTHER CAN TRACE YOU THROUGH YOUR BLOOD THEN THE ONLY WAY TO TRULY HIDE FROM HER IS A FULL TRANSFUSION.
YOU'LL HAVE TO SWITCH OUT YOUR BLOOD WITH SOMEONE ELSE'S.
WHAT AB MY BLOO

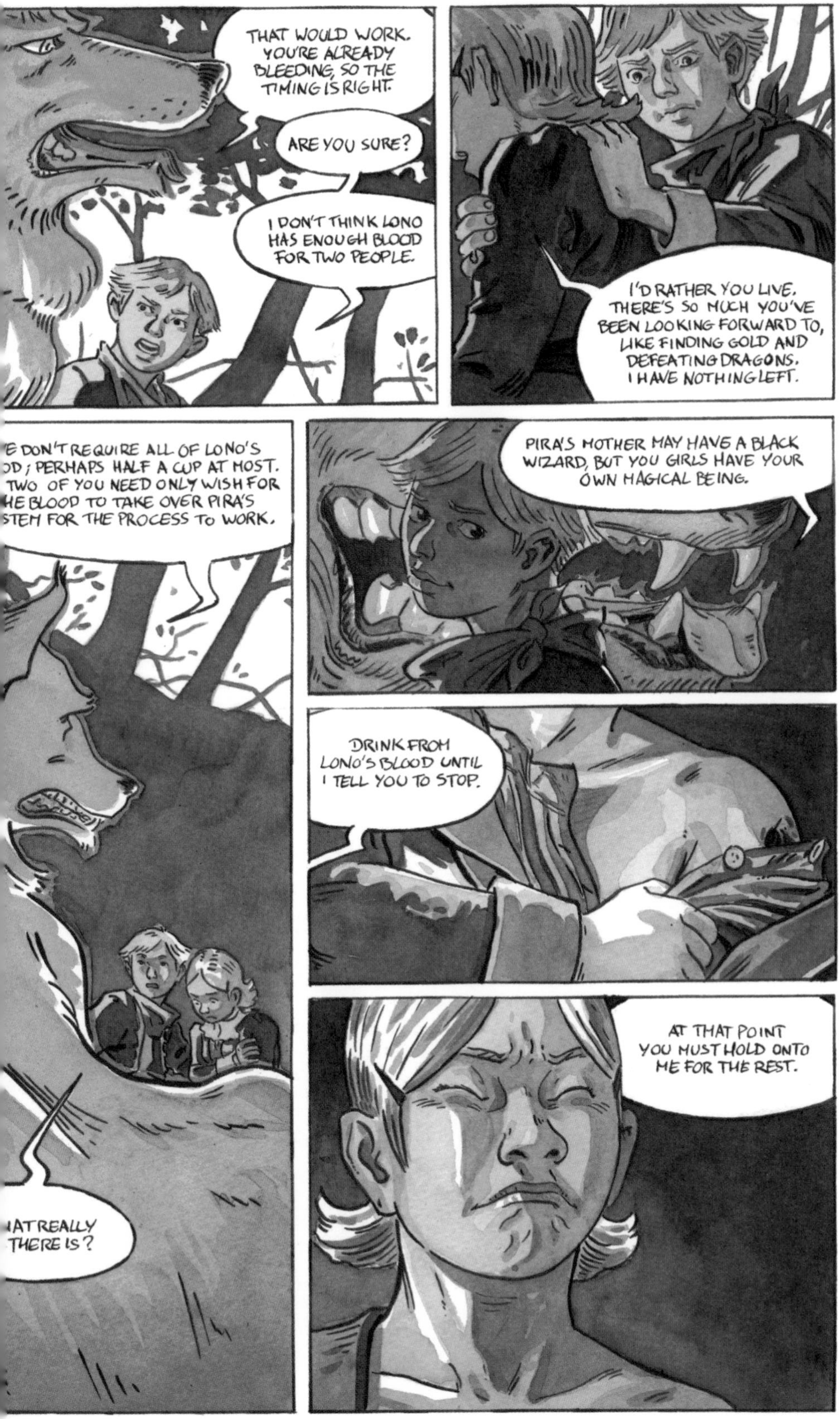
THAT WOULD WORK. YOU'RE ALREADY BLEEDING, SO THE TIMING IS RIGHT.
ARE YOU SURE?
I DON'T THINK LONO HAS ENOUGH BLOOD FOR TWO PEOPLE.
I'D RATHER YOU LIVE. THERE'S SO MUCH YOU'VE BEEN LOOKING FORWARD TO, LIKE FINDING GOLD AND DEFEATING DRAGONS. I HAVE NOTHING LEFT.
E DON'T REQUIRE ALL OF LONO'S OD; PERHAPS HALF A CUP AT MOST. TWO OF YOU NEED ONLY WISH FOR HE BLOOD TO TAKE OVER PIRA'S STEM FOR THE PROCESS TO WORK.
IAT REALLY THERE IS?
PIRA'S MOTHER MAY HAVE A BLACK WIZARD, BUT YOU GIRLS HAVE YOUR OWN MAGICAL BEING.
DRINK FROM LONO'S BLOOD UNTIL I TELL YOU TO STOP.
AT THAT POINT YOU MUST HOLD ONTO ME FOR THE REST.

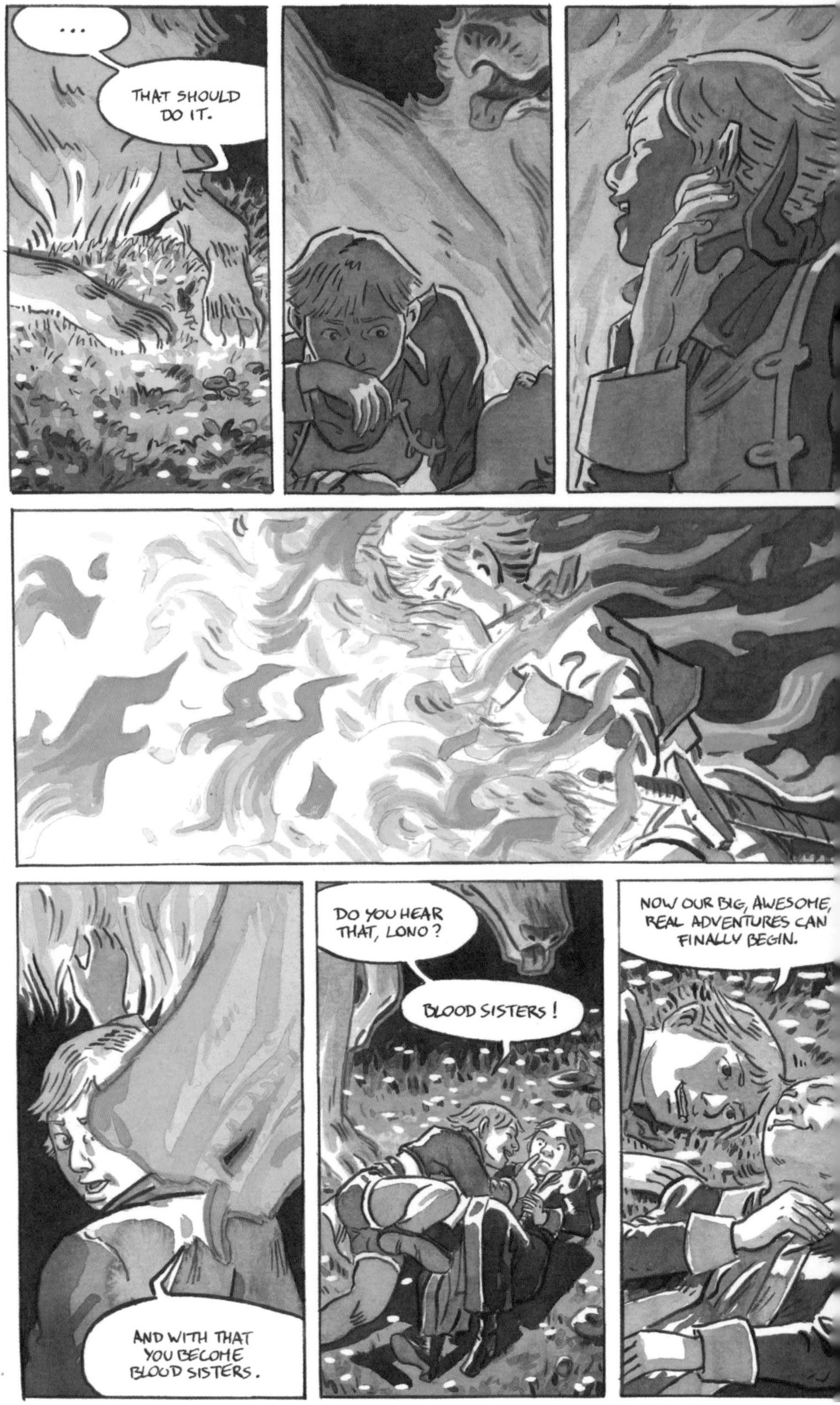
...
THAT SHOULD DO IT.
AND WITH THAT YOU BECOME BLOOD SISTERS.
DO YOU HEAR THAT, LONO?
BLOOD SISTERS!
NOW OUR BIG, AWESOME, REAL ADVENTURES CAN FINALLY BEGIN.

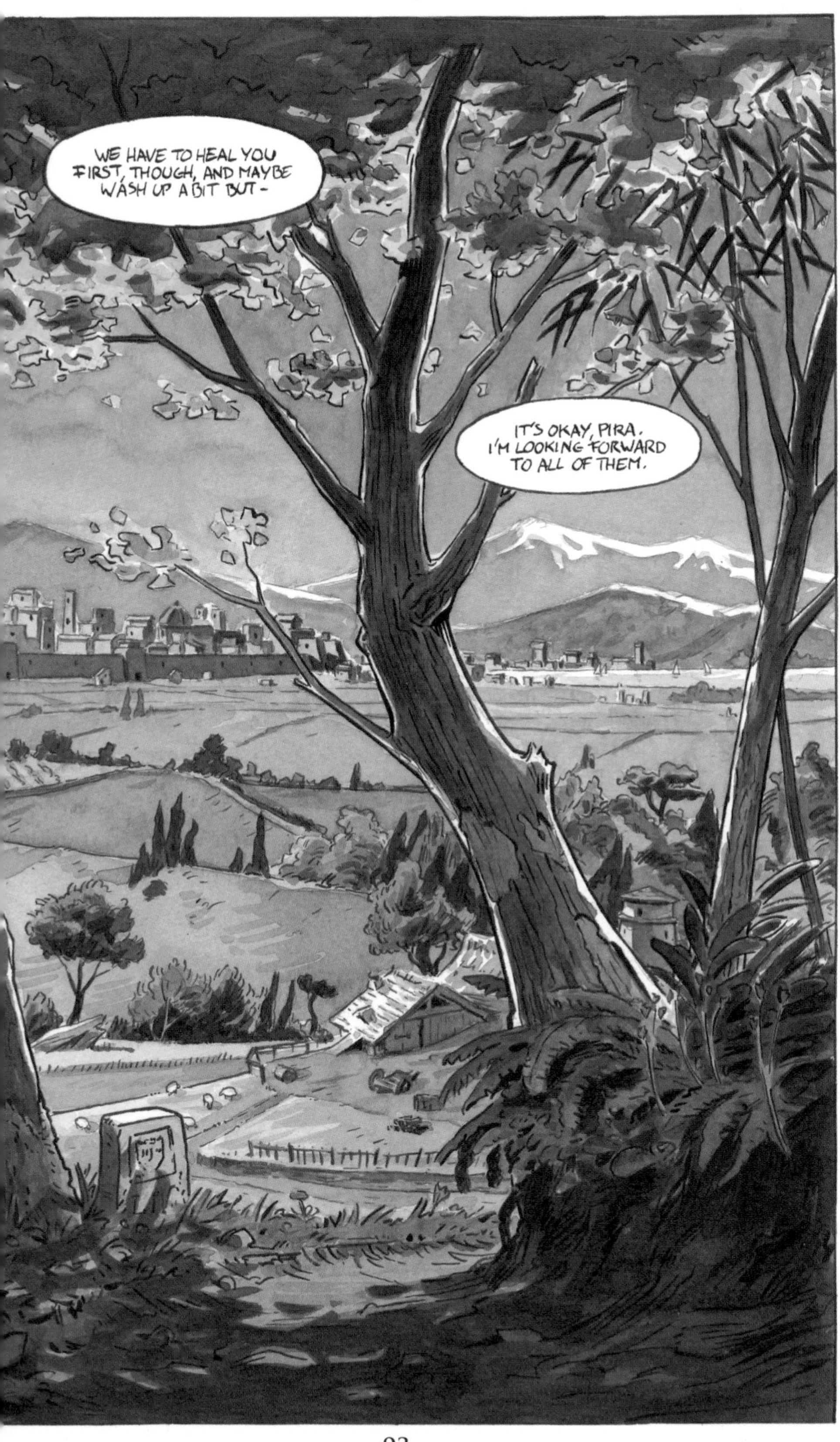
WE HAVE TO HEAL YOU FIRST, THOUGH, AND MAYBE WASH UP A BIT BUT-
IT'S OKAY, PIRA. I'M LOOKING FORWARD TO ALL OF THEM.

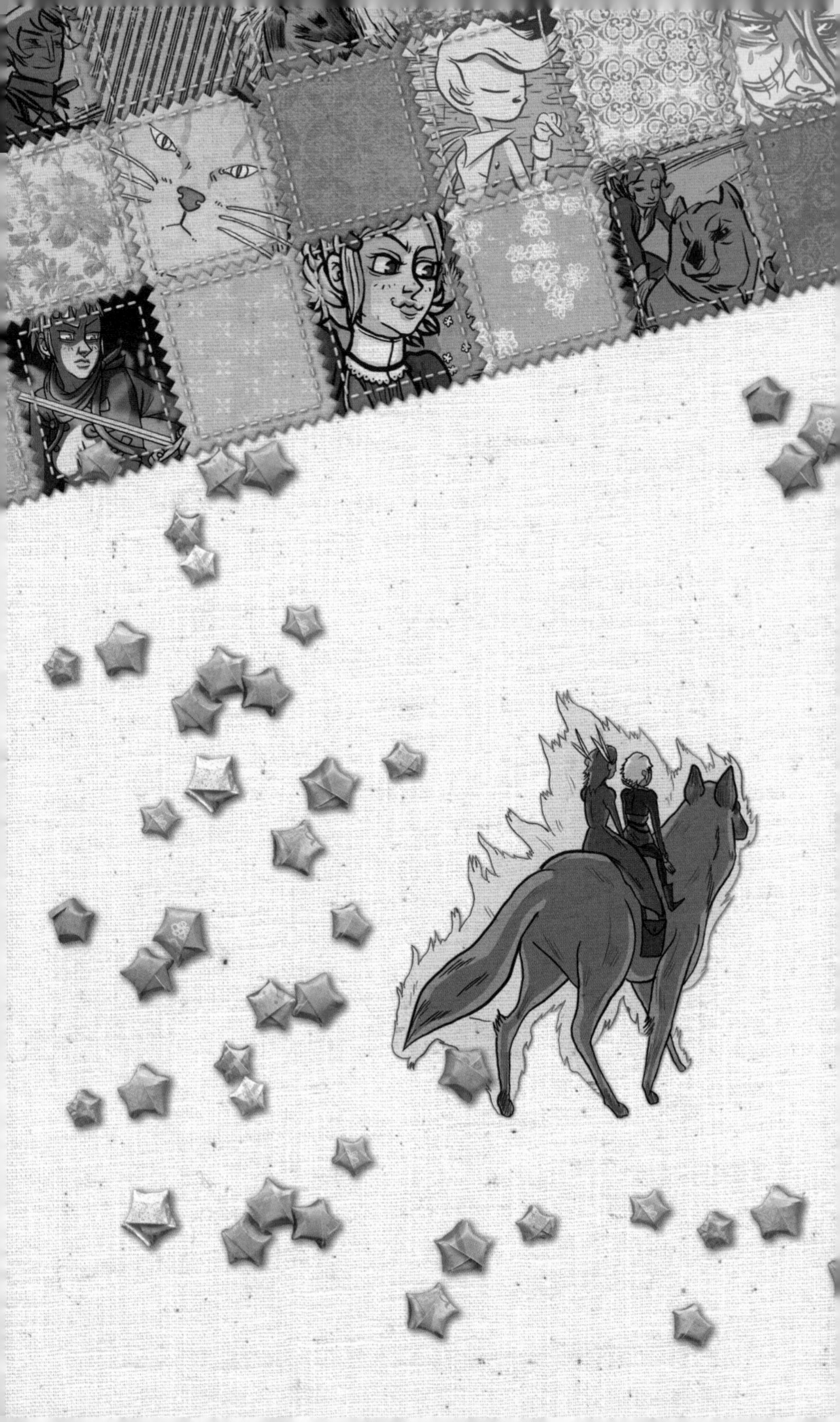

TABLE of CONTENTS
Rubies & Other Tales

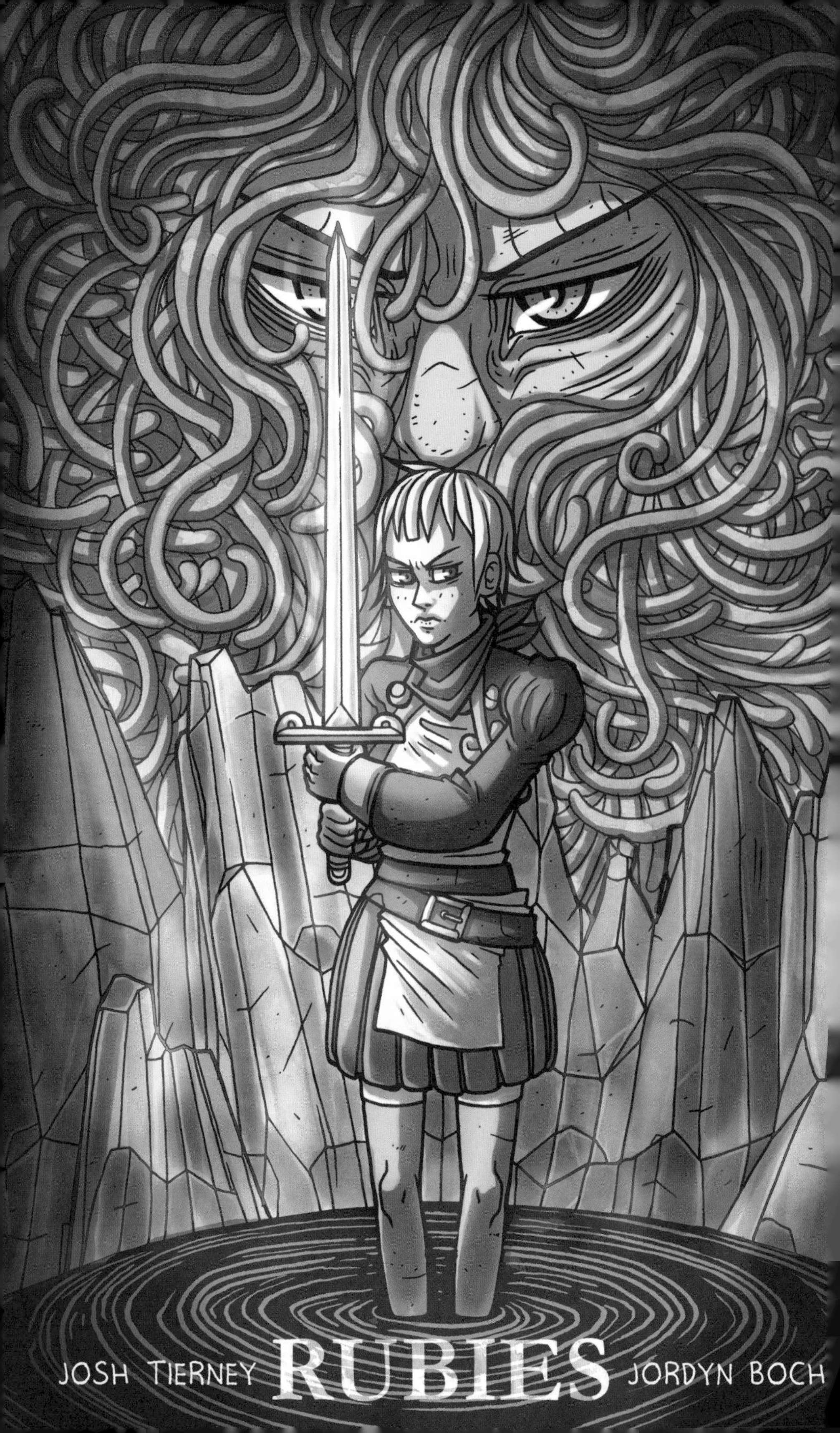
JOSH TIERNEY
RUBIES
JORDYN BOCH

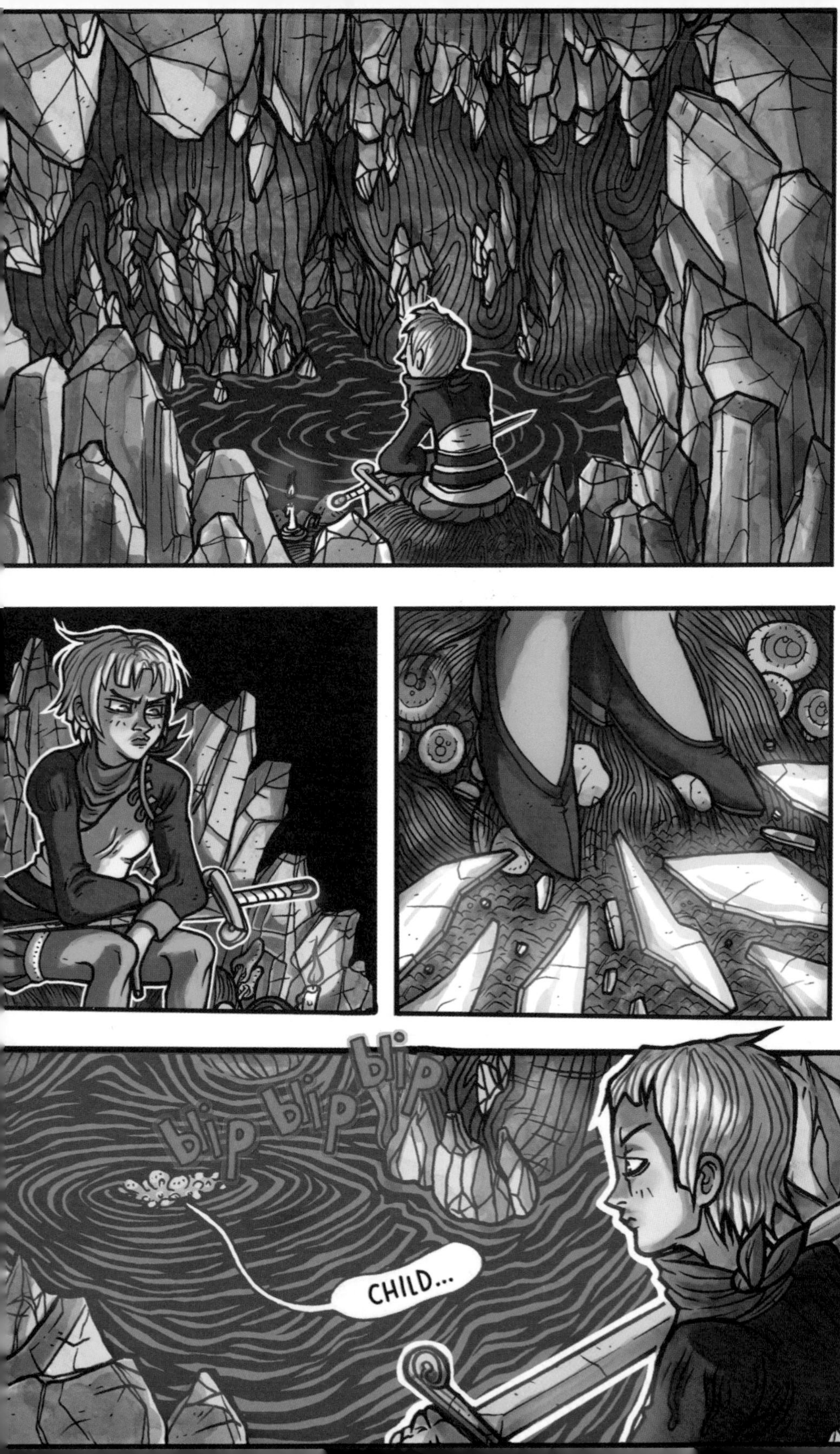

BLIP BLIP BLIP
CHILD...

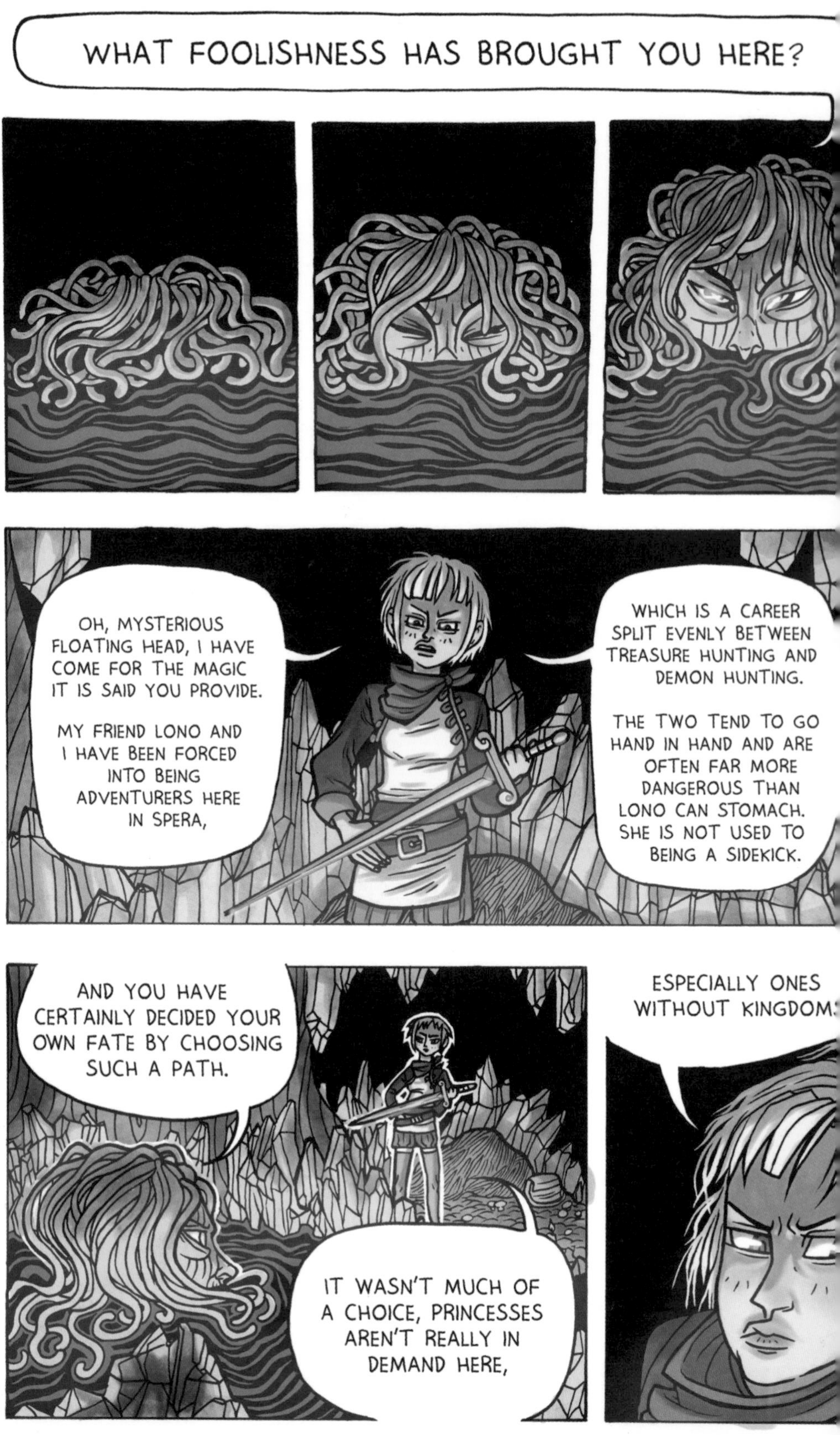
WHAT FOOLISHNESS HAS BROUGHT YOU HERE?
OH, MYSTERIOUS FLOATING HEAD, I HAVE COME FOR THE MAGIC IT IS SAID YOU PROVIDE.
MY FRIEND LONO AND I HAVE BEEN FORCED INTO BEING ADVENTURERS HERE IN SPERA,
WHICH IS A CAREER SPLIT EVENLY BETWEEN TREASURE HUNTING AND DEMON HUNTING.
THE TWO TEND TO GO HAND IN HAND AND ARE OFTEN FAR MORE DANGEROUS THAN LONO CAN STOMACH. SHE IS NOT USED TO BEING A SIDEKICK.
AND YOU HAVE CERTAINLY DECIDED YOUR OWN FATE BY CHOOSING SUCH A PATH.
IT WASN'T MUCH OF A CHOICE, PRINCESSES AREN'T REALLY IN DEMAND HERE,
ESPECIALLY ONES WITHOUT KINGDOM

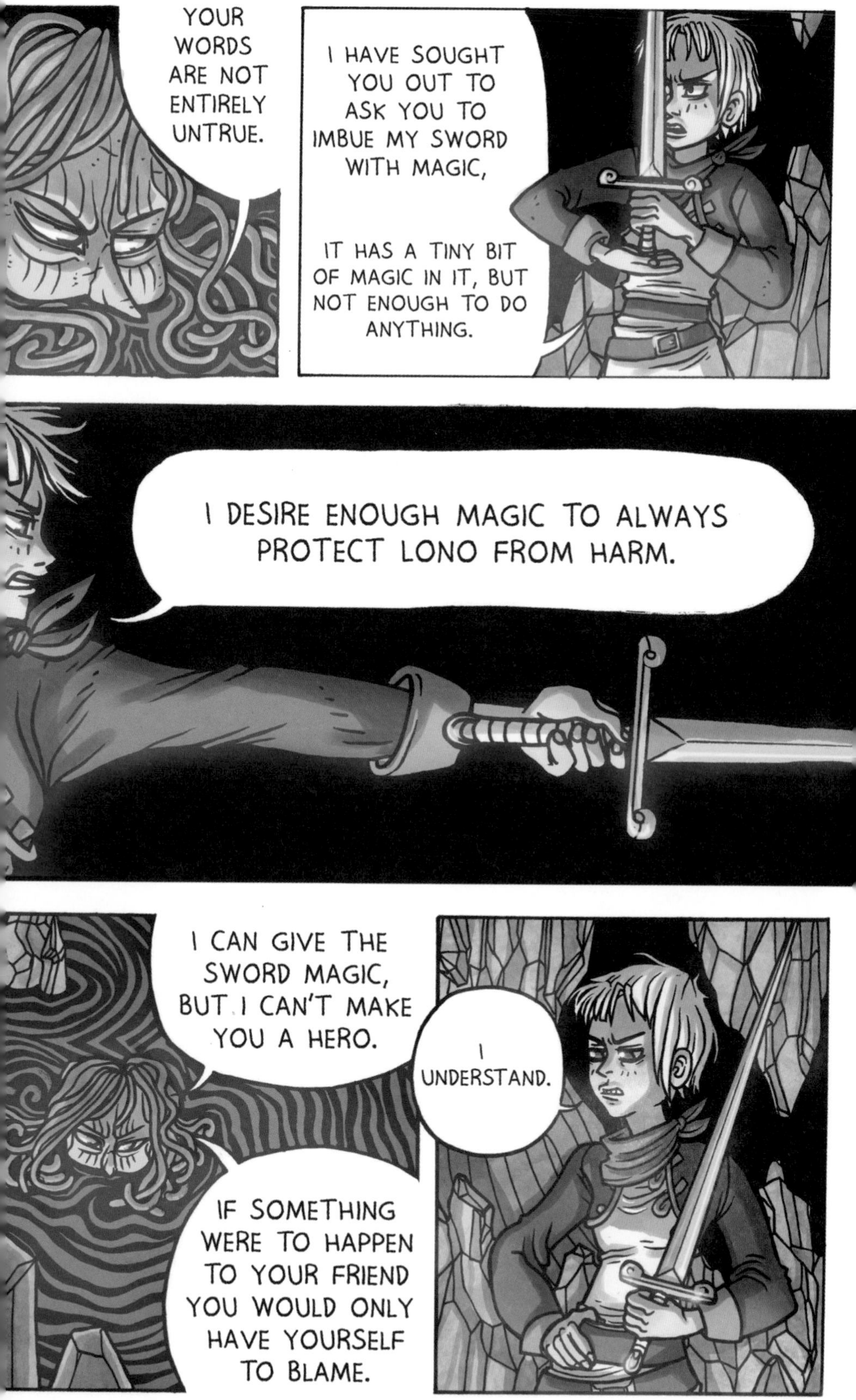
YOUR WORDS ARE NOT ENTIRELY UNTRUE.
I HAVE SOUGHT YOU OUT TO ASK YOU TO IMBUE MY SWORD WITH MAGIC,
IT HAS A TINY BIT OF MAGIC IN IT, BUT NOT ENOUGH TO DO ANYTHING.
I DESIRE ENOUGH MAGIC TO ALWAYS PROTECT LONO FROM HARM.
I CAN GIVE THE SWORD MAGIC, BUT I CAN'T MAKE YOU A HERO.
IF SOMETHING WERE TO HAPPEN TO YOUR FRIEND YOU WOULD ONLY HAVE YOURSELF TO BLAME.
I UNDERSTAND.

YOU CHOSE THE
THREE CORRECT PATHS

AND BROKE ONE OF THE
SEVEN MIRRORS THAT
CONTAIN MY POWER,

YOU'VE RISKED
INSTANT DEATH BY
COMING HERE

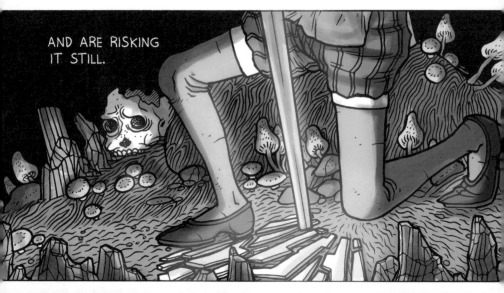

AND ARE RISKING
IT STILL.

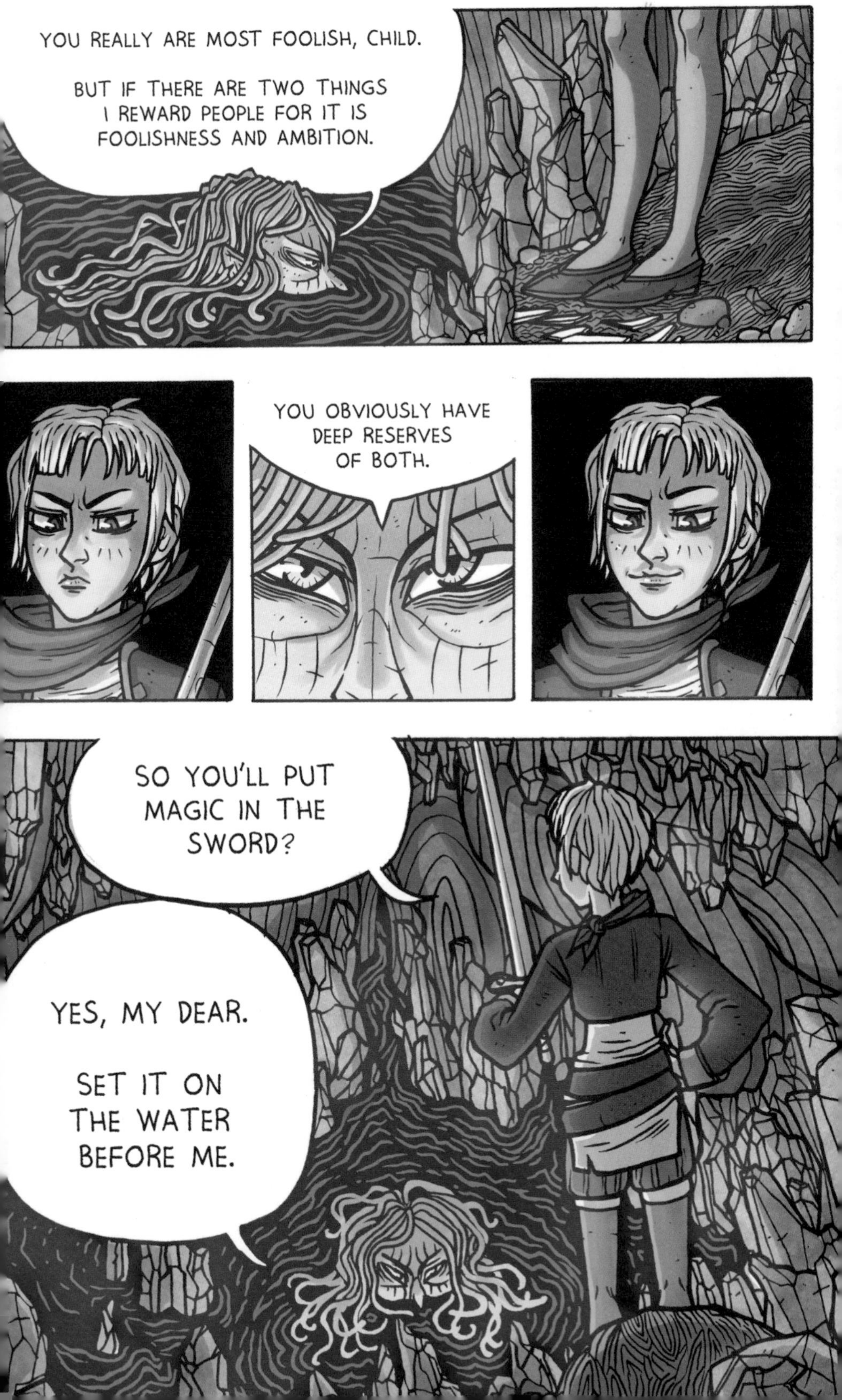
YOU REALLY ARE MOST FOOLISH, CHILD.
BUT IF THERE ARE TWO THINGS I REWARD PEOPLE FOR IT IS FOOLISHNESS AND AMBITION.
YOU OBVIOUSLY HAVE DEEP RESERVES OF BOTH.
SO YOU'LL PUT MAGIC IN THE SWORD?
YES, MY DEAR.
SET IT ON THE WATER BEFORE ME.

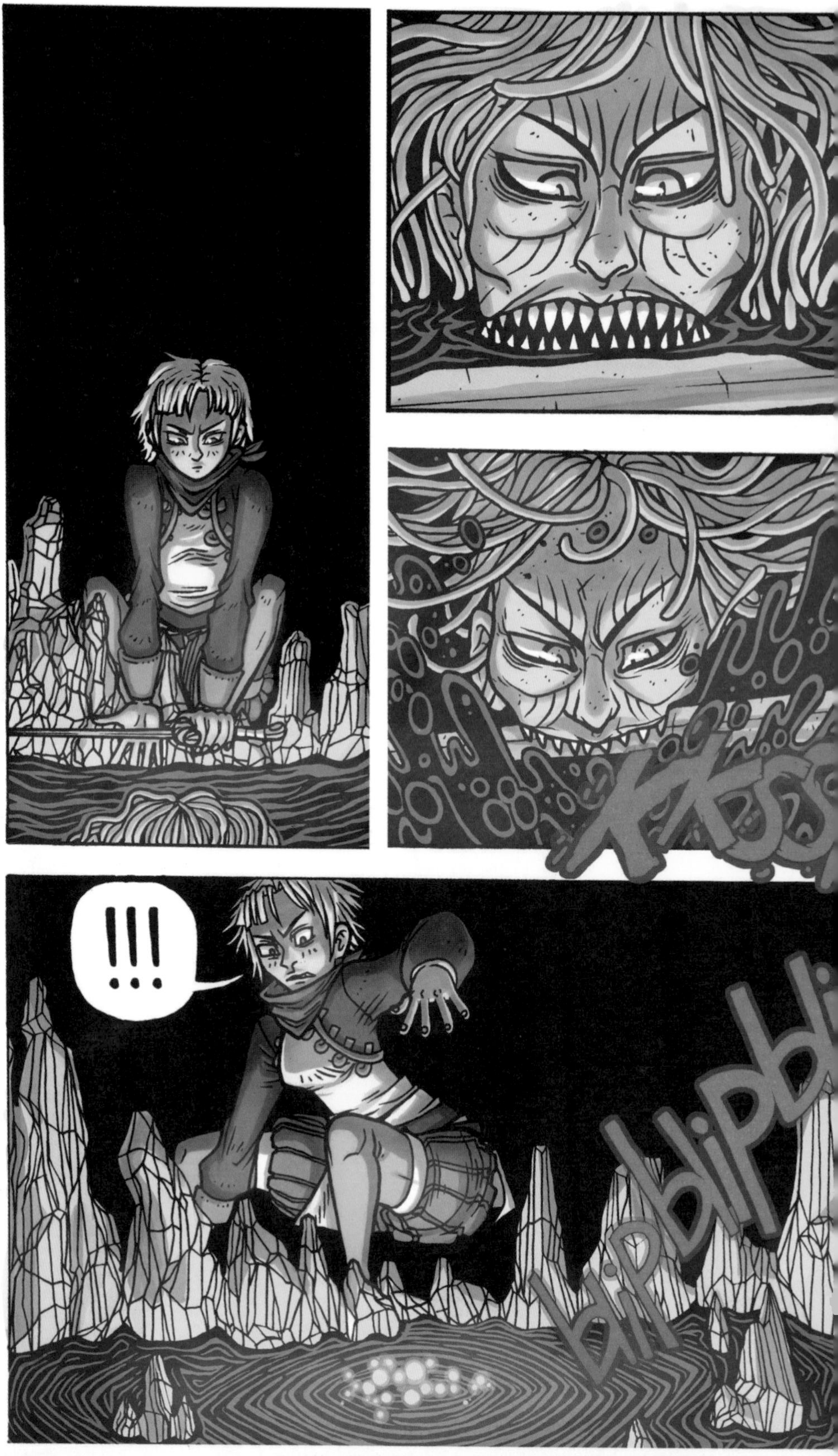
KKSS
!!!
bliPbliPbli

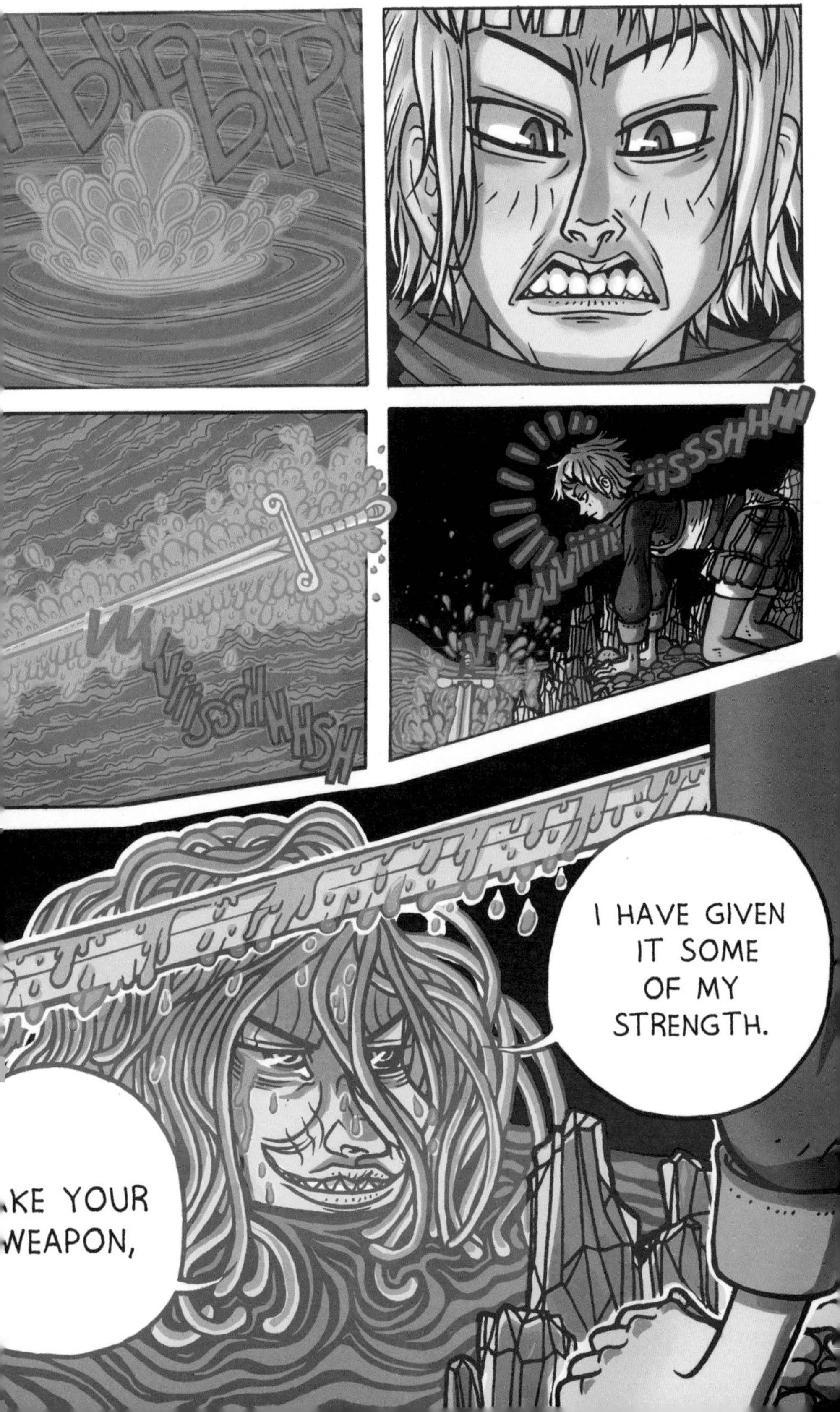
bliP bliP
WHiiSSHHHSH
VVVVVViiiiiiiSSSHHHH
I HAVE GIVEN IT SOME OF MY STRENGTH.
KE YOUR WEAPON,

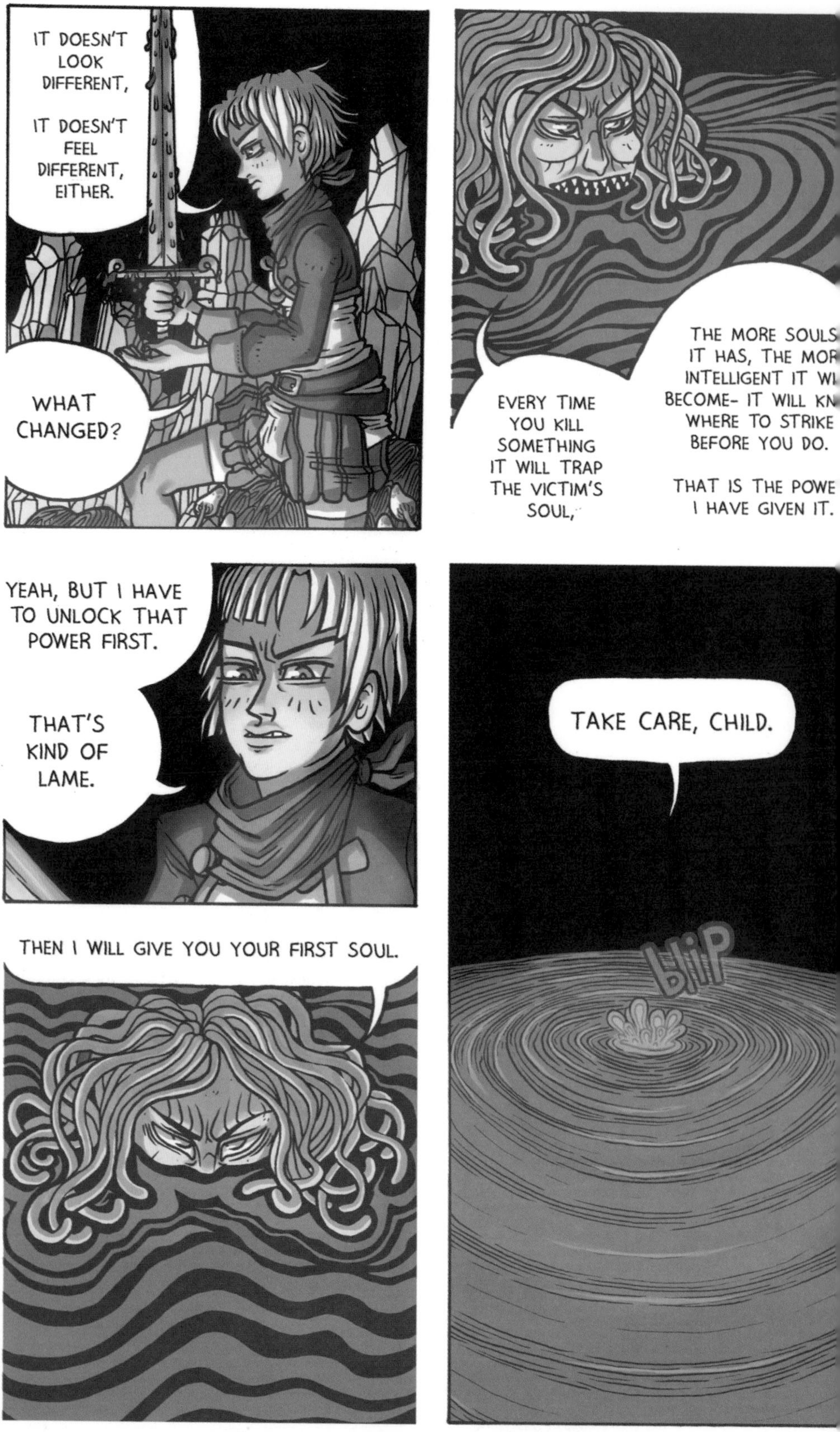
IT DOESN'T LOOK DIFFERENT,
IT DOESN'T FEEL DIFFERENT, EITHER.
WHAT CHANGED?
EVERY TIME YOU KILL SOMETHING IT WILL TRAP THE VICTIM'S SOUL,
THE MORE SOULS IT HAS, THE MOR INTELLIGENT IT WI BECOME- IT WILL KN WHERE TO STRIKE BEFORE YOU DO.
THAT IS THE POWE I HAVE GIVEN IT.
YEAH, BUT I HAVE TO UNLOCK THAT POWER FIRST.
THAT'S KIND OF LAME.
THEN I WILL GIVE YOU YOUR FIRST SOUL.
TAKE CARE, CHILD.
bliP

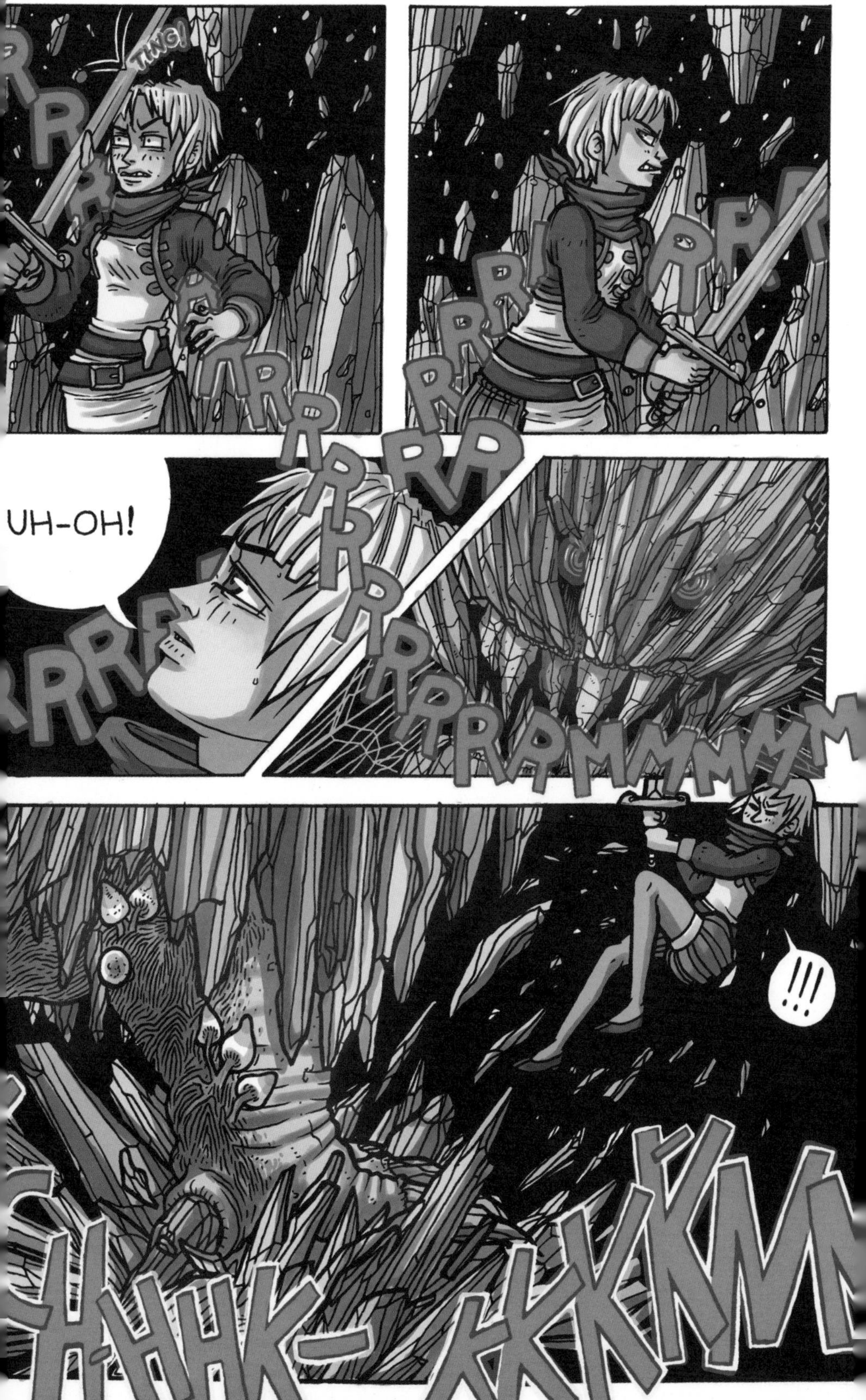
TING!
UH-OH!
!!!

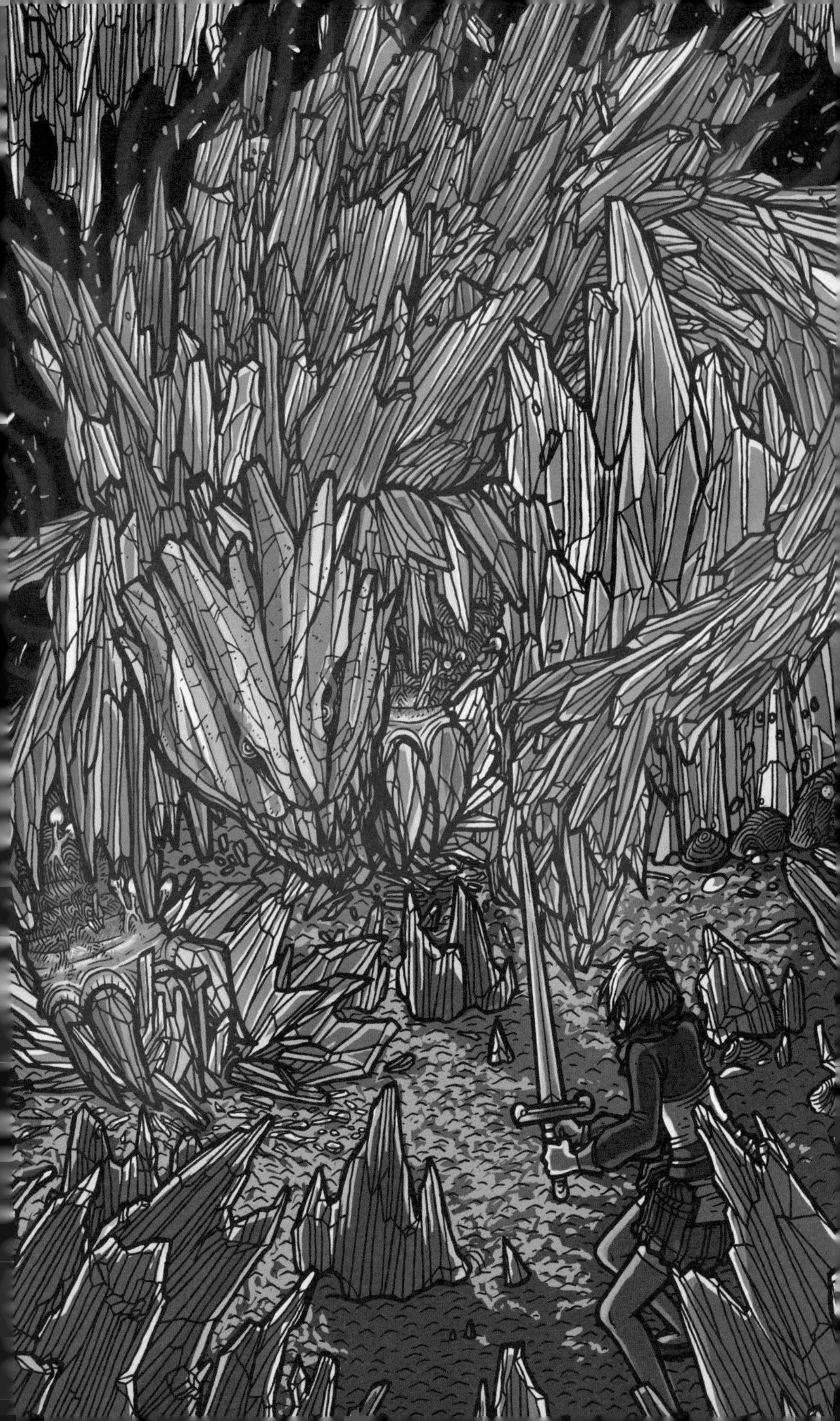

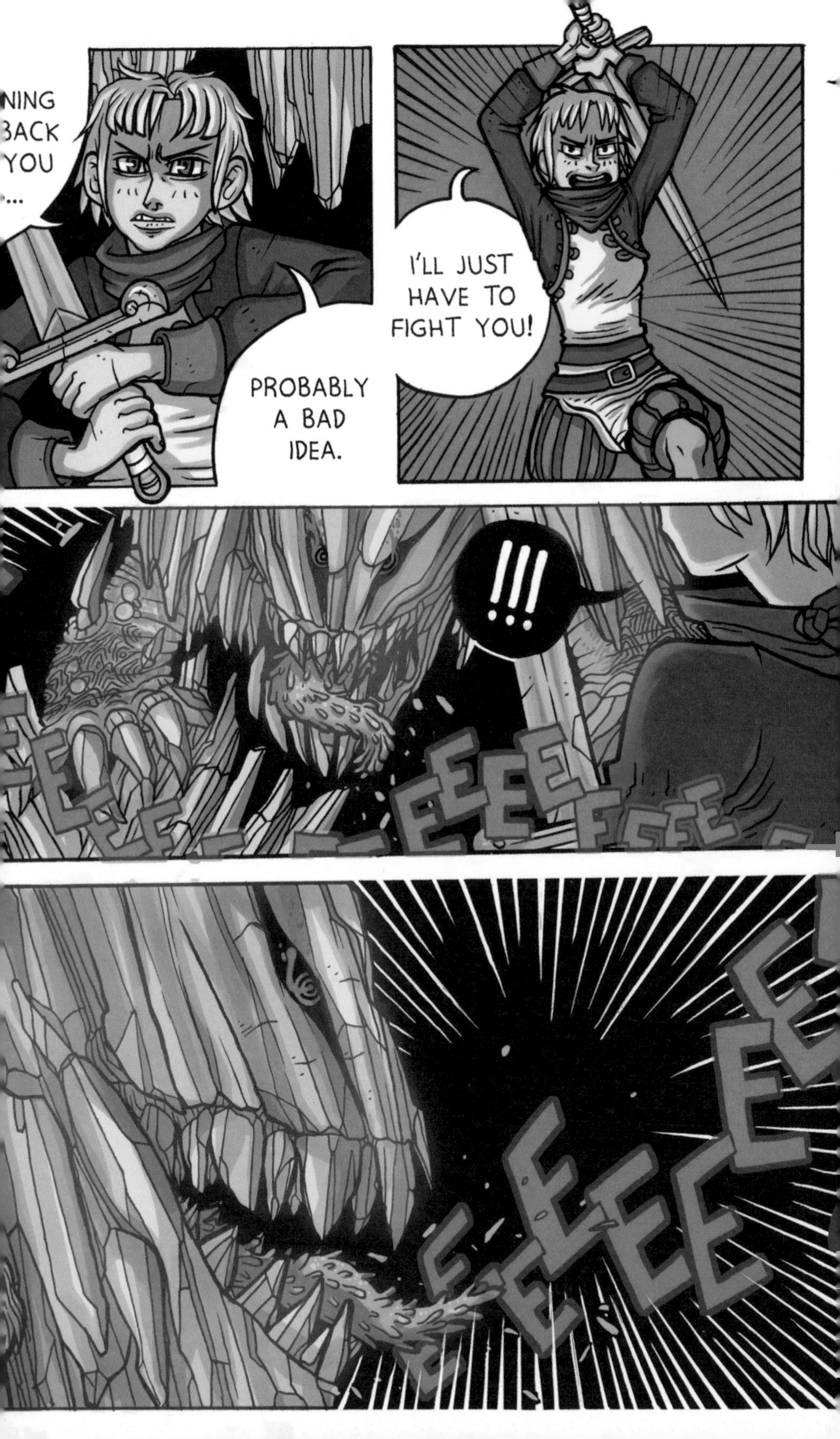

NING
BACK
YOU
...
PROBABLY
A BAD
IDEA.
I'LL JUST
HAVE TO
FIGHT YOU!
!!!
EEEEEEEEEEEEEE
EEEEEEEEE

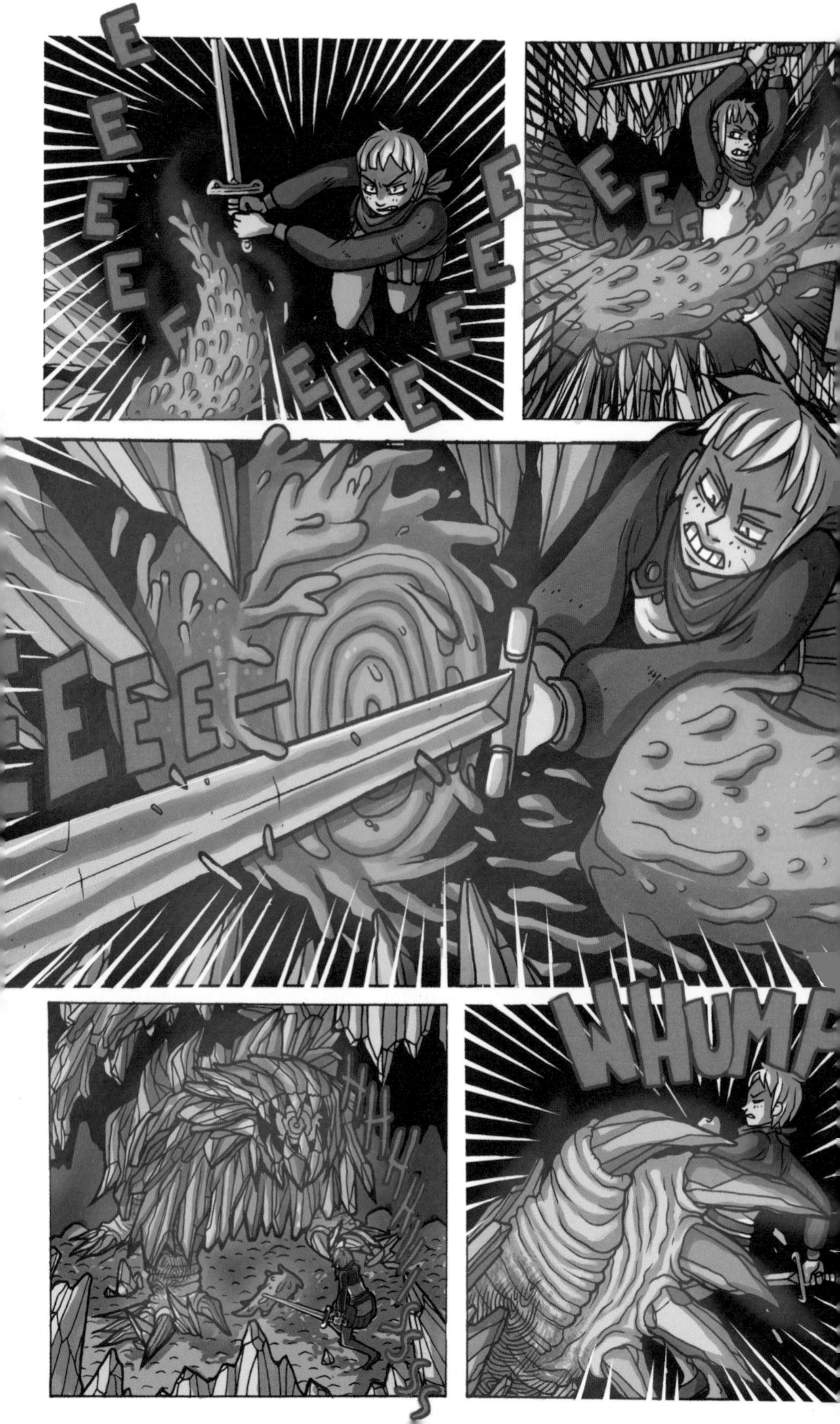
EEEEEEEEEEEE
EEEE
EEE–
WHUM

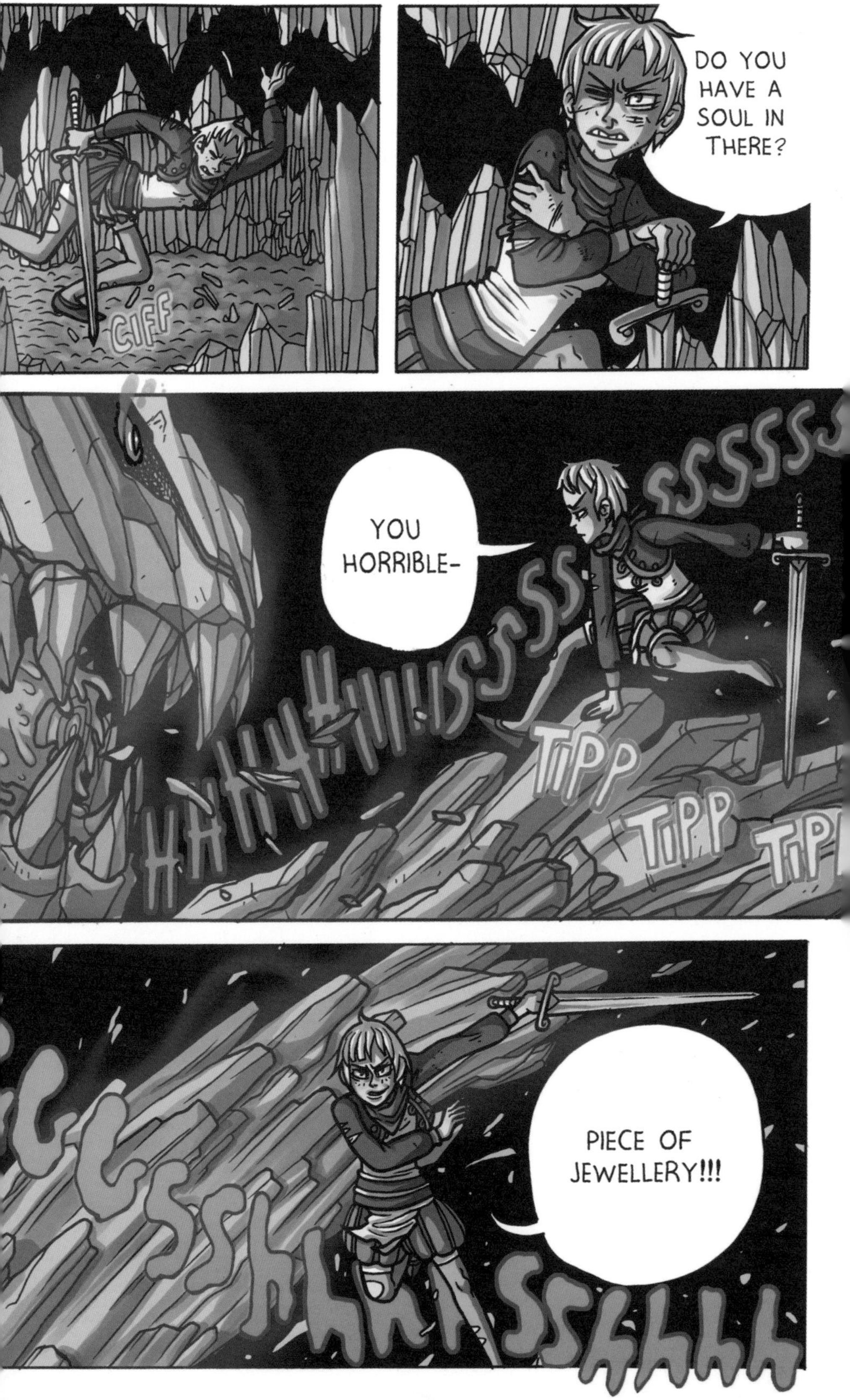
CIFF
DO YOU HAVE A SOUL IN THERE?
YOU HORRIBLE-
HHHHHHHISSSSSSSSSSS
TIPP
TIPP
PIECE OF JEWELLERY!!!
SSHHHSSHHHH

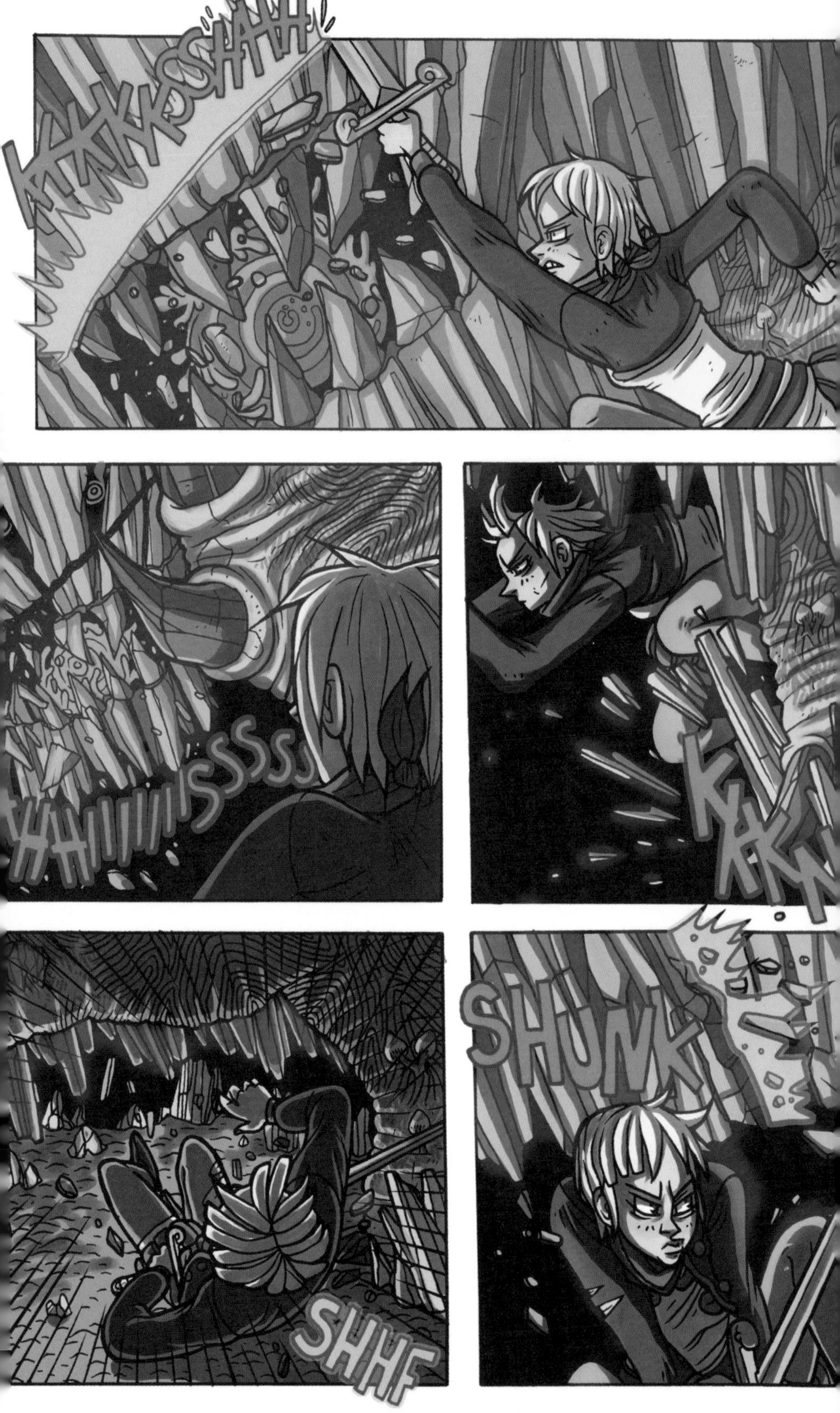
KKKKSHHH
HHHIIIIISSSSS
KKKK
SHHF
SHUNK

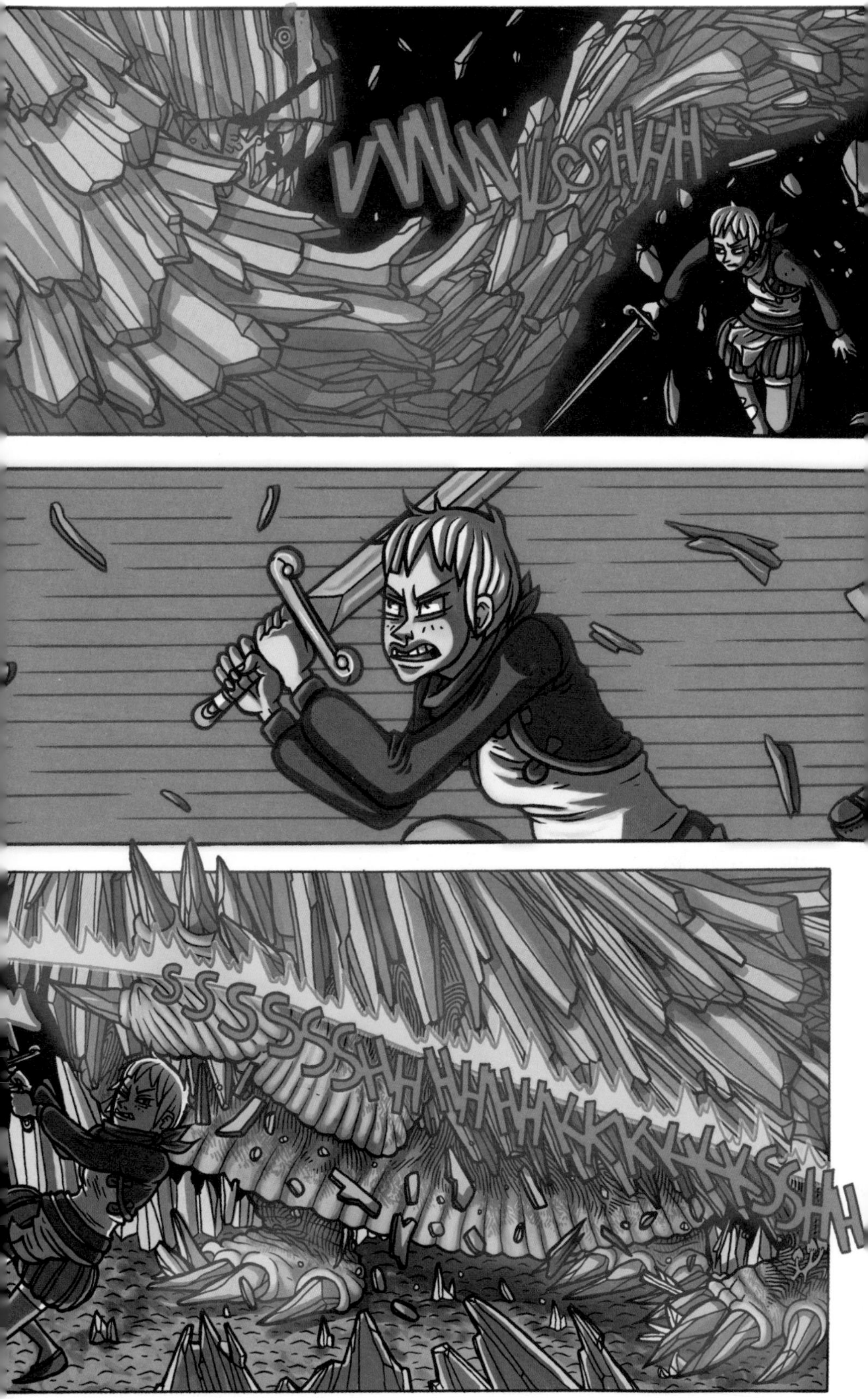
VVVVVSSHHH
SSSSSSHHHHKKKKKSHH

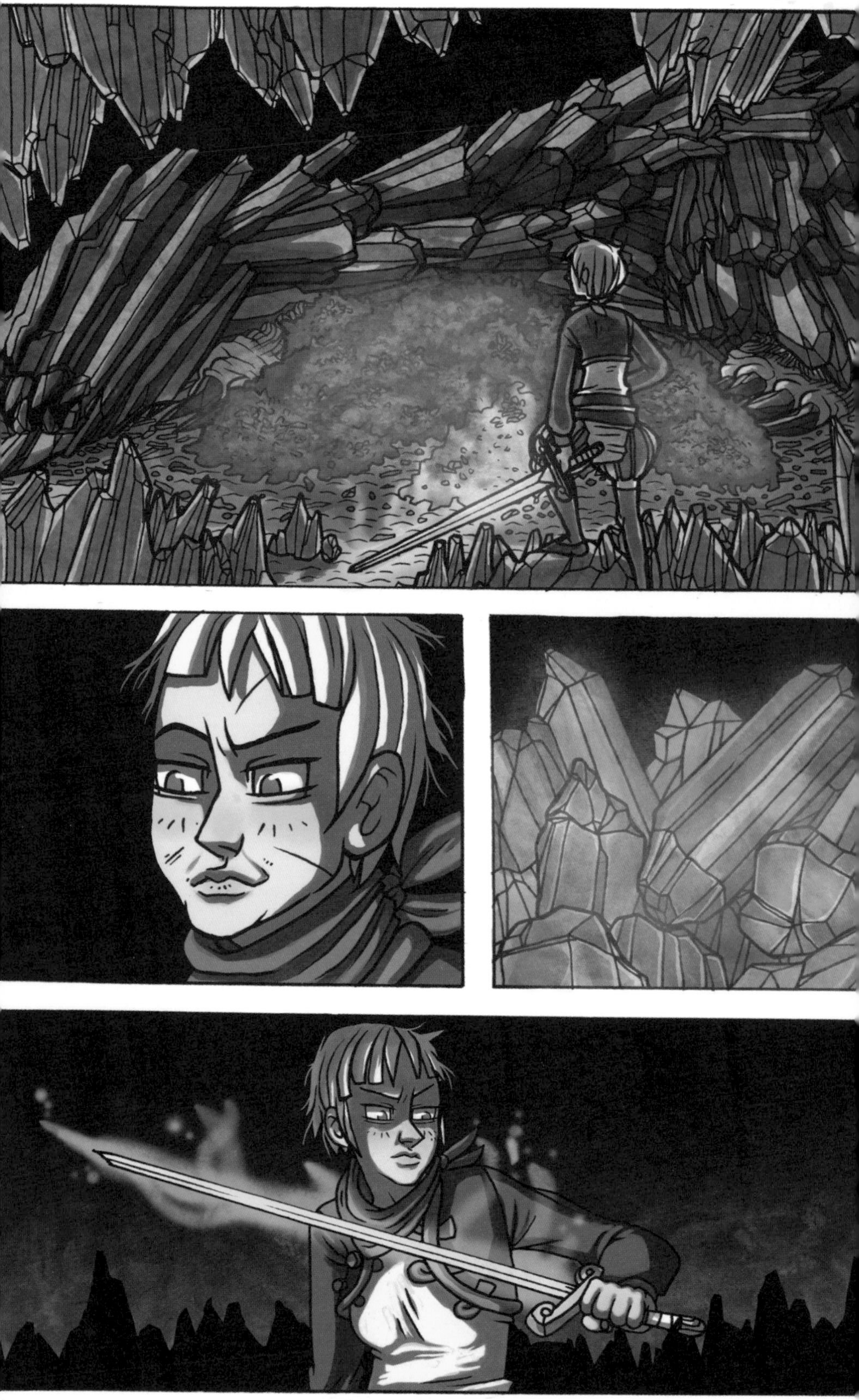

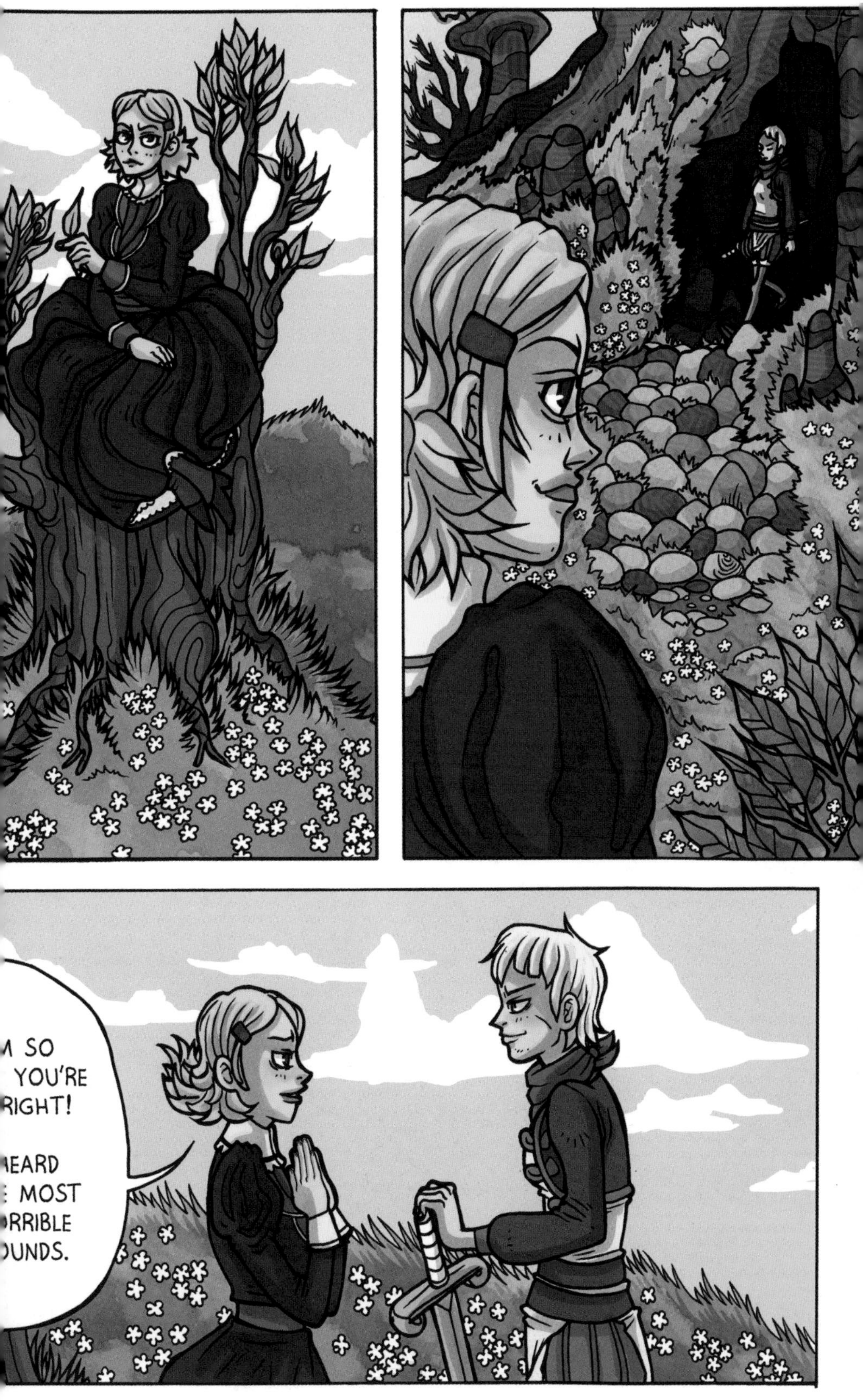
M SO YOU'RE RIGHT!
HEARD E MOST RRIBLE UNDS.

JUST DON'T TELL
ME I NEVER DO
ANYTHING
FOR YOU,

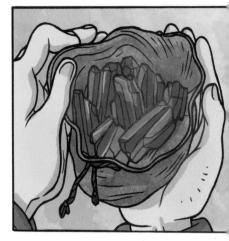

THE END

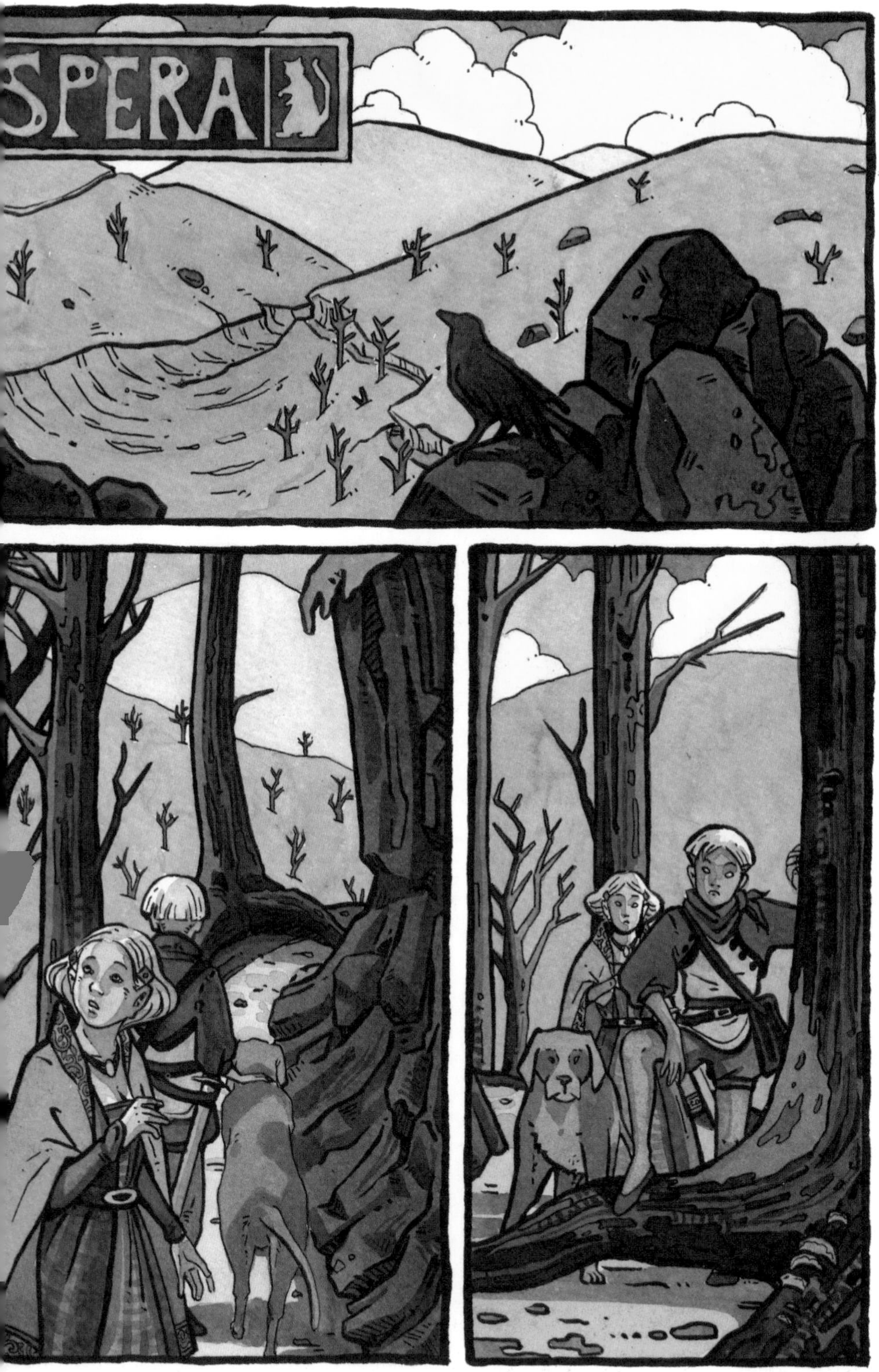
SPERA

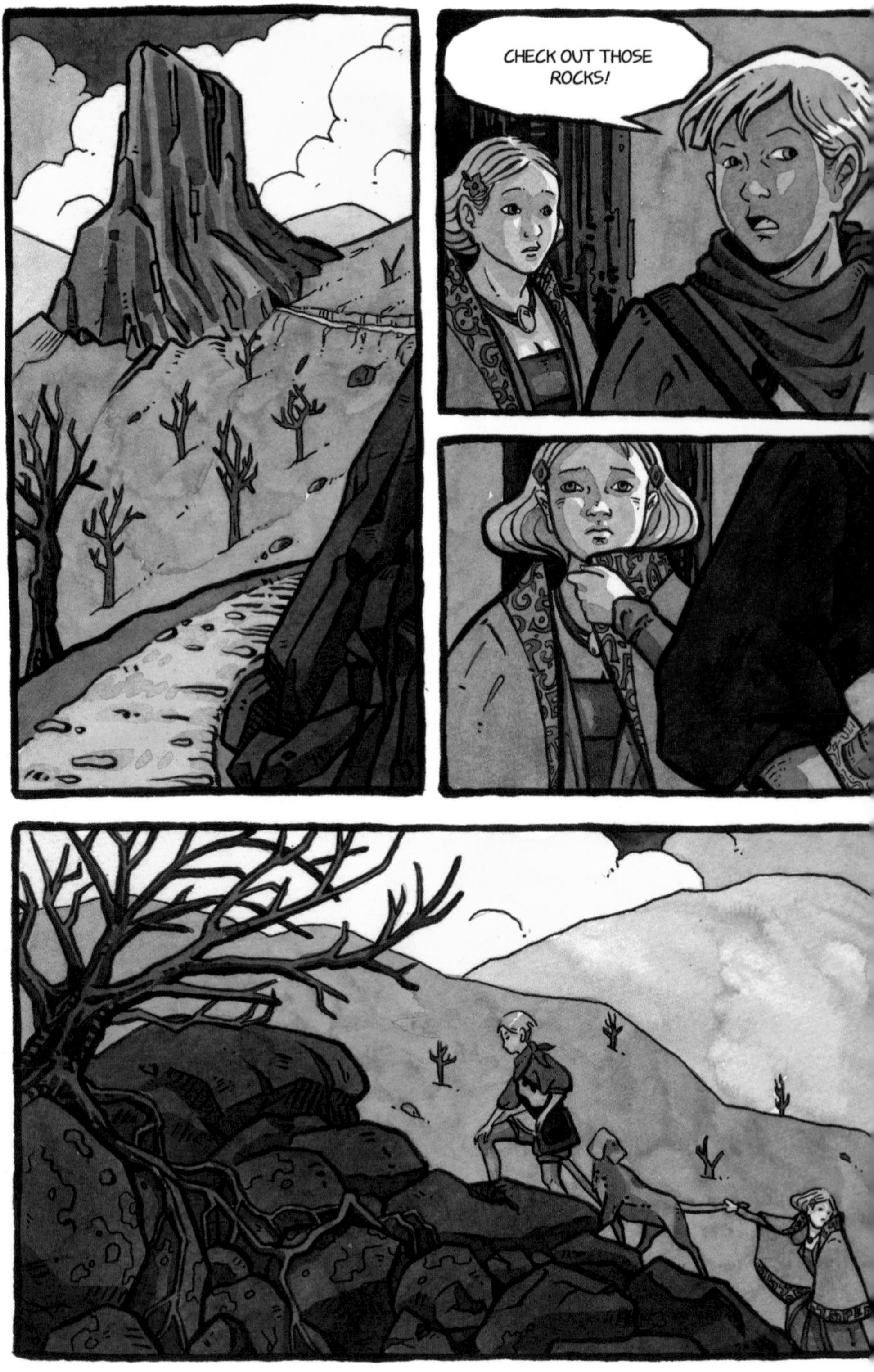
CHECK OUT THOSE ROCKS!

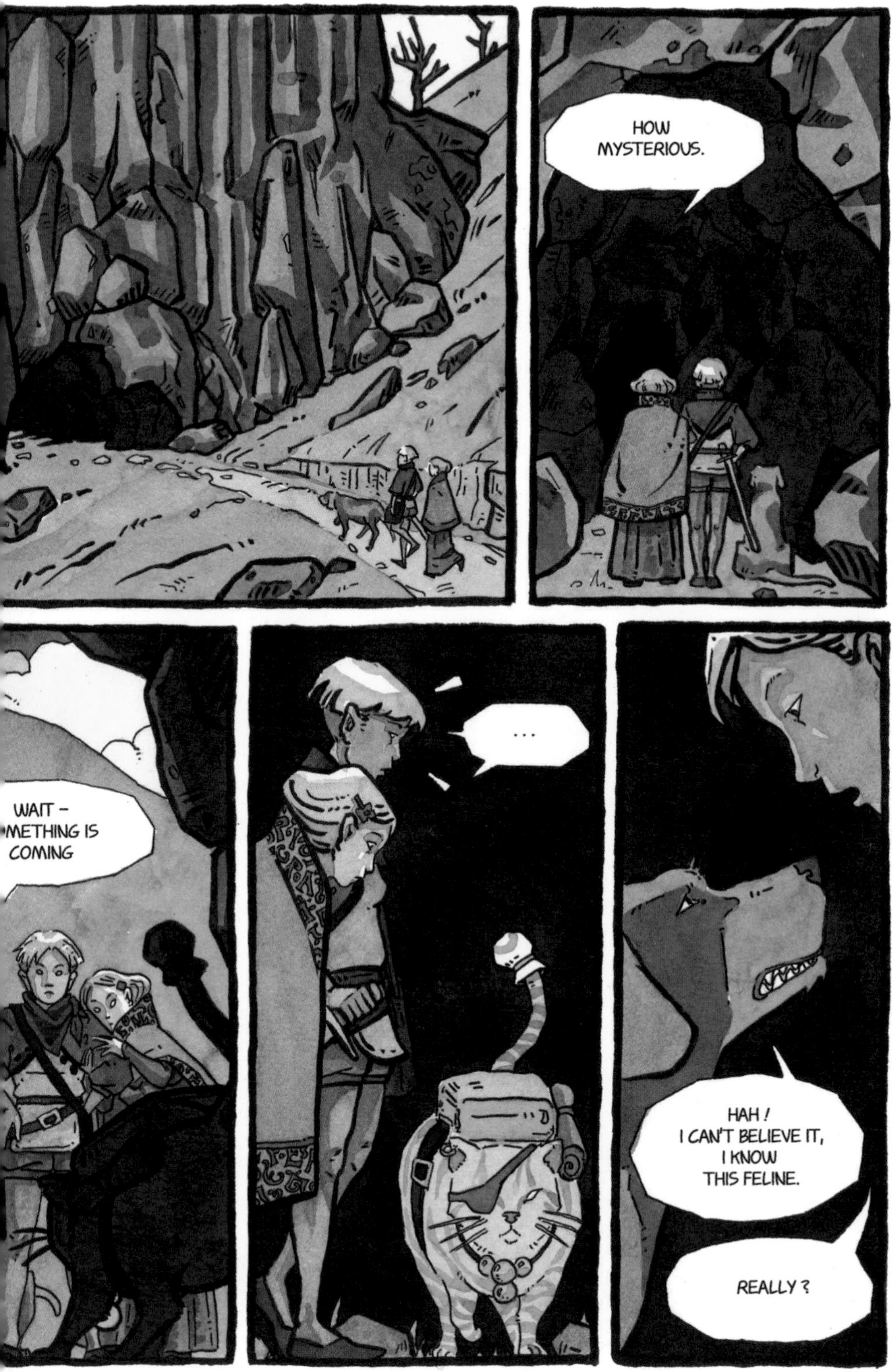
HOW MYSTERIOUS.
WAIT - METHING IS COMING
...
HAH ! I CAN'T BELIEVE IT, I KNOW THIS FELINE.
REALLY ?

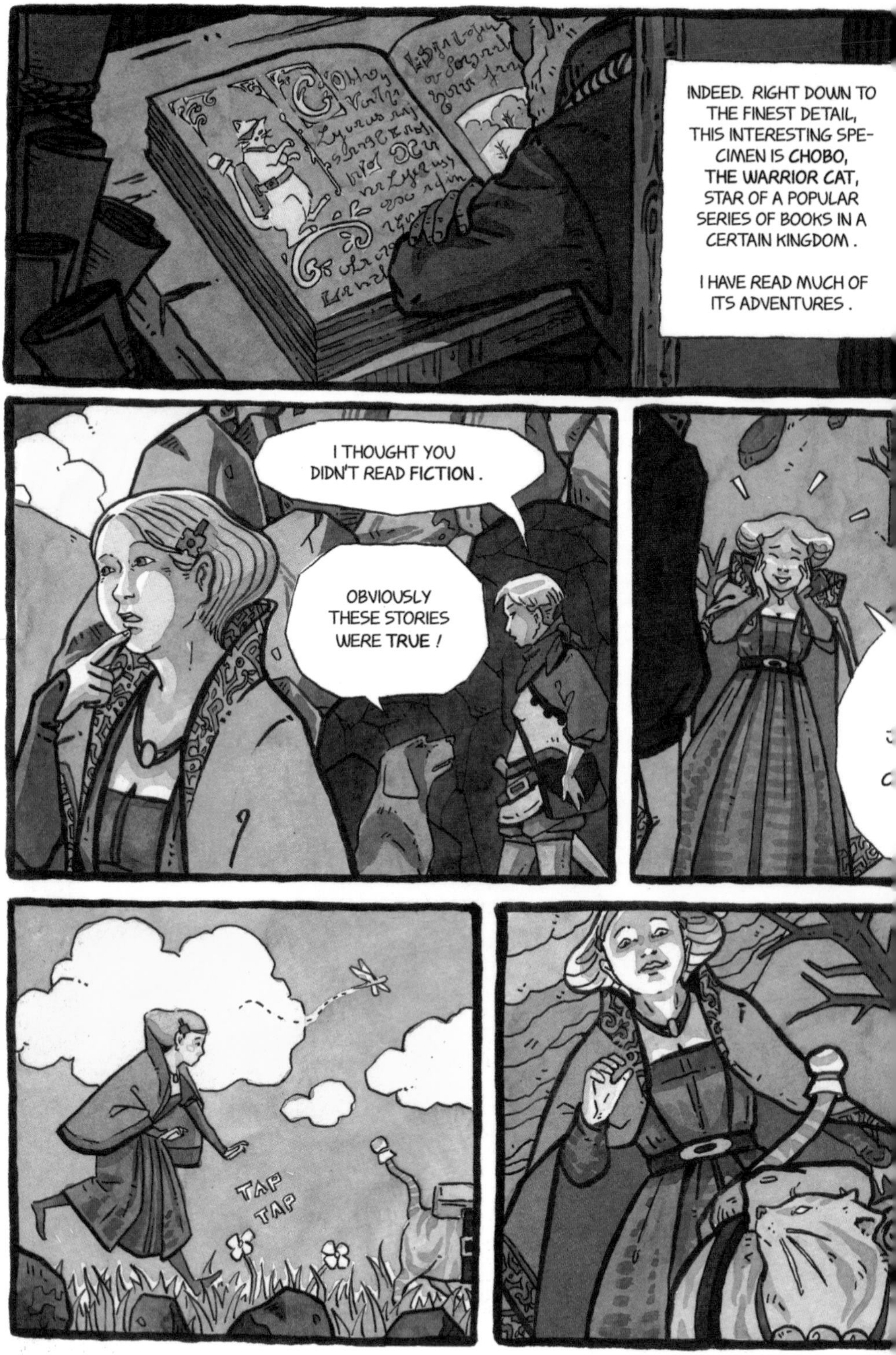
INDEED. RIGHT DOWN TO THE FINEST DETAIL, THIS INTERESTING SPECIMEN IS CHOBO, THE WARRIOR CAT, STAR OF A POPULAR SERIES OF BOOKS IN A CERTAIN KINGDOM.
I HAVE READ MUCH OF ITS ADVENTURES.
I THOUGHT YOU DIDN'T READ FICTION.
OBVIOUSLY THESE STORIES WERE TRUE!
TAP TAP

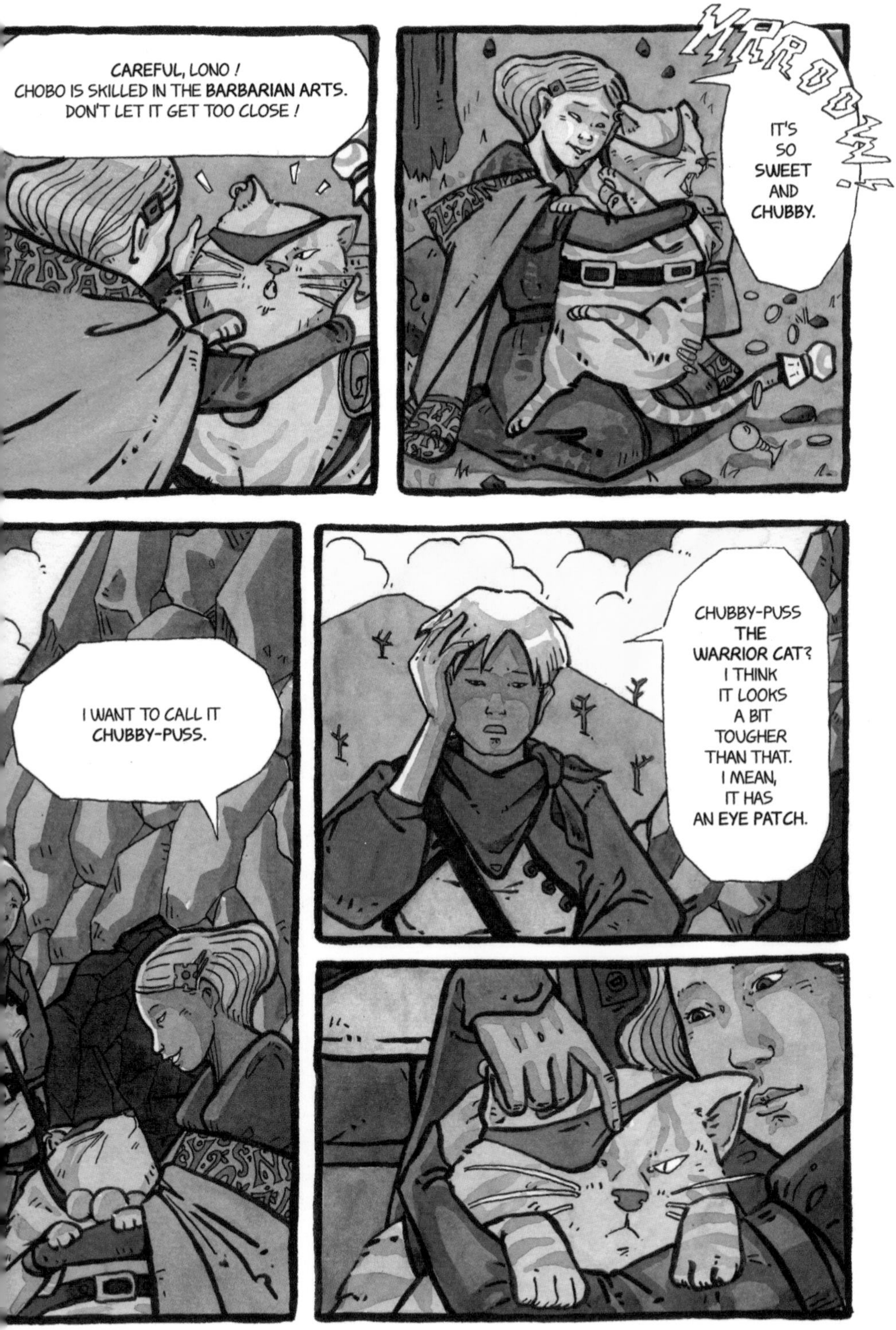
CAREFUL, LONO ! CHOBO IS SKILLED IN THE BARBARIAN ARTS. DON'T LET IT GET TOO CLOSE !
MRROOWL
IT'S SO SWEET AND CHUBBY.
I WANT TO CALL IT CHUBBY-PUSS.
CHUBBY-PUSS THE WARRIOR CAT? I THINK IT LOOKS A BIT TOUGHER THAN THAT. I MEAN, IT HAS AN EYE PATCH.

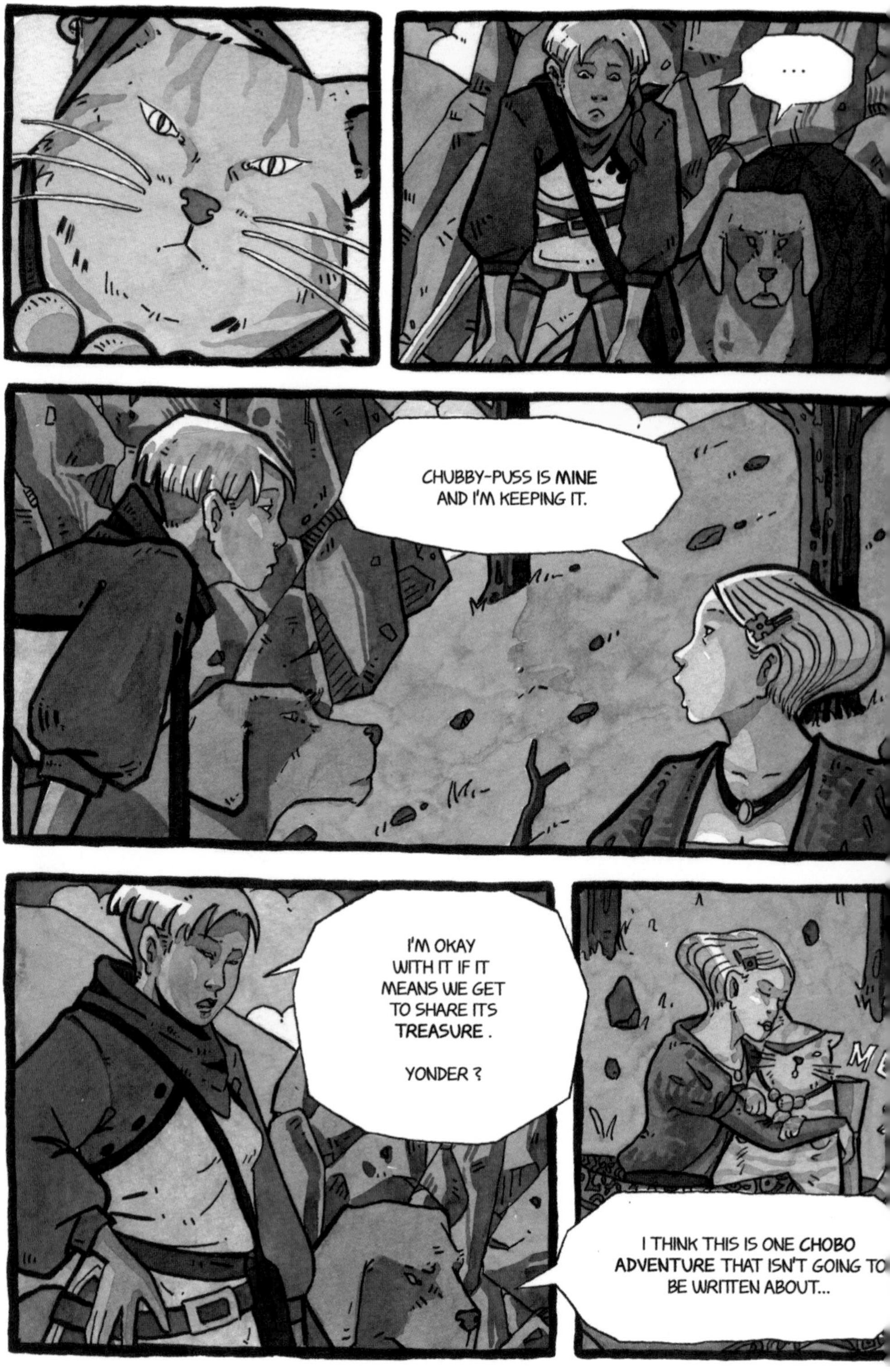
...
CHUBBY-PUSS IS MINE AND I'M KEEPING IT.
I'M OKAY WITH IT IF IT MEANS WE GET TO SHARE ITS TREASURE .
YONDER ?
I THINK THIS IS ONE CHOBO ADVENTURE THAT ISN'T GOING TO BE WRITTEN ABOUT...

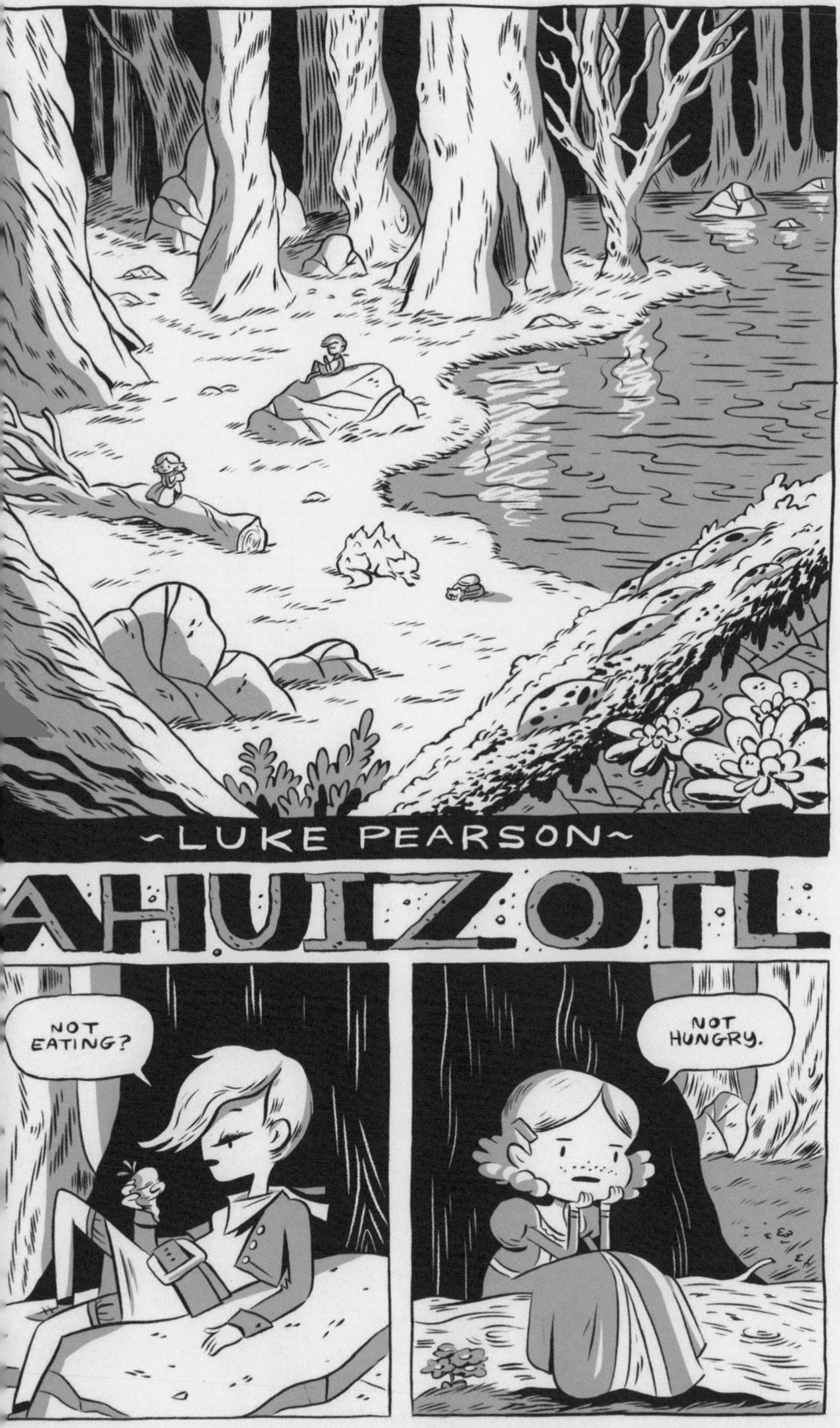
~LUKE PEARSON~
AHUIZOTL
NOT EATING?
NOT HUNGRY.

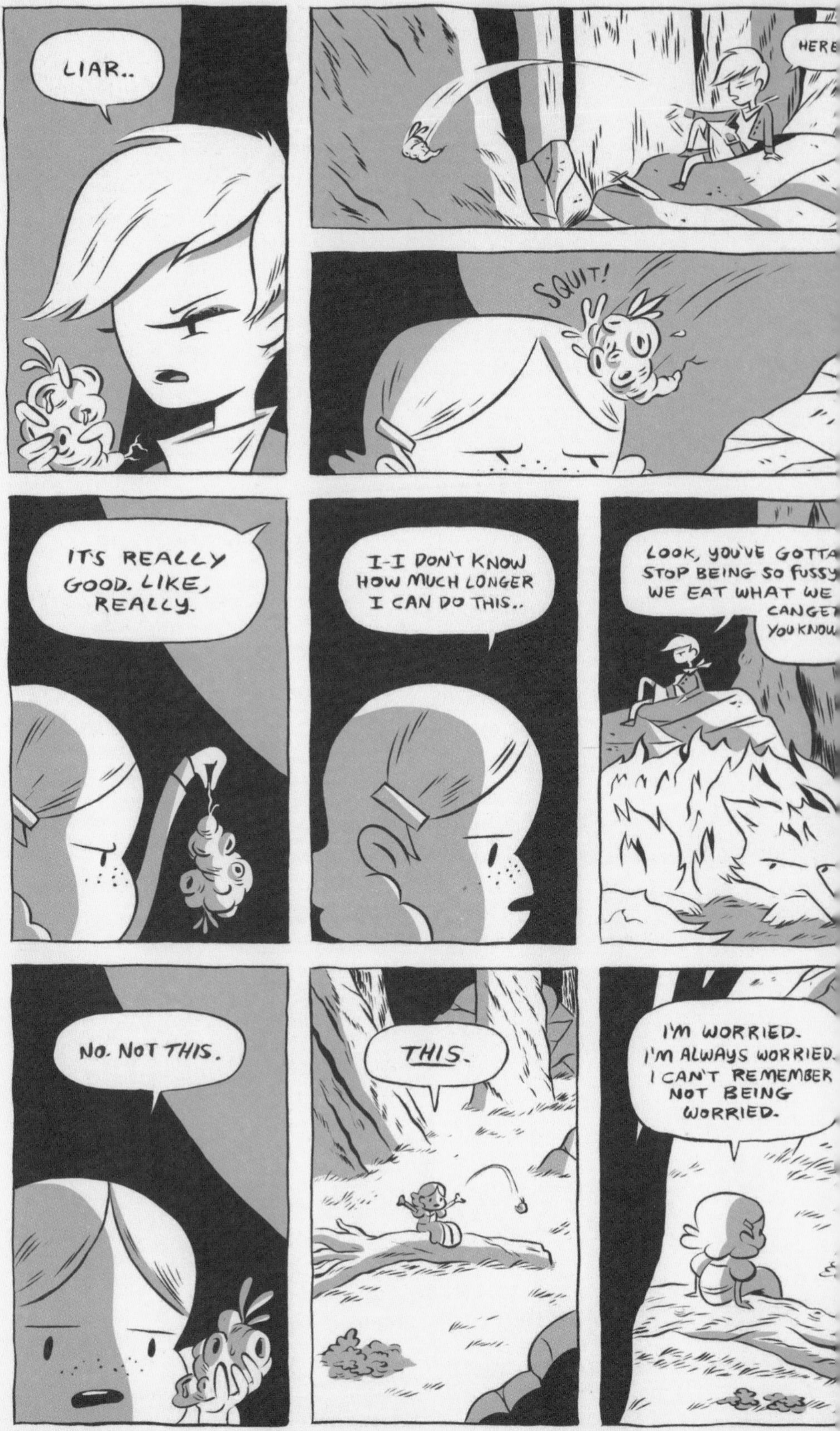
LIAR..
HERE
SQUIT!
IT'S REALLY GOOD. LIKE, REALLY.
I-I DON'T KNOW HOW MUCH LONGER I CAN DO THIS..
LOOK, YOU'VE GOTTA STOP BEING SO FUSSY. WE EAT WHAT WE CAN GET, YOU KNOW.
NO. NOT THIS.
THIS.
I'M WORRIED. I'M ALWAYS WORRIED. I CAN'T REMEMBER NOT BEING WORRIED.

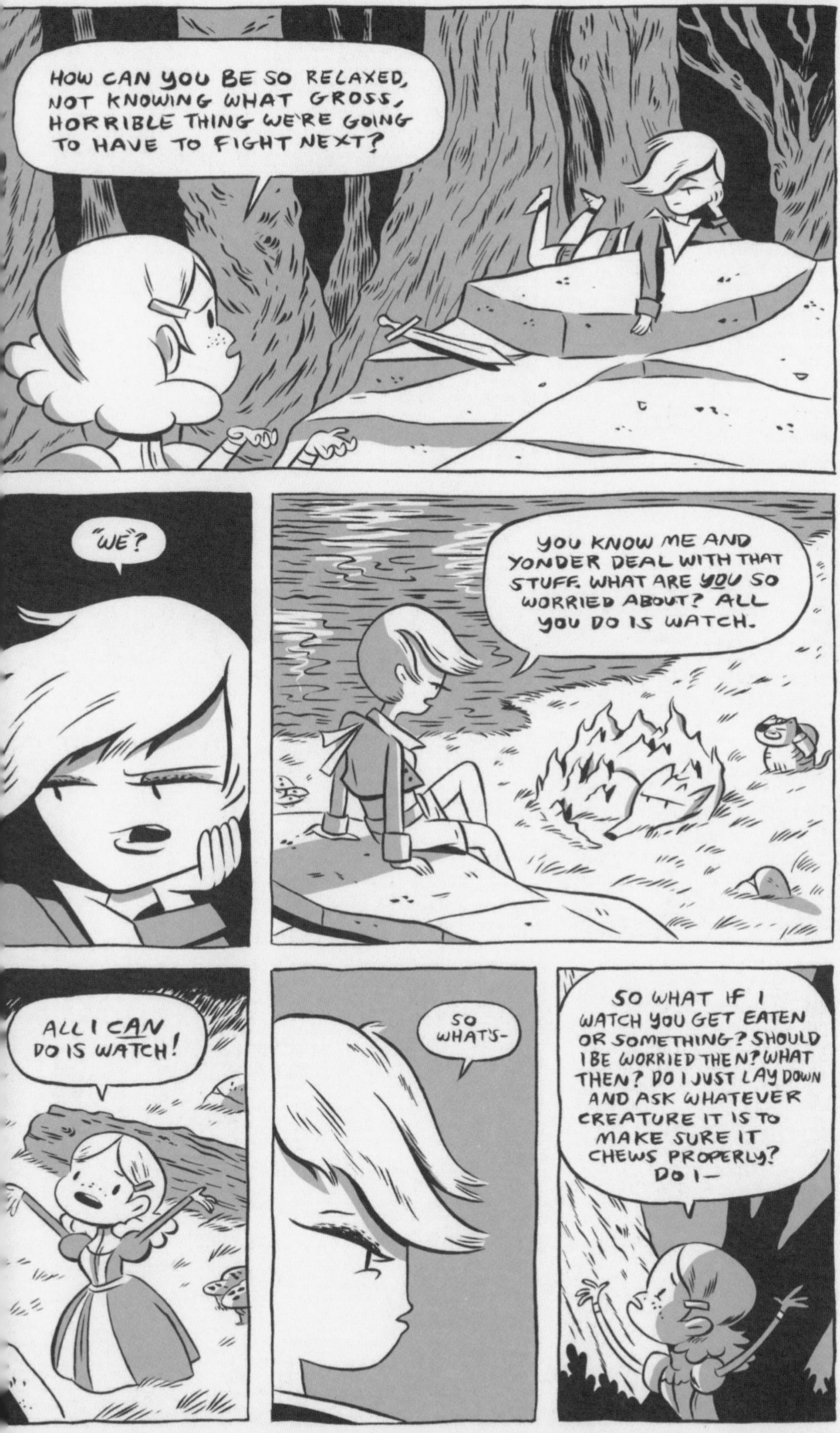
HOW CAN YOU BE SO RELAXED, NOT KNOWING WHAT GROSS, HORRIBLE THING WE'RE GOING TO HAVE TO FIGHT NEXT?
"WE"?
YOU KNOW ME AND YONDER DEAL WITH THAT STUFF. WHAT ARE YOU SO WORRIED ABOUT? ALL YOU DO IS WATCH.
ALL I CAN DO IS WATCH!
SO WHAT'S-
SO WHAT IF I WATCH YOU GET EATEN OR SOMETHING? SHOULD I BE WORRIED THEN? WHAT THEN? DO I JUST LAY DOWN AND ASK WHATEVER CREATURE IT IS TO MAKE SURE IT CHEWS PROPERLY? DO I—

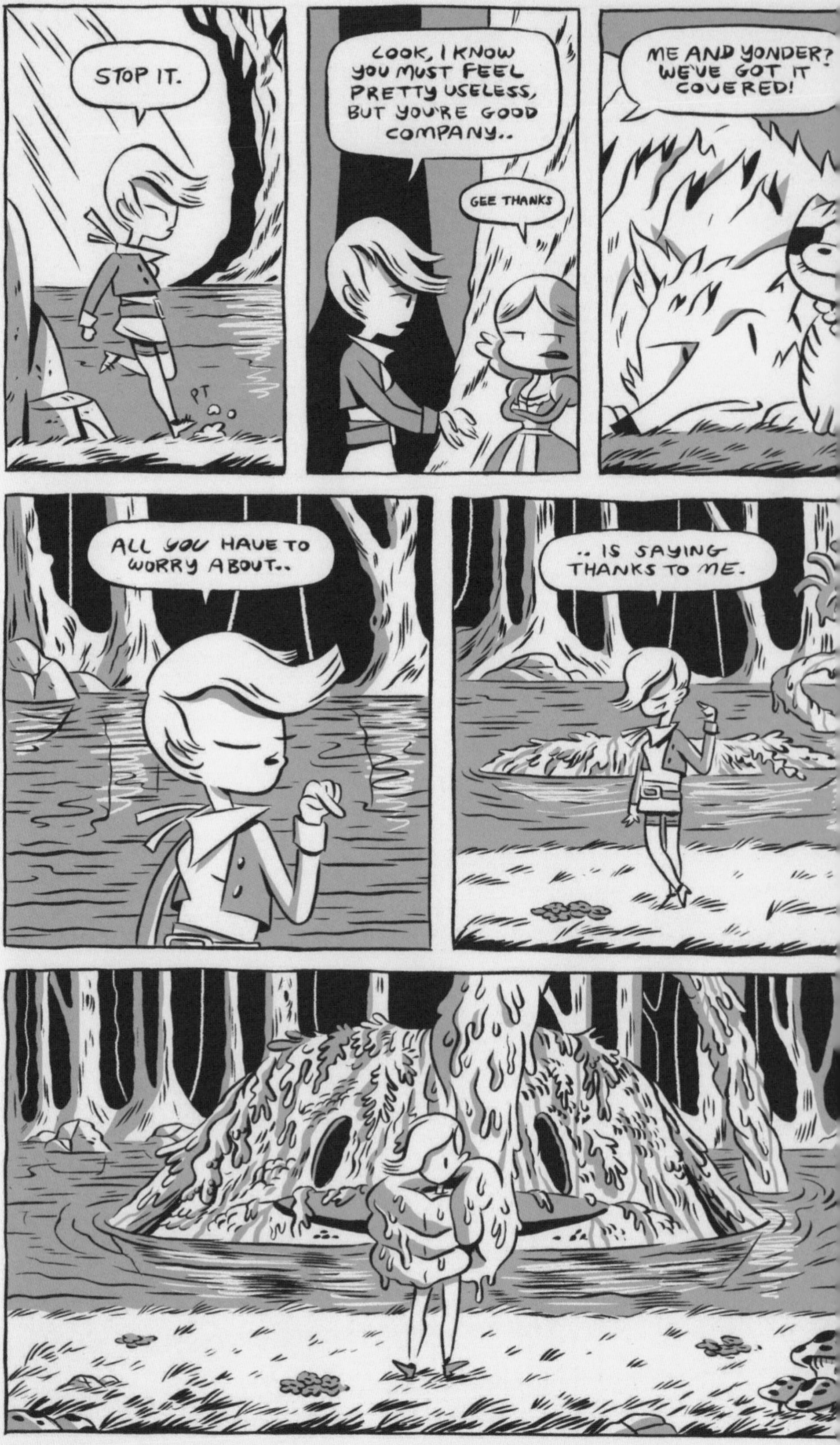
STOP IT.
LOOK, I KNOW YOU MUST FEEL PRETTY USELESS, BUT YOU'RE GOOD COMPANY..
GEE THANKS
ME AND YONDER? WE'VE GOT IT COVERED!
ALL YOU HAVE TO WORRY ABOUT..
.. IS SAYING THANKS TO ME.

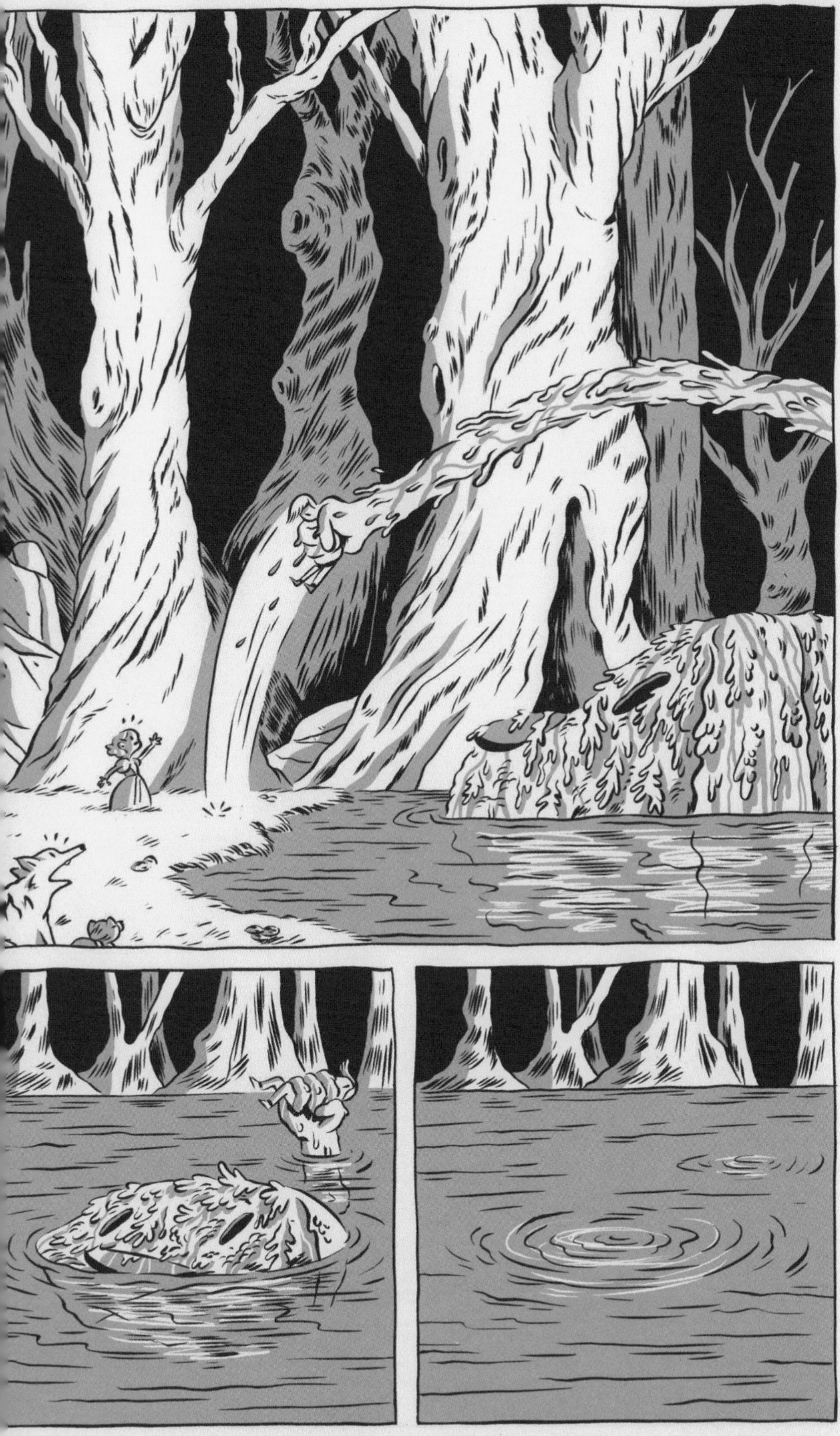

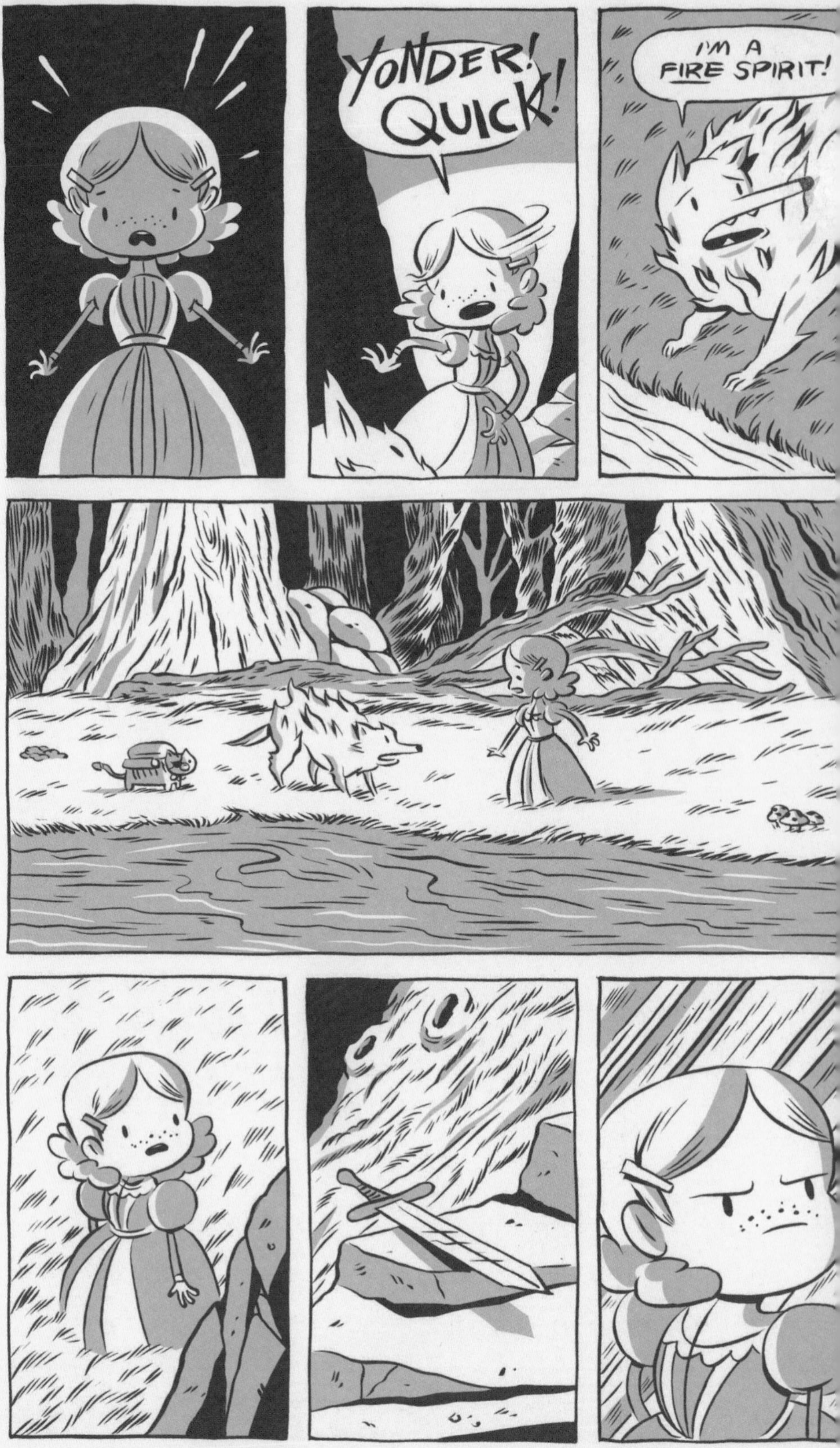
YONDER! QUICK!
I'M A FIRE SPIRIT!

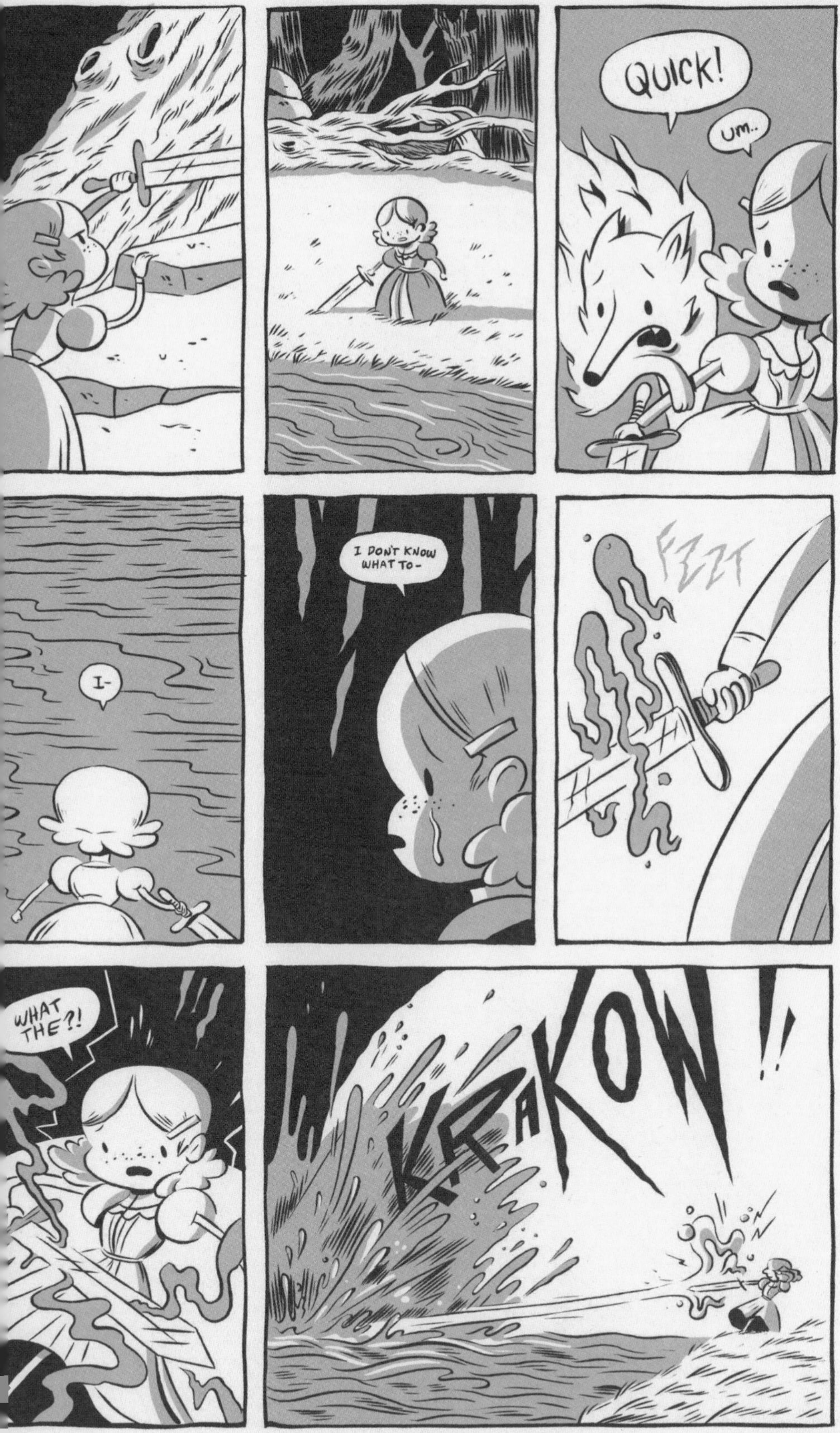
QUICK!
UM..
I-
I DON'T KNOW WHAT TO-
FZZT
WHAT THE?!
KRAKOW!!

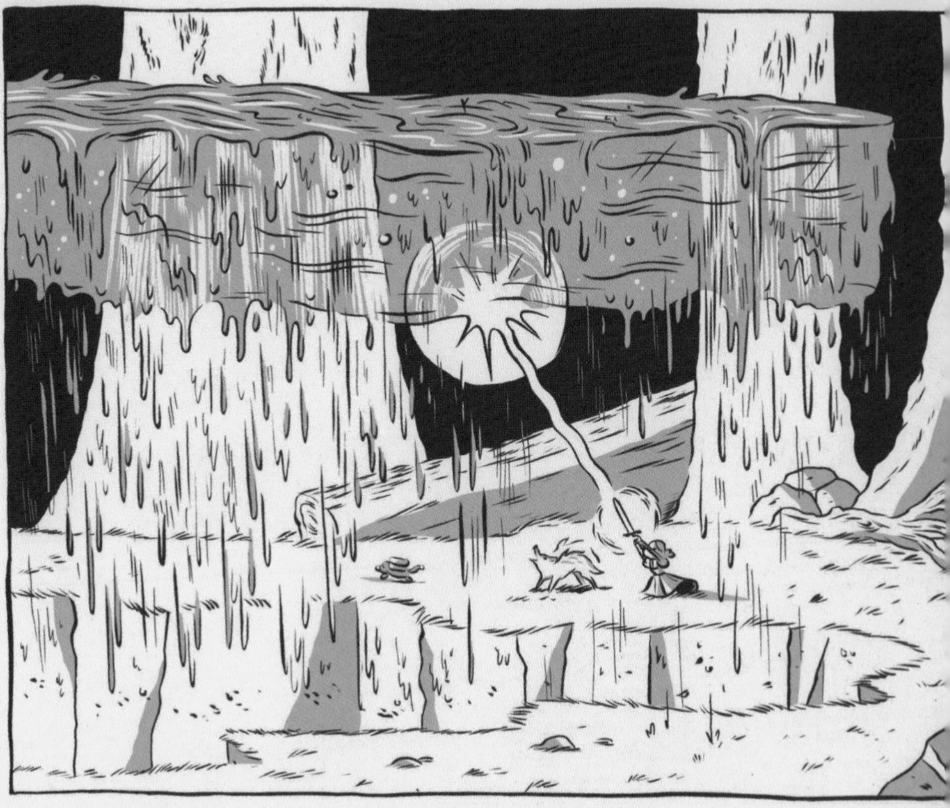

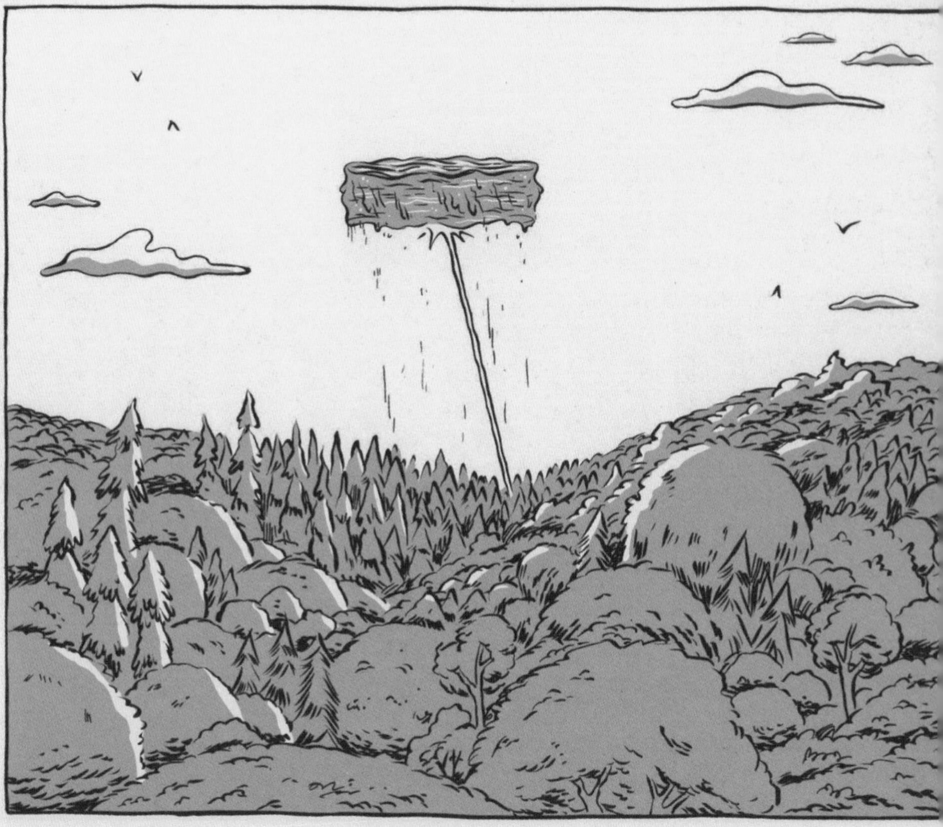

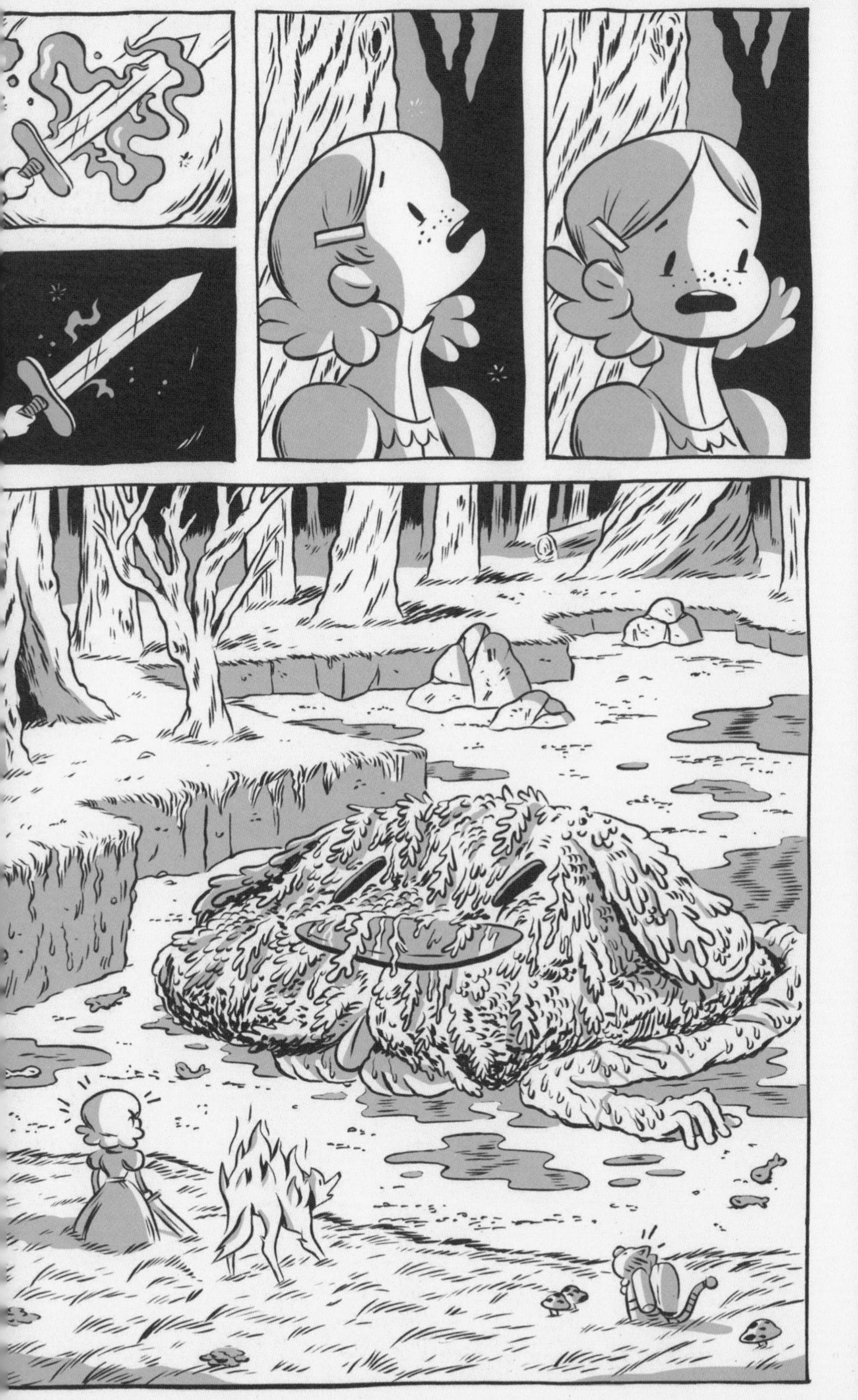

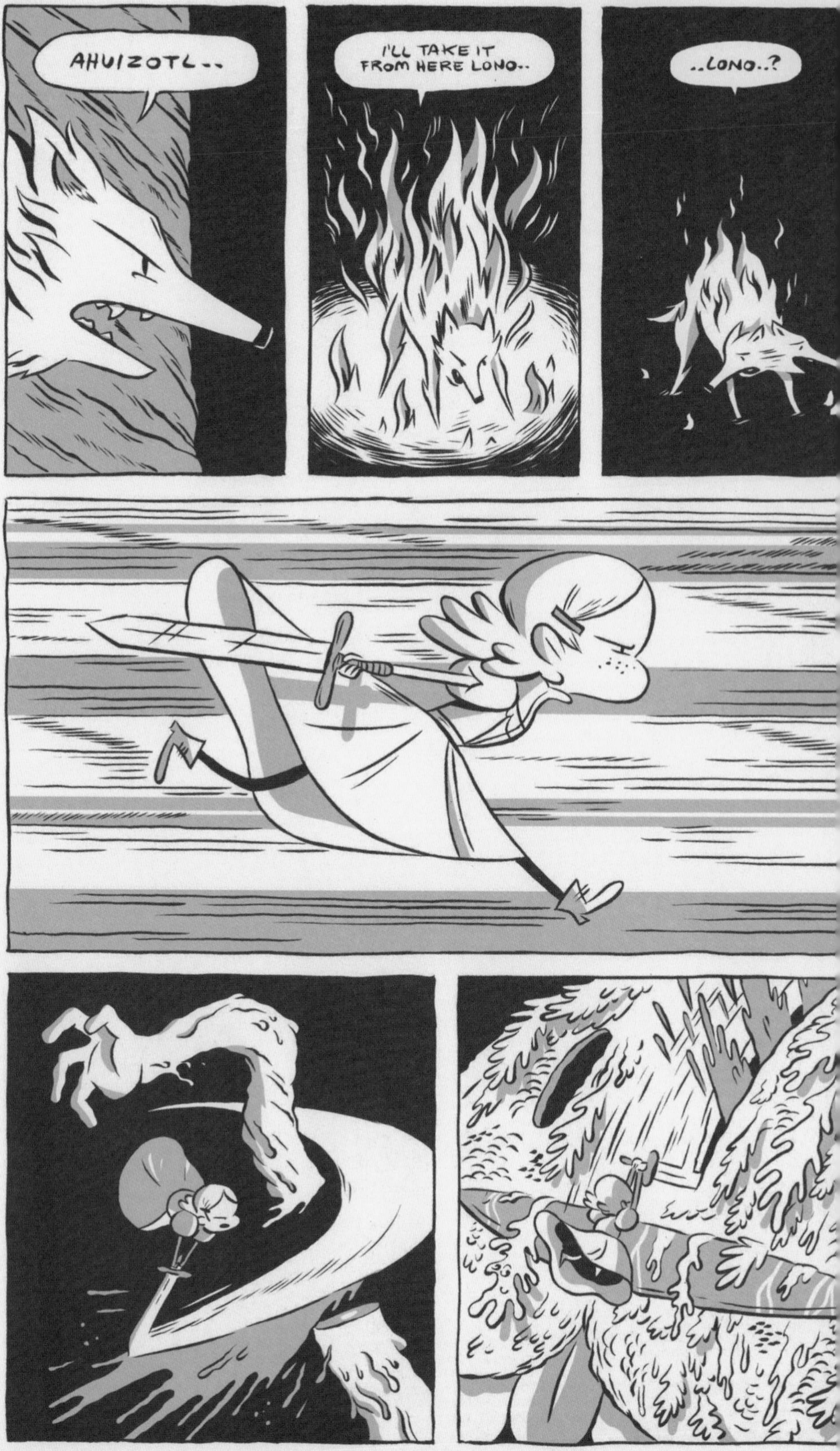
AHUIZOTL..
I'LL TAKE IT FROM HERE LONO..
..LONO..?

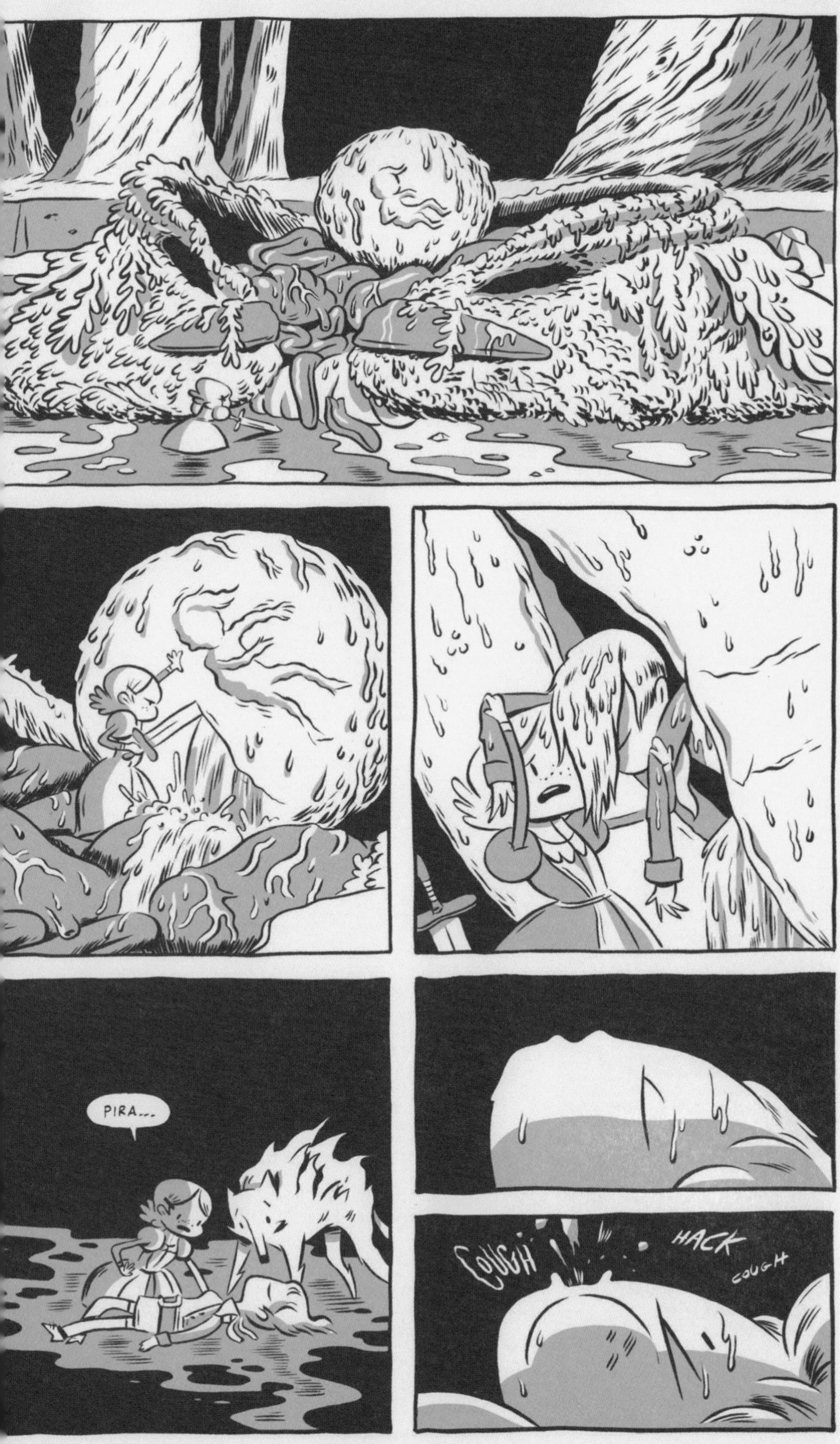
PIRA...
COUGH
HACK
COUGH

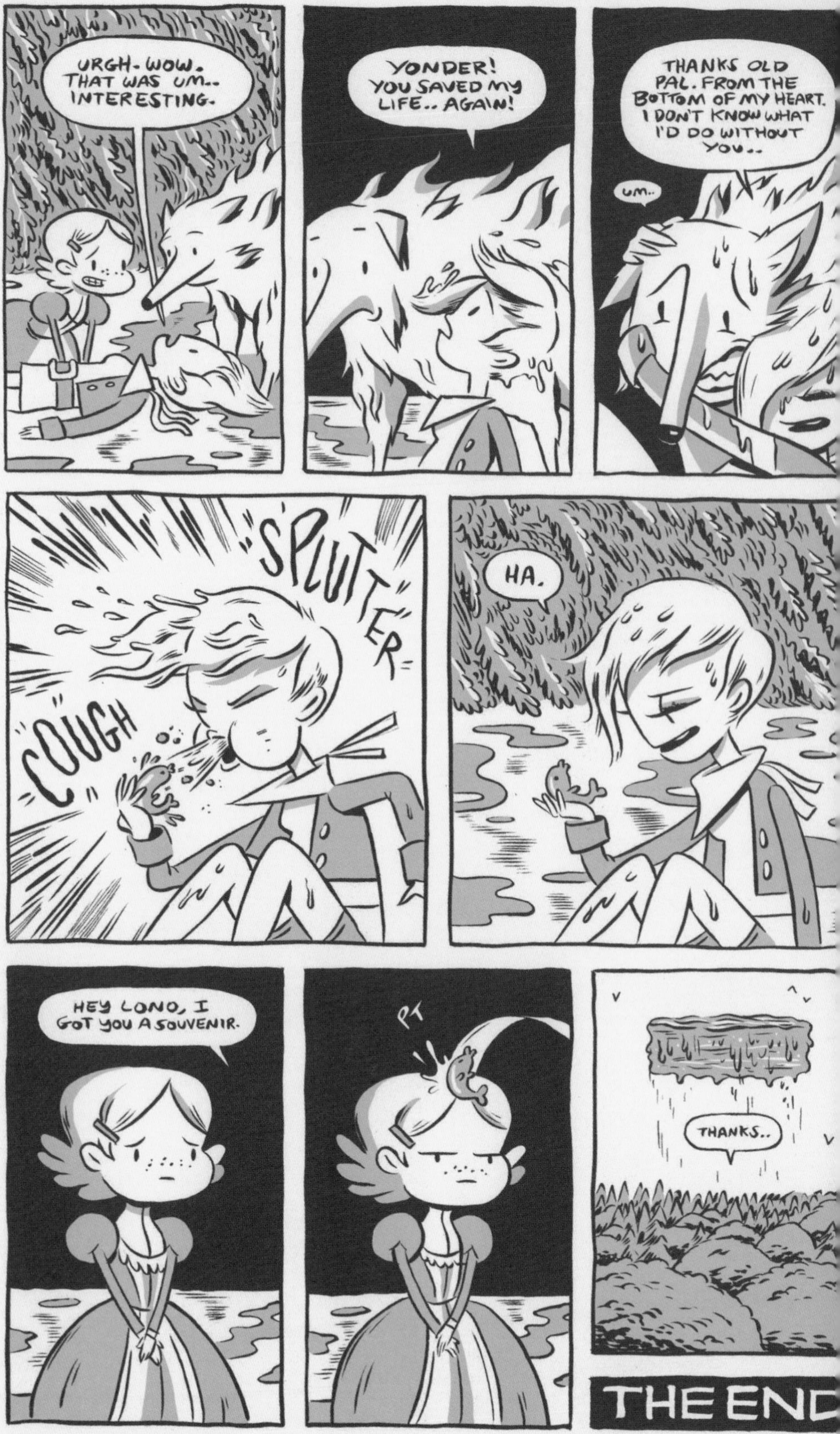
URGH- WOW. THAT WAS UM.. INTERESTING.
YONDER! YOU SAVED MY LIFE.. AGAIN!
THANKS OLD PAL. FROM THE BOTTOM OF MY HEART. I DON'T KNOW WHAT I'D DO WITHOUT YOU..
UM..
"SPLUTTER"
"COUGH"
HA.
HEY LONO, I GOT YOU A SOUVENIR.
PT
THANKS..
THE END

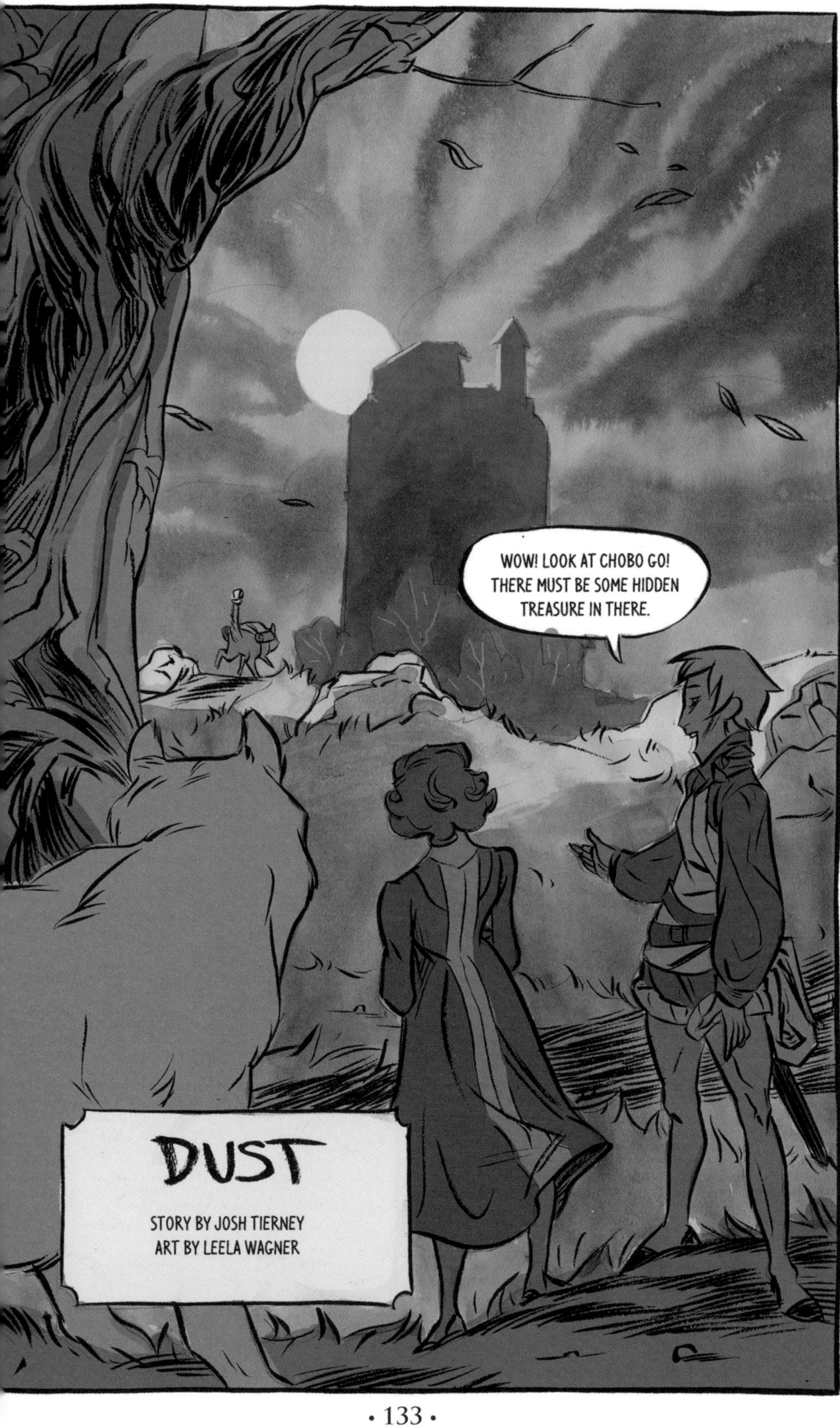
WOW! LOOK AT CHOBO GO! THERE MUST BE SOME HIDDEN TREASURE IN THERE.
DUST
STORY BY JOSH TIERNEY
ART BY LEELA WAGNER

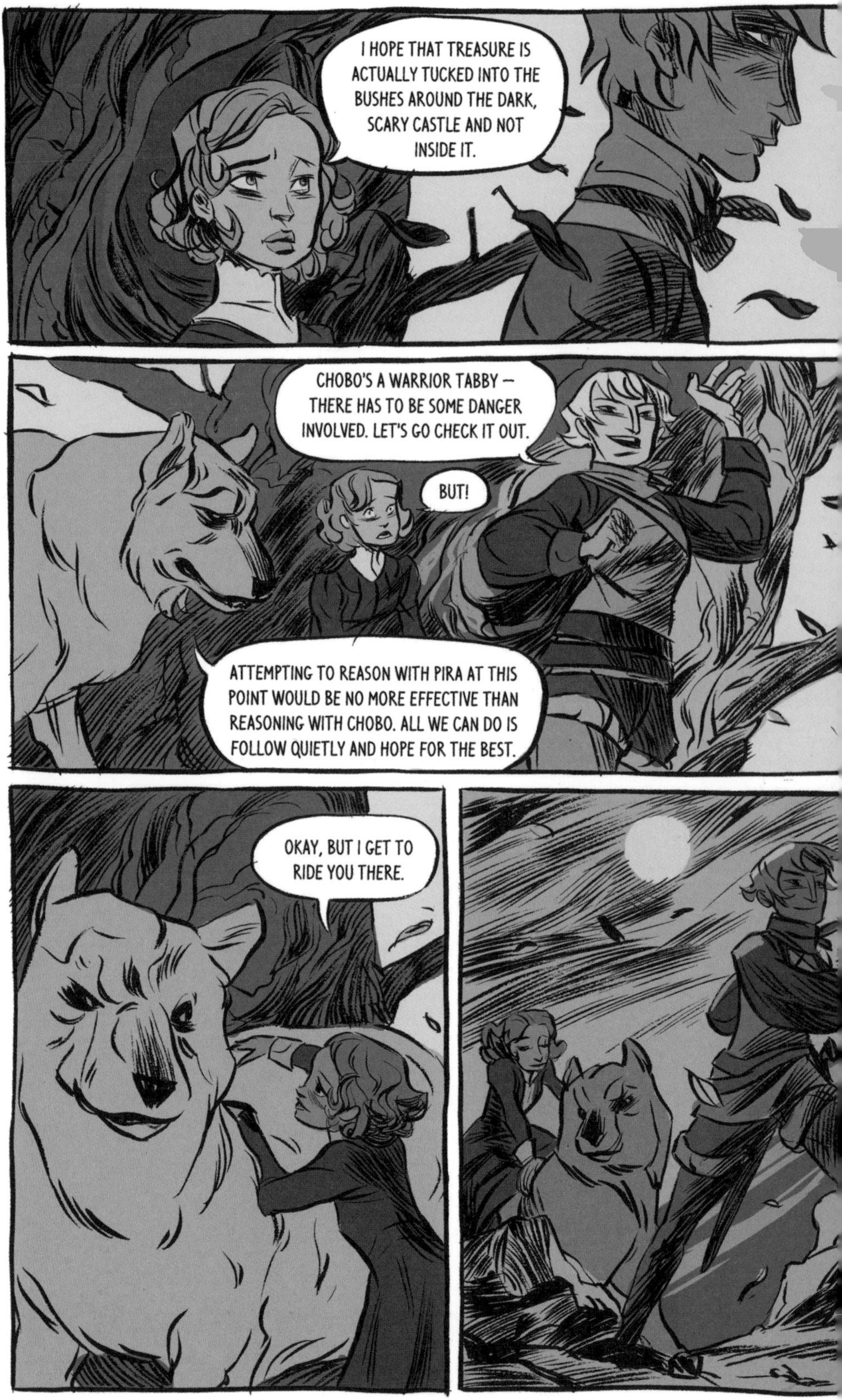
I HOPE THAT TREASURE IS ACTUALLY TUCKED INTO THE BUSHES AROUND THE DARK, SCARY CASTLE AND NOT INSIDE IT.
CHOBO'S A WARRIOR TABBY — THERE HAS TO BE SOME DANGER INVOLVED. LET'S GO CHECK IT OUT.
BUT!
ATTEMPTING TO REASON WITH PIRA AT THIS POINT WOULD BE NO MORE EFFECTIVE THAN REASONING WITH CHOBO. ALL WE CAN DO IS FOLLOW QUIETLY AND HOPE FOR THE BEST.
OKAY, BUT I GET TO RIDE YOU THERE.

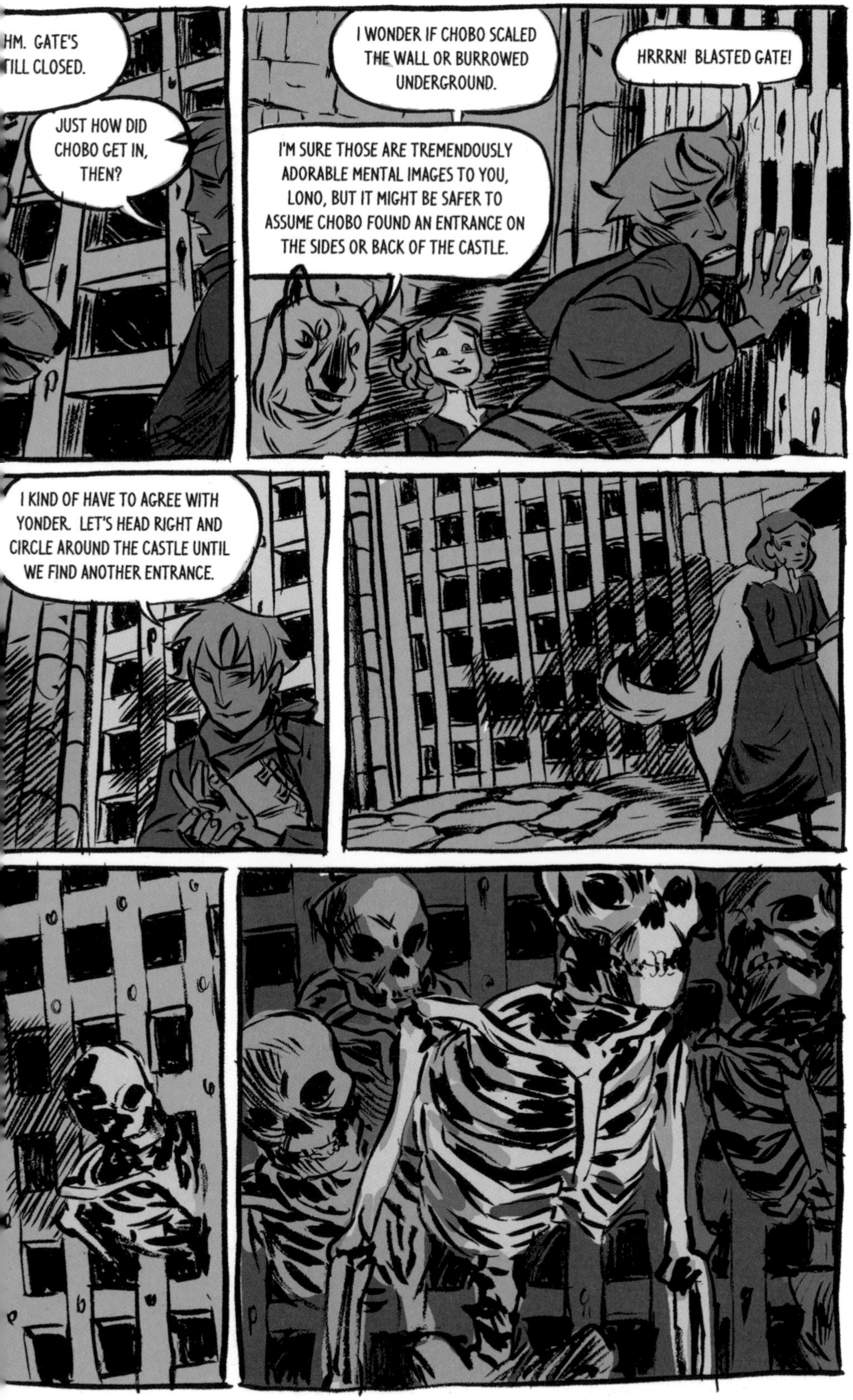

HM. GATE'S TILL CLOSED.
JUST HOW DID CHOBO GET IN, THEN?
I WONDER IF CHOBO SCALED THE WALL OR BURROWED UNDERGROUND.
I'M SURE THOSE ARE TREMENDOUSLY ADORABLE MENTAL IMAGES TO YOU, LONO, BUT IT MIGHT BE SAFER TO ASSUME CHOBO FOUND AN ENTRANCE ON THE SIDES OR BACK OF THE CASTLE.
HRRRN! BLASTED GATE!
I KIND OF HAVE TO AGREE WITH YONDER. LET'S HEAD RIGHT AND CIRCLE AROUND THE CASTLE UNTIL WE FIND ANOTHER ENTRANCE.

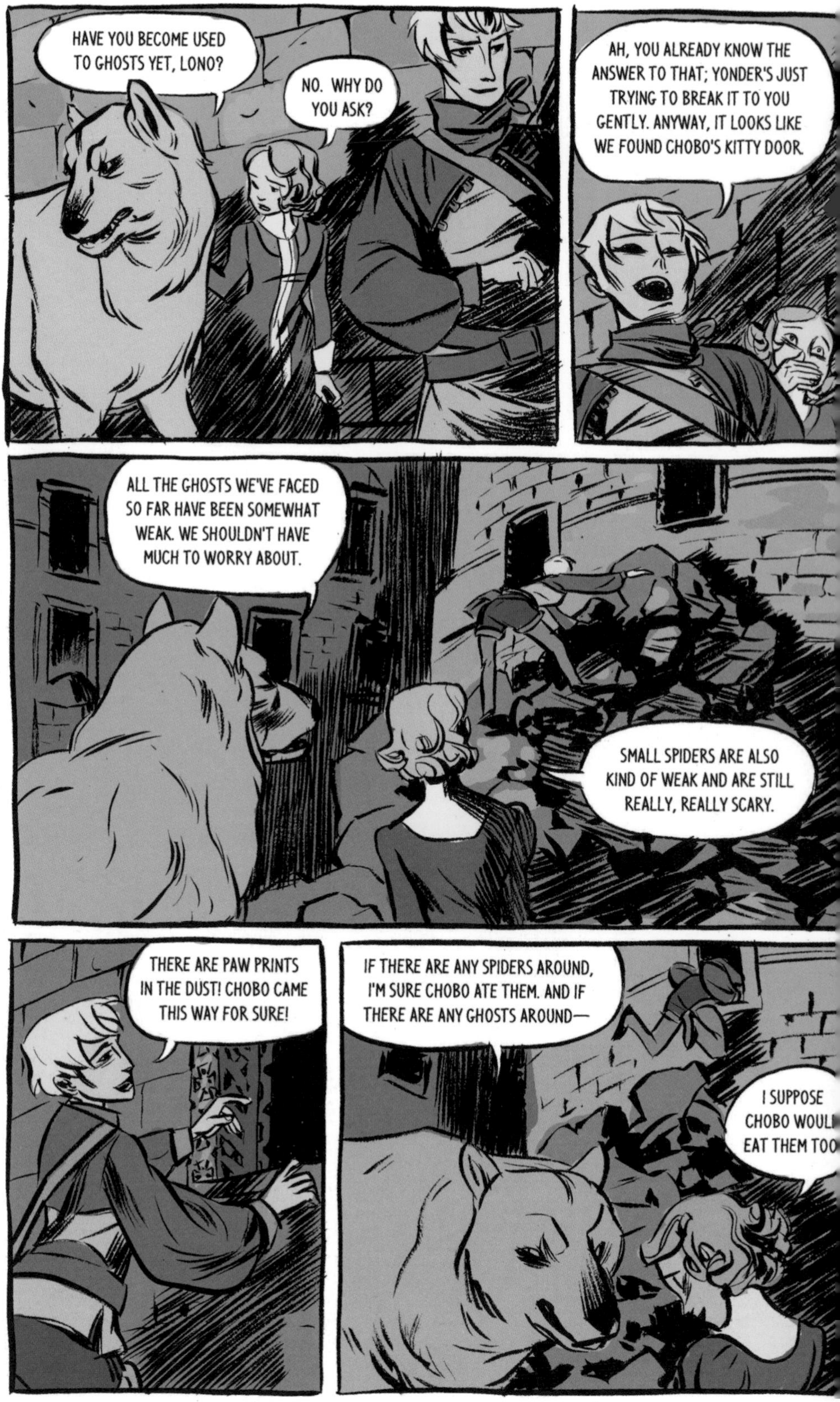

HAVE YOU BECOME USED TO GHOSTS YET, LONO?
NO. WHY DO YOU ASK?
AH, YOU ALREADY KNOW THE ANSWER TO THAT; YONDER'S JUST TRYING TO BREAK IT TO YOU GENTLY. ANYWAY, IT LOOKS LIKE WE FOUND CHOBO'S KITTY DOOR.
ALL THE GHOSTS WE'VE FACED SO FAR HAVE BEEN SOMEWHAT WEAK. WE SHOULDN'T HAVE MUCH TO WORRY ABOUT.
SMALL SPIDERS ARE ALSO KIND OF WEAK AND ARE STILL REALLY, REALLY SCARY.
THERE ARE PAW PRINTS IN THE DUST! CHOBO CAME THIS WAY FOR SURE!
IF THERE ARE ANY SPIDERS AROUND, I'M SURE CHOBO ATE THEM. AND IF THERE ARE ANY GHOSTS AROUND—
I SUPPOSE CHOBO WOUL
EAT THEM TOO

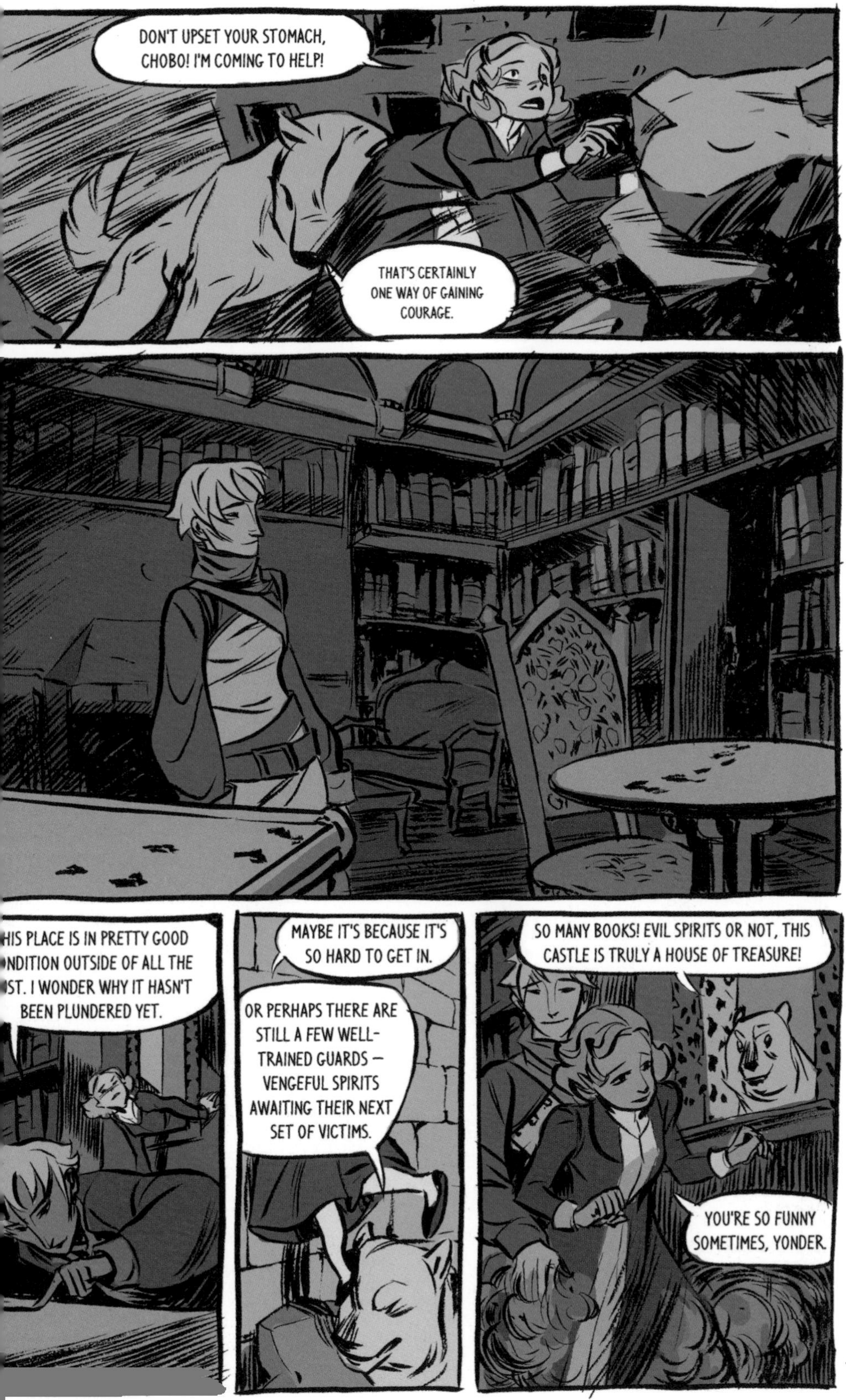
DON'T UPSET YOUR STOMACH, CHOBO! I'M COMING TO HELP!
THAT'S CERTAINLY ONE WAY OF GAINING COURAGE.
HIS PLACE IS IN PRETTY GOOD NDITION OUTSIDE OF ALL THE ST. I WONDER WHY IT HASN'T BEEN PLUNDERED YET.
MAYBE IT'S BECAUSE IT'S SO HARD TO GET IN.
OR PERHAPS THERE ARE STILL A FEW WELL-TRAINED GUARDS — VENGEFUL SPIRITS AWAITING THEIR NEXT SET OF VICTIMS.
SO MANY BOOKS! EVIL SPIRITS OR NOT, THIS CASTLE IS TRULY A HOUSE OF TREASURE!
YOU'RE SO FUNNY SOMETIMES, YONDER.

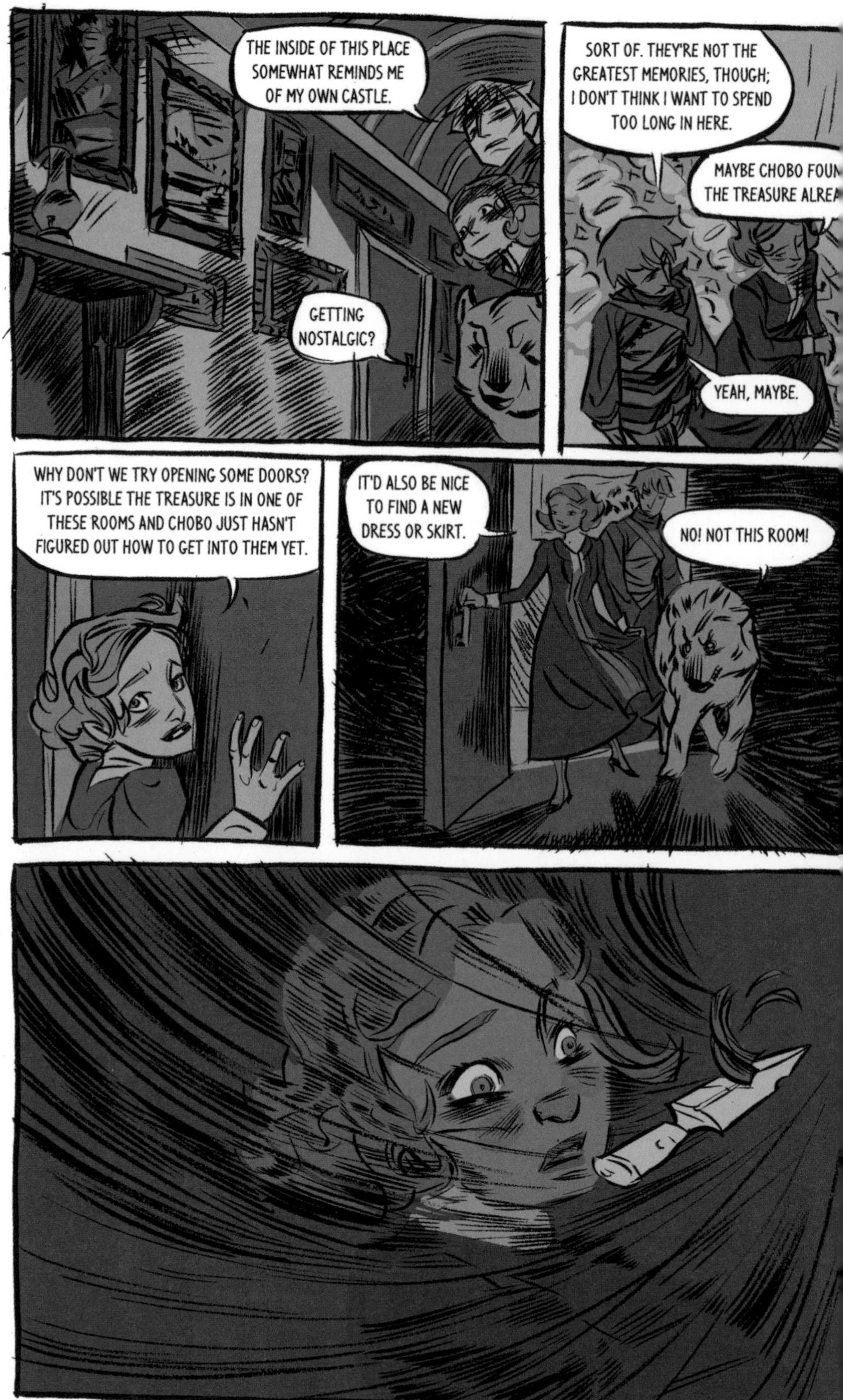
THE INSIDE OF THIS PLACE SOMEWHAT REMINDS ME OF MY OWN CASTLE.
GETTING NOSTALGIC?
SORT OF. THEY'RE NOT THE GREATEST MEMORIES, THOUGH; I DON'T THINK I WANT TO SPEND TOO LONG IN HERE.
MAYBE CHOBO FOUN THE TREASURE ALREA
YEAH, MAYBE.
WHY DON'T WE TRY OPENING SOME DOORS? IT'S POSSIBLE THE TREASURE IS IN ONE OF THESE ROOMS AND CHOBO JUST HASN'T FIGURED OUT HOW TO GET INTO THEM YET.
IT'D ALSO BE NICE TO FIND A NEW DRESS OR SKIRT.
NO! NOT THIS ROOM!

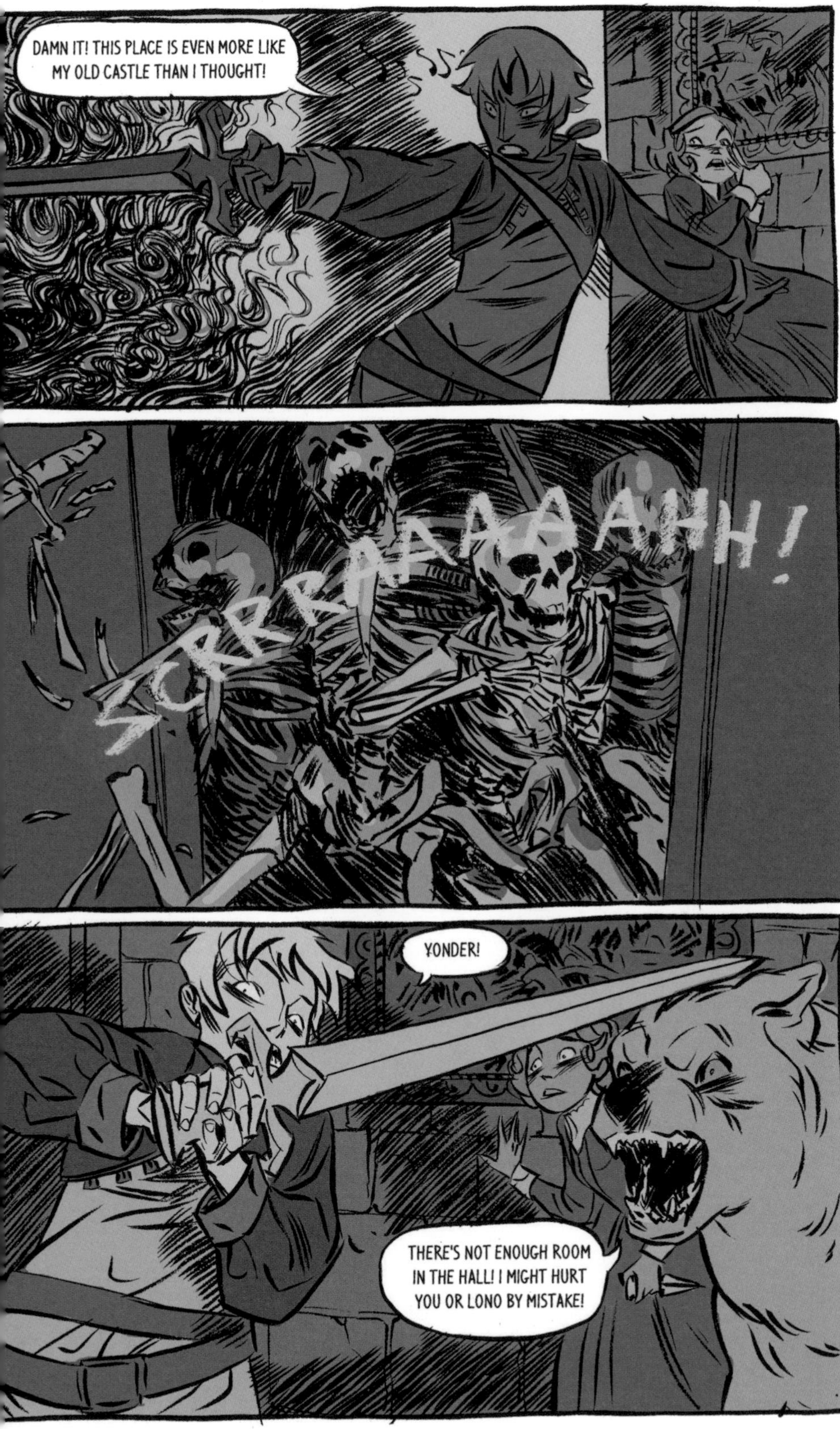
DAMN IT! THIS PLACE IS EVEN MORE LIKE MY OLD CASTLE THAN I THOUGHT!
SCRRRAAAAAHH!
YONDER!
THERE'S NOT ENOUGH ROOM IN THE HALL! I MIGHT HURT YOU OR LONO BY MISTAKE!

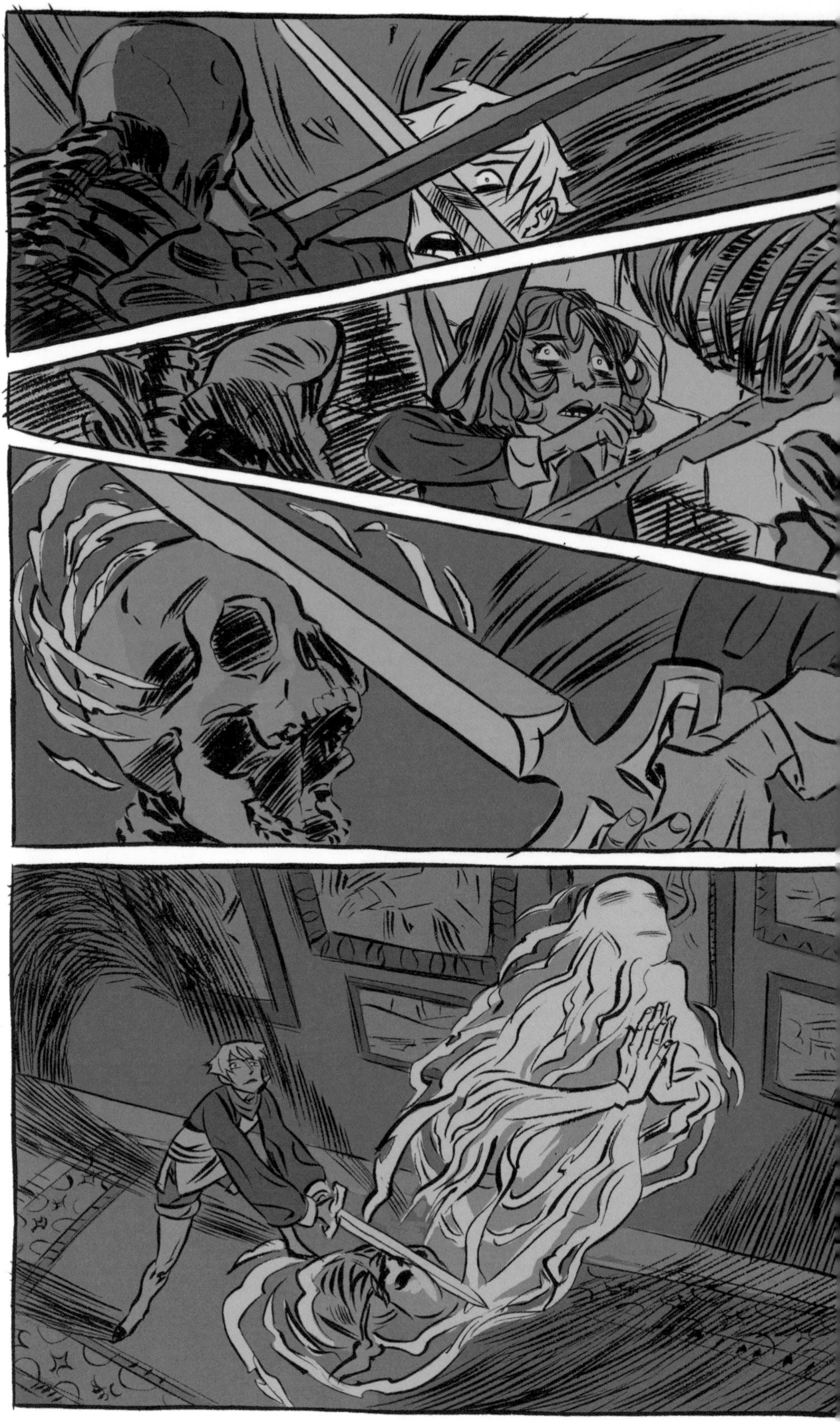

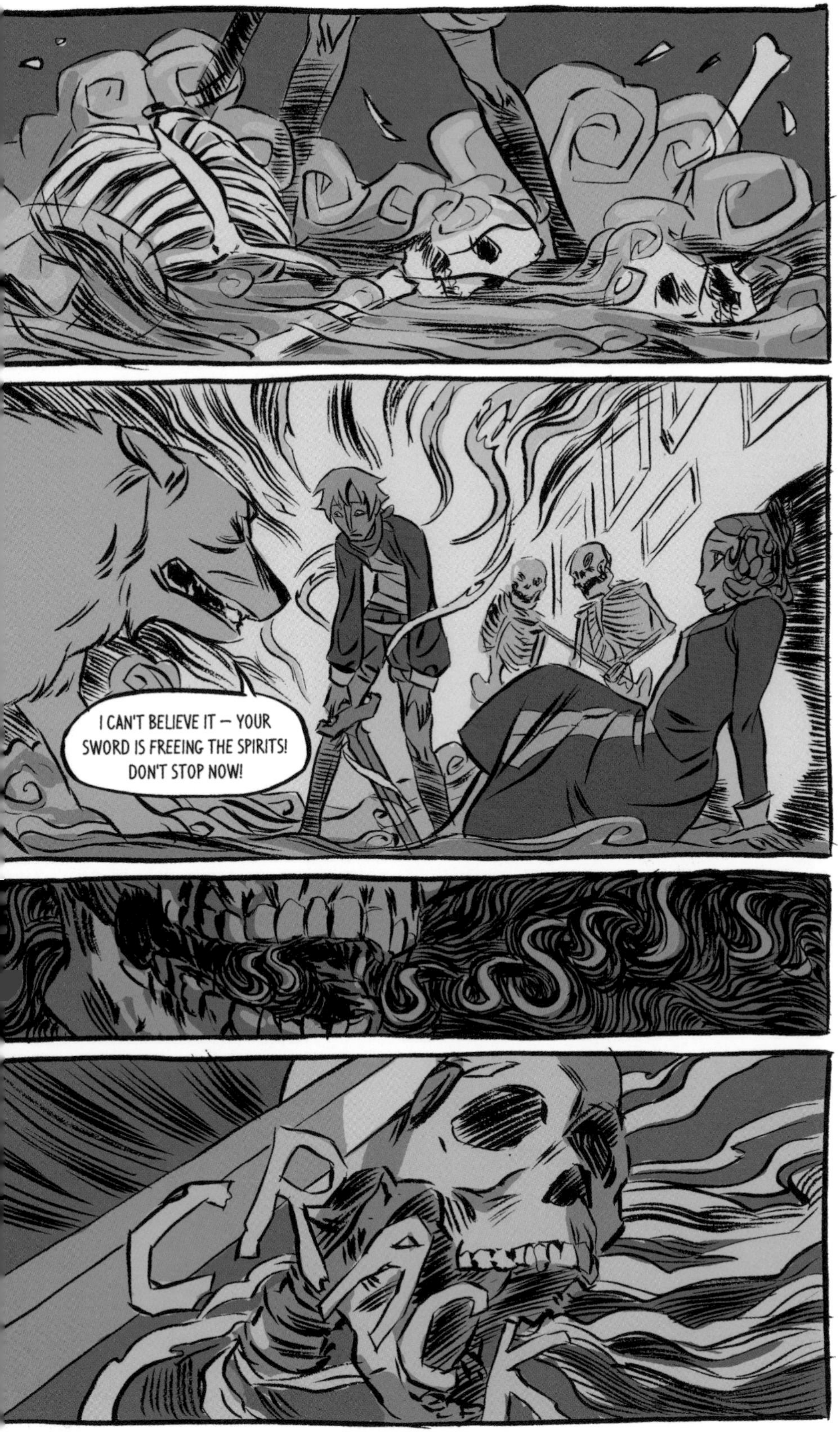
I CAN'T BELIEVE IT — YOUR SWORD IS FREEING THE SPIRITS! DON'T STOP NOW!

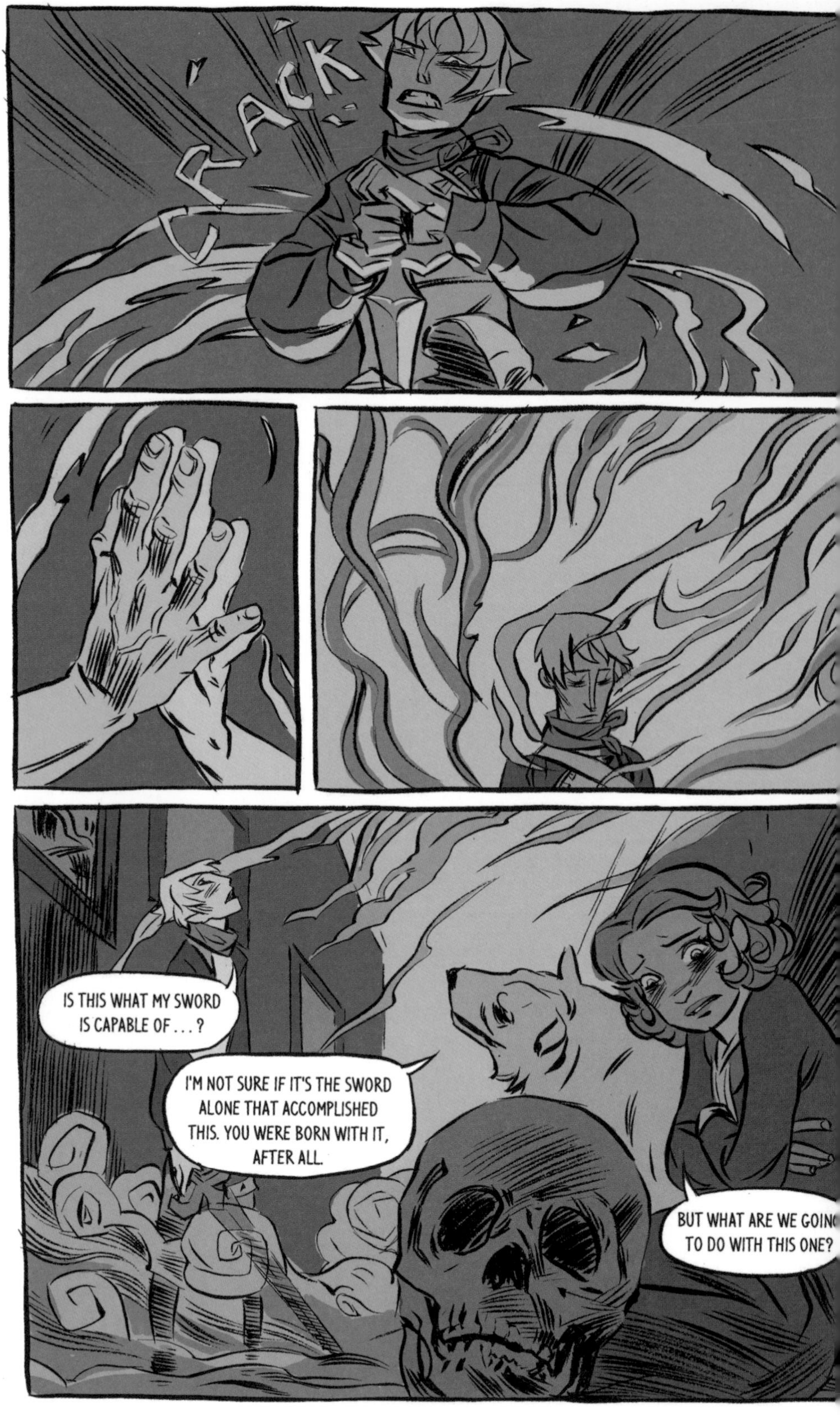
CRACK
IS THIS WHAT MY SWORD IS CAPABLE OF . . . ?
I'M NOT SURE IF IT'S THE SWORD ALONE THAT ACCOMPLISHED THIS. YOU WERE BORN WITH IT, AFTER ALL.
BUT WHAT ARE WE GOIN
TO DO WITH THIS ONE?

YOUR DAGGER WILL NO DOUBT PASS THROUGH IT; THERE IS NO MAGIC IN IT, NOR IS THERE MAGIC IN YOU. PIRA WILL HAVE TO SHATTER IT WITH HER SWORD.

LIKE THIS?

THAT'LL DO.

Grummmmble

WHAT'S THAT SOUND?

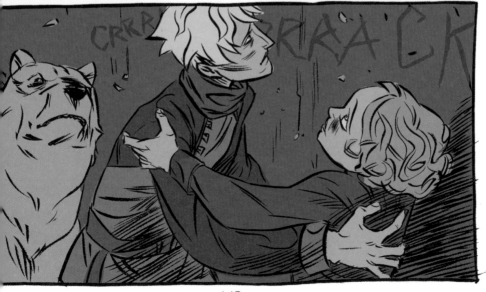

CRRR BRAACK

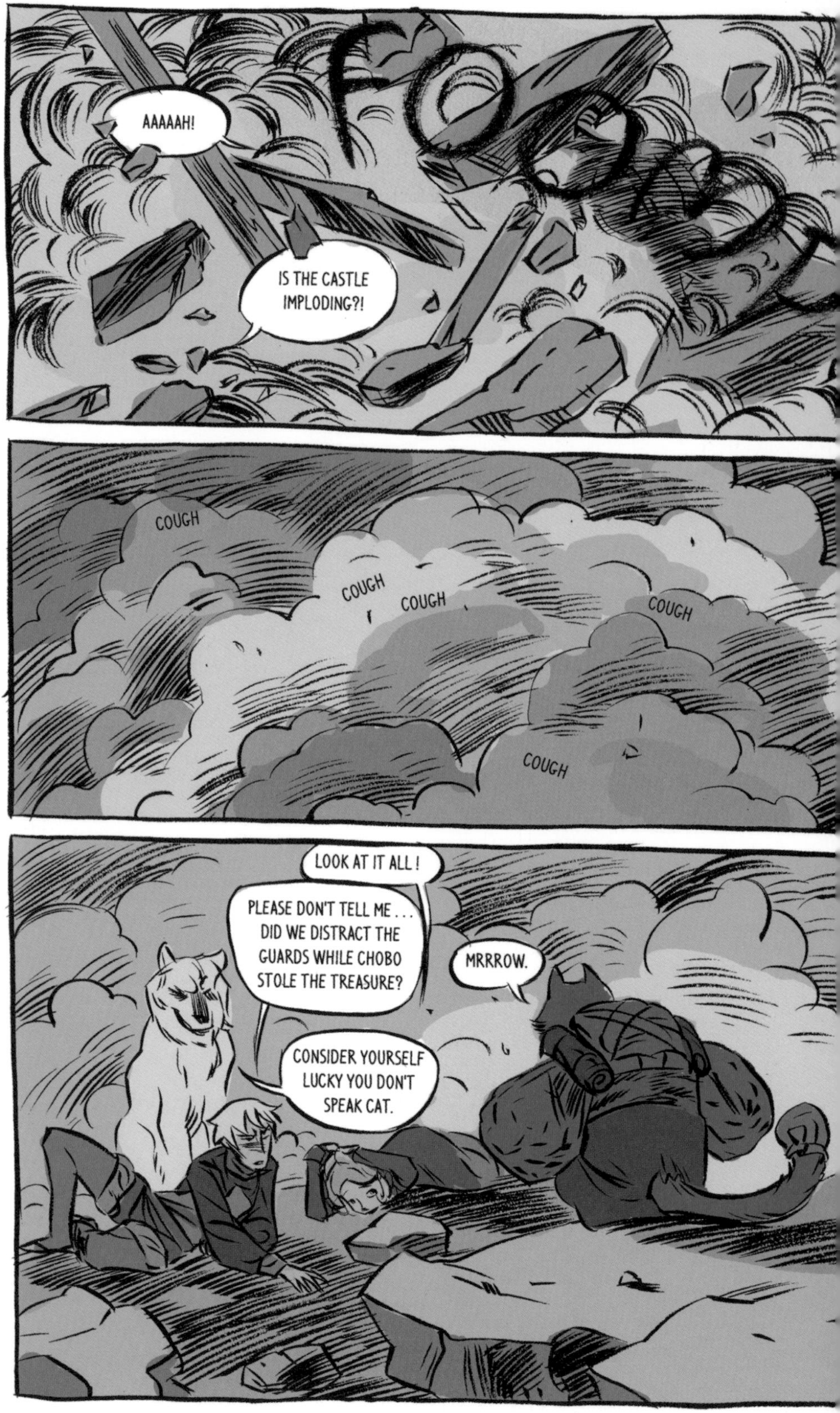
AAAAAH!
IS THE CASTLE IMPLODING?!
COUGH
COUGH
COUGH
COUGH
COUGH
LOOK AT IT ALL!
PLEASE DON'T TELL ME . . . DID WE DISTRACT THE GUARDS WHILE CHOBO STOLE THE TREASURE?
MRRROW.
CONSIDER YOURSELF LUCKY YOU DON'T SPEAK CAT.

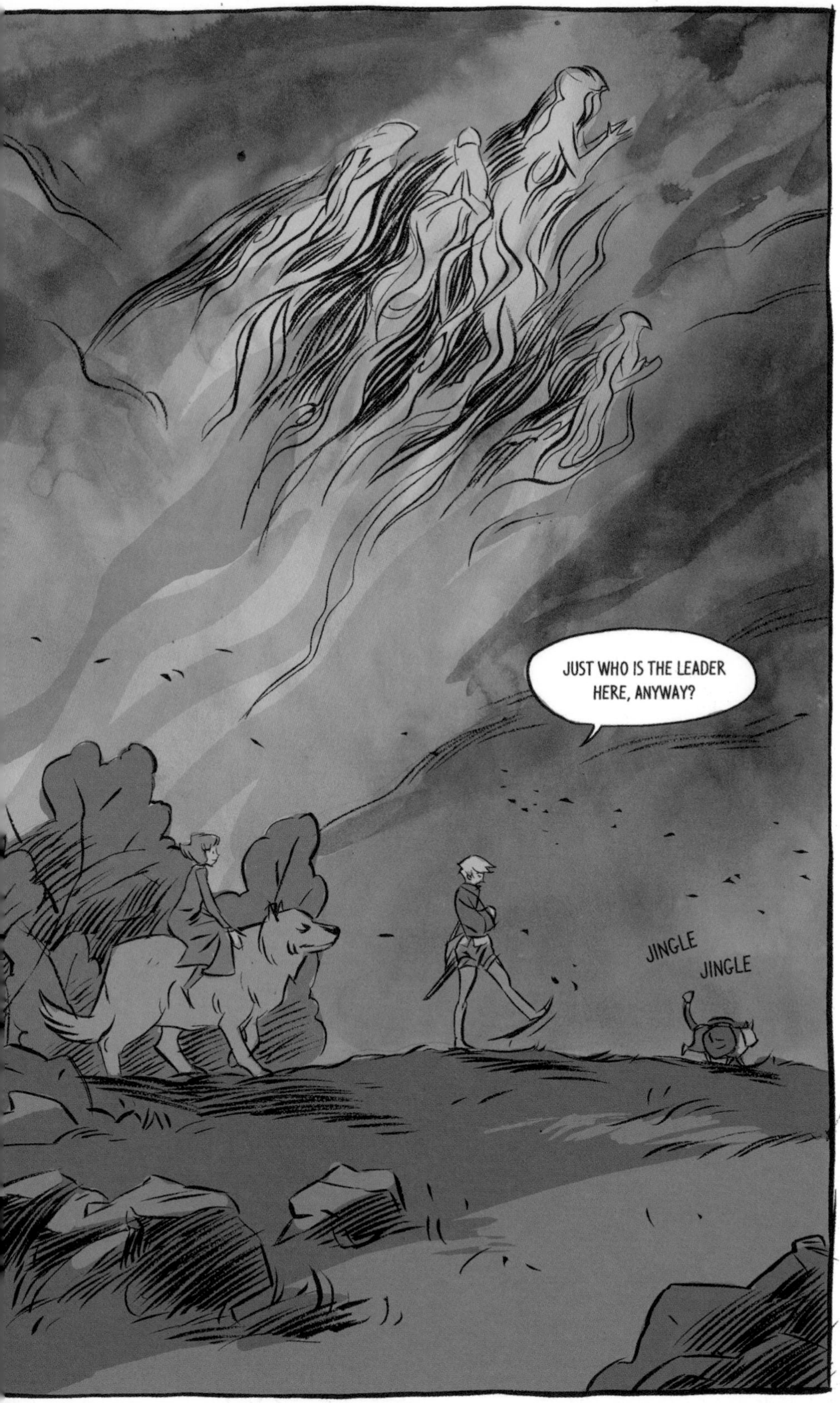
JUST WHO IS THE LEADER HERE, ANYWAY?
JINGLE
JINGLE

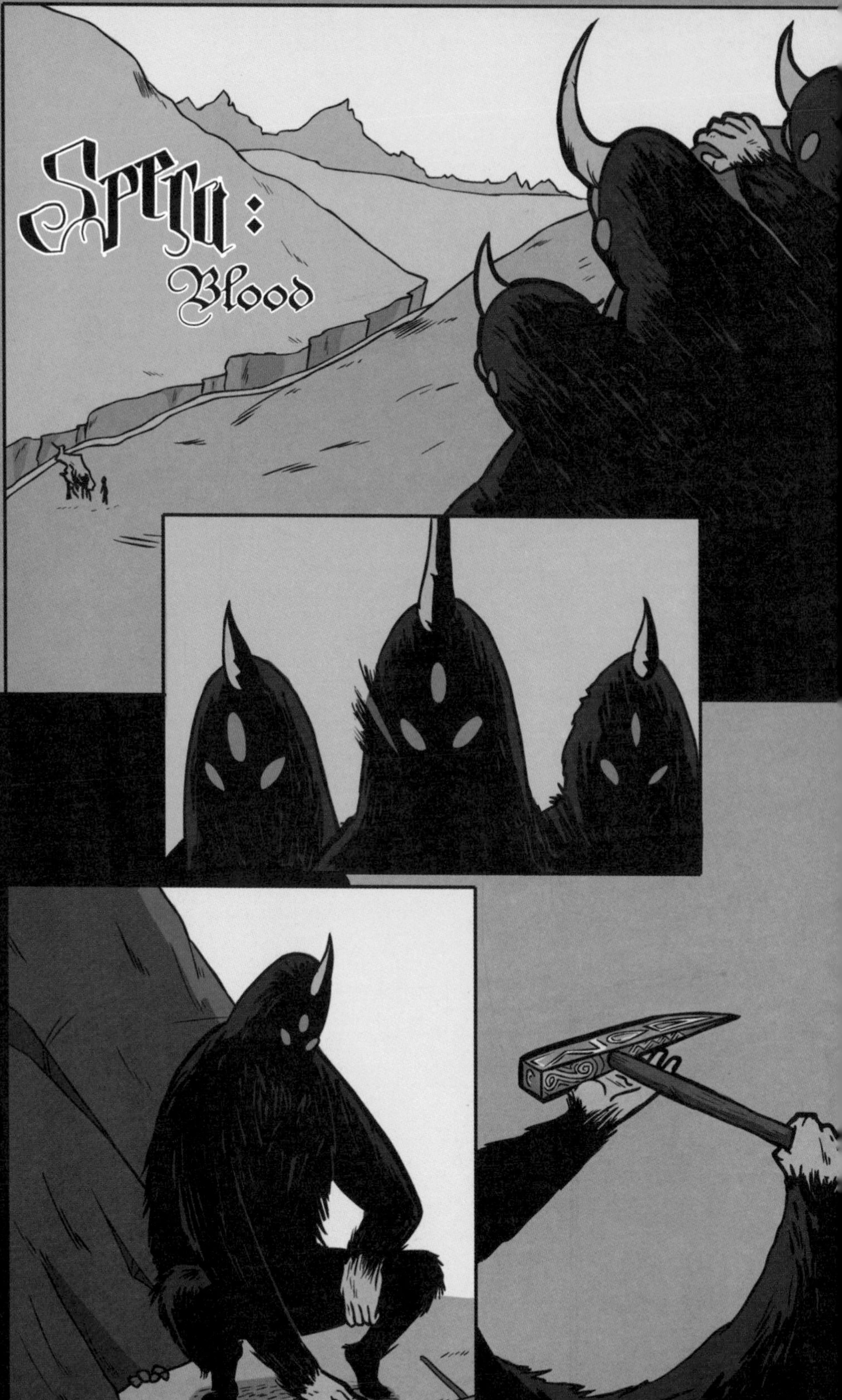

Speru :
Blood

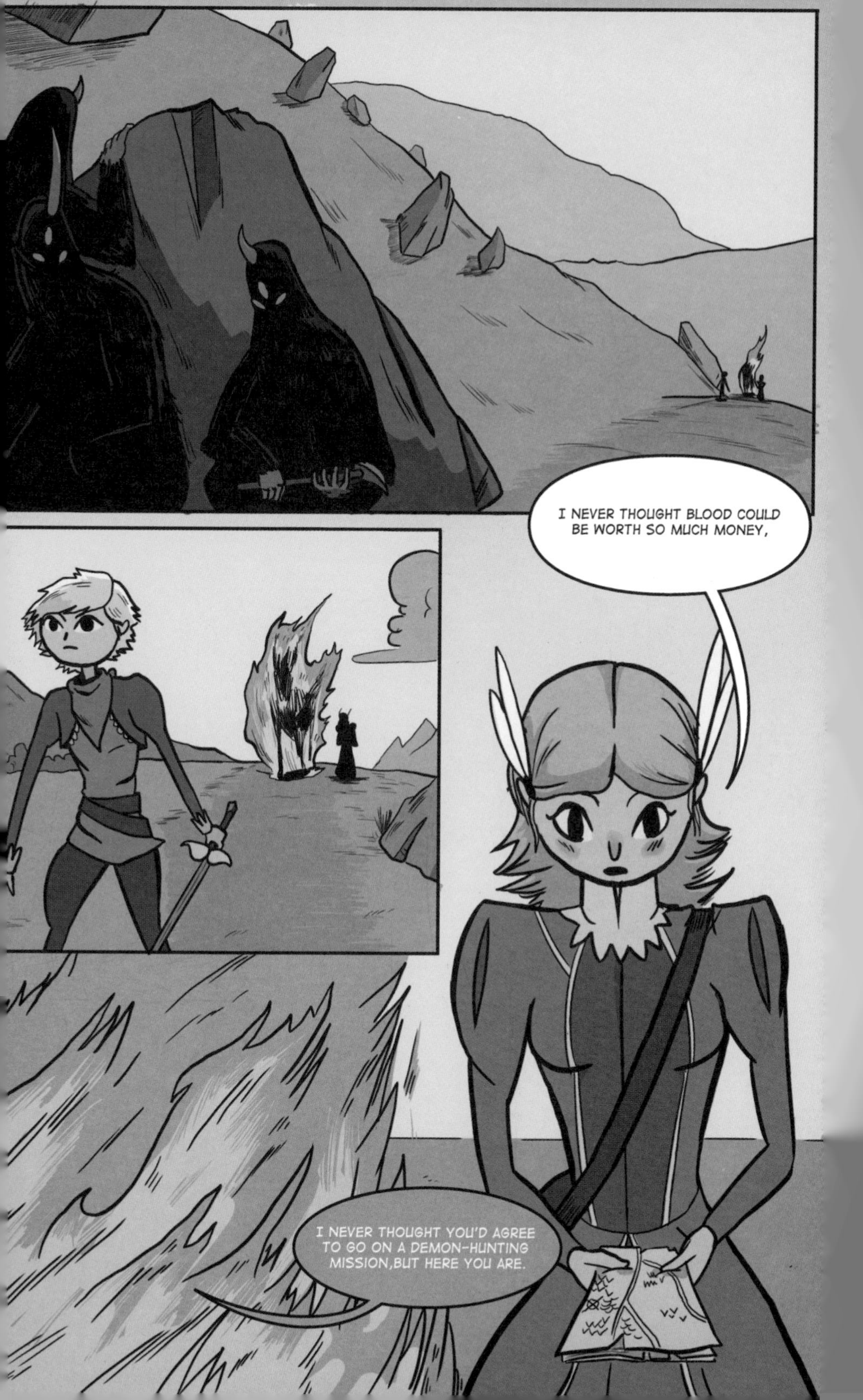
I NEVER THOUGHT BLOOD COULD BE WORTH SO MUCH MONEY,
I NEVER THOUGHT YOU'D AGREE TO GO ON A DEMON-HUNTING MISSION,BUT HERE YOU ARE.

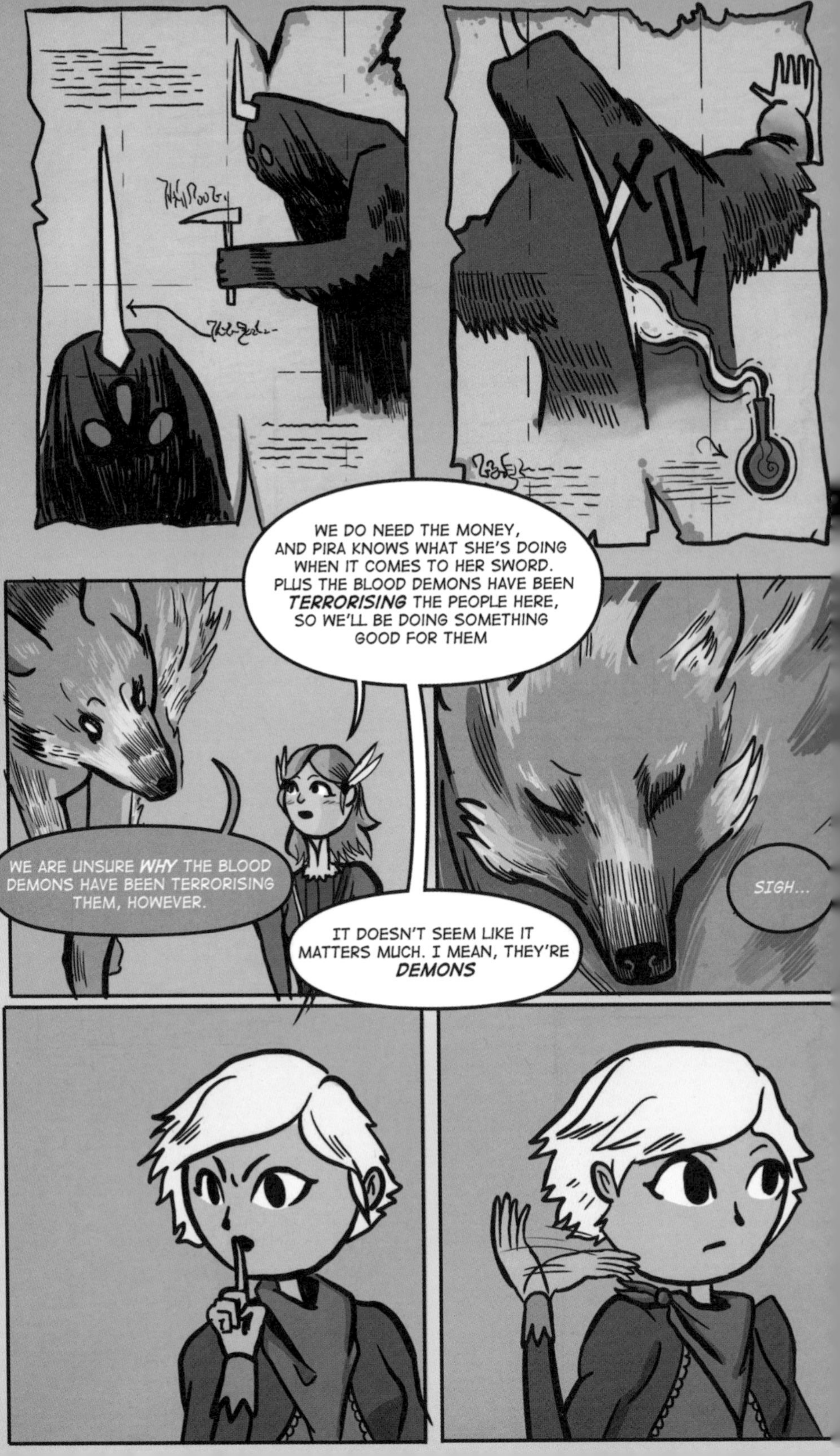
WE DO NEED THE MONEY, AND PIRA KNOWS WHAT SHE'S DOING WHEN IT COMES TO HER SWORD. PLUS THE BLOOD DEMONS HAVE BEEN *TERRORISING* THE PEOPLE HERE, SO WE'LL BE DOING SOMETHING GOOD FOR THEM
WE ARE UNSURE *WHY* THE BLOOD DEMONS HAVE BEEN TERRORISING THEM, HOWEVER.
IT DOESN'T SEEM LIKE IT MATTERS MUCH. I MEAN, THEY'RE *DEMONS*
SIGH...

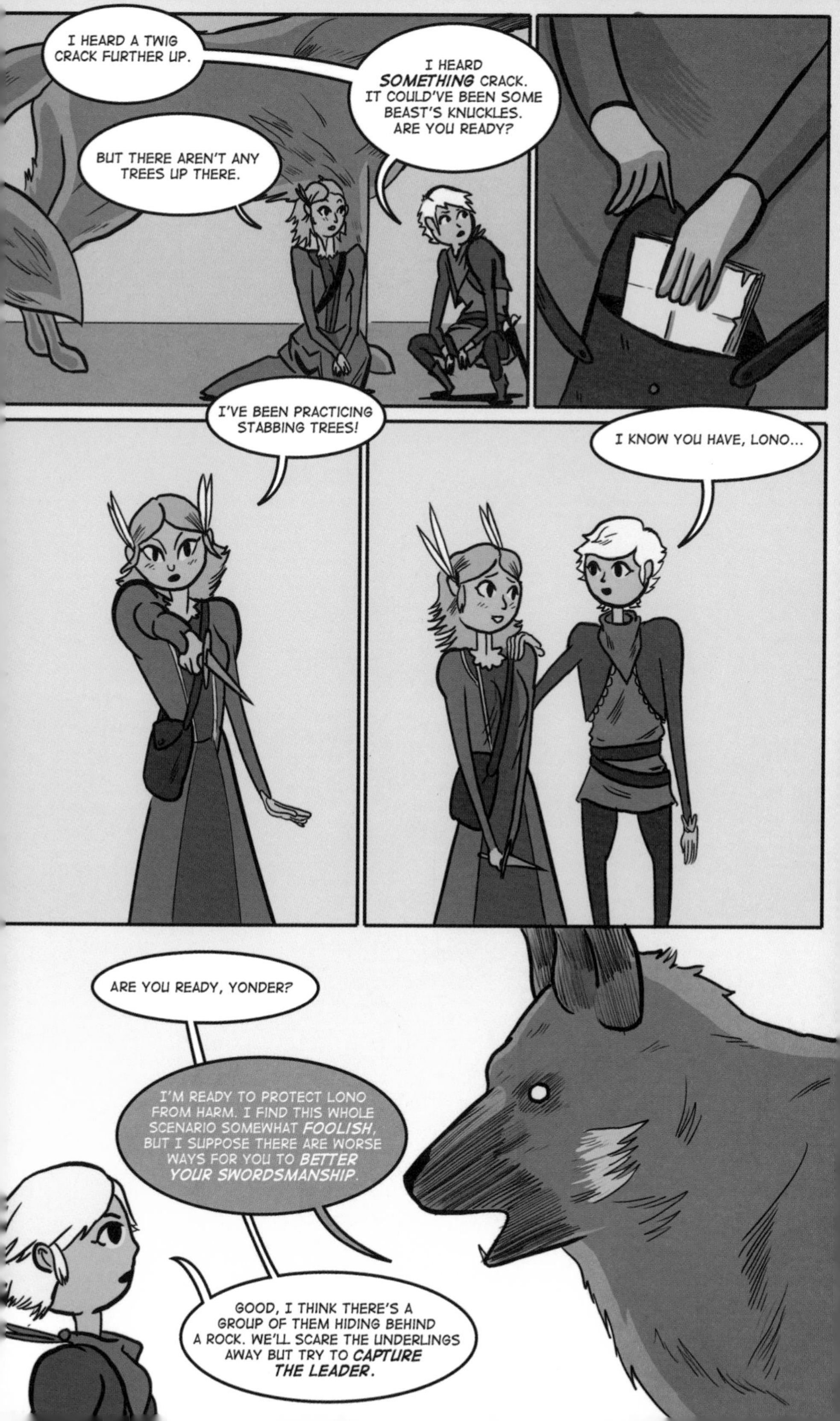
I HEARD A TWIG CRACK FURTHER UP.
I HEARD *SOMETHING* CRACK. IT COULD'VE BEEN SOME BEAST'S KNUCKLES. ARE YOU READY?
BUT THERE AREN'T ANY TREES UP THERE.
I'VE BEEN PRACTICING STABBING TREES!
I KNOW YOU HAVE, LONO...
ARE YOU READY, YONDER?
I'M READY TO PROTECT LONO FROM HARM. I FIND THIS WHOLE SCENARIO SOMEWHAT *FOOLISH*, BUT I SUPPOSE THERE ARE WORSE WAYS FOR YOU TO *BETTER YOUR SWORDSMANSHIP*.
GOOD, I THINK THERE'S A GROUP OF THEM HIDING BEHIND A ROCK. WE'LL SCARE THE UNDERLINGS AWAY BUT TRY TO *CAPTURE THE LEADER*.

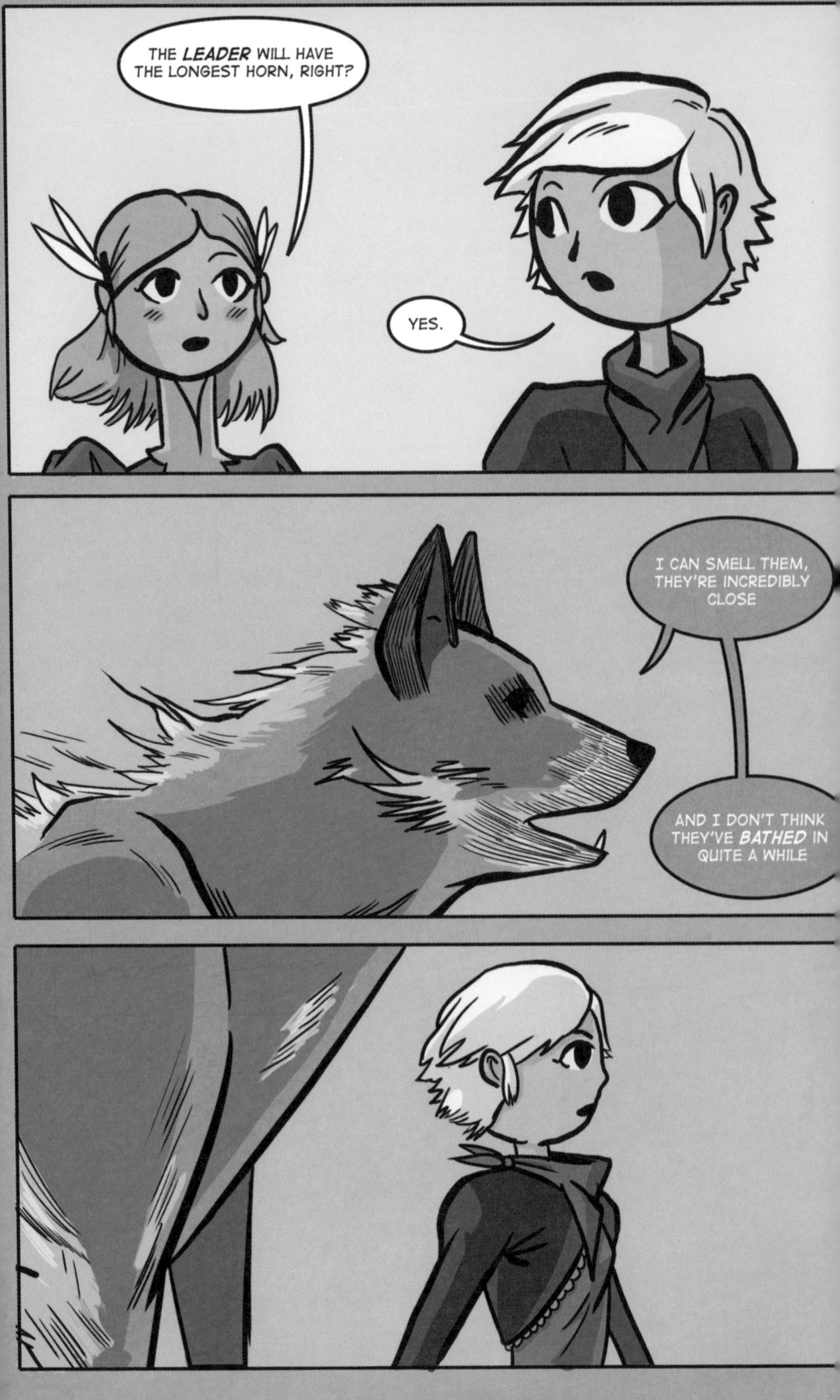
THE LEADER WILL HAVE THE LONGEST HORN, RIGHT?
YES.
I CAN SMELL THEM, THEY'RE INCREDIBLY CLOSE
AND I DON'T THINK THEY'VE BATHED IN QUITE A WHILE

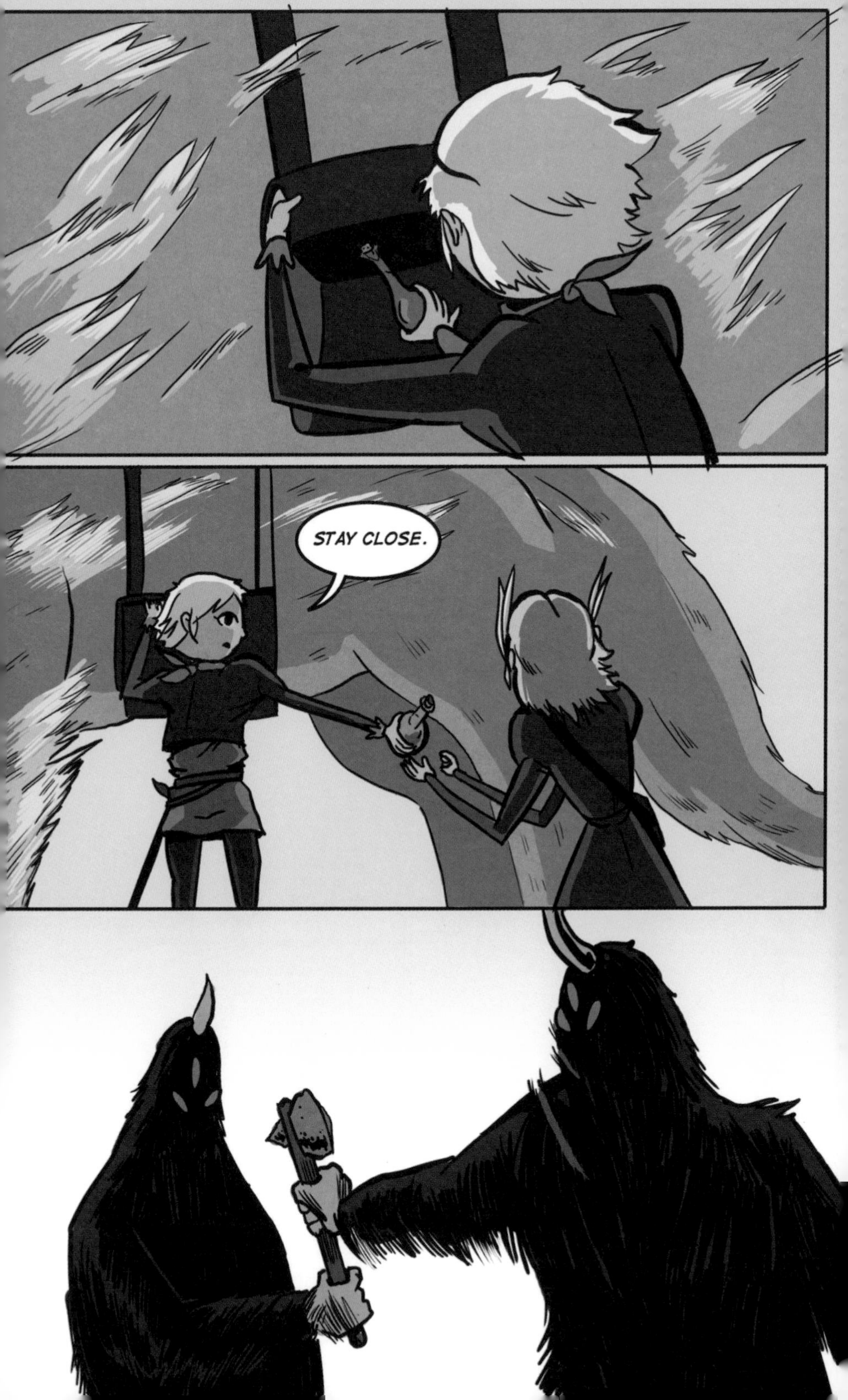
STAY CLOSE.

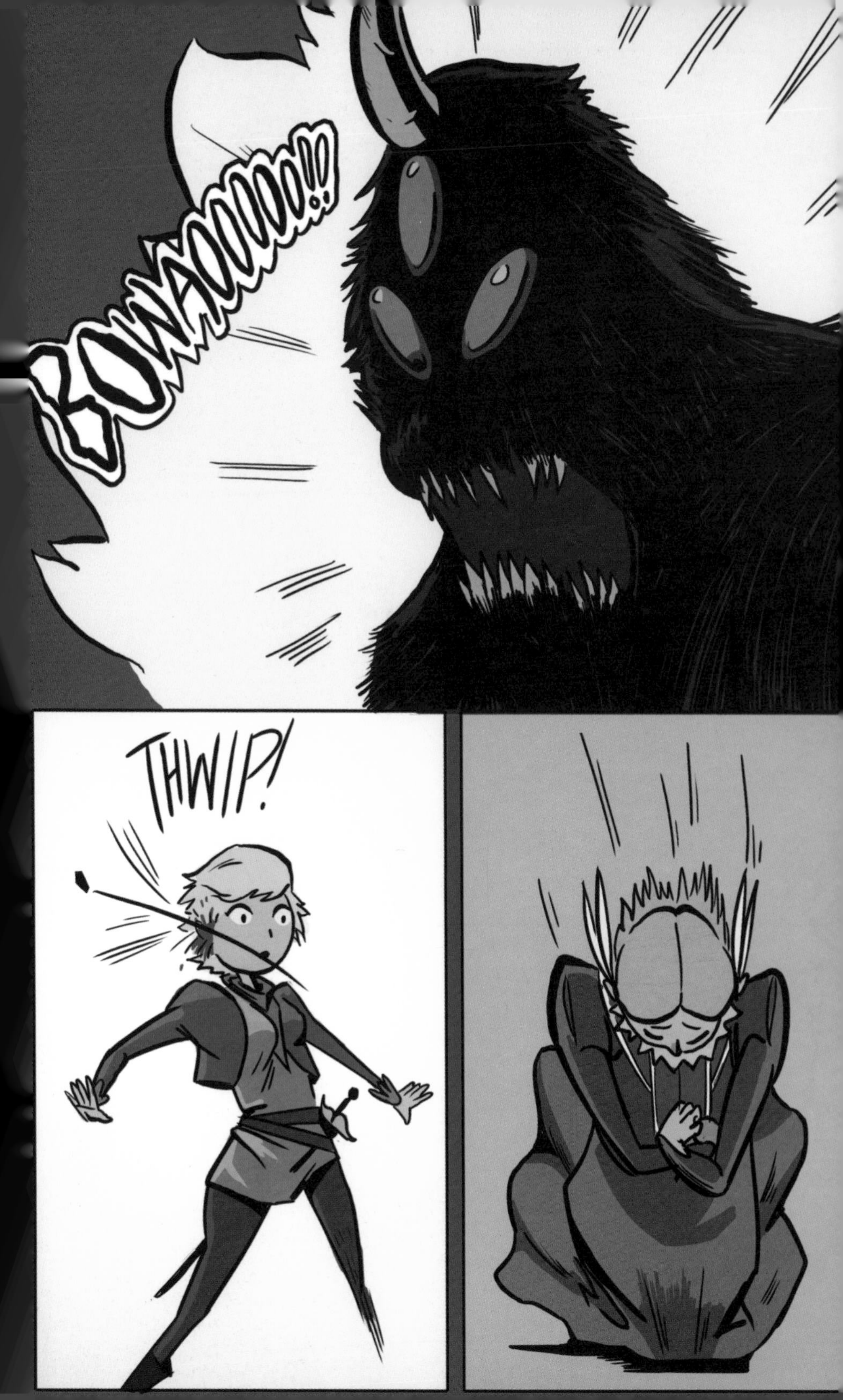
BOWAOOOO!!
THWIP!

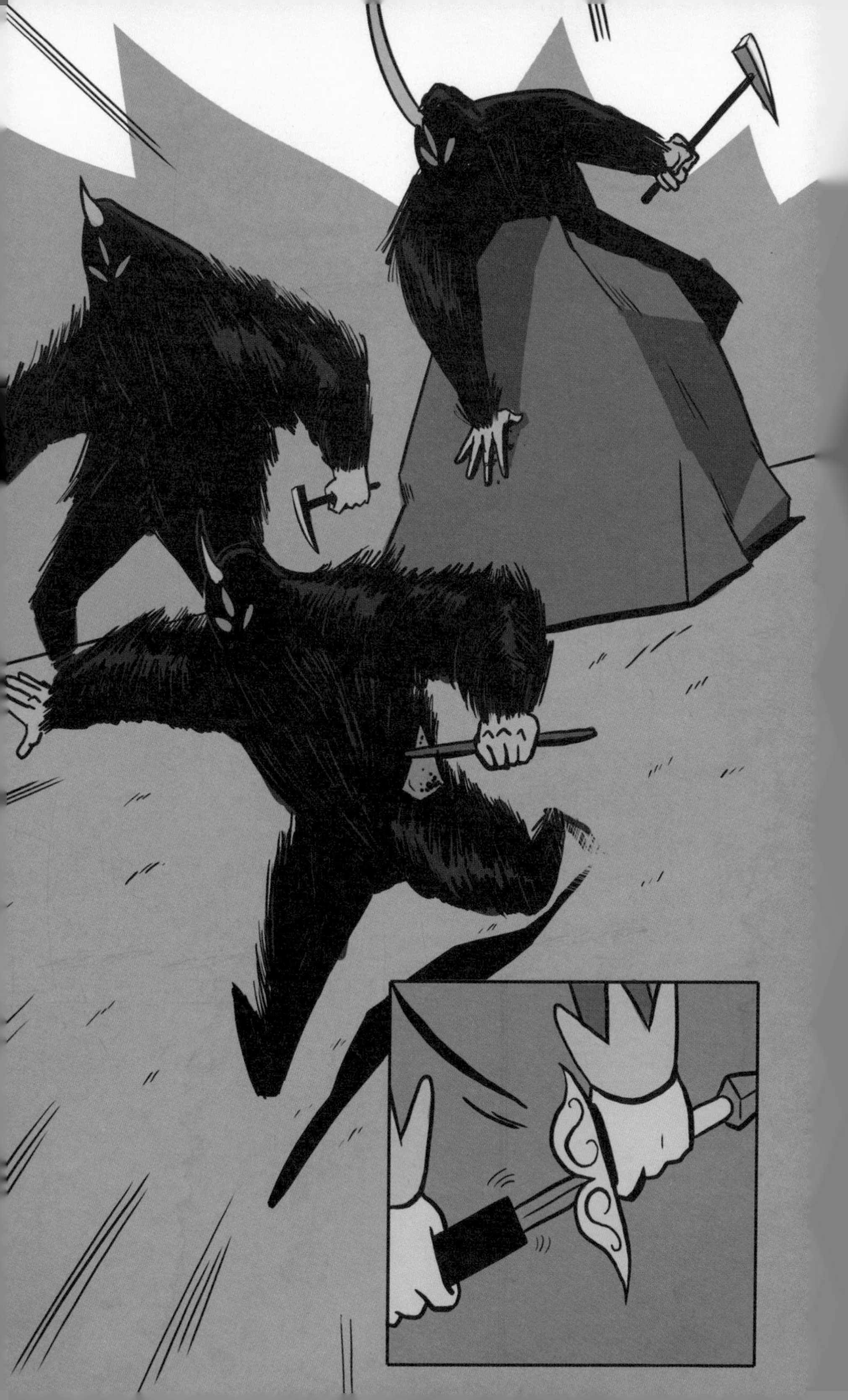

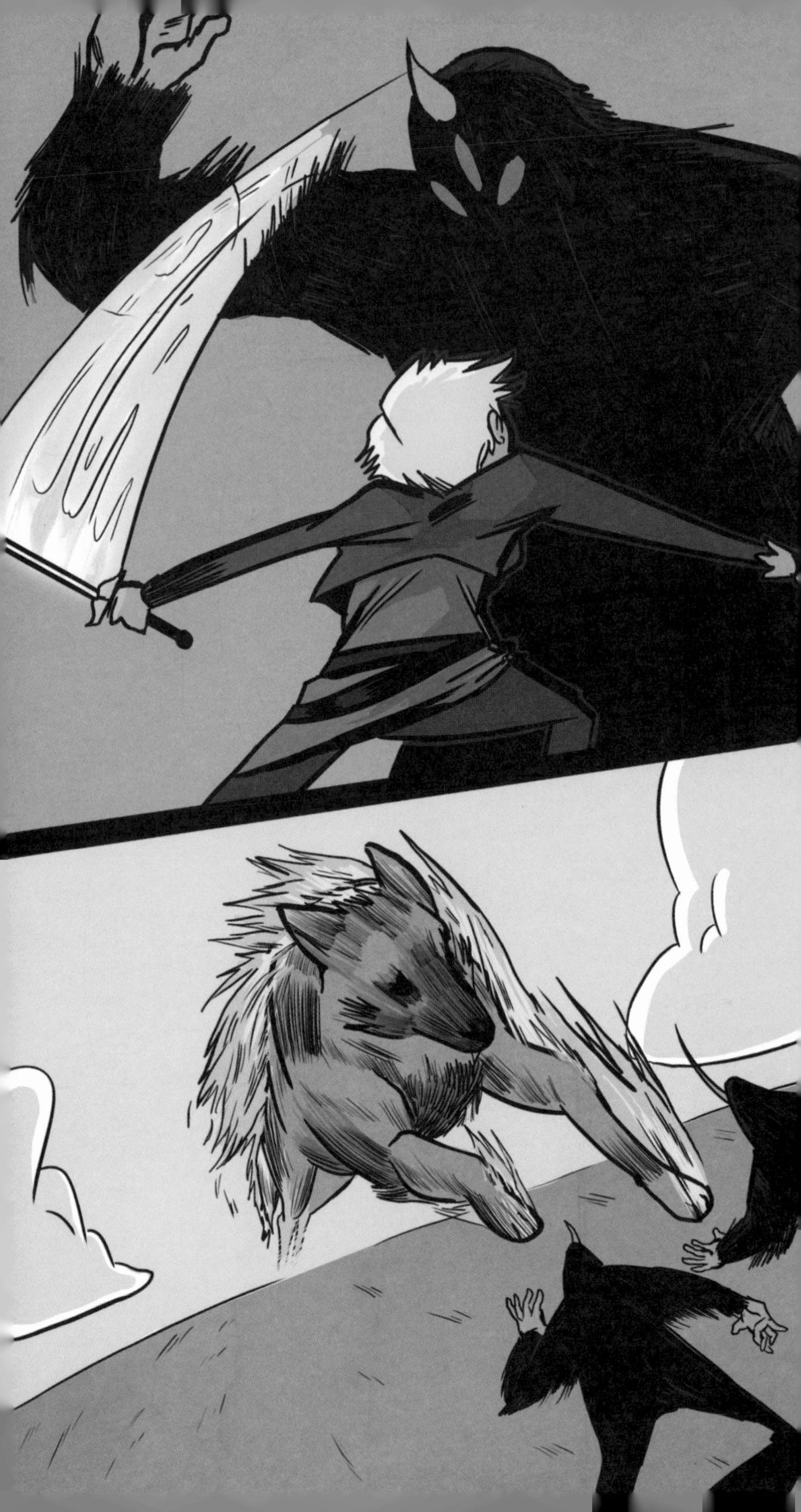

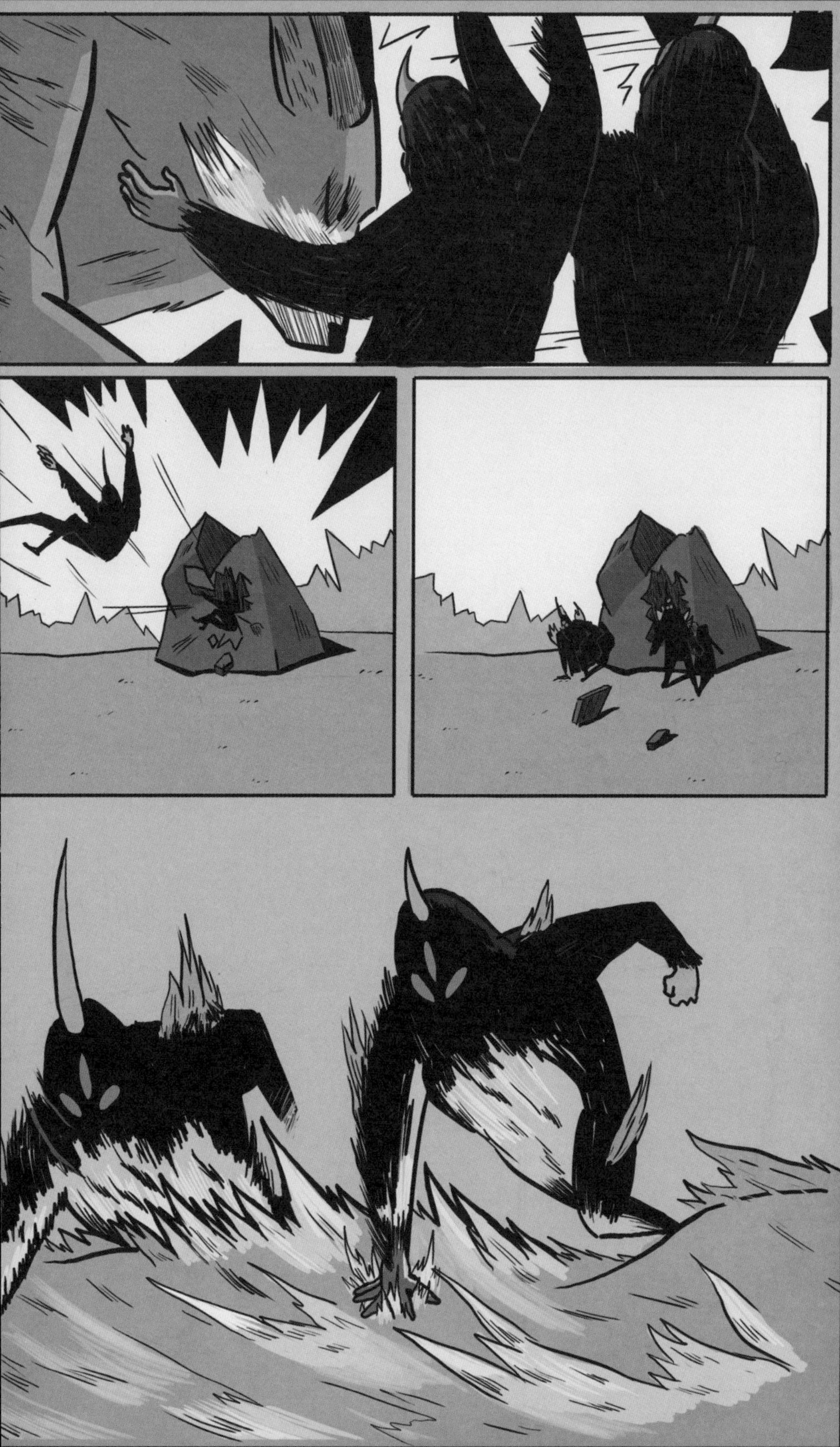

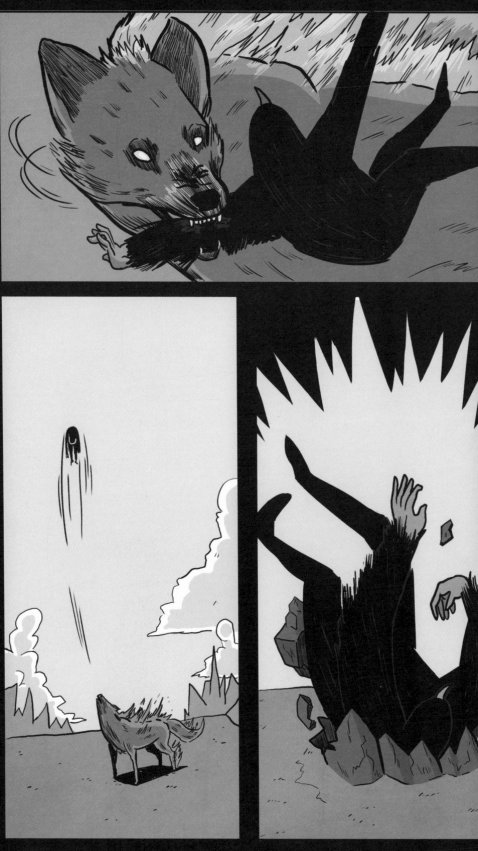

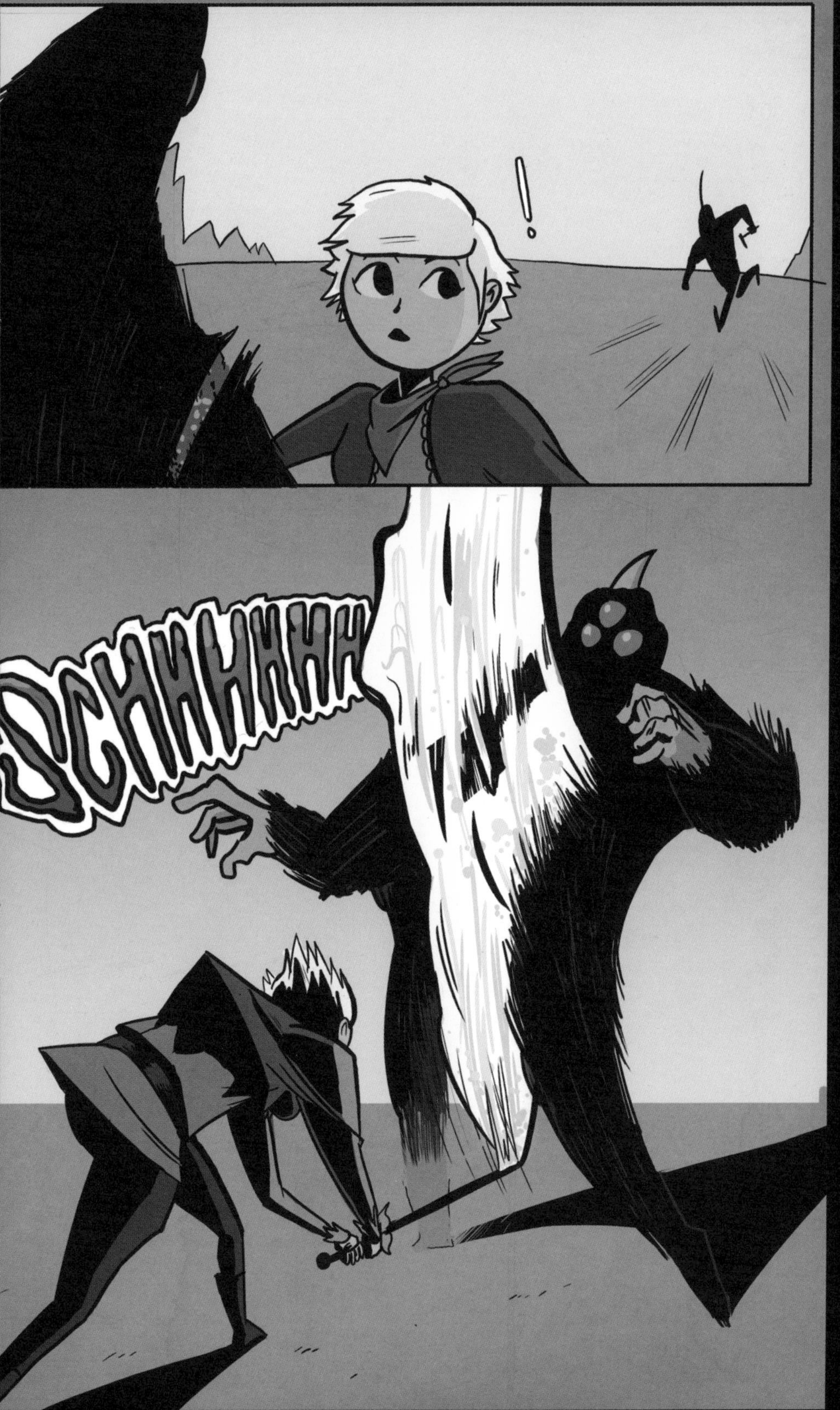
!
SCHHHHHH

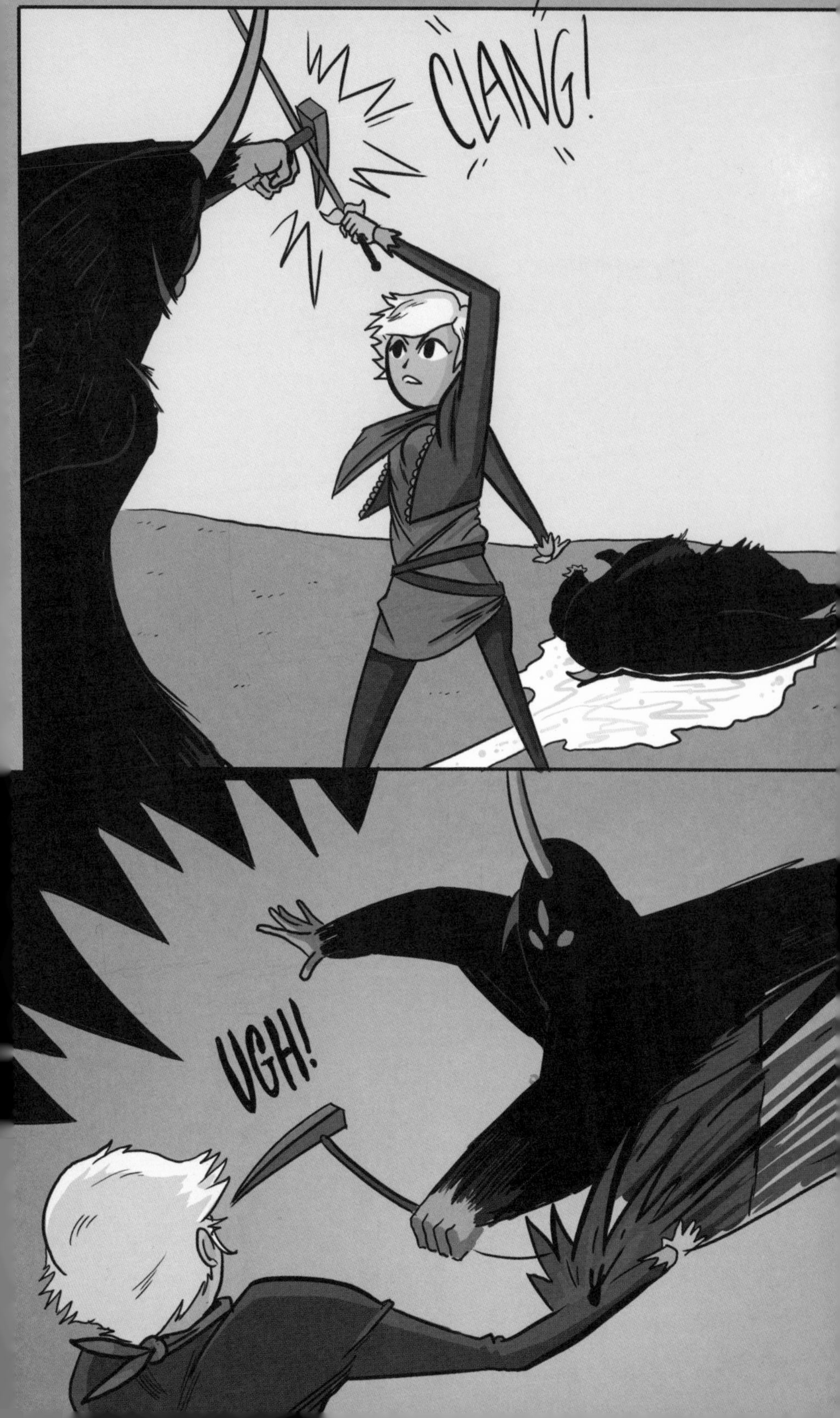
CLANG!
UGH!

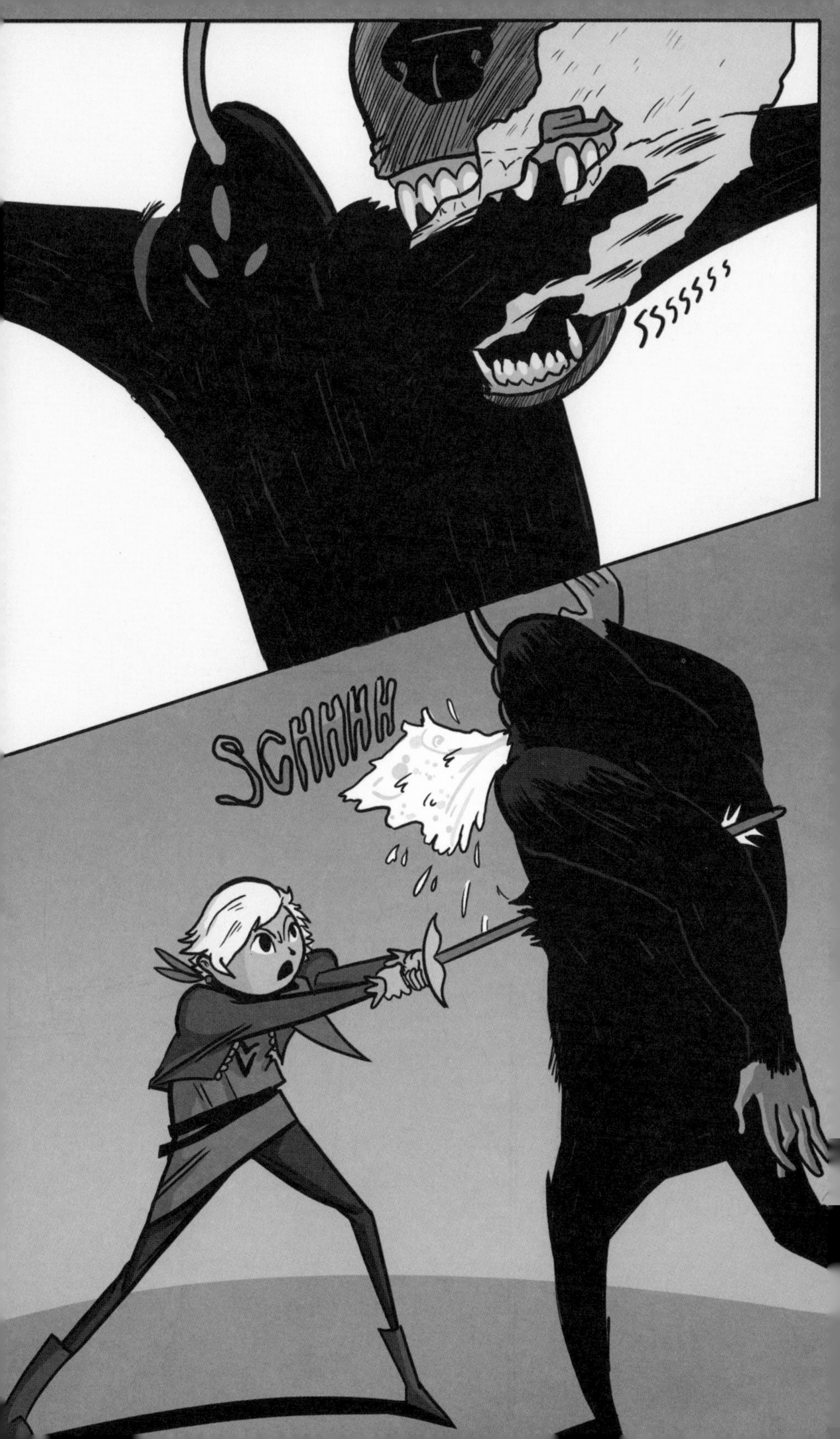
SSSSSSS
SCHHHH

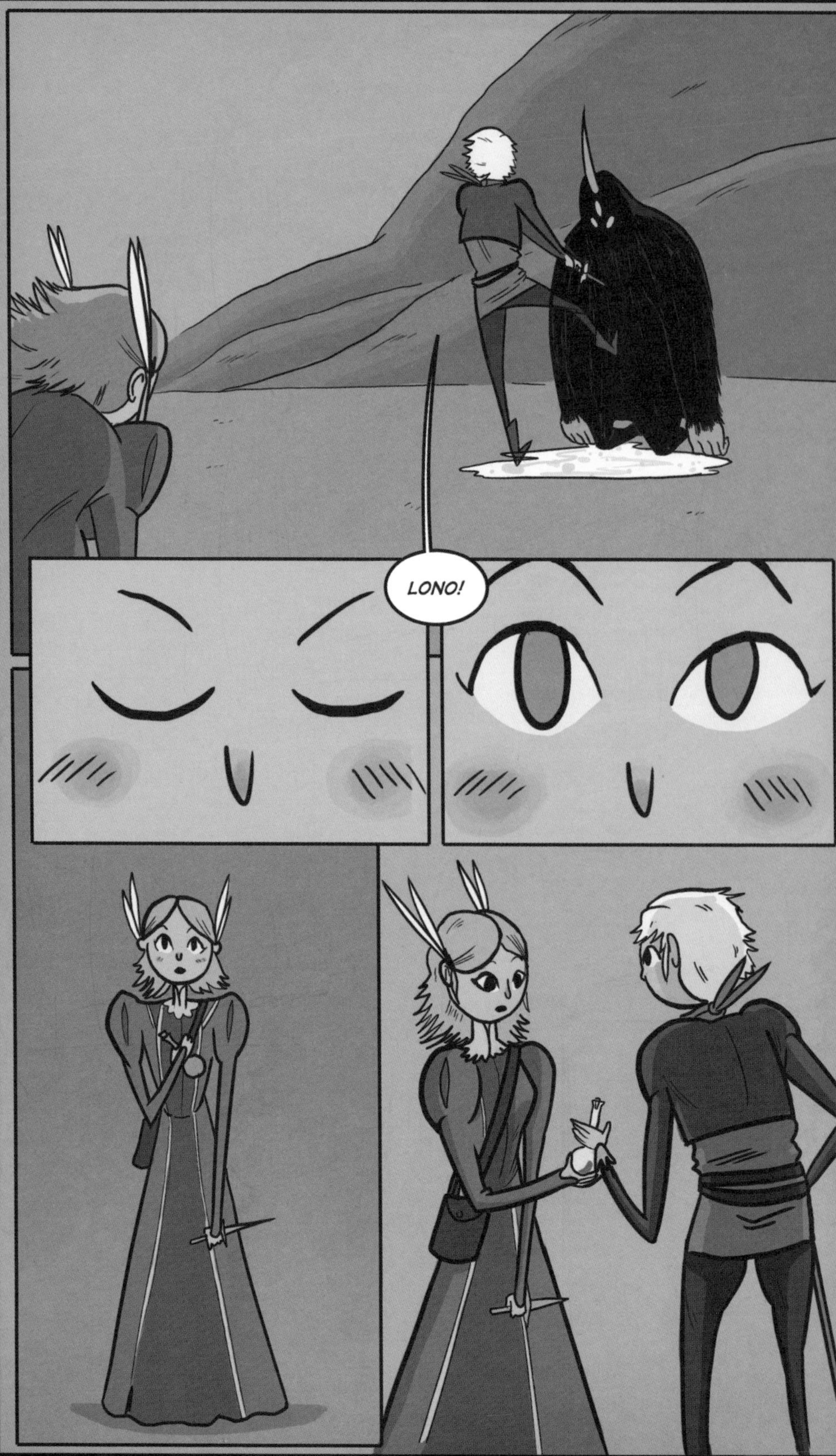
LONO!

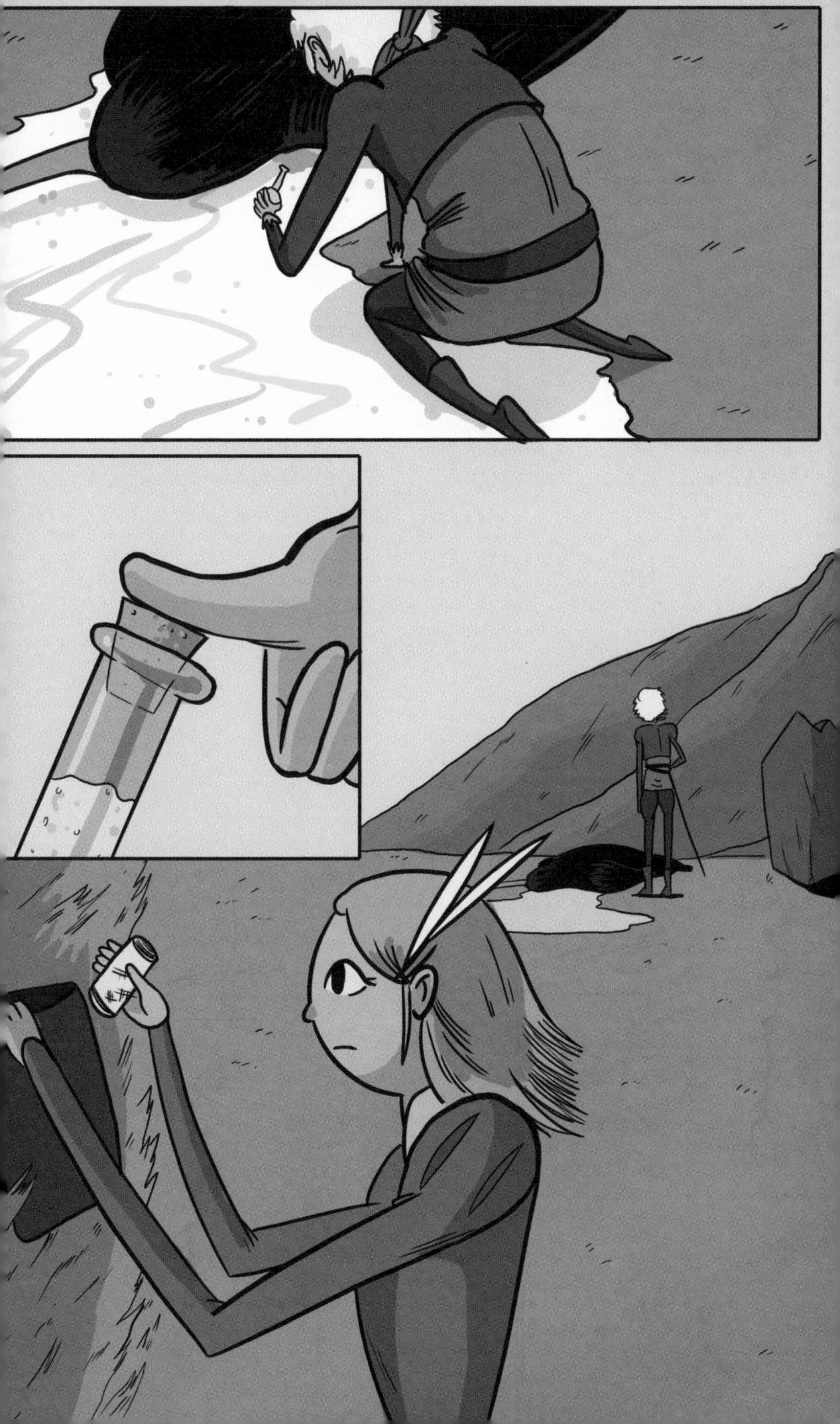

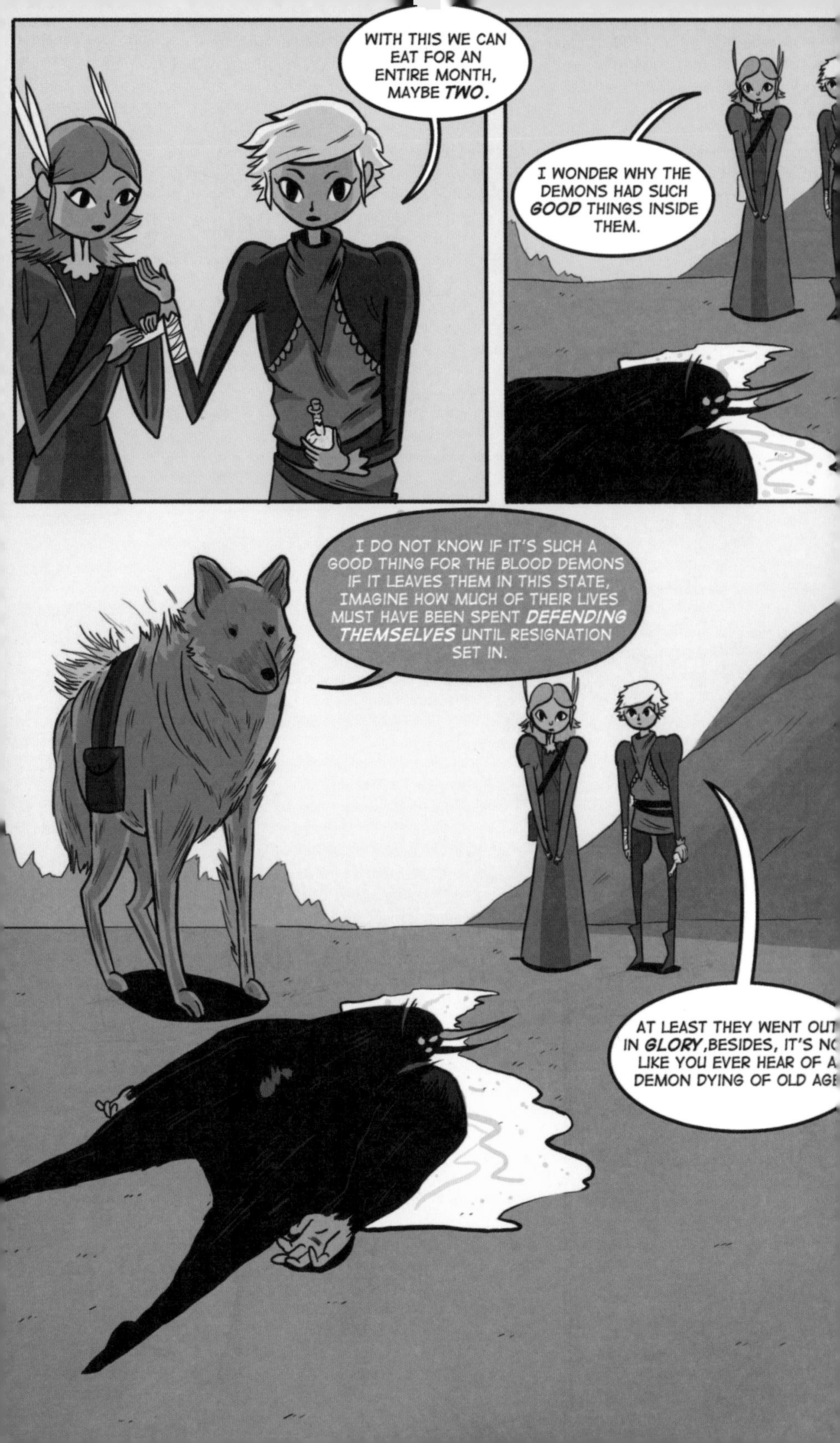
WITH THIS WE CAN EAT FOR AN ENTIRE MONTH, MAYBE *TWO*.
I WONDER WHY THE DEMONS HAD SUCH *GOOD* THINGS INSIDE THEM.
I DO NOT KNOW IF IT'S SUCH A GOOD THING FOR THE BLOOD DEMONS IF IT LEAVES THEM IN THIS STATE, IMAGINE HOW MUCH OF THEIR LIVES MUST HAVE BEEN SPENT *DEFENDING THEMSELVES* UNTIL RESIGNATION SET IN.
AT LEAST THEY WENT OUT IN *GLORY*,BESIDES, IT'S NO LIKE YOU EVER HEAR OF A DEMON DYING OF OLD AGE

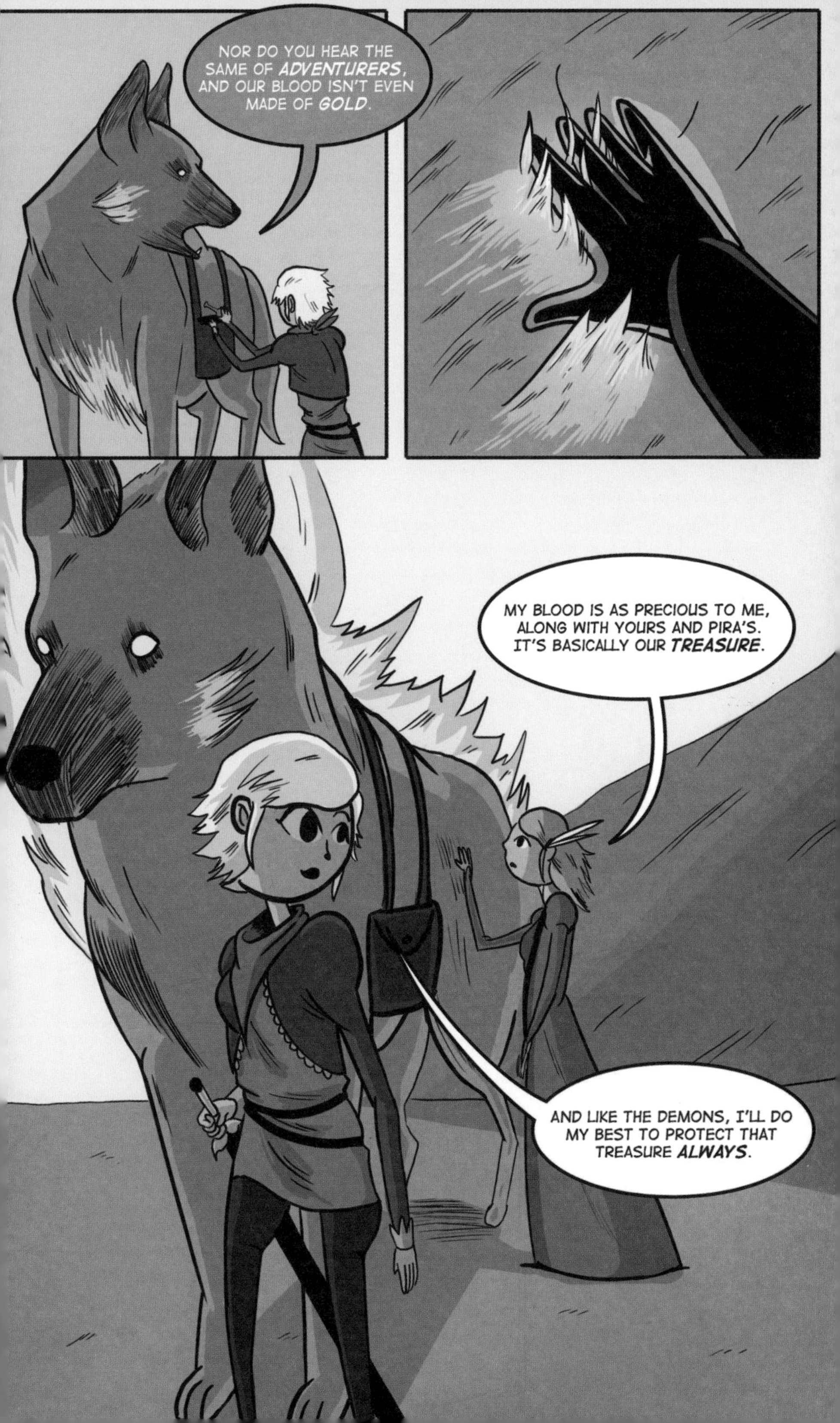
NOR DO YOU HEAR THE SAME OF ADVENTURERS, AND OUR BLOOD ISN'T EVEN MADE OF GOLD.
MY BLOOD IS AS PRECIOUS TO ME, ALONG WITH YOURS AND PIRA'S. IT'S BASICALLY OUR TREASURE.
AND LIKE THE DEMONS, I'LL DO MY BEST TO PROTECT THAT TREASURE ALWAYS.

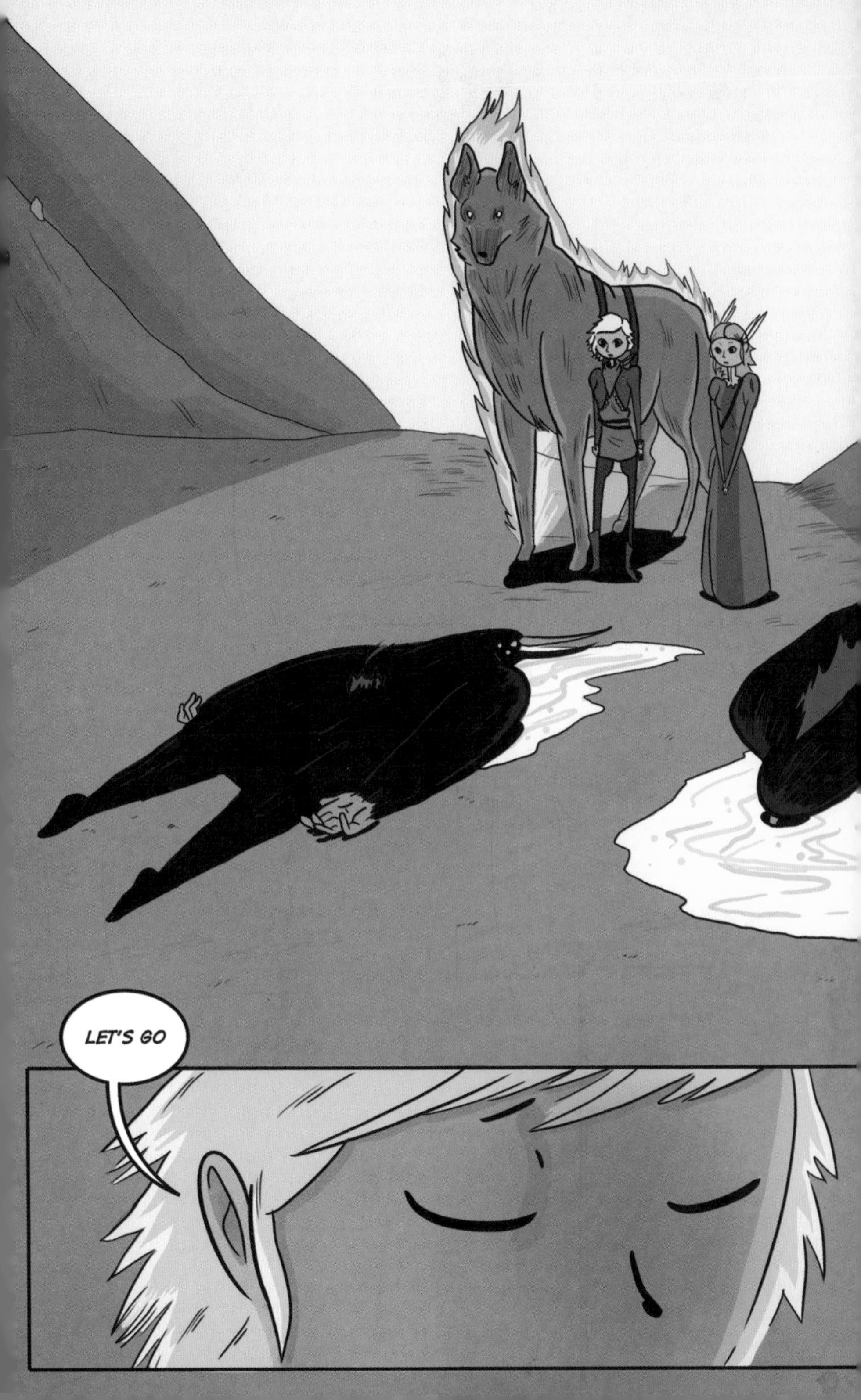
LET'S GO

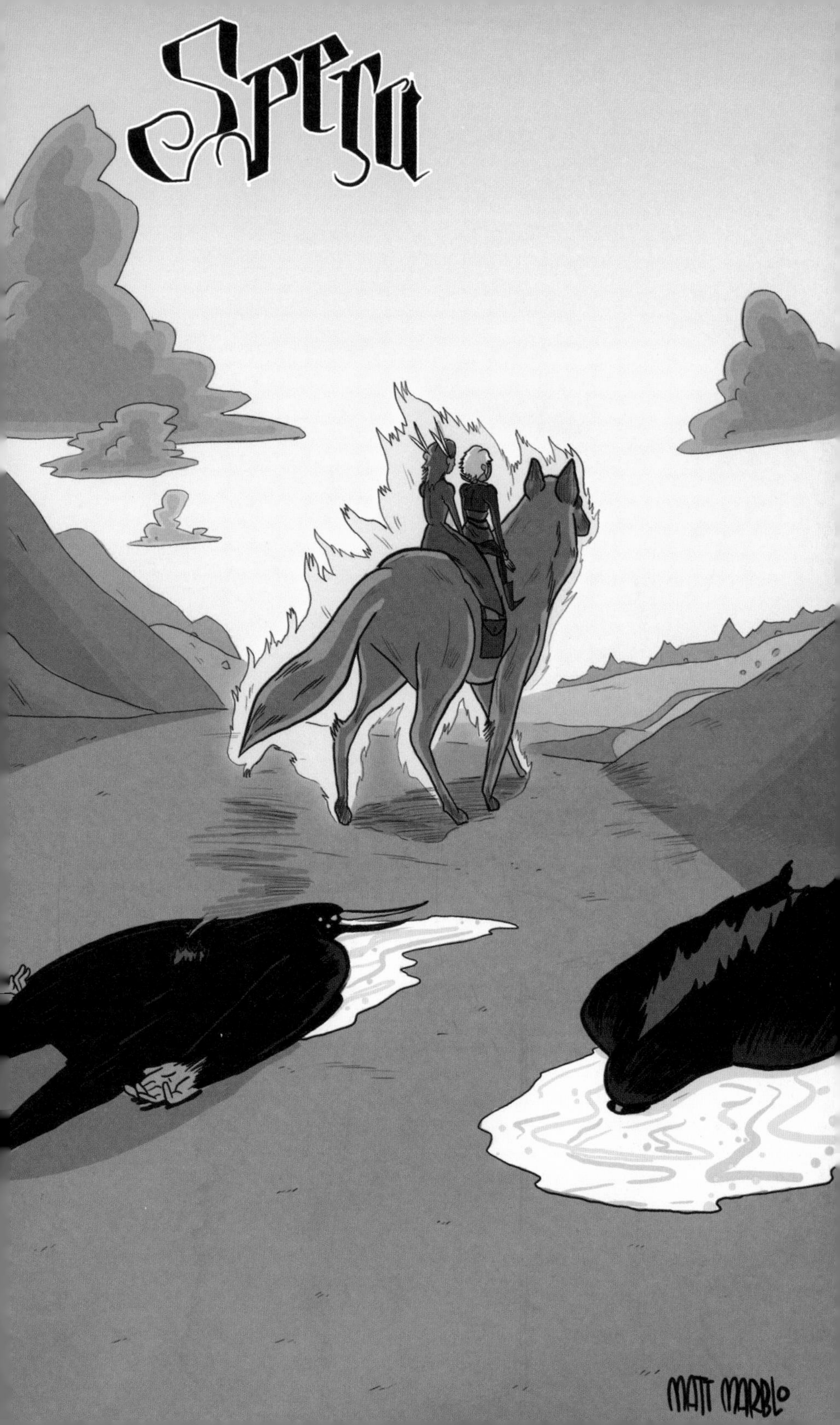
Spera
MATT MARBLO

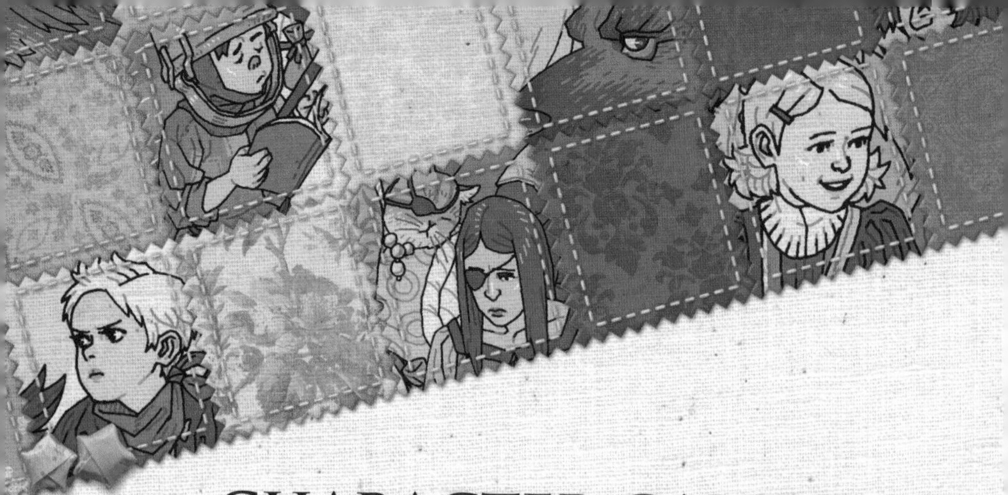

CHARACTER GALLERY

character designs and illustrations by AFU CHAN

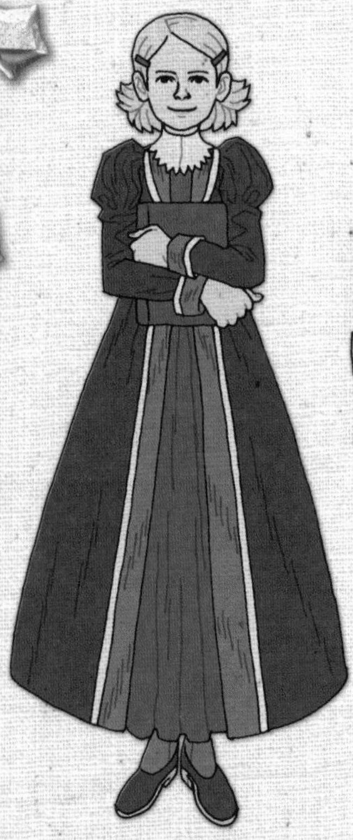

• lono •

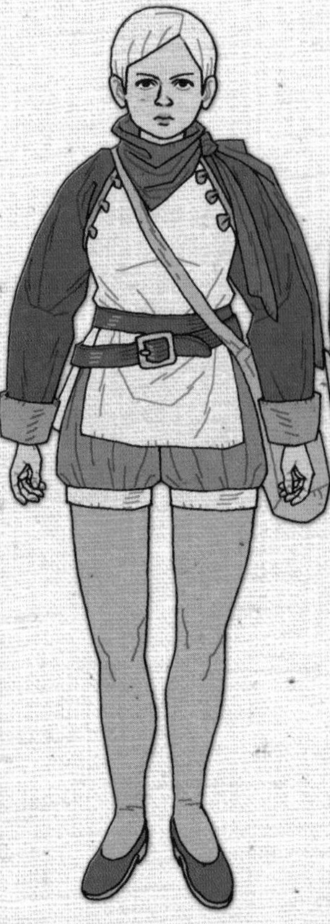

• pira •

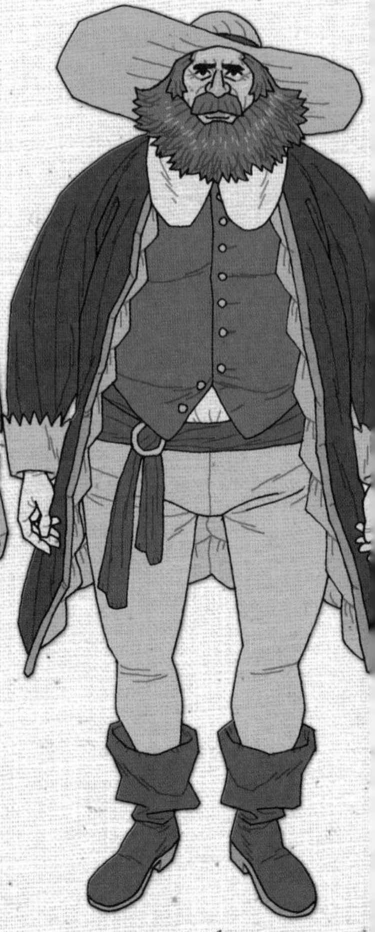

• yonder •

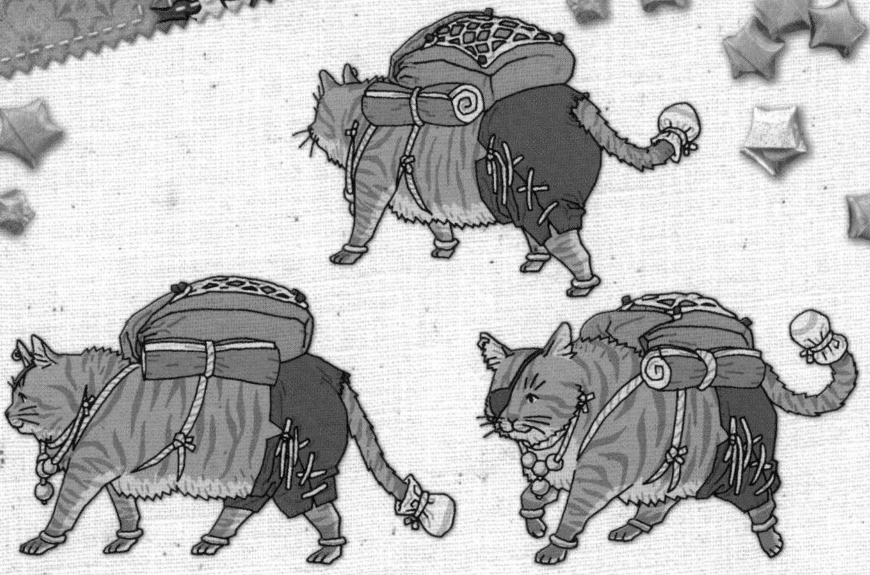

• chobo •

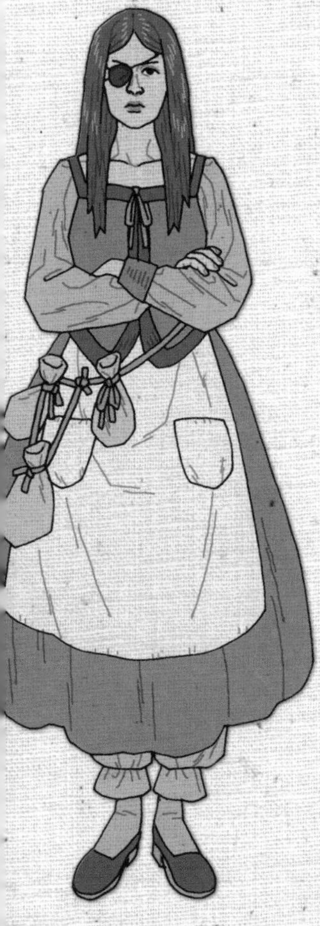

• sana •

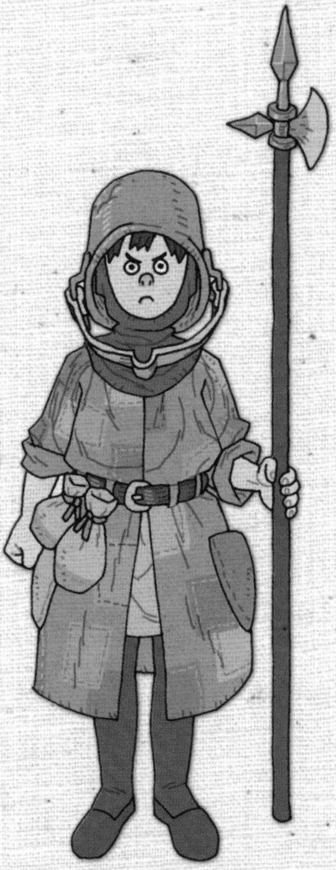

• watchboy •

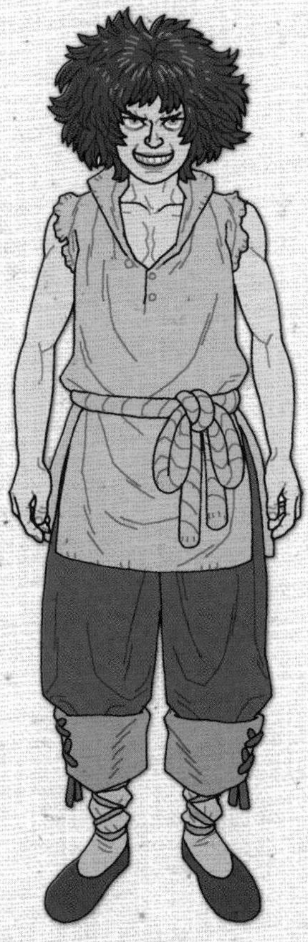

• darkboy •

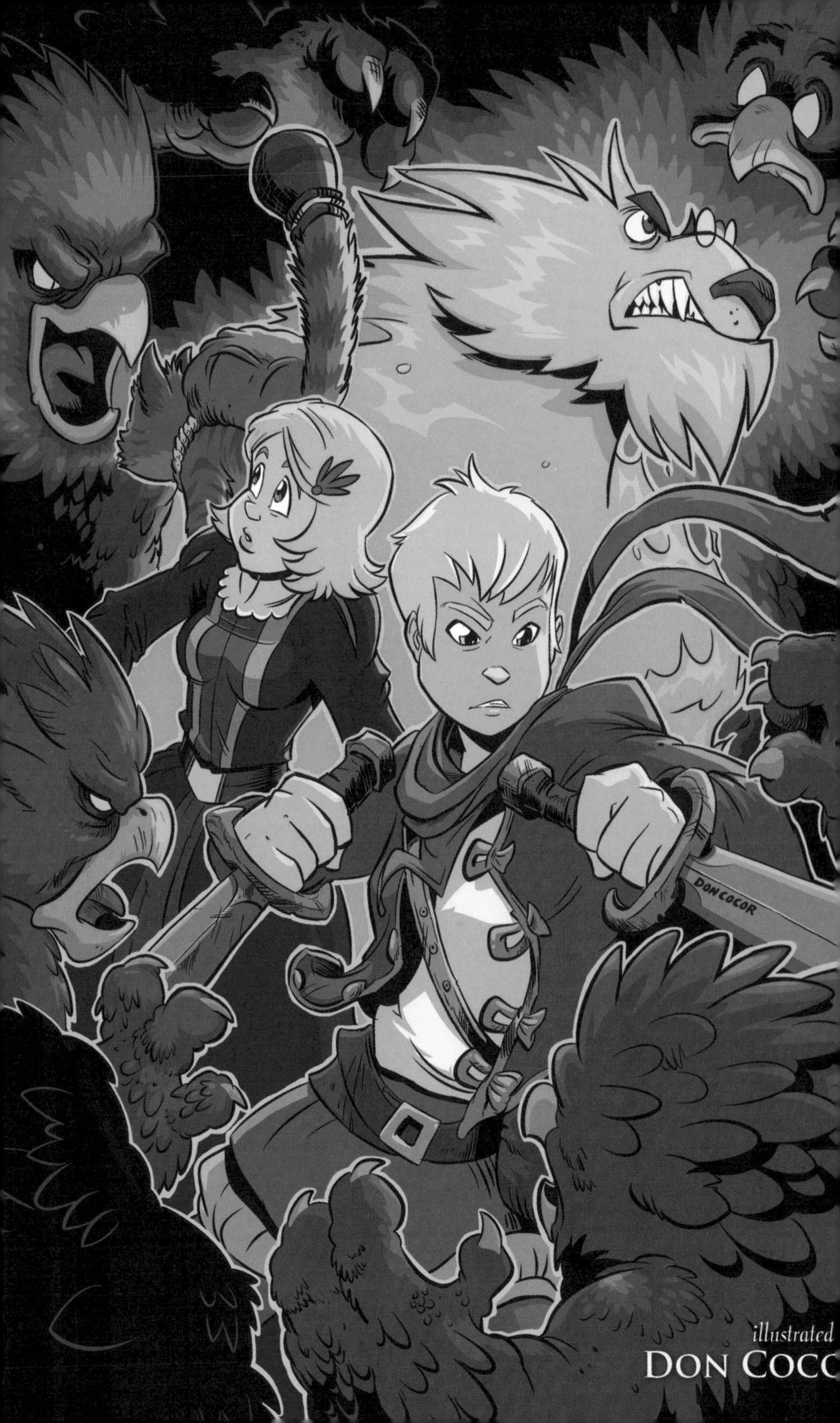
DONCOCOR
illustrated
DON COCO

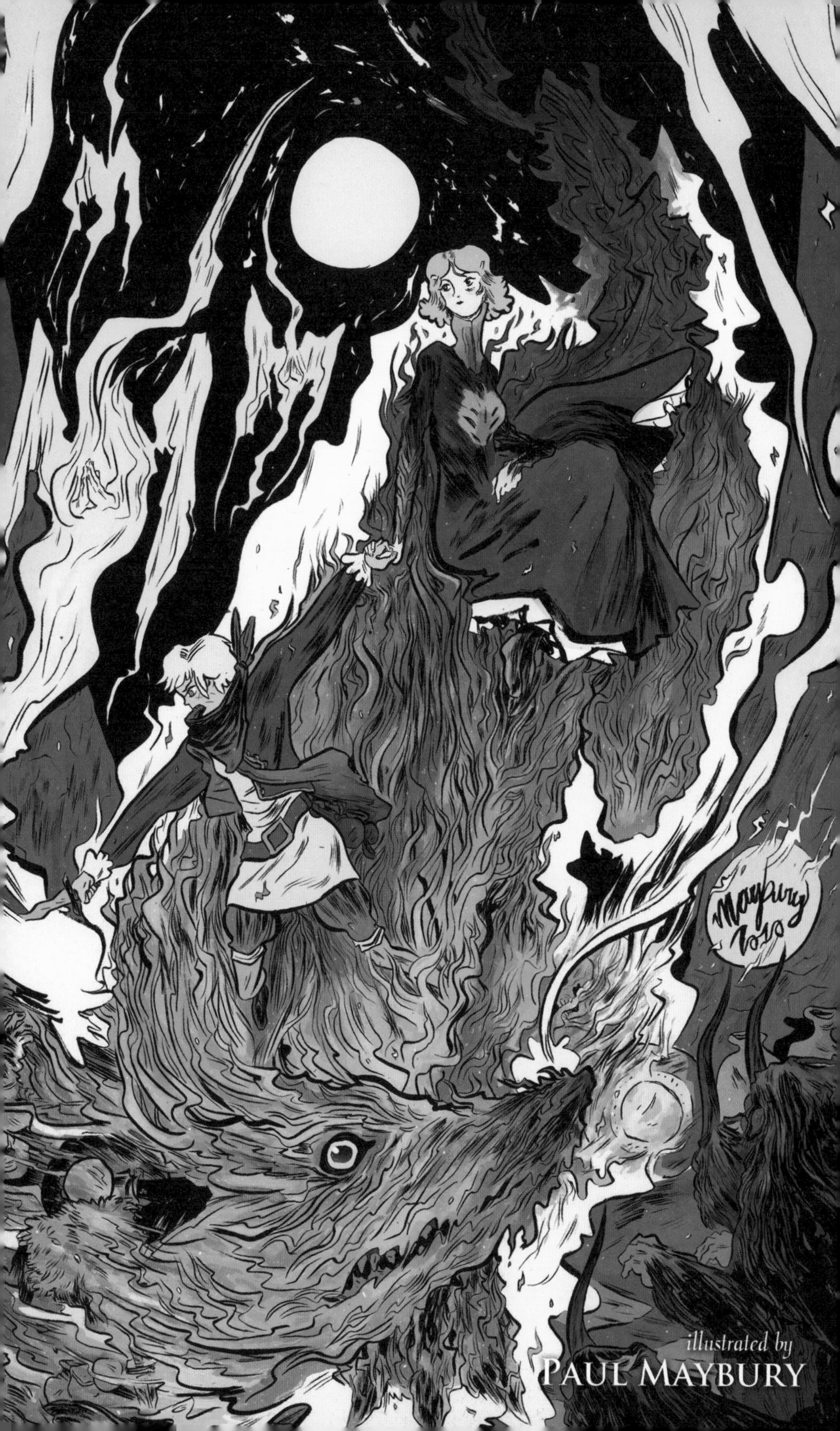
illustrated by
PAUL MAYBURY

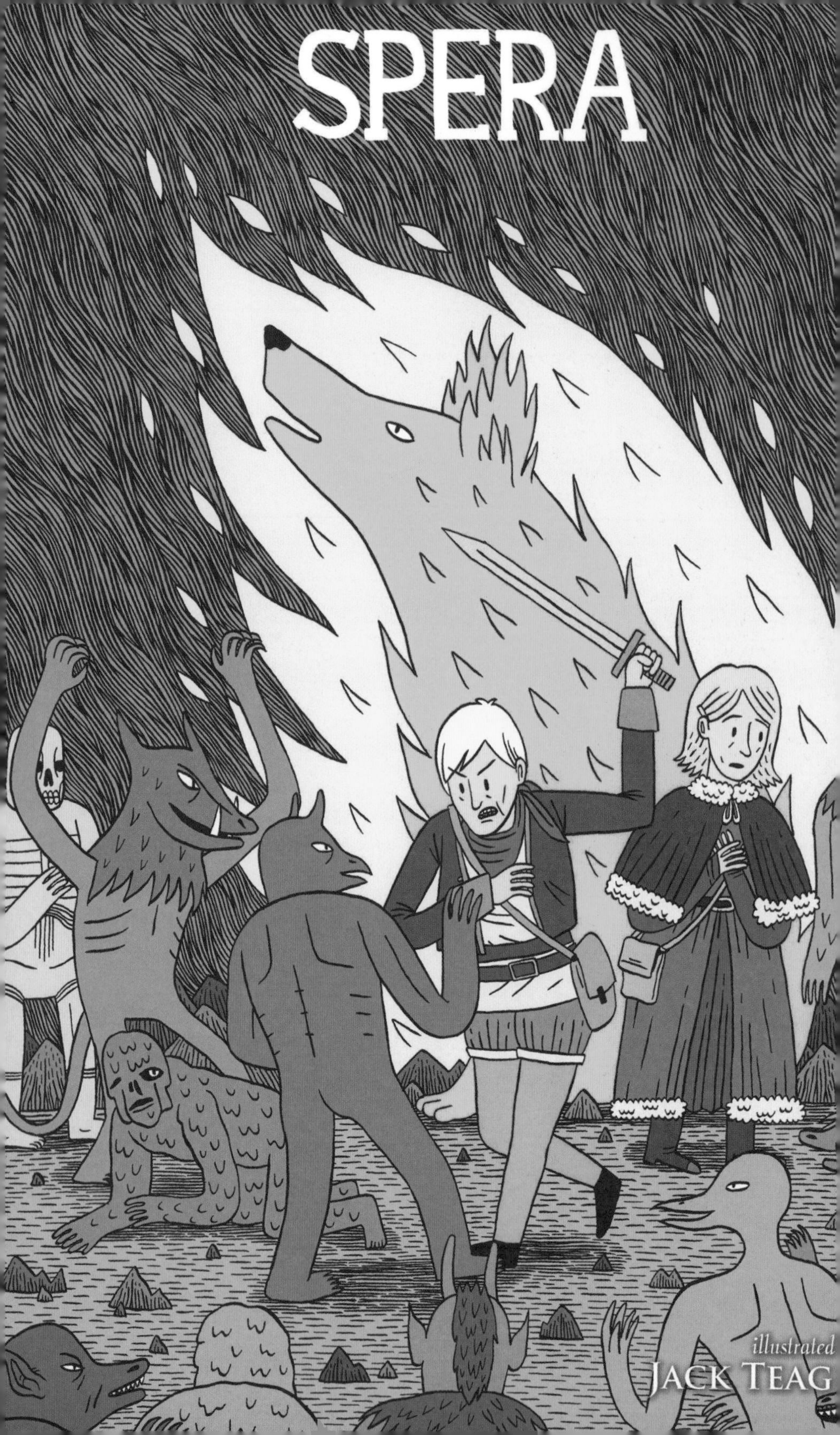
SPERA
illustrated
JACK TEAG

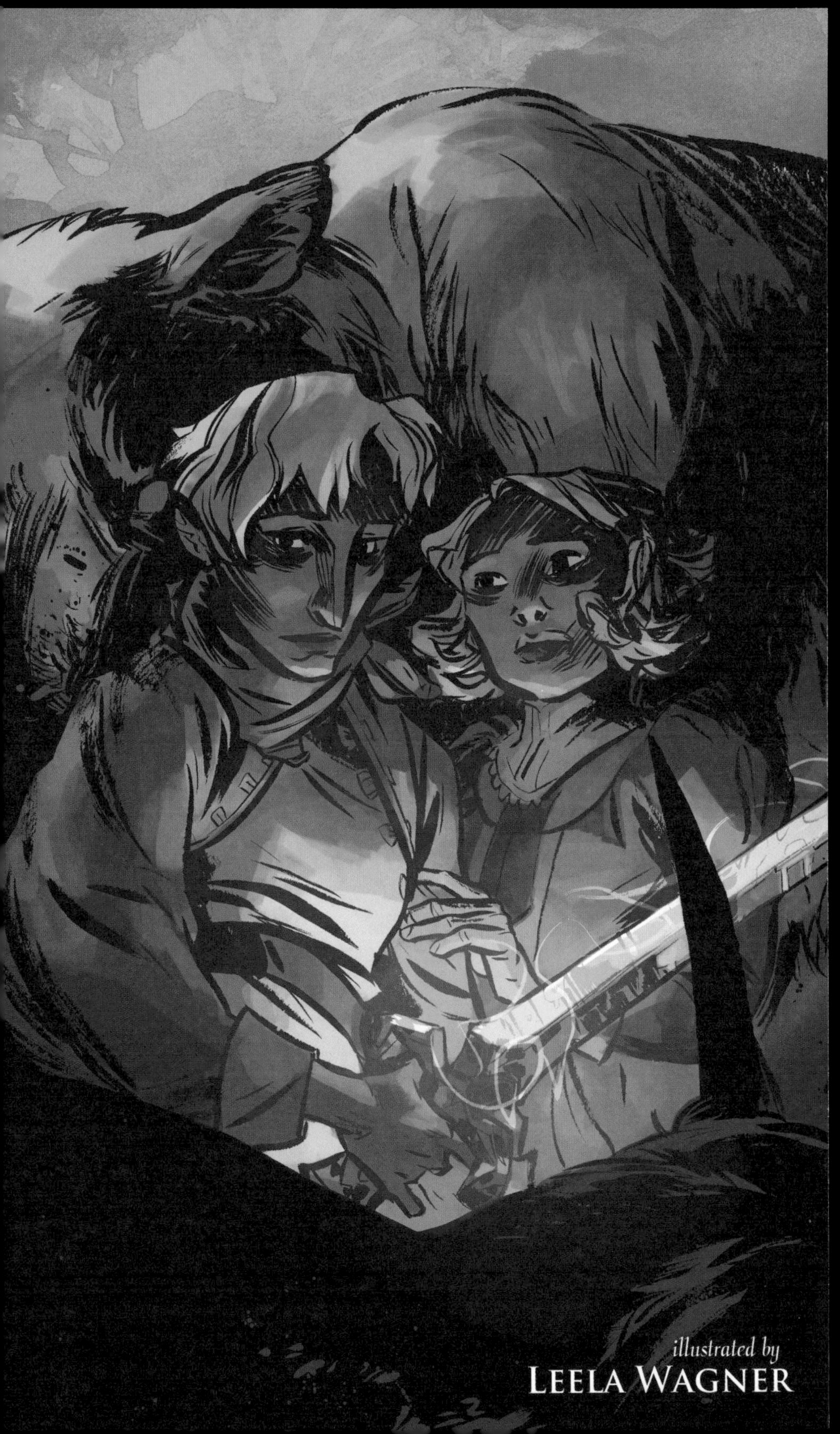
illustrated by
LEELA WAGNER

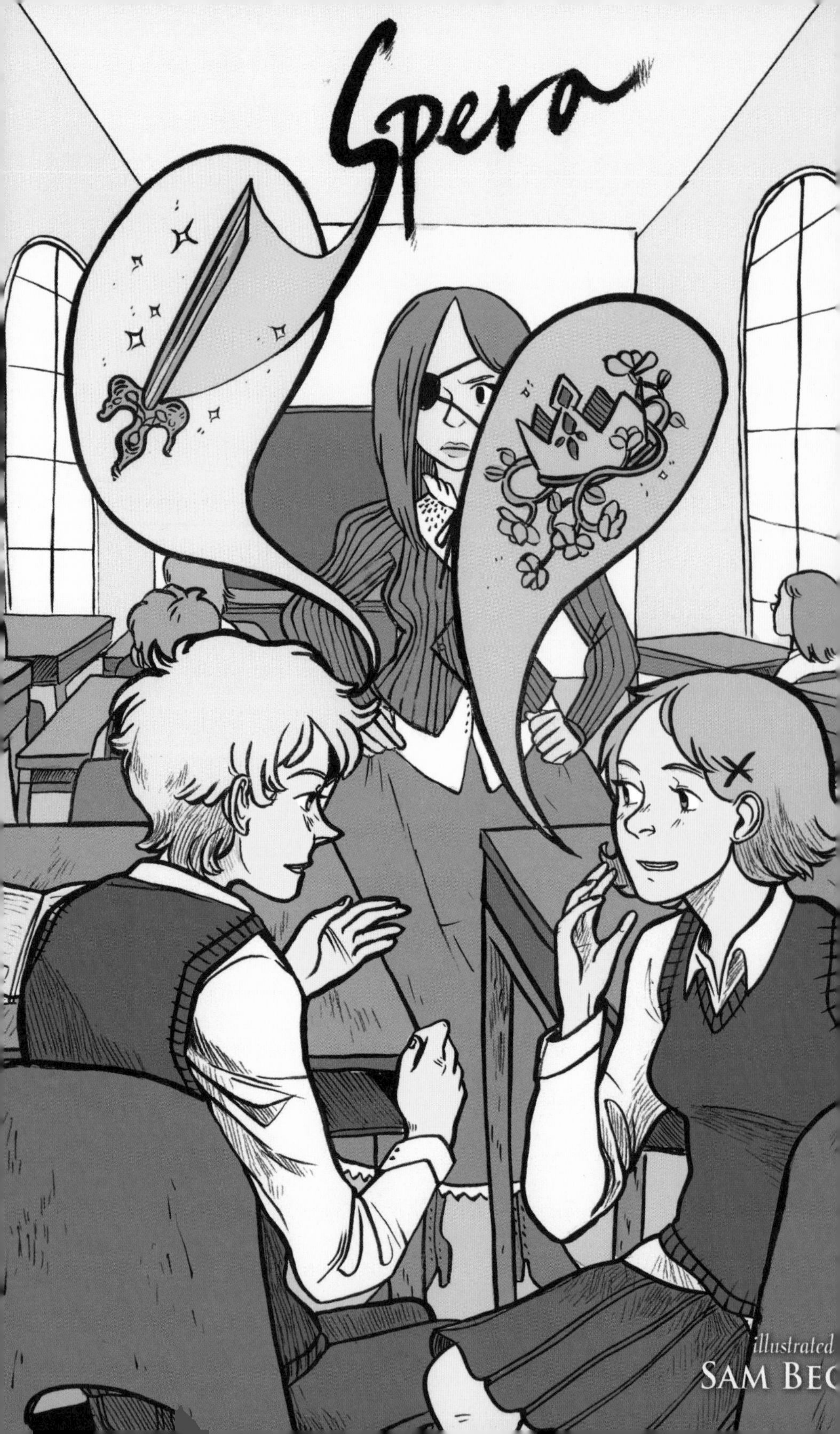
Spera
illustrated
SAM BEC

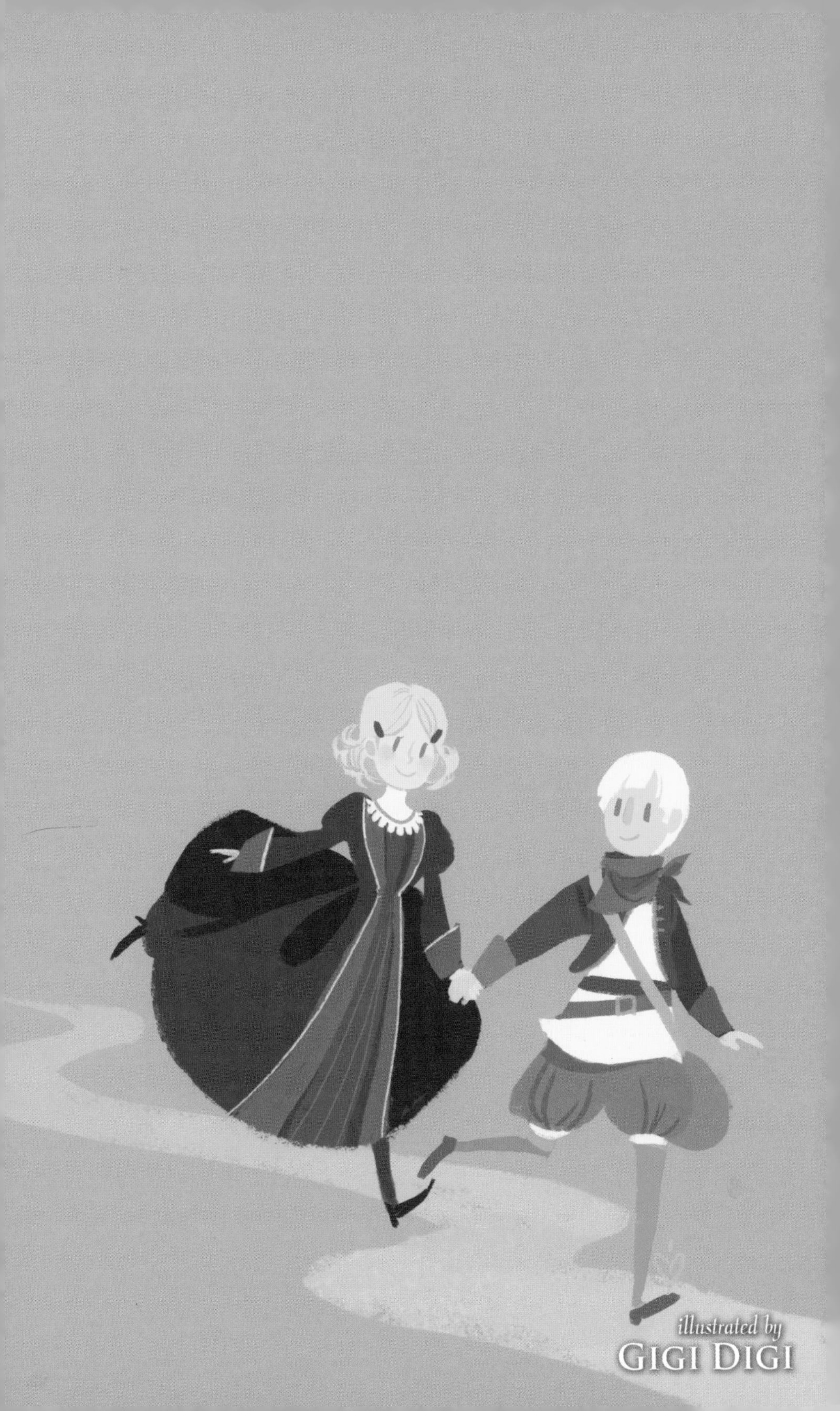
illustrated by
GIGI DIGI

ABOUT THE AUTHORS

the storytellers who have spun our tales...

JOSH TIERNEY resides in London, Ontario with his wife and cat. He purchased his first ever comic book at the age of six and *Spera*: **Volume I** is his first published graphic novel twenty-one years later. Josh is grateful to be able to work with some of the finest artists he knows on *Spera*, which he considers a love letter to all that is unique about fantasy, fairy tales and the limitless medium of comics.

AFU CHAN is an illustrator and freelance artist. He is a fan of the films of *Wong Kar Wai* and *Johnnie To* due to their quirky storytelling and distinctive styles, which serve as some of the biggest inspirations for his work. Afu designs the characters and creates the covers for *Spera*.

KYLA VANDERKLUGT is a Toronto-born freelance illustrator and comic artist now working out of her ramshackle little studio in the country. She takes inspiration from her surroundings, and mostly the things she is surrounded by these days are animals and trees – and the tottering piles of books of her overflowing library. You can visit her online at *www.kylavanderklugt.com*

HWEI lives in Malaysia, drawing and writing comics. Her art and stories are usually about the ocean and its inhabitants, tragedies of the Three Kingdoms and Sengoku historical periods, videogames, and the unbearable absurdity of being. Hwei's website is *lalage.org*

EMILY CARROLL is a Vancouver-based cartoonist and animator who graduated from Sheridan College for Classical Animation in 2005. A fan of urban legends and world mythology from a young age, she takes a particular interest in fairy tales and fables when it comes to her own work. Emily can be found online at *www.emcarroll.com*

OLIVIER PICHARD is a French comic artist interested in the Occult Science of Perspective. He travels regularly to other planets and lives in a dilapidated manor in the hollow of an old European plain. From his tiny attic window, he watches and laughs at the madness of modern times.

JORDYN F. BOCHON currently lives in Halifax, Nova Scotia. Author of comics such as Gene Day Award-nominated *The Day After V-Day* and *Finnegan Strappe And The Gni'ehn Dagger*, her work has been described as quirky and dark, often dealing in tense relationships, the beauty of inner-city life and scientific fictions.

CÉCILE BRUN would like to be a comic artist, if she had more free time. Sadly, most of her time is spent on collages, photography, cooking, sewing and gardening, as well as teaching Japanese, making short movies, travelling, taking a nap and trying to find things she has lost . . . However, it does seem she is working on several secret projects, such as illustrated books and the like.

LUKE PEARSON is an illustrator and cartoonist from the UK. Since graduating with an illustration degree in 2010 he has drawn a bunch of stuff. He is the creator of the comics *Hildafolk* and *Everything We Miss*, both published by Nobrow Press.

LEELA WAGNER is uncomfortable making predictions about her life by the time this book is in your hands so here are the facts: she has recently made the transition from "student" to "recent grad" and is living in a place, in a time, in a world. Chances are good she is drawing stuff. The rest is unknown.

MATT MARBLO is an animator and comic artist based in New York City. He likes to draw silly things and watch cool Sci-Fi movies. He can be found online at *mattmarblo.blogspot.com*

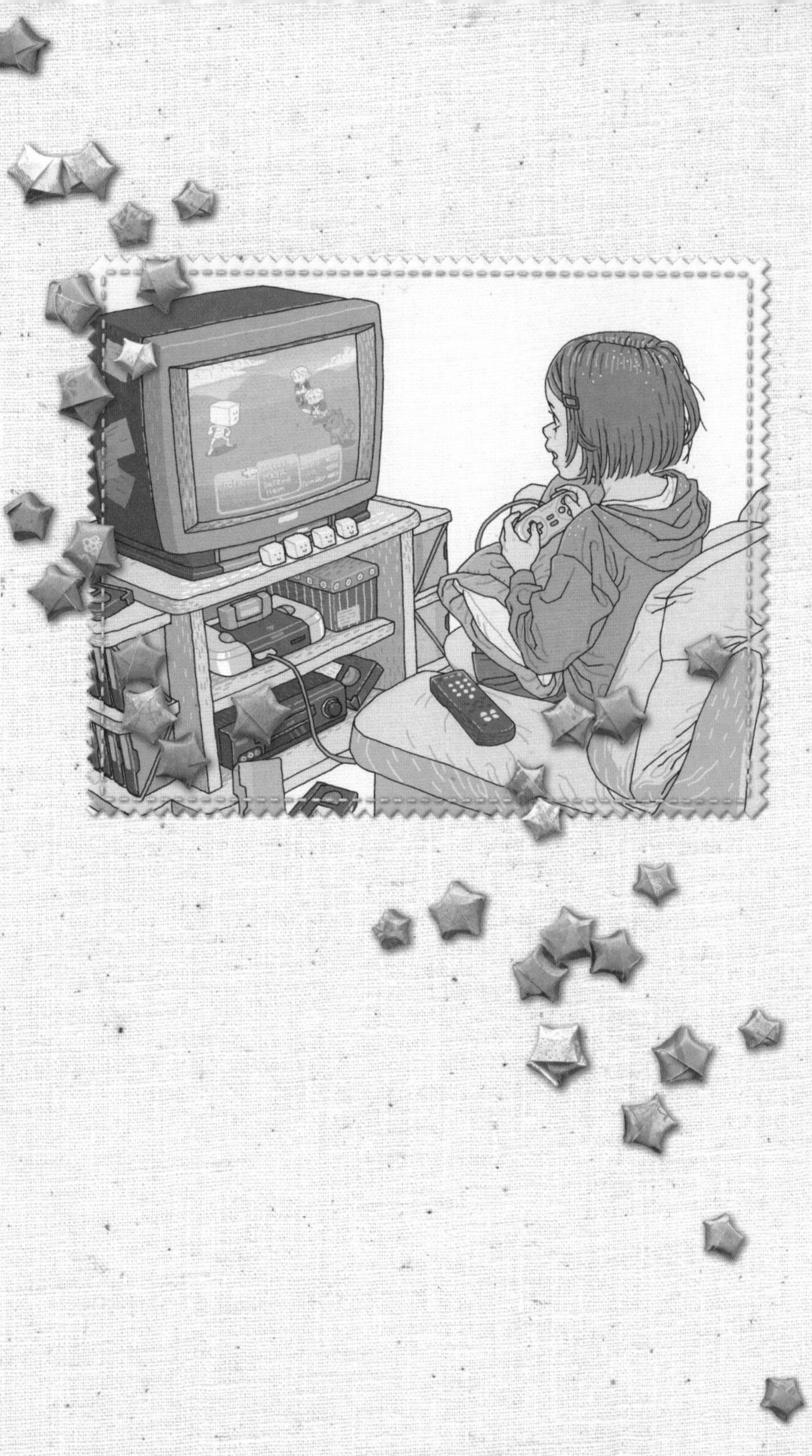